MEDICINE MAN

SAFFRON A. KENT

Copyright

Cover Art by Najla Qamber Designs
Photography by Rafa G. Catala
Editing by Leanne Rabesa
Proofreading by KC Enders & Virginia Tesi Carey

September 2018 Edition
Print ISBN: 978- 1727409161
Published in the United States of America

Books
by
Saffron A. Kent

A War like Ours
(Dark enemies to lovers romance)

The Unrequited
(Sexy student-teacher romance)

Gods & Monsters
(Un-conventional coming of age romance)

Blurb

Willow Taylor lives in a castle with large walls and iron fences. But this is no ordinary castle. It's called Heartstone Psychiatric Hospital and it houses forty other patients. It has nurses with mean faces and techs with permanent frowns.

It has a man, as well. A man who is cold and distant. Whose voice drips with authority. And whose piercing gray eyes hide secrets, and maybe linger on her face a second too long.

Willow isn't supposed to look deep into those eyes. She isn't supposed to try to read his tightly-leashed emotions. Neither is she supposed to touch herself at night, imagining his powerful voice and that cold but beautiful face.

No, Willow Taylor shouldn't be attracted to Simon Blackwood at all.

Because she's a patient and he's her doctor. Her psychiatrist.

The medicine man.

WARNING: This book discusses sensitive issues including, but not limited to, depression and suicide.

Dedication

To all the fighters and warriors who battle silently; I see you.
And of course, my husband.

Disclaimer I

Although care has been taken to adhere to the facts and general workings of a psychiatric hospital, some liberties were taken to fit the story.
Please note that the author does not intend any harm or offense.

Days spent on the Inside = 14

Days *left* to spend on the Inside = 28

Days since The Roof Incident = 17

Chapter 1

I remember the day I lost my mind.

The sun was out, and the day was bright. It was fucking miserable.

Through the window of my apartment, I saw people jogging, cycling, laughing in Central Park. The birds were chirping and there wasn't a single cloud in the sky.

Did I mention it was miserable?

Yeah, I remember everything about that day. Every single thing. But that's not the worst part.

The worst part is that everyone else remembers it too. And the thing about everyone else remembering is that they don't ever forget it. And they don't let *you* forget it, either.

As if you need any more reminders.

As if you don't relive those moments in very vivid and graphic detail. The day you crossed over to the other side.

The side where the crazies live.

I've always straddled that line and done a great job of staying on the sane side. Because unfortunately, everyone else in my family is sane and un-crazy. I've always wanted something in common with them. Other than my silver hair, that is.

I come from a family of silver-haired and green-eyed women. Also, tall.

Taylor women are tall and willowy and stunning and have been for generations. It's our signature, actually. Not to mention fashionable and successful.

We own a boutique clothing store called *Panache* on Madison Avenue that caters to the old-money New Yorkers and Upper East Siders.

When I was born, my mom, my grandma, my aunt, my older cousin who was eight at the time, they all thought I'd be like them. In fact, they were so confident about my Taylor-ness that they'd already decided on a name suitable for a Taylor baby: Willow.

They shouldn't have.

There's nothing willowy about me. I'm not delicate or graceful or tall.

Except for the legendary silver hair, I don't possess any of the Taylor qualities. My eyes are a startling shade of blue. I'm too short and my fashion sense is a pair of shorts, sneakers, and t-shirts with Harry Potter quotes.

But the thing that bothers me the most is that I was born with something more than blood in my veins. Something extra-terrestrial, alien, quite possibly blue-colored – hence the weird, un-Taylor color of my eyes. Something dark and shadowy, with long claw-like fingers. Something that has weighed me down all my life.

"Have you thought about it?"

"No," I say.

"Have you thought about harming yourself in any way?"

"No."

"Are you ready to talk about what happened that night?" she asks.

I look up from where I'm playing with my short nails. They don't let us keep long, sharp ones on the Inside.

"What's that?" I ask, like I haven't heard her loud and clear.

"About your attempt."

"It wasn't an attempt."

"So what do you think it was?"

"An accident," I tell her. "It was an accident."

Josie, my therapist, gives me the look.

That look.

The look where they think I'm crazy and I'm lying, and they pity me. They think that if they poke me too much, I might explode.

I don't like that look.

It makes me *want* to explode. It makes me want to snap my teeth, grow my nails to the point where my hands look like talons. It makes me want to scratch and bite and scream.

But I won't.

That's not me. I don't explode. I'm a peacekeeper. I'm sweet and quiet. I keep my head down and don't make any ripples.

I am calm. I'm cool. I'm a cucumber.

Happy thoughts.

Thoughts about... my bunny slippers that I brought from home, *Harry Potter and the Prisoner of Azkaban* that I'm reading for the thirty-sixth time, and the pigeons that I feed in the gardens when they let us outside.

Slowly, I deflate.

"Okay, then." She nods. "It was an accident. Are you ready to talk about it?"

It being The Roof Incident.

People have been asking me this a whole lot ever since The Incident happened. My doctors back at the state hospital, my therapist, my mom. Everyone.

I've already told them, and they still sent me here.

On the Inside.

"If I talk about it, will you let me go? Will you recommend that I be released?" I ask.

"You know I can't do that."

I look at my bunny slippers. "Didn't think so."

"We still have a lot of ground to cover, Willow, and your contract says another four weeks. So I'm sorry."

"Are you, really?"

"Yes, of course."

I make a non-committal sound because I don't believe her.

"Why? You don't believe me?" she asks, reading me accurately.

"Not really, no."

"Why not?"

"Because frankly... you're not my friend. You don't care."

She doesn't care that I've been stuck here for two weeks

now and that my every move is monitored. She doesn't care that they feed me pills twice a day and then, ask me to open my mouth and actually, *show* them that I've swallowed them.

What am I? An animal?

She doesn't care that I have to participate in group therapy and art therapy and recreational therapy and all kinds of fucking therapy all day when I clearly don't need to.

So yeah, nope. I'm not talking. Thank you very much.

"I care. I do care, Willow," she says.

I lick my lips and sit up straight. "Do you have a boy-friend?"

She looks taken aback.

Well, maybe I shouldn't have been so abrupt. But it's a valid question.

My therapist is pretty. She's got straight blonde hair that she keeps tied up in a no-nonsense ponytail. Her light-colored eyes are hidden behind big, black glasses and her lips are usually very lightly painted pink. That's the only touch of make-up on her beautiful face. It doesn't matter. She doesn't need any.

I bet guys must lose their minds over her. Figuratively.

She twists on her couch and clears her throat. "Um, no. Not right now."

"Why not?"

"I haven't met anyone interesting in a while."

"So, what do you do for sex?"

I can't believe I said that but I'm genuinely curious. I've always been curious.

If I'm stuck here with a therapist, I might as well make

some use of it. If she wants to talk, we can talk about interesting stuff. Stuff that I've always wanted to ask and never got a chance to.

I couldn't ask my mom. She wouldn't have liked it. I think according to her, I'm still a pre-teen who hasn't even gotten her period and thinks kissing could make babies.

Josie laughs. "I'm sorry?"

Not gonna lie. I like that this question is making her a little uncomfortable, if her squirming is anything to go by. This is a complete win-win.

"For sex. What do you do? One-night stands? Masturbation? I'm in the masturbation camp. You know, because I'm stuck here and all."

She smiles, adjusting her glasses. "Ah, is this your revenge strategy? I asked you questions you didn't like and you're trying to make me uncomfortable."

Yes.

I shrug, innocently. "I'm just making conversation. You said you cared."

"Well, to answer your question, masturbation is keeping me happy for now, so I think I'm managing," she says.

I jump topics. "What about my books? There's not a single Harry Potter book in your library. You guys should do something about it. It's a travesty."

Ah, Harry Potter.

The source of everything good and holy in the world.

She smiles. "I'll talk to someone about that, okay?" She folds her hands in her lap. "Now, are you ready to talk about it?"

I sigh. "Can we just move on from it already? It's been like, two weeks."

"Exactly, only two weeks."

"If I keep talking about it, I'm never gonna forget it. You realize that, don't you?" I raise my eyebrows.

Josie raises her own eyebrows. "Forgetting is not the goal. The goal is to talk about it and confront it *and* get help."

Help.

Pfft.

I can help myself, and the first thing I need to do is forget that The Roof Incident ever happened. Talking about it and re-hashing it is not going to make me feel better.

Personally, I think therapists and psychiatrists have a very twisted way of treatment.

Besides, The Incident is not going to happen again, any-way.

I sigh, tired.

So tired.

I've got a full day of this. When I leave here, I've got community group, process group, education group – *all* the groups – where all they ever talk about is your illness, your meds, your *feelings*.

And it's not as if I can get some sleep at night, either. The meds they have put me on are sleep-stealers. I can't sleep until the wee hours of the morning and even if I do manage to fall asleep before that, the whimpers and noises of the ward jerk me awake.

Okay, happy thoughts.

All the fucking happy thoughts.

In my most monotonous voice, I tell her, "There's nothing

to talk about. It was an accident. I was very emotional that day. I'm a very happy individual, otherwise. You know, my illness aside. So yeah. Again, for the thousandth time, it was an *accident*. I'm not crazy. I don't belong here. You need to pick up your phone and call my mom. You need to tell her that I'm fine and she should come here, break the contract and take me home."

She sighs, too. Her sigh is patient but long. "Okay. So, not today. All right. I'm not going to force you. That's not my style. But I do want to tell you that what happened has nothing to do with the circumstances. Your life might be very happy but that has no bearing on it. It's like an itch, Willow. It's there. Constantly. You can ignore it but then, one day it becomes so big, so irritating, that you'll do anything to get relief. Including scratch it." She smiles, gently. "But then again, I don't have to tell you that, do I? Because you already know. So I'm here when you want to talk about it."

The itch.

Interesting description. Personally though, I like the one I came up with: Magic.

I thought it was magic. That *something* in my blood.

Granted, it was during the time I'd first discovered Harry Potter books and I was in a major Harry Potter phase. Well, to be honest, Harry Potter isn't a phase, it's a lifestyle. But still.

I thought I was born a witch and that's why I was so different from my family. I was almost convinced that when I turned eleven, they'd come for me like they came for Harry. They'd take me to the world's biggest school of witchcraft and wizardry, Hogwarts. I'd learn about all the spells and incantations and potions and the right way to wield a wand.

But instead of going to my dream school for magic at eleven, I ended up here at the age of eighteen: Heartstone Psychiatric Hospital.

"Can I go now?" I ask.

"Sure. See you next week."

Because that something in my veins is not magic. It's anything *but* magic.

It's a curse and the only thing that I can do to get rid of it is to not think about it at all. And somehow get through the remaining twenty-eight days of my incarceration, so I can be Outside again and get my life back.

Chapter 2

Heartstone Psychiatric Hospital — my home for the next four weeks — is a very small private facility located in the Middle of Nowhere, New Jersey.

Fine, it's located in the *scenic* town of Heartstone, and is surrounded by woods and ugly open grounds on all sides.

Okay, *fine*. Not ugly.

It pains me to say this because I want to hate everything about this place and I do, but the grounds surrounding Heartstone are pretty and spacious. The perimeter is lined with tall trees and brick walls. The grass is a sharp green shade, like the color of my family's eyes and *unlike* the color of mine.

I haven't seen so much space in my entire life. You don't find something like this in the city. And neither do you find taller and blacker metal gates that keep the Outside world, outside.

I remember seeing them for the first time when my mom drove me up here. They opened on their own when she spoke into the intercom, like something controlled by dark magic. Slowly, they revealed the vintage-looking Victorian style building with a red pointed roof and white bricks, making me wonder how something so pretty, something that might belong in a fairy tale, could be so scary and hellish.

The moment we passed through the gates, I knew. I *knew* in my heart, in my soul that I'd spend the rest of my life here and even if I did manage to get out, I'd never be the same.

I wanted to make a run for it.

But, of course, I didn't run. My mom would've had a heart attack, and I love her too much to do that to her. With my illness and now The Incident, I've already put her through enough as it is.

Besides, I'm getting out in just four weeks. No matter what my overactive imagination makes me believe. Four short weeks and I'll be out of here. On the Outside.

Away from this stupid hospital that creaks and shakes at night when the wind blows and the rain batters the roof. Well, what else do you expect from a building that was built in the early 1900s?

In any case, Heartstone is *way* better than the state hospital where I stayed for forty-eight hours before they transferred me here. The staff over there, the patients, the smell of bleach, everything was the stuff of nightmares.

At least, this facility is pretty to look at.

According to history, this was a house long before it was turned into a hospital. The original owner had it built for his mentally ill wife. He'd loved her more than life itself and he hated the little town of Heartstone that shot his beloved wife wary looks. So he said *fuck it, I'm gonna build my wife a castle* and he did.

This I'll admit – without any sort of pain – that I find romantic. Kind of epic, really.

A man who builds castles to keep the woman he loves safe. Whoever she was, she was pretty fucking lucky.

This castle has three levels, sixty-seven rooms that house about forty patients, and two separate wings, east and west. I'll never understand why they needed so many rooms but whatever.

We live on the second level. It's a long corridor, running from the east wing to the west, flanked by rooms on either side, with a nurses' station at the end. It's simple and straightforward, and very white and beige-y.

The third level is what everyone calls 'The Batcave.' They usually put patients who require extensive monitoring up there. I don't know very many people from the upper level. But every time I see someone from The Batcave with their checked-out looks and almost translucent eyes, I try not to make it obvious that I'm staring.

It's not polite to stare. Ask me. I've been stared at a lot ever since The Incident.

My favorite place – relatively – is the ground level. All the offices, dining hall, rec room, TV room, all sorts of rooms are located on this level. Basically, it's a hub of activity and is the loudest of all the levels.

It's where I hear the name Simon Blackwood for the first time.

I'm in the dining hall, waiting in line for a breakfast of watery oatmeal and cut-up fruit when I hear it. The name, I mean.

It comes out of one of the nurses talking and keeping an

eye on the long breakfast queue. For some reason, these lines are a breeding ground for meltdowns, so they always have someone watching them. I have yet to see it, though, and I pray that it never changes. Just the thought scares the fucking crap out of me.

"By Blackwood, you mean, The Blackwood?"

"Yup," says one of the nurses as I trudge my feet past them.

"Oh geez. Like I needed more problems in my life. I bet he's got a huge ego."

"I know."

"Ugh. I don't wanna deal with him. I was only now getting adjusted to the long hours they put me on two weeks ago. Why's this Simon Blackwood coming here? Is it permanent?"

"Who knows? Beth is super hush-hush about it. Which I don't understand, by the way. We're the ones who have to deal with him, not her. She's gonna be locked up in that big administrative office of hers, while he'll be roaming around the floor as if he owns the place."

"Exactly! Why are the nurses last to know about these things?"

"I don't know. Like we don't matter, right?"

Then they start bitching about the fact that they were last to know the changes in their yearly vacation days. *As if nurses aren't overworked as it is.*

And just like that, it's over. The topic of Simon Blackwood.

A little thing about me: I've overheard a lot of conversations in my life. During family gatherings and at school. I'm an expert eavesdropper. I don't do it intentionally. It's just that I'm kind of invisible and a weirdo, what with my pale, almost translucent skin and silver hair. People don't notice me or don't take me seriously if they do notice me.

So they talk and, well, I've got ears. So I listen.

Generally, I forget about these conversations as soon as they occur. Not this one, though.

Nope.

It sticks in my head.

Not the conversation itself, but the name.

I don't know why. I've never heard it before. I don't know who it belongs to, except that whoever he is, he's coming here. And Beth, the administrator, isn't telling the nurses about it, and they are pissed.

Whatever.

Time to forget it and move on. So I do. Move on, I mean.

I don't forget though. I remember the name for some very strange reason.

Floorboards creak under my bunny slippers as I get my breakfast and walk over to the table by the large windows. They overlook the gray skies and the wet grounds.

Ever since I got to this place, it's been raining every day. Maybe it's the universe's way of making me even more miserable.

It's no secret that I hate the sun; I burn too easily. Rain's my only respite. I love the rain. I love the water droplets crashing into my body, sliding down, clinging to my skin, washing me clean, making me new.

It's raining now, more like drizzling, and I wish I could go outside and feel it, but I can't.

I put my tray onto the Formica-topped table and plop

down on my seat. Plucking a strawberry from the fruit bowl, I pop it into my mouth.

I'm sitting next to Renn Deschanel, my red-headed neighbor.

She was the very first person to talk to me the day I arrived here two weeks ago. She saved me from the creepy stare of a guy who lives on the other side of the hallway and is here for some sort of addiction. I don't know his exact diagnosis though.

At the time, I was panicked, angry and completely devastated that my own family thinks that I'm crazy enough to be locked up. I thought they'd believe me when I told them that I didn't need to be here.

Anyway, Renn as usual, is staring at her crush of the week. Her crushes come and go, and she has a type. Silver fox – her words, not mine. This week, it's Hunter, one of the techs, who's probably closer to her dad's age than hers.

I shake my head at her. "What's the damage?"

She sighs. "I'm guessing at least twenty-five years. He's like, a couple of years younger than my dad. I can't believe I didn't notice him before. Like, this guy's been around forever. How did he not catch my eye?"

Yeah, forever is right.

Renn loves Heartstone. She loves it so much that she keeps coming back.

I think this is her fourth time on the Inside. Every time she comes in for a couple of months, has the time of her life – according to her – and gets out to come back in again.

This time she's in here because her dad is getting married

and she can't stand her new step-mother. So, in her infinite wisdom, she made herself throw up and she's severely anorexic. When her dad found her passed out in her bathroom, he did what he always does: sent her on the Inside.

She knows everything and everyone. Nurses are her best friends. Techs can't get over how pretty she is. Renn's the queen bee.

I pop another strawberry in my mouth and say, "Could be the fact that you didn't know he was married until last week."

"Hmm." Renn drums her fingers on her chin. "You might have a point. I like a challenge. It makes me feel better about myself if I can get an unavailable guy to like me. It's my pathetic self-image." She stabs her fork into a piece of watermelon. "Maybe I should somehow try to get Hunter as my escort after meals. Imagine the things I can do to him while he's watching me with those dark eyes."

After every meal, a tech stays with Renn for about an hour to see that she's keeping her food down. She's known to give them the slip and throw up every chance she gets. She's super proud of her pokey bones and the fact that you can count all her ribs.

"Or you can shut up about it and not force us to listen to what is clearly one of the most inappropriate things ever," Penny chimes in, glaring at her from across the table.

She's got a book in her hands and up until this second, her eyes were glued to it and her lips were moving as she muttered the words to herself.

Penny, aka Penelope Clarke. She was the second person I talked to after I got here. Actually, all we did was say hi to each other after Renn introduced us, and Penny went back to doing what she always does: read.

From what I've gathered in my time here, Penny loves reading. I love reading too so I definitely get that. But her love and my love are vastly different.

For Penny, reading is oxygen. She can't live without it. She needs to be reading something or I've seen her get shivery.

On the Outside, she read textbooks; she was a pre-med. On the Inside, she reads all the cookbooks that she can find in the small library. She says it's to keep her mind sharp and active for when she gets out of here in fall. A few weeks after me.

Penny suffers from crippling anxiety with a touch of paranoia mixed in there. When she failed one of her classes, which she claims was a set-up against her, she broke down. Renn told me she tore pages out of her biochemistry textbook and ate them. Literally.

"Um, hello. How's liking someone inappropriate?" Renn turns her focus on Penny.

"He's a tech and you're a patient." Penny flicks the page angrily. "Not to mention, he's married and older. You're not supposed to like him."

"Well, as Willow said, I like him *because* he's married. It's a sickness. My heart happens to beat for him, okay?"

"Oh please." Penny rolls her eyes. "Last week your heart beat for that homophobe with homicidal ideation from The Batcave."

"Roger isn't a homophobe. He was assaulted by a man. Excuse him for not liking it up his ass and being angry about it!"

Penny's ready with a retort and I've had it. I know if I don't stop them, they'll go on for hours. That's what Renn and Penny do.

They fight.

I don't like fights. It's bad for my inner equilibrium and everyone's peace. And I'm the peacekeeper and the avoider of confrontation.

So I raise my arm in the air like a referee and blurt out the very first thing that comes into my head. "Simon Blackwood."

"What?" Renn turns to me, frowning.

"If you guys stop fighting, I'll tell you," I say.

"You have gossip." Renn's eyes widen.

Shrugging, I say, "I might have some, yes."

"Oh my God, tell us!"

Again, Penny rolls her eyes. "Really, Willow? I didn't know you were interested in gossip. I thought only Renn was the blabbermouth."

"Hey, don't call me blabbermouth. Let her talk," Renn admonishes.

"Don't fight." I stab my finger at both of them. When they both nod, I say, "So I heard the nurses saying that a new guy might be coming in. I mean, they didn't sound very happy about it. Beth never told them and they're like, nurses are always the last to find out and –"

"Oh God, who's coming?" Renn stops my rambling.

"Right." I clear my throat. "Someone named Simon Blackwood."

Simon. Blackwood.

I roll that name around in my head.

If names were an indication of someone's personality, then this Simon Blackwood would be strong, masculine, and regal. But then, names aren't everything.

Take me, for example. Willow clearly, isn't the name for me. Although, I can't imagine what else could be my name.

"Is he like, The Blackwood?" Penny asks.

"What is *The Blackwood*? What does that mean?" I ask.

"How can you not know what The Blackwood means?" Renn's face scrunches up in disgust. "He's the guy who founded this place, Willow. Dr. Alistair Blackwood. Well, you know, along with Dr. Martin. I bet Simon Blackwood is related to him in some way."

Dr. Martin is the psychiatrist in here who oversees things. I've only met with him once, when I first got in and thank God for that. I generally spend my time with a therapist or in group therapy.

Doctors are the worst kind of people. Pretentious, arrogant, obnoxious. Most of them have a God-complex. They think everyone needs saving and they are the only one who can do it.

They think that they can ruin your life whenever they want to. Turn your mom against you because they really *think* you'd benefit from in-patient treatment.

Fucking assholes.

I shift in my seat, feeling embarrassed. "Well, I just heard the nurses talking."

Renn sits back with a smile. "Oooh. Do you think he's a doctor too?"

"Could be." This comes from Penny.

Damn it.

If someone new is coming, I don't want them to be a doctor. This stupid hospital doesn't need another evil overlord.

Renn widens her eyes before craning her neck toward the door, as if whoever Simon is, he's gonna come striding in. "Oh my God, I'm so intrigued. Oh, please let him be handsome. And older. Like, at least ten years older. I've got a thing for older guys," she informs us, like we don't know.

"Or maybe he's not a doctor. He's a patient. Not everyone follows in their parents' footsteps," I say.

"Whatever. I just want him to be older."

"Yes, let him be older," I agree and Renn fist-pumps. And then, just to tease her, I add, "Oh, and wrinkled. Yup, a wrinkled old man who farts twice every hour."

Renn flips me the bird and my smile widens.

"Why don't you guys want me to eat?" Penny pushes her tray away in disgust. "If he's a doctor, then this kind of talk is inappropriate."

"How about we bet on it? We can play for lime jello." Renn grins.

On the Outside, I hated lime jello. It looks like puke, tastes like puke. It's plain puke. But on the Inside, it's all I ever wanna eat. I don't know why.

Could be the meds. They started me on a new cocktail as soon as I got here and that's always a disaster. My first week here wasn't pretty what with all the withdrawal-like symptoms that I went through after being taken off my old meds. They say my drugs aren't addictive but still, it felt like I was attacked by a stomach bug.

Meds have fucked with my life a lot. My body is thirty percent me, and the other seventy is what meds made me. I wouldn't be surprised if they fucked my palate too. Renn calls it The Heart-stone Effect; fuckery of drugs and psychotherapy.

Penny thinks about Renn's offer. "Fine. My money's on a new doctor, only five years older than Renn," she says, before picking up her book and resuming reading.

Renn sticks her tongue out at her, before turning to the fourth occupant of our table. "What about you, Vi? You want in on this?"

Vi, aka Violet Moore. She doesn't talk much. In fact, she's the one I've got a lot of things in common with. She's quiet. She's more or less invisible. People pass her by without noticing.

But unlike me, I think she chooses to be invisible. It's because she's grieving. Her fiancé died a few months ago and she might as well have died with him. No one knows what caused his death, not even Renn, and I haven't had the courage to ask Vi.

I wish I could.

I wish I could ask her what she thinks about when she stares out the window. She clearly isn't watching the rain like me. I wish I could ask her why she always has an empty chair next to her. Is it for her fiancé? Is she waiting for him as if he were alive and might walk over any second to take his place?

When Renn calls her name, Vi turns away from the window, bringing her flat brown eyes to us. "I'm with Renn. He's a handsome new doctor with at least fifteen years on us."

"Perfect. I'm so excited," Renn squeals.

Just as Renn sets out the rules, Beth enters the hall. She's Dr. Martin's wife and the hospital administrator.

Usually, she has a smile on her weathered face but today she looks a tiny bit frazzled. "Happy Monday, everyone," she begins, her greeting sounding less than enthusiastic. "Hope we're all doing well and enjoying our breakfast."

At this, she gets cut off as a couple of people boo her. It doesn't deter her, though. "I tell you this with a very heavy heart, that…" She sighs. "Friday night, Dr. Martin suffered a sudden heart attack and had to be hospitalized over the weekend, and…"

She swallows, trying to gather herself, as a shock wave runs through the room. "And, well, he's doing fine right now, and he's expected to make a full recovery. But it means that he won't be able to come back to work for a few weeks."

The murmurs and boos that had died down before Beth started talking come back to life, louder, more agitated.

Even though I'm not the one contributing to the ruckus, I'm kind of shocked, too. He was fine the last time I saw him. He smiled at me in the hallway, his white mop of hair glinting in the afternoon sun that was filtering through the big window in the TV room. He was chatting with a few patients, who all looked at him like he hung the moon. For them, he probably did.

He is super popular with the patients and the staff.

I remember thinking, how can you love your doctor? I mean, he's a doctor. A psychiatrist, no less. Someone who prescribes you meds and arranges your life in a series of therapy sessions. But even I wouldn't wish any harm on him.

Beth manages to calm people down with the help of techs and continues, "I know you guys are upset and I understand. Of course I do. I'm upset, too. Some of you have been very close to him, and I promise you he's fine. I'll let him know how much you guys love him. He'll appreciate that."

Smiling sadly, she takes in a deep breath. "But for now, I'm here to tell you that we've been very fortunate to have found a replacement for him. He's due to arrive today and he's an excellent doctor. I'm sure you guys will love him, and everybody will get along in this difficult time, okay?" She shoots a couple of pointed stares around the room. "If you have any questions, come find me or any of the staff members. We're all here to help you."

She's ready to leave when Renn calls out, "Hey, Beth! Who's the new guy? The one we're supposed to love and get along with."

Beth turns around and raises her eyebrows. "Right. Thank you, Renn, for shouting out that question. The doctor you're supposed to *love and get along with* is Dr. Blackwood. Dr. Simon Blackwood. He's coming to us from Boston. Mass General, to be specific. They have one of the most reputable psych departments in the country." She throws a pointed stare again. "As I said, you're in more than excellent hands."

With that, she leaves, and noises recommence.

Renn murmurs, "Well, we already guessed the doctor part. Ugh. Is he age-appropriate for me to fantasize about or not?"

Penny spits back, "He's a *doctor*. All talk about his looks is off-limits."

They begin fighting but I tune them out. I'm frozen, trapped by the sound of a name.

Simon Blackwood.

Dr. Simon Blackwood.

He's a doctor.

Actually, no. He's an *excellent* doctor.

And he's coming here.

Damn it.

Chapter 3

The weather is miserable, and I love it.

It's raining like it won't rain ever again. The winds are battering against the window, shaking the whole hospital.

I hate that I love it so much. Because I can't be outside and feel the sky fall on my body. I almost want it to take this stupid Victorian house apart, even though it's a testament of a great love and all, so I can escape. We can all escape. I'm sure forty determined patients will be able to move a certain automatic gate up front.

We've been cooped up inside the entire day and it blows. Not to mention everyone is wary and shaken up about the new arrival.

Community group was really agitated today. This group is basically where they explain and re-explain the hospital rules and take in complaints from the residents. And today every complaint was against a man who managed to upset everyone, and he isn't even here.

Sophie, a girl with severe insomnia, burst into tears, saying she came here to get better and not deal with this shit. If she wanted to deal with change, she would have stayed with her mom and her ever-changing boyfriends. Roger, the guy with homicidal ideation and Renn's crush of the week *last* week, was worried about the vibe he'd get from the new doctor. He's big on vibes and auras.

I'm usually quiet in such groups because my only complaint is that I don't belong here. I'm sure it won't go over too well with the therapist who handles the group. But then people started getting agitated when Renn expressed her own faux fears to rile things up: *what if he does something to us in our sleep? I'd be so scared to fall asleep now.*

I decided to intervene. "You guys, stop. He's not that bad. I met him," I said. "In the hallway. And you know, he looked pretty non-threatening to me. So yeah."

Yes, I was lying but it was okay. It was for a good cause.

My lies are always for a greater purpose.

Renn threw me a suspicious look but whatever. At least I got everyone to calm down. For about two seconds, and then, the questions started.

Where did you see him? The nurses said he hadn't arrived yet. How'd he look?

What do you mean non-threatening? What'd he look like exactly?

How old is he?

The last one came from Renn.

I answered them the best I could: I met him when he was just arriving, five minutes before this meeting, and maybe that's why no one knows he's here yet. He looked pretty okay. Short and bald and yes, old.

Although I didn't get a lot of time to embellish my lies, which I'm very good at by the way, because the therapist handling the group got us to shut up, with the help of a few techs.

All in all, this day sucks.

Now, I'm clutching *Harry Potter and the Prisoner of Azkaban* to my chest as I make my way toward the rec room at the end of the hall. Two nurses are standing in the corner, talking to each other, along with a couple of patients from my floor loitering about.

I pass by Beth's office. Usually, all staff offices are located in the area that's not freely accessible to the patients. But Beth told me when I first got here that she considers Heartstone a family and she wants to be available to everyone without having to jump through the hoops of appointments and whatnot.

Through her half-open door, I hear her talking to someone. But more importantly, I hear the same name I overheard a few hours earlier at breakfast.

Simon.

My feet come to a halt.

My eyes go wide.

"How's he doing?" Beth asks to someone in her office. Someone who she called Simon a second ago. "I'm sorry I haven't been in to see him this week. You know, with everything."

There comes a rustling and that someone clears his throat. "He's exactly the same as he was last week."

Oh my God, is that Simon?

Is he here? Is he actually *in* there?

A long sigh. Then Beth says, "He likes to be difficult. I'll give you that."

"Well, he always liked you," he says.

Simon says. No, Dr. Blackwood. Dr. Blackwood says. For some reason, I don't want to be on a first-name basis with him. Even in my head.

Anyway, so Dr. Blackwood says. Or rather rumbles.

In a voice that's deep and rough.

"And who can blame him." Beth chuckles.

There's a puff of air followed by a low grunt. I don't think it should've made it out of the room for me to hear, but it did. That low, scratchy sound. Somehow, I know that it's his laugh, rusty and unpracticed.

I swallow as my heart pounds more than it was already pounding.

There's a prolonged silence. Seconds and minutes of silence. Or maybe it only feels like that to me. Because I'm frozen, unable to move. Then I remember that I'm standing in the middle of the hallway, trying to eavesdrop on a conversation. Twice in one day.

But how can I resist? He's the new doctor, my new enemy. I *have* to listen.

I whirl on my feet and face the wall. I can't be eavesdropping when there are people around. Or rather, I can't make it obvious, so I try to make it look like I'm studying the collages on the wall.

It's the photographs of the patients, hospital staff, previous doctors, therapists with their names written on colorful strips.

"I've said this before, but I'm glad you're back. So glad,

Simon. And I can't tell you how excited I am that you're here, at Heartstone. This is your place. You belong here." Beth sounds nostalgic and so full of emotion.

"You've said this before, yes," Dr. Blackwood says wryly.

She chuckles. "I think you should tell him. You know, about everything that happened."

"No," he clips.

"I keep saying it but… it's okay. Whatever happened."

"Doesn't matter."

"It does matter, Simon," Beth insists. "I practically brought you up. I can see it."

"It's over."

"I think, if not him then you should talk to them. I think you should explain and maybe they will –"

"No."

Beth goes silent. I don't blame her. Even I jerked when I heard it – no, clutching the book to my chest and rubbing my arms. It's the way he said it. So shortly and loudly. So final.

"It's over, Beth," he says in a much calmer voice. "There's nothing to explain. Let it go."

What the hell are they talking about?

Whatever it is though, it has to be something extremely serious. I can say that much.

I wonder –

Suddenly, I feel a hand on my shoulder and I squeak, my thoughts disintegrating and my book falling to the floor with a thwack.

I whirl around to find an amused Renn looking back at me.

"What are you doing?" I screech at her.

"What are *you* doing?" In contrast to me, her voice is relaxed and so is her posture.

"You scared the c-crap out of me." I press a hand to my chest, trying to control my out-of-control heartbeats.

"Were you eavesdropping?"

"No," I lie. "And what happened to the no-touching rule?"

There's a rule here prohibiting touching between patients because some of them freak out when touched.

"As if. No rules can bind me."

"Maybe they should because –"

I stop talking when the door to Beth's room opens up and she stands in front of us. "Hey, guys. What's happening? Is everything okay?"

"Hey, Beth," Renn chirps. "It's nothing. I just touched Willow and she freaked out."

"Renn." Beth shakes her head. "You know there's a no-touching rule."

"Willow doesn't mind. She's my BFF." She turns to me. "Aren't you?"

Despite myself, I flush with pleasure at being called a BFF. I've never had any BFFs before. In fact, I never had any friends period.

Though I won't let Renn off the hook so easily. "Yes. But she scared the crap out of me, Beth." I press a hand to my chest, dramatically, before smirking at Renn. "Rules are rules for a reason."

"Traitor," Renn mutters, just as Beth launches into the importance of rules.

Chuckling, I bend down to pick up my fallen book. It's an old copy, with a questionable spine, and the fall has caused some of the yellow pages to come loose. They are scattered on the hardwood floor, black lettering flowing like a river. I grab hold of them and begin arranging them in the right order.

Over me, Beth and Renn continue to argue about rules and how Renn should be more conscious of them. But all conversation is lost when he steps out of the room.

Simon Blackwood.

I'm still bent down on my knees, putting my book back together, page by page, but I feel him standing over me. My fingers slip, causing a few collected pages to spill on the floor again.

Taking a deep breath, I tell myself to chill out. He's the enemy. I can't show him fear.

But him towering over me bothers me more than I'd like. Maybe it's because the air has moved around me, to make space for him. I feel his body casting its own shadow, creating its own awareness.

Discreetly and still arranging the papers, I look at the lower half of him. He's wearing black dress pants and brown wingtip shoes. Moisture and droplets of water cling to the fabric, and to his pointy and put-together footwear.

Outside.

He has come from the Outside.

Well, where else would he have come from? But God, he's brought rain with him, crisp and so pretty. I wish I could feel it on my skin.

And then, as if he can hear my thoughts, he makes it rain. He comes down on his knees by my side and I feel the cool, fresh droplets that shake down from his body, falling on mine. One plops on my scalp, another on my forehead and cheek, and a couple on my bare arms.

I move away from him fractionally.

I don't want him close. And neither do I want to notice how his dress pants are stretching across the expanse of his thighs. I've never seen cloth do that to a body before, mold around the bulging muscles like it were clay.

He should wear looser pants; I should tell him.

"You missed a few," he says, and I forget about his thighs.

From this close, his voice sounds more potent, more grainy, more rough, more deep.

Just more.

He reaches out his arm, and his fingers fold around the yellowed pages, lying on the side. Gently, he plucks them off the floor, arranges them in order, exactly the way I was doing a moment before. The way he grips the thin strips with such care, such finesse, wakes up my goose bumps.

I whip my eyes up to look at his face.

I breathe out a relieved, suspended breath. I didn't know I was even holding it. My gaze catches on to his square, rock-hard jaw, tracing the stubble that roughens up the slant of it. My eyes move up and I see his cheekbones, high and cliff-like.

Royal, masculine, stunning. Just like his name. He reminds me of the timeless statues I've seen in my history textbook.

His eyelids are lowered, as he's still focused on his task, and a couple of stray rain droplets shine on his eyelashes. In fact, I don't even think he's looked at me once. Not once. It prickles me that he finds a book worthier of his attention than me. Which is the most ridiculous thing I've ever felt.

Ever.

Once he's done, he offers the pages to me. Again, barely looking at me. "Here."

His eyes are gray in color.

Gray.

Like the clouds up in the sky. The man – my new enemy – who's wearing the rain has eyes the color of rainy clouds. One of my favorite things.

Damn it.

He frowns, giving me a distracted glance. "Are you okay?"

I blink, embarrassed, and take the pages from his hands before sliding them somewhere random in the book. "Yeah, sorry. Thanks."

"You might want to fix it."

"Huh?"

"The book," he explains, tipping his chin toward the object in my hand. "So it's not broken anymore. A little glue on the binding should help."

I swallow, my throat dry. "Right. Yeah, okay. Thanks."

I'm aware that I'm somewhat repeating my words, but my brain is mush. It's like the time when my anti-depressants made me almost manic, and they had to give me something to bring me down. I was in a fog the entire time.

Besides, he didn't even stop to hear my answer. As soon as

he doled out his piece of advice, he stood back up, his gaze slipping away from me. Not that it was there for more than a microsecond, but still.

Except I caught a word in all of this, and now it's stuck in my brain like his name: *fix*.

"Well, Renn, as much as I'd like to argue, I think I'll pass." Beth smiles before turning to the man beside her. "All right, I'm going to do the honors. This is Renn, our resident troublemaker. Watch out for this one. And that's Willow, our resident good girl. In fact, I don't think we've ever had a patient as well behaved as Willow."

I look away from him. I'm embarrassed now. The way Beth described me sounded lame. Although, I *am* a good girl. I've always followed the rules, listened to my mom and teachers, taken my meds on time.

So, good girl. That's me.

I don't know why hearing that bothers me though.

Or the fact that he barely even throws us a smile. He nods, twitches his lips half-heartedly, hardly making eye contact. You can't call it rude; all of it is polite.

Except, I don't like it.

Beth continues, "And girls, this here is our new doctor, Dr. Blackwood."

Even though I knew who he was, my heart races as if I'm hearing it for the first time. The shock of who this man is, is still new and vivid. It'll probably never wear off.

Again, Dr. Blackwood throws out a slight nod and a small smile. It's all right and well-timed and nice. And I bet he forgot our names as soon as he heard them. I bet he won't even remember this encounter tomorrow.

Dear God, it bothers me so much. *So* fucking much and it doesn't make sense.

The way he's not looking at us… at me. The way he said, *You might want to fix your book.*

"Oh, so *you* are Dr. Blackwood," Renn muses. "Can you confirm your age for me? Like, really quickly?"

"Renn!" Beth chides, glaring, and I do the same, forgetting my strange irritation at the man in front of us.

"What? I didn't ask *your* age." Renn rolls her eyes at Beth, pointing to me. "We've got a little bet going."

Damn the bet. I'd completely forgotten about it until Renn popped her stupid, inappropriate question.

"Are you kidding me?" I snap, pointedly looking away from Beth and Dr. Blackwood.

"What? It's the truth." Renn shrugs like she's so innocent. "Besides, you should be worried right now, dude. You lost."

"I did not lose." I look at Beth and reassure her, "I wasn't even playing."

"Are *you* kidding me now? Didn't you say he was short and bald? You put your money on that."

Beth gasps. "Renn! Willow? Why would you –"

Renn doesn't let her speak. "No, actually. She said he likes to fart twice in an hour. Then, in the group she said she'd met him and he was short and bald."

My eyes bug out. "What? I…"

"Both of you –" Beth begins but this time, it's me who talks over her.

"First of all, the bet was Renn's idea." I glare at her, my face flaming, *flaming*. "And second of all, everybody was freaking out in the group. They were worried about his aura, okay? It was a mess. I had to do something. So I kinda made things up. I did get everyone to calm down, didn't I?"

"Is that what you do?"

This is the first time he's said something ever since this non-sensical argument sprouted up.

It's a wonder I even hear him over my own pounding heart-beats. Somehow, someway, I turn my eyes to him. That's a wonder too, given my level of embarrassment.

Is it weird that I'm sweating everywhere, even under my bangs? I blow on them and he glances at the fluttering strands before looking into my eyes. Not in passing, but really. Like he's really seeing me.

The earth tilts slightly but I plant my feet wide and refuse to be moved as he takes me in. My loose topknot, with strands of hair sprinkled around my face, clinging to the nape of my neck. Even though, his gaze flicks along my features and he doesn't look anywhere else below that, I still try to remember what I'm wearing. I think I've got a white t-shirt on with the quote across my breasts, *"Just a wizard girl, living in a muggle world."* Oh, and sweatpants with my bunny slippers.

In my outrageous nightmares, I saw them putting me in a straitjacket as soon as I arrived at the facility. But apparently mental hospitals don't do that anymore. They told me to bring my most comfortable clothes and, well, what's more comfortable than my

Harry Potter t-shirts and sweatpants?

But oddly, I'm regretting my wardrobe choices now. Which obviously means that I've lost my mind. Well, more than usual. I lift my chin in defiance and something flashes across his impassive face. I can't say what, however.

"Do what?" I ask.

"Make things up?"

I want to fidget under his gray eyes but I control myself and hug my book tighter.

What kind of a question is that?

See? Psychiatrists ask stupid, irrelevant questions.

I frown. "I don't make things up. I elaborate."

He stays silent for so long that I think he'll never speak again. But he does, very casually. "And that's clearly very different from each other."

"Yes." I smile. "As a matter of fact, they are very different from each other."

"You do that often – elaborate, I mean?"

"Is that a trick question?"

"No, just a regular, run-of-the-mill question."

I can't figure out if he's serious or not. I mean, he looks serious but there was something there on his face, in his voice, some kind of amusement, wryness, that makes me think he's having fun with this.

Well, whatever.

"Then the answer is no. I don't elaborate." A voice in the back of my mind disagrees but I squash it. "Besides, I was only doing it to make people feel better. Isn't that your whole job? I was basically doing it for you."

Beth gasps and Renn snorts.

But Dr. Blackwood ignores both of them and asks, "You were, huh?"

"Yes."

For a beat, all he does is scan my face without a word, jacking up my heart even more. Like his stare is a certain drug.

But then he ducks his head, his dark, wet hair glinting under the hallway lights. He looks back up with half a smile. One-fourth of a smile, actually. "Well, then I owe you one. Thank you for doing my job for me. I appreciate it very much."

Before I can say anything, Renn jumps in, highly amused. "Just give her a lime jello, she'll be happy."

But Dr. Blackwood doesn't pay her any attention. "Maybe I will," he says to me.

He steps back, probably ready to put this whole conversation behind him. "It was nice meeting both of you. And... I'm thirty-three, by the way."

Renn fist-pumps. "Yes."

Before he leaves though, his eyes drop to the book in my arms and I clutch it tightly, as if he'll take it away. "Let me know if you need any help fixing your book."

This time, however, I'm having a hard time keeping my face blank at the word fix. So I might have pursed my lips; I'm not sure.

Stop saying fix, you moron.

I swear, I see a distinct twitch on his mouth as he glances at me one last time and leaves. I glare after him and his ridiculously tall and broad body, encased in clothes that seem to be made just for him.

It's like he knows that word affects me. He knows how much I hate it.

Fix.

That's what people have been saying to me for the past two weeks. Especially my mom.

We need to fix this, Lolo. What if it happens again?

Why won't you let the doctor fix you, Lolo?

A few weeks at Heartstone is going to fix you right up, Lolo.

But that's stupid because there's no way he could've known. We've only just met.

Oh and he's fifteen years older than Renn… and me. But that doesn't matter.

Not at all.

I clutch my book even tighter. My precious book.

My precious perfect book.

My *fucking precious perfect* book.

God, I hate all doctors.

Chapter 4

Everyone's watching him. Like he's a celebrity or something.

Well, almost everyone.

Me? I'm not watching except for occasional glances here and there.

A tech comes up to me with a plastic cup, taking my focus away from the new doctor. The cup holds the key to making my brain happy. The pills. Prozac, lithium, Zoloft, Effexor. I can't keep track of them anymore.

I take it from him and gulp the sour-tasting, magic medicine down that's going to steal my sleep all in the name of side-effects. When he doesn't go away, I shoot him a look. He shoots me a look of his own.

Gah.

Narrowing my eyes at him, I open my mouth and stick my tongue out for him to examine. When he's satisfied that I've swallowed my pills like a good girl, he walks away.

"Do you think he's taken?" That's Renn.

At her words, I switch my focus back to my enemy.

He's standing in the hallway with Beth and a few of the staff members. And we're in the TV room. I'm supposed to be reading my precious book, but all the murmured and hissed conversation is messing with my mojo.

"It doesn't matter if he is," Penny says and goes back to reading. I have no idea how she does it. I wish I had her focus.

"Exactly. I mean, he's hot enough, older enough, and un-available enough for me. I'm gonna go for him anyway." Renn shrugs, balancing her chair on the back two legs.

Vi snorts, flicking the channels on TV.

"God, he's handsome. Like, really handsome, you know. I'll really have to stop myself from not calling him daddy at our appointments."

"Ew. Stop," Penny snaps.

I'm right there with Penny as I toss my book on the table. "Yes. Stop. He's like every other jerk doctor I've ever met."

"Don't be a sore loser. Besides, I thought I was dead to you." Renn throws me a flying kiss.

I roll my eyes at her. After what she did to me in front of Beth and Dr. Blackwood, I'm super mad at her. But of course, she doesn't care. She's Renn.

"You are. I just like talking to dead bodies."

"You've got issues."

I stick my tongue out at her and that only makes her laugh. When I go to glance really quickly at the group standing in the hallway, I find Dr. Blackwood staring straight at me. I feel a jolt run through my body.

He's all gray eyes and cool face. Of course, from here I can't really see their color, but I remember it from before. I remember it from every time I look up at the rainy sky.

Why did his eyes have to be the color of my most favorite thing? It's really not fair. It's like hating someone dressed like Hagrid, the friendly half-giant from Harry Potter. You can't hate Hagrid; he's too nice.

I look away from him, disgusted.

"I don't think he's like every other doctor you've met. I mean, his dad founded this place. Hello? Genius alert. So technically, it's in his blood. Science and medicine," Renn concludes.

She is right.

Medicine is in his blood. Like illness is in mine. My blood is tainted with poison and his is laced with the antidote.

The fucking contrast. Don't know why it even occurred to me, let alone bothers me.

"Yup, Dr. Alistair Blackwood was one of the best psychiatrists. They teach one of his books in med school. I wonder where he is these days," Penny says.

"What happened to him? Did he retire?" I ask, despite myself.

"Kinda. He just stopped practicing a few years ago," Renn contributes. "My dad was pretty broken up about it. The hospital board wasn't happy with the change. Meaning, my dad wasn't happy about the change."

Renn's dad is one of the board members of this hospital. Sometimes I feel that Renn keeps coming back here because she wants to get his attention. And he keeps sending her here because he just doesn't care.

But then, what do I know of fathers? I've never met mine. I don't know anything about trying to get your dad's attention, like Renn, or following in his footsteps, like Dr. Blackwood.

Cool and aloof, Dr. Blackwood.

He's barely talking to the group of people. He's simply listening, punctuated with polite nods. I bet he doesn't even remember their names. I bet he doesn't even remember *our* names, Renn's and mine, and we met like a couple of hours ago.

Anyway, it's none of my business. I don't care.

I've got enough problems of my own. For example, being stuck on the Inside. Away from everyone and everything. Where you only get to talk to your family or see them once a week. I've asked my mom not to visit – I draw the line at her seeing me like this, locked up and crazy – so talking on the phone is my only option.

Today's that day. I call it the phone call day. Another thing about being on the Inside is that days run together. I don't know if it's Monday or Tuesday or if they even follow the normal calendar like on the Outside. It's all the same.

The only reason I know it's phone call day is because people keep disappearing down the hall with either a huge smile or apprehension on their faces, and they come back ten minutes later with either that smile in place or with tears or anger in their eyes.

I dread phone call days. I want them too much and when it's over, I'm left feeling bereft and homesick. And angry.

A few minutes later, I find myself in a small room with a

couple of couches and desks and old-fashioned rotary dial phones. Black and monstrous things.

I take a seat at the small table, just under the rainy window. Swallowing, I pick up the receiver, lying on its side. "Hello."

"Lolo. Hey, sweetheart," my mom says.

A sting in my eyes and gravel in the back of my throat steal my breath away for a second. I miss her so much. So freaking much that I have to press the receiver tightly, hold on to the arm of my chair, so I don't fall off.

"Hey, Mom," I whisper, thickly.

"How are you, baby?"

Her voice is soft, softer than usual. It gets that way when she's tired or sad. Right now, it's the latter. She's sad because of me. Because of how fucked up I am.

"I'm okay. How are you?"

"I'm good, too."

"Yeah? How's work?"

"You know, busy. We have a huge wedding coming up so we're all scrambling."

If it were two weeks ago, I would've asked who's getting married. Or maybe she would've volunteered that information herself. But it's not two weeks ago. It's now. And we don't talk more than what's necessary.

"Good. I'm glad," I offer, lamely.

Awkwardly.

My mom and I, we hardly ever have awkward moments. In fact, she's been my best friend – my only friend – ever since I was born. She tells me everything and so do I. Well, almost everything.

There are certain things I can't ask her or tell her because she'll freak out.

But The Roof Incident has changed everything.

It came as a major shock to her. Even more than my diagnosis that I got at the age of fourteen.

My mom was so shaken up that day at the hospital. She looked at me like I'd vanish any second. Like, I was *planning* to vanish any second. She didn't leave my side even once. Not until they took me away for a forty-eight hour mandatory admission to the psych ward.

I don't know if she'll ever trust me again. I don't know if *I'll* ever trust her again.

"How're things for you? Are they... are they treating you well?"

I wanna say that they are evil, all of them. I wanna tell my mom that they keep me chained to my bed, give me electric shocks. They're making me crazier. Day by day, I'm losing my left-over sanity.

But I won't.

I won't lie. Not about this. I can't burden her any more than I already have. No matter how mad I am at her for sending me here.

"They're treating me well," I say, finally.

"Okay. Okay, that's good."

There's silence and I'm dreading that this will be the end of our conversation.

God, how did this happen?

I hate this. I hate myself for being so fucked up.

I hate my mom for not believing me.

"So, I…" my mom begins and I sit up straight, eager to hear her talk. "I'm, uh, painting your room light yellow. I read it in this magazine that it's supposed to bring calmness. It's good for your… thoughts."

I grit my teeth as tears spring in my eyes.

Thoughts.

Yeah, everything is happening because of my fucking *thoughts,* isn't it?

"Mom, you don't need to do that. I'm… Honestly, I'm fine. I don't… I'm not…"

Crazy.

It hurts me so much that I've hurt her. That she doesn't trust me when I say I don't need to be here.

"I'm just trying to do everything I can, honey. Everything that I can possibly do to make it easier," she whispers.

"Mom, everything is easier. It's fine. I keep telling you. I don't… I don't need to be here."

Her sigh is frustrated. "Lolo, not this again, please."

"But it's true, Mom. I don't belong here. I don't need to be here. I'm fine. It was a one-time thing and…" I look up at the ceiling. "Please, Mom. Let me come home."

I haven't been home in two weeks. Two fucking weeks.

It might not sound like much but I've never lived apart from my mother. In fact, I was going to stay home while attending college. We had it all worked out. I was going to spend my summer working at the bookstore like I always do. Then, Mom was going to take some time off from the store and we were going to do something fun together before my college started.

But now, I'm trapped here.

All because of one foolish mistake.

"I want you home too, but you need to be there. You need to fix it, Lolo. I can't... I can't go through that again. I can't get that day out of my head. I can't forget how you looked. So pale. So... lifeless. Lying in that bed. I just... It gives me nightmares. And all because of a boy? I still can't believe it. I can't believe that my daughter would lose her mind over a boy. In fact..." She takes a deep breath. "I drove by your school. I know I promised that I wouldn't. But, God, I couldn't stop myself. I want to track him down and —"

I sit up straight, clutching the phone to my ear, dread prickling the nape of my neck. "Mom, no. You promised."

"I know. But it's because of him you're... Everything happened because of him. You lost your mind because of him, Lolo."

I wipe my nose with the back of my hand. I'm shaking. I'm cold and sweating. I don't want to think about *him*.

I don't want her to think about him, either.

Why the fuck did I even tell her? Why? All I can say is that I was so panicked that day at the hospital that I didn't even realize what I was saying until the words came out. But then, it was too late to take them back.

"Mom. You gave me your word. You said if I went to Heartstone, you'd forget about it. I am at Heartstone and you have to keep your promise."

She sighs.

God, please let her give up. Just please. I can't have her

thinking about *him*.

"Fine. But in the future, you can't keep secrets from me. Do you understand, Lolo? We can't have you jeopardizing your health over a guy. They are not worth it. Boys, men, relationships… nothing is worth your health, Lolo. Love is a very stupid thing to lose your life over."

My family is all super independent types. My mom and grandma, my aunt, my cousin. They date but they don't fall in love. They've got their priorities straight. Work and family. A man is only good as a stress reliever.

My father was one. I think she met him on a trip to Paris. She was there for business and when she wanted to wind down, she found him at a bar. All I know about him is that he was tall and handsome. I like to imagine him as a dashing Frenchman by the name of Jean-Claude, with blue eyes.

I can't say that I miss him or want him in my life but I would've loved to know him. Maybe he could tell me about my illness and how I got it when no Taylor has ever suffered from it before.

I deflate, my body going loose. "Okay. Yeah. No secrets about boys."

A rush of air escapes her. Long and full. She has probably been holding that breath ever since The Incident.

I can almost see her slouching down in relief. She must be sitting in her favorite armchair in the living room, by the fireplace. "Good. That's good. I just want you to get better. You do everything they tell you to do, okay? We have to fix it. No more refusing treatment. And when you go to college in fall, we're getting you a counselor there, as well. Promise me, okay? Promise me you'll get better."

I grit my teeth. Again.

Refusal of treatment is a very unfair assessment. I never refused treatment.

I hated the therapist at the state hospital, so I might have poured water on her charts because she was being condescending. And I may have called her a few choice names.

That's it. That's all I did. But I never *refused* treatment.

And yes, I might have created a little bit of a ruckus when at the end of the forty-eight hour period, my mom came to see me at the psych ward. I thought she was taking me home, but she said she wanted me to do a six-week in-patient program at Heartstone, based on the doctor's recommendation.

But can anyone blame me? I thought I was finally going home, not to a psych facility in the middle of the woods.

"I promise, Mom. I'll get better. You don't have to worry," I reassure her again, instead of arguing.

Ten minutes later when I have to hang up, I have such deep longing to go back home and hug my mother that I have to clench my eyes shut.

Four weeks.

Four fucking weeks before I can go Outside.

But I have a feeling that even when I get out, I'll never leave. The Roof Incident will always haunt me. My mom will always be worried about me. She will always be watching me.

God, I'm such a fuck up.

On shaky legs, I stand up, ready to leave, when I spot a tall figure in the rain.

Like the trees, the figure's blurred and I have to press my face to the cold, permanently-shut window to get a better look.

It's a man.

He doesn't have any protection against the deluge as he stands on the grass, looking up at the pouring sky. It's almost as if he's daring it to fall, to do his worst to him. My lips part and my breaths fog up the glass as I watch him.

When he looks down, appearing frozen in the moment, I wonder what he's thinking about. I also wonder why they matter, his thoughts.

Nothing about this man should matter to me. In fact, I hate this man.

Simon Blackwood.

It's him.

His clothes are soaked, the mud brown shirt and dress pants, and they cling to his body like skin made of fabric. Every bulge, every carved muscle is on display. His hands are shoved down into his pockets and there's a messenger bag slung over one of his shoulders.

He's leaving for the day, I think. Usually, people wait for the rain to pass or the wind to become less vicious, but not him, I guess.

I claw my fingers on the glass in jealousy. The nurse tells me to move away from the window and the phone. She tells me it's someone else's turn. I don't listen to her. I smash my nose into the glass, standing my ground.

I hate that he gets to feel the rain whenever he wants, and I can't even see it without someone telling me to back off.

I hate that he can leave through those tall gates whenever he wants to and go back home. While I'll be stuck here, forcing myself not to miss my mom too much.

Most of all, I hate that when he reads my chart, he'll come to know everything about me.

Every single thing.

He'll know I'm crazy.

So crazy that the nurse finally gives up warning me and physically removes me from the window, muttering, "Do you want me to call the techs?"

Medicine

Man

When I stop at the cemetery in the pouring rain, I don't expect to see anyone there.

Let alone a small boy – a boy I know – in a black suit with his head bent and his knees drawn up, sitting under the tree as the lightning streaks through the sky.

He's my neighbors' kid. Well, my father's neighbors' kid. I don't live in that house anymore.

My first thought is that he is lost; I don't see his parents around. In fact, I don't see anyone around. Then I spot a bicycle toward the far end of the dismal place. Must be his.

My second thought is that maybe he's meeting someone here. A friend. Girlfriend? But a cemetery is an odd place to meet someone. Then again, I have no idea what kids are doing these days.

At last, I decide it doesn't matter. It's none of my business what he's doing here. All alone, in the storm, with hunched shoulders.

I get out of my car, water beating down on me. When I walk through those gates, I have every intention of not caring and heading to the grave I came here to see. I have every intention of doing what I haven't been able to do ever since I moved back from Boston a couple of days ago. I'm thinking today is the day I'll do it.

But I pass by the grave I'm supposed to stop at. In fact, I don't even pay attention to it. I keep walking.

My focus is the kid sitting under a tree.

I've only seen him once. Yesterday, when I stopped by the house because Beth said that the pipe in the upstairs bathroom was leaking and the plumber wouldn't be there until tomorrow. I told her I'd fix it.

Although it wasn't any of my business. What happens to that house, which looked to be in pretty bad shape – leaking roofs, broken stairs, loose floorboards – and the man living in it. Even the willow tree in the backyard looked like it was about to die.

The kid looks up as I approach, and I gauge his age to be twelve. His eyes are swollen; he's been crying.

I clamp my jaw shut and tip my chin at him. "Hey."

He sniffles and glares at me. "My mom said not to talk to strangers."

I thrust my hands in my pockets and nod. "She tell you to sit under a tree during a thunderstorm, too?"

"No." He shrugs. "I can do whatever I want. She's not here to stop me."

He looks away angrily, and I tell myself to move on. There's nothing I can do here. He's grieving, for whatever reason, and grief's not something I can do much about.

Definitely not as a doctor. There's even a thing called Bereavement Exclusion in the Diagnostic and Statistical Manual of Mental Disorders. Meaning, there's a fuck ton of debate over diagnosing bereaved individuals.

Grief is not something I can fix – not medically. I should know for more reasons than one.

Still, I take a seat beside the boy.

"Where is she?" I look at the ocean of graves, resting my elbow on my upturned knee. "Your mom."

He rips the drenched grass out of the ground and spits out, "Dead."

I knew he was going to say something like that. But it doesn't make it any easier to hear. Death never gets easier. Duller, perhaps. The pain of losing someone. But it's always there.

"How'd she die?" I ask, running my hands through my soaked hair.

The boy doesn't say anything for a while. I don't know if he'll talk. I wouldn't. I haven't, even after nineteen years. I've buried it like these dead bodies.

"Cancer," he says at last, in a small voice. But then it rises, matches volume with the storm around us. "The doctor said she'd be fine. He said he was gonna do everything."

"And he didn't?"

"No. It was a minor procedure. I looked it up. She was supposed to be better after surgery. But she never even made it out." Ripping out the grass once more, he snaps, "Fucking moron." Then, "Sorry. I know you're a doctor."

I raise my eyebrows at him.

"I was being a dick. I saw you yesterday. The first time I ever saw that house getting any visitors." He shrugs sheepishly. "And heard you. You were talking about hospital and patient charts and cases or whatever. Didn't mean to insult your kind, but I also kinda did. I'm Dean, by the way."

I chuckle, despite myself – a dry sound – and rest my head against the tree trunk. "Simon. And I don't mind. Doctors are morons, yes. They think they can save everyone. They have this God complex. They think they are heroes. They think the whole world depends on them. Like they aren't capable of making mistakes."

"Do you have a God complex?"

"Yeah. I do."

"So, you've never made a mistake?" he asks with disbelief.

"No," I lie, making him chuckle.

He rests his head against the tree. "I miss her."

For some reason, I'm compelled to tell him, "Yeah. My mom died when I was fourteen."

Dean spins his head toward me. "No way."

I jerk out a shrug.

"What happened?"

I sigh, thinking about it.

What happened?

She was there one minute, and then, she was gone. I remember tucking her in for the night. I remember turning off the light and going back to my room.

There was a party one of my friends from school invited me to. I didn't usually party. I never had the time to. Besides, I didn't jell with most of the guys from my school. They kept away from me because they liked their faces and their big mouths, and I liked talking through my fists.

But that night, I was debating whether to go or not. I thought she'd looked good today. She'd been having a streak of good days so maybe I could go, blow off some steam.

But after that everything's hazy.

I passed out in my bed and when morning came, for some strange reason, I was frantic. Anxious. I dashed to my mom's bedroom and there she was. On the bed, the same way I'd left her. Only difference was that she wasn't breathing.

"I can't remember. All I remember is that a doctor was supposed to save her, but he didn't," I reply, hardly believing that I'm having a conversation about my mother with a twelve-year-old boy.

I haven't talked about my mom with anyone in years.

"Were you pissed at him? The doctor," he asks.

"Yes."

"Did you do something about it?"

I think about not telling him, but maybe it will help in a small way, knowing someone else has felt the same. "Punched him in the face."

I want to rip off the grass like Dean did. My hands tremble with the need. But I fist them and shove them in my pockets instead.

"Oh man, that's awesome," he says in awe. "I wish I could punch him too. But my dad wouldn't be too happy about it."

I wonder what his dad is thinking about right now. He must be freaking out. But I have a feeling if I point it out to his son next to me, this strangely rebellious boy is not going to like it.

"So, why'd you become a doctor?" he mutters after a moment.

"Because I wanted to be better than the man who killed my mother." I look at the pouring sky. "I wanted to show him that I could do a better job than him. Save everyone."

"Did you?"

Something moves in me. I can't name it. Or rather, I don't want to name it. Naming it would mean… it's real.

I've failed. I'm like him, and I can't deal with that.

I can't *deal* with being like him.

"Yes. I did," I lie again, and he smiles.

We sit in silence, after that.

"That your bike?" I point toward the red bike leaning against the brick wall.

"Yeah."

"So what? You waiting for someone? Ran away? What?"

Dean narrows his eyes at me. "Are you gonna lecture me about the dangers of running away like a boring old man?"

This time my chuckle is louder, surprised; I can't help it. "If you want to run away, kid, that's your problem. Just don't be stupid about it."

"I'm not stupid."

"Are you planning on going back?"

"Maybe."

"Ah, so you're just trying to kill your remaining parent."

He swallows, looking guilty. "I'm not."

I shake my head at him. "Look, either run away because you really mean it, or just don't do it at all. Temper tantrums don't look good on anyone."

He glares at me for a few seconds and I want to laugh out loud.

Which is a feat in itself.

I wasn't looking forward to today. I knew it was going to be excruciating, walking through the same hallways I'd visited as a child. I hated being at Heartstone. The smell, the walls. Nurses, techs. The patients.

Visiting Heartstone meant that my father wasn't home, and my mother wanted him to be. So either she'd take me with her when she went to see him, or I'd go look for him in the hope that I could convince him to come home.

If it weren't for Dr. Martin and his sudden heart attack, I wouldn't be here. Even though back in Boston I was basically out of a job, coming home, walking through the doors of my father's legacy, was never the plan.

But plans don't always work out.

"I hated the funeral, okay?" Dean snaps, his eyes welling up again. "I hated staying back there. My dad wouldn't say anything. My sister wouldn't stop crying. I had to get away. Not that it's any of your business."

It's not. He's right.

By experience, I know that this isn't the last time he'll cry or run away. This isn't the last time he'll be angry. My body goes tight at the thought of all the times he'll want to punch something or someone. All the times he'll want to forget the pain of losing his parent by either being reckless or so fucking numb that even his veins would freeze over.

"Your sister. Is she younger than you?"

"Yes. Why?" he asks suspiciously.

"She likes balloons?"

"Yes."

I nod, my body relaxing at having something to do. "Come on. I know a place where we can buy balloons." I come to my feet, my clothes sticking to me; I fucking need a shower to wash this day off.

We walk to the car and I think, tomorrow. Tomorrow I'll come back and visit the grave. Tomorrow, I'll tell her all about what happened at Mass General and why I came back when I promised I never would.

But then again, telling her would be admitting failure, admitting that I might be like my father – a fraud – and I already know that tomorrow will never come.

We get to the car and I load his bicycle in the back. Dean loves my car, if his *ooh*s and *ahs* are anything to go by. It's a Mercedes sl550 convertible. My father never drove a Mercedes. That was the only reason I bought it. To prove that I've got a better car than him.

I drive Dean to the store, where we buy a bunch of balloons. By the time I drop him off at the funeral home, the rain has stopped.

I help him with his balloons and bike. Fishing my card out of my pocket, I say, "Call me if you ever run into trouble."

"Are you gonna stick around for a while?"

I look at the overcast sky, thrusting my hands inside my pockets. Back in Boston, I was supposed to be promoted. I was going to be the head of their psychiatry department. Youngest in their history. Until I stepped down.

I don't know if there's anything left for me in Boston. But I can't stay here, either. Not in this town.

I can't say that to this boy, though. No idea why. But I can't take away his hope when he's looking at me like that.

"I think so, yeah."

He grins, ties the balloons to his bike and take off pedaling. I stay there until I see him walking through the door, and then drive off.

Not to the house though. To the hotel.

A couple of hours later, I'm fresh out of the shower and in bed. I've got patient charts to read before the upcoming meetings this week.

Opening my laptop, I log into the system. The words seem blurry, like I'm looking through a lens of water. I reach out and pluck the glasses lying on the nightstand. No matter how much I try to deny it, I do need glasses for reading now.

My eyes have gone weak. Like *his*.

I put the glasses on; the words on screen make sense. Crystal clear. I pull up the only chart I'm interested in, for some unfathomable reason.

Name: *Willow Audrey Taylor*.

Age: *18*

The girl with the silver hair and a tattered book.

The girl who likes to make things up.

Chapter 5

The next morning I'm summoned by the king.

The ice king.

That's what I'm calling him now.

He's trying to get to know the patients, that's what Beth and one of the nurses told me at breakfast.

I'm at his door right now. A brown, polished door that still says Dr. Martin's name. Though the man inside is nothing like Dr. Martin. The man inside is much harsher, much colder.

Hence the name.

But it's gonna be okay. Who cares if he's cold and wooden? I don't have to spend an eternity with him in that room. Get in. Get out.

"Be calm and sweet and gentle," I mutter to myself. "Don't get provoked. Don't pour water on his papers. Don't be defensive, Willow. He doesn't think you're crazy, okay? I mean, he probably does think that but whatever. You're not here to impress him. So relax. It's going to be okay. Don't be an idiot. He's probably gonna ask a few *very* general, *very* casual questions. Answer them. Just –"

I'm cut off mid-speech as the door whips open, blowing up my bangs. I look up and come face to face with the ice king.

Dr. Simon Blackwood.

If I thought he couldn't get colder and more unapproachable than yesterday, then I was wrong. He's even more distant than before in his horn-rimmed glasses. Big, square-shaped. Old-fashioned and timeless.

Kind of like him.

"Were you talking to someone?" he asks in his deep voice, his storm-colored eyes even more vivid from behind his specs. Which is totally ridiculous and nonsensical. A layer of barrier should lessen their effect, not enhance it.

"No."

It's not a lie. I mean, technically, I was talking to myself, not *someone*.

He looks up and down the hallway, which is pretty much empty except for the bustle at the nurses' station at the end. His office is located in the area, which is not freely accessible to patients, unless they have a prior appointment.

"You sure?"

"Yes. There's no one here but me." And then, just because I can't stop myself, I add, "Why, you think all crazy people talk to themselves?"

His sharp gaze finds mine. "Why, are you crazy?"

"Now is *that* a trick question, given where we are right now?" I fold my arms across my chest, mentally kicking myself.

Why the hell do I have to go and be defensive like that?

Not everyone's out to get me.

He studies me. His gray eyes flick across my face and my overgrown bangs. I blow on them and his jaw ticks. A slight, almost invisible tick. I probably wouldn't have caught it if I wasn't standing so close to him.

That's the whole problem, actually. That I'm standing too close to him. I want to take a step back, be away. We should probably have a one-arm distance between us. Two-arm distance.

I'm about to inch back in a way that he doesn't notice when he speaks, bringing my attention to his lips. "One thing you'll learn about me, Willow, is that I don't ask trick questions. And neither do I like trick answers. And I usually know when I'm getting one."

My spine goes rigid, even as something very similar to flutters races down the length of it.

I should've moved away from him; I know that now.

Or at least not been so close to him when he said my name. First of all, his lips are the softest, most pillowy lips I've ever seen. They contrast so well with his face. So well and so effectively that it's hard not to focus *only* on them.

And second of all, I've never seen anyone's lips mold around my name the way his did. So carefully and so deliberately that the rest of the words almost disappeared.

But I ignore all of those things because they are inconsequential. Besides, the rest of the words almost disappeared. *Almost.* Meaning I did catch a few, and was that arrogance I heard in them?

"Are you saying that you've got a superpower or something? That sniffs out trick answers?" I ask, raising my eyebrows.

He straightens his glasses with his long, manly fingers as he rumbles, "Or something."

I swallow at the gesture and how stern it is. If this is his way of intimidating me, he's kind of succeeding. I *do* have things to hide.

"Well, then." I unfold my arms and sweep my bangs off my forehead. "Good thing you've got me for the next hour. I'm as straightforward and truthful as you can get."

Nothing, not one thing changes on his face so I don't know if he's being sarcastic or what when he says, "Good thing."

With that, he steps back and lets me in, and I enter with my heart lodged in my throat.

I've been inside this room once. The day I came here two weeks ago, when I had a meeting with Dr. Martin.

I don't know what I was expecting when I walked in here, but it wasn't the rich browns and greens and cozy leather couches that look like a throwback from the 90s. Most likely, this room used to be a study with the rows and rows of bookshelves, a nook for reading, complete with a fireplace and its own washroom. Dr. Martin has plants in every corner, making the room so welcoming and warm.

I remember being shocked. I remember thinking it was a trick to lull patients into a false sense of security, so they stay here forever or admit to things that aren't true. Namely, that they are crazy. Now, I'm thankful for the warmth.

I turn around to face Dr. Blackwood when I hear the click of the door being shut. Suddenly, all the sounds, chatter and murmurs of the hospital, are gone. There's complete silence. Like we're in a bubble. A vacuum, maybe.

The air seems thicker in here, with a distinct scent. I can't quite figure out what it is but it's pleasant. Not like the moldy and bleach-y smell of the rest of the hospital.

It fills me with… happiness.

Dr. Blackwood is still by the door, standing tall and large, his hands inside his pockets, his rich, dark hair brushing against the collar of his shirt. I wonder what we're waiting for when I realize his face is ducked and his eyes are glued to my bunny slippers. Inside the soft haven of my footwear, my toes curl.

"Can we get started?" I ask, feeling self-conscious.

Without lifting his face, he shifts his gaze to me. I wish I was good at reading people but I'm not and I can't tell what he's thinking. But I do notice that his eyes are glinting. Or maybe it's the light shafting through the windows. Today's a bit sunnier than yesterday; I hate it. But at least I might get to go outside and feed my pigeons.

He nods and walks to the desk. "Sure."

I nod back, wiping my hand on my black yoga pants. My t-shirt says, "*Snuggle this muggle.*" I thought I needed something cozy today.

I'm about to take my seat when I notice something at the desk. Something green and in a plastic cup, placed exactly where I'm supposed to sit.

My lips part on a small breath and I look up at him, standing by his chair, composed as ever.

"Is that… a lime jello?" I manage to ask in a hoarse, compressed voice.

"That is what the label says, yes," he replies, coolly.

I narrow my eyes. "Why's there a lime jello where I'm supposed to sit?"

At this, I notice something twitch. His lips.

There's a very, very small smile on his lips as he bows his head again before looking back up, and his hair gets caught up in the sunrays. I'm almost stunned to see that it isn't all black; there are slices of rich chocolate brown in there.

"Are you always this suspicious of snacks?" he asks.

"Only when they are given to me for no reason. And by a doctor, no less."

"You have something against doctors?"

Say no. Say no. Say no.

I offer him a tight smile. "Yes. Especially psychiatrists. Not to mention, psychologists too. I think they're wacked."

Then the sound I heard yesterday echoes around the room. His chuckle. It's short and sharp. Such a burst of bright sound that I don't even regret outing my true feelings about people like him.

Dr. Blackwood shakes his head once, a small lopsided smile lingering on that soft mouth. "Yeah? How's that?"

"They spend their days figuring out the crazy. It's clearly not because they want to help people."

"Clearly."

I let his sarcasm go. "It's because there's something wrong with them. Who wants to spend hours upon hours sitting on a couch, analyzing the shit out of insanity? Insane people."

"I sit in a chair."

I throw him a mock smile. "Whatever. Doesn't make you any less wacked."

"Noted." Then he shrugs, keeping his eyes on me. "Well, I owed you, and your friend – Rachel, is it? – said lime jello is the way to go."

Right.

Stupid, freaking Renn. I still haven't forgiven her for throwing me under the bus yesterday.

But that's not important right now. What's important is that he forgot Renn's name. I mean, I knew he would. I *knew* it. And it pisses me off. How dare he forget my BFF's name?

"Renn."

"Excuse me?"

"Her name's Renn," I inform him.

"Right. I apologize. I'm not very good with names, apparently," he says in a tone that's laced with both self-deprecation and arrogance, somehow. Like he's apologizing but not *really* apologizing.

"You remembered my name."

As soon as I blurt it out, I wanna take it back. I wanna find those words in the air – the thick, scented air – and shove them back inside my mouth.

This is what happens when you talk too much. You say the wrong things. I was supposed to be calm and cool and a cucumber.

Now I can't stop thinking about the fact that he did remember my name. In fact, I still can't get over the way he said it, like that name really suited me. Not to mention, he remembered the whole nonsensical conversation from yesterday.

For an unknown reason, all of this makes me flush and I look away from his penetrating eyes.

He's not supposed to affect me this much. I've always hated doctors with their judgmental looks and God complexes. But not like this.

"I had a weeping willow in my backyard while I was growing up," he says after a few seconds, and I shift my focus back to him. "Broke my leg on it when I was ten. Not an easy thing to forget."

"What were you doing up on the tree?" I ask, despite myself.

It's so hard to imagine Dr. Blackwood doing something fun like climbing a tree. In fact, just by looking at him I can say that he never, ever did anything carefree or impulsive. He's too severe, too intense for that.

Too straight-laced.

"Trying to impress someone with my athletic abilities," he murmurs, his eyes somewhere off my shoulders. Like there's a portal to the past behind me.

"A girl?"

His eyes come back to me. "Yeah. Kind of."

"Did you? Impress her, I mean."

"I think so, yes."

I want to ask if she was pretty. I don't know why. It's a stupid thought. Shouldn't even enter my mind. But it did, and now I'm even more agitated.

I look at the lime jello, and the plastic spoon beside it, and almost lunge for it. If I'm eating, then I'm not thinking about him climbing trees to impress a girl.

Things boys do for pretty girls and not for girls like me.

Not that he's a boy or anything. He's thirty-three. A man. A man much older than me.

"Good for you," I congratulate him on impressing this unknown girl who may or may not have been pretty, and march to the chair, pull it out, and drop down in it before plucking the jello from the table and digging into it.

I shovel a mouthful of it in before looking up at him and raising my eyebrows. "Shall we?"

He studies me for a beat before taking his hands out of his pockets, pulling out his own chair, and sitting on it way more gracefully than I did.

Rolling the chair forward, he opens a file, probably filled with notes on me and my sessions and hits a few keys on his laptop. He's getting my entire medical history together.

I hate that.

So I look at something else. The watch strapped to his wrist. It's one of those large dial ones with a brown leather band, which make him look even more severe, manlier. Older.

"It says here that you have trouble falling asleep?"

I swallow my lime jello. "Yes." Then, "No thanks to your stupid meds."

He looks away from the chart and at me. "Stupid meds."

I try to stay quiet. I really do.

Four seconds later, I blurt out, "Yes. Stupid meds. They are ruining my life *and* my sleep. Thank God, I'm not throwing up anymore. I'm pretty sure I lost an organ last week while you guys kept saying that it will pass."

He waits a second, all silent and studying me. "It did pass, correct?"

Damn it.

I stab the spoon at my jello. "Not before I lost one-fourth of my liver. It came right out of my mouth."

"It will grow back."

"I'm sorry?"

"Liver. It exhibits regenerative properties. Meaning, it can grow itself back. But let me see what we can do about your sleep."

He's laughing at me; I know that. Although his expression is very smooth and serious.

Narrowing my eyes at him, I ask, "What *exactly* are you going to do about it?"

"What do you think I'm going to do about it?"

"Sing me a lullaby?"

Closing his laptop and the files, he puts them aside and laces his fingers together. This time there was definitely a crease on the side of his eyes. "Yeah, singing. Not my forte. Let's try some medication first."

God, why does he have to be so… unruffled?

"I don't want your meds. I told you they are ruining my life," I say in my bratty tone.

I didn't even know I had that tone until right now.

"This one will save your life, I promise," he says. "And fix your sleep."

Fix.

There's that word again. The look in his eyes shows he's doing it on purpose. Jerk. I do want to come at him with a snappy statement, but I won't.

Don't engage the enemy. Well, not more than what you already have.

I eat more lime jello and look away.

"Tell me about the night of your eighteenth birthday."

The question jolts me, and I pause mid-swallow, glancing up at him. At his gorgeous, ice-cold, expressionless face to see if he's kidding. Or maybe he didn't speak at all and I'm hearing things.

Crazy people hear things, right?

Bringing my lime jello to my chest, almost hugging the tiny cup, I gulp whatever I had in my mouth. "I'm sorry?"

"What happened that night?" he repeats.

I see his lips move. With my own eyes. Meaning I'm still sane enough to not hear things. Though for the first time in my life, I wish I weren't.

Swallowing, I wedge my plastic spoon in between the green jello and put it back on the desk. There was a tiny tremble in my fingers but I'm not focusing on that. I bring my hands back to my lap and clasp them, tightly.

In a calm tone, I say, "It's all there in my chart."

There. Nice and polite.

I'm proud of myself.

"It is. But I prefer to hear it from you."

"Well, Dr. Martin and I, we've already had this conversation. And I talk about it with Josie all the time," I lie.

Dr. Martin talked about it and I listened but never spoke. And Josie and I, we don't talk about it all the time. I mean, she tries to, but I ignore her.

Basically, all I've done is ignore this conversation and rightfully so. I don't wanna talk about it. Why don't people get that? Why do they think they have a right to poke and prod into my psyche like this?

Across the desk, he's cool, composed. Almost sprawled in his chair. Like this is his domain, which it is but he doesn't have to flaunt it. "That's excellent," he rumbles, dryly. "That you talk about it. But I'm not Dr. Martin or Josie. Why don't you tell me what you told them?"

Without my volition, my eyes flit over the contents of his desk. There are mountains of files on either side of his workspace. A pen holder. A closed laptop. His phone. A desk phone, again a throwback from the 90s. A crystal-clear paperweight.

The last one's the most interesting one. It's the object I can use to do the most damage. I blow on my bangs as I stare at it. If I snatched it off his desk and hurled it at him really quickly, what's he gonna do? He wouldn't have time to stop me. I'd be really fast.

And I'm already locked up. He can't lock me up twice, can he?

As if he knows what I'm feeling, Dr. Blackwood picks up the paperweight and rolls it in his palm. There's something on his face that's meant to provoke me. That *does* provoke me. A slight arrogant, knowing smile as he plays with the object. Like he's almost daring me to do something about it.

Fucking Voldemort. The lord of everything evil and dark, according to Harry Potter, of course.

"You like it?" he asks, watching me carefully with shrewd eyes.

"Yes. Very much."

"Yeah? I got it as a present when I graduated med school."

"How touching."

His slight smile broadens, stretching his pink lips, making him look so classically handsome and appealing and… devilish, that I want to throttle him.

Happy thoughts.

Peaceful thoughts.

"It is." He nods, setting it down, out of my reach. "Though I can't say I've ever met anyone so interested in it before. But then again…"

He trails off and I know he's done it on purpose. He *wants* me to ask. I decide that I won't give him the satisfaction.

I won't.

I will not.

My clasped hands are digging into my lap. My knuckles have probably formed dents on my thighs. I grit my teeth but still, the question flows out. "Then again, what?"

"I don't think I've ever met anyone like you."

My breath catches in my throat. "I-I'm sorry?"

"It's in your file." He raises his eyebrows. "Your therapist at the state hospital wasn't very happy with you."

My cheeks heat up.

"Though, I really want to know something," he says, thoughtfully.

Sniffing, I ask, "What?"

He cocks his head to the side. "Did you really destroy her charts?"

I squirm in my seat. Curse him for bringing it up. I'm pretty sure he's going to judge me and be condescending. It's not like it hasn't happened before. Everyone has already lectured me about it, including my mom in her phone call yesterday. About my supposed *refusal* of treatment.

But the thing is, I'm not like that. I'm not aggressive or prone to fights. I'm not real proud of all the things I've done to avoid talking. All I want is to be left alone.

All I want is peace.

"Why?"

"People can exaggerate sometimes. I tend not to believe everything I hear. And everything I read."

I wasn't expecting him to say that. No one has said that to me or given me the benefit of the doubt. They just assumed I did it because that biatch therapist told on me. I *did* do it. That's not the point, though.

The point is that he's asking instead of assuming.

"Yes," I tell him, feeling bad.

I'm searching for judgment or condescension. Maybe some sort of a reprimand. There's nothing except genuine curiosity.

It throws me off. It kind of… relaxes me.

"How?"

The way he said it, *how*. Like he's so baffled and he really wants to know and that just makes me want to smile. I bite my lip so I don't give in. I don't want to smile at the enemy. "I poured water on them."

He presses his lips together as if he wants to smile too, but he's not going to. "All of them?"

Damn it.

I didn't want to have anything in common with him. But our desire to not give in to our smiles is poking holes in my hatred of him.

"All of them," I confirm.

"You're dangerous," he murmurs.

Okay, I give in.

I smile, shaking my head. "You bet I am. But in my defense, I was going for her head."

His lips twitch. "Were you?"

"Yes. She was annoying. I didn't like her voice."

Willow, how can I help you if you don't help me?

College is hard. Don't you want to go to college without the burdens of what happened and what you did?

Talk to me, Willow. I can help you.

But I like his voice. I'm not going to tell him that, though. Nope.

I shrug. "Anyway, I changed my mind and went for the charts."

"What made you change your mind?" he asks.

He sits back in his chair and does something that I can't look away from. He rubs his lower lip – his pillowy, dusky pink lip, with which he said my name in that enticing way – with his thumb, and despite myself, I follow the gesture.

Swallowing, I say, the words slipping out of my mouth, "My mom."

"What about her?"

"I thought she wouldn't like it. She, uh, worries about me a lot."

"Why's that?"

His question makes me look away. Good thing, too. I don't want to be obvious that his inconsequential gesture is captivating me.

"I don't know." I shake my head and clear my throat. All of a sudden, emotions are filling up my chest; it happens when I think of my mom.

"I mean... I know," I continue. "She loves me, and I'm her only child. So yeah, she worries."

Poor Mom.

"What about your dad?"

"He's not in the picture," I say, swallowing again. "I don't think he even knows about me."

"Why not?"

Shrugging, I stare at my bunny slippers. My mom bought them for me before coming here, actually. She bought everything new: new toiletries – they let you bring your own as long as the packages are brand-new and never been opened before, new clothes, as if she was sending me off to college and not to a psychiatric facility.

I remember the way she showed them off, all the new, shiny things she bought for me. So I could go and spend six weeks of my life, locked up and trapped.

"I came out of a one-night stand. My mom met this man in France and they hooked up. She was on a business trip." Then I find myself adding, "My entire family is like that. They don't need a man, you know, to complete them. They are already complete. They achieve all their goals and dreams and... well, they are pretty fucking spectacular. They were born complete, actually."

Bunny slippers are making me cry for some reason, so I focus on him. He's listening to me with such attention, I feel goose bumps rising on my skin.

"And you weren't? Born complete, I mean."

"No. I was born with something else."

"What's that?"

My eyes feel grainy, heavy, and that pile of emotions in my chest moves up to my throat. "Something more than blood in my veins. That's why my eyes are blue." He frowns and I explain, "No one in my family has blue eyes. No one in my family is ill either, so I'm the odd one out."

He's watching me.

I know I've given him a lot to think about. He might be having one of the best days of his psychiatrist life. I'm fucked up. I know I've got issues. But it's okay. As long as we're not talking about The Roof Incident, I'm okay.

"Not that you'd know anything about it. About being the odd one out," I say.

"And why wouldn't I know that?" His voice sounds rusty, like he's talking after ages.

"Because you're a doctor. And your dad was a doctor too, wasn't he?" I conclude, shrugging. "So you're like him."

Something freezes in him. Something subtle. But I catch it. I catch the instant stiffening of his shoulders and the fact that his chair was rocking from side to side. It's not doing that anymore, and I honestly don't know why.

Did I say something wrong? It wasn't my intention. Honestly, I wasn't saying it to throw my doctor – my enemy – off.

Then, as if it never happened, his tightening and rigidity, he goes back to normal. "Not like him. But yeah, he was a doctor."

Okay, color me curious now.

"A good one, too. From what I hear. Penny, one of the patients, she said they teach his books in med school."

"They do."

"So, he's like a genius or something."

He studies me before lowering his eyes to his desk, rearranging his pen and nodding, "Yeah. He was definitely something."

"I like his name, too," I say, because obviously, I can't say that I like *his* name, the man sitting in front of me. And I want to keep talking about this. It's interesting. Mostly because I don't think he wants to talk about it.

"Alistair Blackwood. Regal and, you know, old-fashioned."

He whips his eyes up.

My heart is beating really fast. God, it was stupid to say that, wasn't it?

Well, there's no way that he can know that I'm talking about his name and not his dad's. But there's something in his look that makes me think that he can see right through me.

Which is dangerous, actually. I don't want him to see the things inside me. I don't want *anyone* to see.

"I'm glad you think so," he murmurs.

"I actually –"

"As much as I enjoy talking about my father," he cuts me off with a tight smile. "I'd love to talk more about you. Tell me what happened that night."

Looking at him, I can't say that he enjoyed talking about his father. In fact, he downright didn't want to talk about his father at all.

So he doesn't like the taste of his own medicine, does he?

Fine, I'll feed him lies, then. I'll weave such a story that he won't know up from down.

I stare into his eyes, at his sculpted face. His stubble looks thicker than yesterday. Sunrays hit his jaw, making those bristles look warm, almost reddish. Appealing.

I don't want it to be appealing.

"You wanna know what happened that night?" I begin. "Fine. I'll tell you. It was my birthday and my family threw me a party at our house in the Hamptons. A party I never wanted to begin with. But hey, everyone was like, you only turn eighteen once. You need a party. So I was like, okay. Let's do a party. I'll be the one in the corner, getting bored out of my mind but who the fuck cares. At least my boyfriend will be there with me. So we were hanging out until I asked him if he could bring me something to drink. Like a good guy, he went. But he never came back."

I emit out a sharp laugh. "Because he got stuck on some-one's lips. I caught him making out with one of my classmates. In my bedroom. His tongue was probably touching her tonsils. And she loved it. You know, with the way she was moaning. I got pissed, heartbroken. I thought nothing would ever be the same in my life. The angst of it almost killed me. No pun intended. So I got drunk and stupid, and I jumped."

I don't remember much about the jumping, itself. All I know is that one second I was on the roof and the next, I was in the air, my hair whipping against my face and wind punching my stomach. And then, nothing.

Raising my eyebrows, I keep talking. "When I woke up in the hospital, I told them everything. I told them I was heartbroken and devastated and whatnot. I told them it was spur of the moment. It wasn't going to happen again."

I roll my eyes. "But my mom got stressed out. There wasn't any reason to be. There were very little scratches on my body. They'd kept me under observation overnight and I passed their tests with flying colors. The attending called it a miracle that I escaped unscathed. Instead of celebrating, my entire family looked at me like I'd been planning to kill myself for ages. For no reason whatsoever, they held me in their psych ward for forty-eight hours. So, I might have thrown a bit of a tantrum. And when I thought it was time for me to finally, go home, my mom said that the psychiatrist recommended I be sent here. Because I was unstable, and I'd benefit greatly from an in-patient program."

Smiling tightly, I finish, "So see? I might be a drama queen and I might be 'clinically depressed.' But I'm hardly suicidal. What'd you guys call it? Suicidal ideation? Yeah, sorry. I don't have any such ideation. I'm not crazy enough to take my own life. I'm not crazy enough to be here in the first place. So, if you're half as good as they say you are, you'll recognize the error in your judgment and let me go."

During my fervent speech, Dr. Blackwood didn't move at all. He didn't even blink his eyes. He sat there, like a marble statue he reminds me of.

I almost want to reach out and touch him. See if his skin is warm like other living things or if he really is cold.

But then he moves. As if proving to me that he is, in fact, a living creature and not a museum relic.

"Crazy," he murmurs. "You use that word a lot."

"I didn't know you could only use it a specified number of times."

"I'm just wondering what you think it means. Crazy."

"It means abnormal. Insane. Freak. Maybe you should take a look at a dictionary," I say, licking my lip.

"It doesn't mean anything. Not medically. Medically, it's a waste of a word. Suffering from a mental disease does not automatically mean you're crazy. And I don't care about something that can't be explained scientifically." He tips his chin at me. "But thanks for educating me."

A flush rises not on my cheeks but somewhere inside my body, under my clothes. I'm turning scarlet. I wanna get out of here.

I wanna get away from him.

Of course, I know crazy is a derogatory word. I'm aware of that. But I'm okay with calling myself that because if I don't, then it means there's something seriously wrong with me.

And that's something I can't accept.

"Can I go now?"

He scans my face again. "Where was your boyfriend? When you were at the hospital?"

"He never showed up. In case you don't remember, the asshole cheated on me."

"What was his name again?"

I take a moment to answer. I take a moment to adjust my tone, adjust my whole demeanor. "Lee. Lee Jordan."

"Right," he says thoughtfully, before nodding and getting up from his chair. "Thanks for your time."

Slowly, on trembling legs, I stand up as well. I don't reply or wait for him to say anything else. Although what he would say after dismissing me, I don't know. Either way, I'm not taking a chance. I practically run to the door and open it.

But freeze when I feel him at my back.

His heat.

God, there's no way this ice king is cold to touch. No way.

His heat is radiating out of his body. In a wave, it reaches me, spans across my shoulders and spine, goes down to the back of my thighs. And that scent I've been breathing in ever since I stepped into this room?

That's him, I realize.

It's his smell. Rain, fresh and crisp, mixed in with his musk. It's wafting around the room and all that time I spent in there was dangerous, because I think that scent has made a home in me.

"Willow." He says my name and I have to bite my lip. Hard.

I'm going to ask him to call me by my last name. I have to. I don't like how much I *like* the way he says my name. In fact, a flash of his soft lips shaping it streaks across my brain.

I whirl around to tell him exactly that, my bangs fluttering along my forehead. But my attention is snagged by the fact that he's so tall. So freaking tall. So much so that even with my topknot, I only reach his stubborn chin.

His expression is neutral, professional. I wonder what *my*

expression is.

"I want to see you again."

I blink, all my systems have slowed down as I run his words through my mind.

He wants to see me. Again.

He wants to. See me.

Again.

"What?"

"In my office. Next week."

Aren't psychiatrists supposed to just write you prescriptions and then, send you on your way to a therapist? Why does he want to see me again so soon?

"W-why?" I ask my question, out loud.

"Because I think we have a lot to talk about."

Chapter 6

He's staring at something, Dr. Blackwood.

The man who thinks we have a lot to talk about when I see him next week.

He's by Beth's office staring at the same collages as I did when I was trying to eavesdrop on his conversation with her the day he arrived here.

I'm standing at the mouth of the hallway, having just come down the stairs for breakfast, and there he is. All still with raindrops clinging to his hair and clothes.

It's none of my business why he's so stiff and tight while the world moves around him. Nurses are laughing. Techs are walking up and down the hallway with files. A few patients linger here and there. I see the girl from my floor, a pretty blonde, pacing up and down. A tech is trying to calm her. She gets agitated every morning before breakfast, but I don't know why.

I should be avoiding all conversations with him, and yet, I

find myself walking toward Dr. Blackwood.

Why? Because I'm curious. Super curious about him.

"Hi," I greet him, facing the collages, trying to see what he was seeing. "Interesting photos, aren't they?"

I feel him turning toward me. "Interesting shirt."

I face him, then. All the earlier stiffness is gone from his body. He's cool and unaffected. If I hadn't seen him looking at the pictures with such severity, I wouldn't ever have guessed that he was capable of such a reaction to something.

His eyes are on my t-shirt before he comes to look at my face. But I still feel his gaze there, on my chest, very close to where my heart is along with some... other things. I'm pretty sure he wasn't focused on them. I mean, that would be ridiculous.

Right?

Even so, I feel like my lips are drying out and I've got this weird tingling in my chest.

"Were you looking at something in particular?" I ask.

He shoves his hands down his pockets. "Do you always wear t-shirts with one-liners?"

Something makes me fold my hands at my back, and my spine arches just a teeny-tiny bit. But he keeps his eyes firmly on my face. Not that I wanted him to move them or notice... my assets. But still.

"You don't like to talk about yourself much, do you?" I comment, remembering how fast he closed up when we were talking about his dad.

I've thought about it a lot in the past few days, actually, since we had our meeting. There isn't much to do around here.

And I've concluded that there's something there, between him and his dad.

"You don't like that either," he responds, kind of drily.

I don't fight the smile that comes on. "So what, are we kindred spirits?"

"I wouldn't go so far as that."

"Good. Because I can't imagine the horror." I lean toward him, slightly. "Of us being similar, I mean."

Squinting, he nods. "Right. Because you don't want to be similar to someone who's – what was it – wacked. And psychiatrists are that, aren't they?"

"You know it."

A small smile appears on his lips at my answer, and I already know that it's a rare thing for him. Smiles and chuckles. Laughter.

Like they are for me.

God, he's making it very hard for me to hate him.

I want to hate him. Trust me.

I'm aware he's the enemy. I'm aware that with one signature, he can send me away, to the Outside. But he won't. Because he's like them, like all the other doctors I've known.

Although, he did fix my medicine-induced insomnia. He put me on sleep meds along with my regular anti-depressant and mood stabilizer. So at least I can sleep at night.

Not to mention, Renn loves everything about him and the way he handled her short meeting. I've heard nurses and techs talking about how nice he is. Some patients might still be wary of him, but I've seen him always be polite and courteous, opening doors, nodding, dragging out chairs. Not that he's friendly or chatty but he's well-mannered.

As I said, very hard – extremely hard – to hate someone who's so fucking gentlemanly and makes me want to smile, and puts me to sleep.

Licking my lips, I look away from him and down at the t-shirt I'm wearing. It's a light gray shirt with maroon lettering saying, *On a scale of 1 to 10, I'm 9 ¾ obsessed with Harry Potter.*

I tug at the hem and say, unnecessarily. "It's from Harry Potter."

"I figured."

"You like Harry Potter?"

"I'm not into fiction."

"I figured."

He crosses his arms across his chest. "How?"

I look at him, his face, his put-together hair, his stubble. Then I move my eyes to his starched shirt, his pleated pants, his wingtips. I know I'm checking him out, unabashedly, but I have a good reason.

"You've got the wingtips, dude," I say, smirking.

"Dude."

"Man?"

"Why don't we stick with Dr. Blackwood?"

"What if I don't wanna call you Dr. Blackwood?" I say just to be contrary. "What if I get the urge to call you Simon?"

His name on my lips sounds fresh and new. I've never known a Simon before. He's the first. I like that.

And therein lies the problem.

Just the fact that I *want* to say his name, means I shouldn't ever say it.

"Well, then I'd advise counting to ten," he responds. "That usually helps with the urges. But if not, we can talk about your urges next week."

Urges.

Something about that word brings back the tingles in my chest and I clear my throat. "My point is that I can see my face in your shoes. They're uber polished."

"And that somehow doesn't go with Harry Potter?"

"No, *you* don't go with Harry Potter. I mean, look at you." I wave my hand at him, up and down. "You're dressed like you're a hundred years old, even though you're only thirty-three. All professional and uptight. No way are you cool enough for Harry Potter."

"Is that right?"

"Yes." I nod. "You look like some kind of a… I don't know, old-fashioned medicine guy. Sorry, man. Medicine man."

"Medicine man."

"Yup. That could be your name."

"You've got a thing for names, don't you?"

My eyes widen fractionally. I've been caught out, haven't I? He knows I was talking about his name rather than his dad's at our meeting.

"Nope," I lie.

"My mistake," he says but doesn't look like he believes me. "I've gotta get going. I'm late for Quidditch."

With that, he turns around and walks away, leaving me wide-eyed in his wake.

Did he just say Quidditch?

How does he know Quidditch? He said he didn't like Harry Potter. How does he know about their sport?

No. Wait.

He said he wasn't into fiction. He never said he didn't *read* the books.

Did he just trick me? After the whole don't-give-me-your-trick-answers speech from the other day. I know I should be angry. I *know* it.

But I'm not.

I'm almost in admiration. He knows how to dodge all the questions. He's a pro. Though I don't understand what he could possibly be hiding about Harry Potter. Or his dad, for that matter.

Yup, super curious.

When he disappears from view, I face the collages. I stand where he stood. In the exact same place. I'm not as tall as he is so I have to crane my neck, get up on my tiptoes to look at the photos up top.

There are a bunch of pictures celebrating Christmas and some birthdays. I spy Beth, Hunter, Josie, Dr. Martin, and a few other people. Everyone's grinning with happiness.

These photos don't depict the gritty realities of staying at a psych ward. They don't show the night sweats I suffered from during my first week because they weaned me off my old meds. They don't show Renn's sickly complexion when she had to purge her lunch last week, and they took her to a different room to do that. I don't see the dark circles and hollowed out cheeks of the insomniacs, or puffy, red faces of the patients who can't stop crying after a therapy session.

All these photos show is happiness.

In a place like this. It's incomprehensible. Incredible.

It's exhausting.

I'm exhausted just by looking at the enthusiasm on their faces. How do people even *do* it? How do people get happy and then, *stay* happy? It's not supposed to be this hard, right? Life's not supposed to be this hard.

But then, if I wasn't clinically depressed, would I be happy all the time? Would I be positive? Would I never have bad days?

That's the worst part of being mentally ill: you don't know the real you because the illness and the meds fuck with everything.

There are cute little name tags under the staff members and I run through the names on all of them, until I stop at one. I *have* to stop at one: Dr. Alistair Blackwood.

He's standing by a woman wearing a red dress. I'm not interested in her because Jesus fucking Christ, the man in the photo looks exactly like the current Dr. Blackwood.

So, this is the man who founded this place.

Even if I didn't read his name, I'd still know that he was the current Dr. Blackwood's father. He's got the same hair, rich and dark and a little wavy. Same nose, straight and arrogant. Same jawline, same high cheekbones. The only difference is the color of their eyes. His eyes are green, while his son's are an intense, stormy gray.

He was looking at his father. But why the hell was he looking at his dad like that? With such severity?

There's no time to think about any of this because one of the nurses reminds me that breakfast is about to start.

Which is uneventful, as usual. If you don't take into account that one of the patients from The Batcave had a little bit too much coffee and he was jumpy. Then I have to sit through an hour of process group with a social worker. We talk about how to deal with negative thoughts in the Outside world. Then we do art therapy for an hour.

At last, it's time for lunch. We're at the usual table, by the window, and I'm savoring my lime jello, moving it around my mouth so it settles in every corner of my tongue and chases away the sour taste of medicine.

A moment later though, Dr. Blackwood walks into the dining room and I forget about the meds and their sour taste.

Somehow, he's taller than he was this morning. Taller than yesterday, even.

I have a weird vision of me somehow getting up to his broad shoulders and standing on them. I bet even with my tiny frame I'd touch the roof, the clouds even.

I have a weird vision of saying hi to him, waving my hand at him from across the room.

Ridiculous. I'd never do that.

He isn't wet like he was this morning and his hair has settled into its place. Polished and composed. Shiny. I'm not the only one who notices the glimmer of his hair. Renn notices it too and whistles under her breath, watching his progress through the room.

"God, he's hot. Like, legit hot. I look at him…" She trails off to a sigh. "And I just want him to be my daddy."

I bite down on my tongue at the word *daddy*. The sharp sting makes me jump in my seat and waters my eyes.

Penny groans. "Ugh. I'm gonna punch you in the throat."

Facing her, Renn grins. "Admit it. You were thinking the same thing." Then she nudges me with her elbow under the table while I'm trying to calm down my pounding heart. "At least, our Willow was thinking it."

"I was not!"

This only makes her giggle and I seriously contemplate carrying out Penny's threat.

I was *not* thinking about that.

"Don't call him that," I tell her.

"Why?"

"Because."

"Are you claiming him? Because if you are then I need to know. I don't screw around with what belongs to my friends."

I almost choke on my food again. "He doesn't belong to me. It's such a stupid way to put it. Like he's an object."

"Does he or does he not?"

"If I say yes, will you stop talking about him like that?"

"Yes. Pinky swear?"

She gives me her finger, so I can make the promise if I want to. I think about it a second. Fine, for a microsecond. Then, I entwine my finger with hers really quickly before snatching my hand away lest a tech notices us breaking the no-touching rule.

"He's mine," I say, my heart on the verge of explosion. "Don't talk about him like that."

Renn whoops. Penny gasps and Vi grins.

Me? I blush and look away.

Then I notice something. Every single jittery and squirming eye is trained on Dr. Blackwood. There's not a single person in the room who's not watching him. Myself included. Most of them are wary. Some of them are curious. All of them are chattering and murmuring. The sounds of the room have increased.

Something akin to sympathy rises in me.

For the enemy. First, I struggle with hating him and now, I'm sympathetic.

What is happening to me?

Maybe because I know what it feels like when every eye is on you. I've felt it not very long ago. I know what it feels like when every eye turns into a microscope, inflating you and your flaws. Every eye tries to see your cracks.

I know.

I feel like I want to claw at those eyes. Claw at those faces. Scream and kick and thunder.

But Dr. Blackwood appears cool. Extremely cool, in fact.

Nothing on his expression suggests that he even knows about the attention he commands or the sudden increase in the chatter. The scattered staff around the room has become more attentive, though.

"Good afternoon, everyone." His voice rises above the din, crisp and loud, as he stands in the middle of the room. "I hope you're having a pleasant day so far. Some of you'll be seeing me in my office later today, so please don't let me keep you from enjoying the delicious lunch. As much as I love the attention, we don't want to offend the cooks."

With that, he strides over to where Beth's watching him with a motherly smile, shaking her head. There's no other option but to watch him after he handled that so smoothly.

Again, I can't help but think this man knows stuff. He knows how to handle being under scrutiny.

I watch him lower his head to listen to what Beth's saying. He has his large hand on her lower back as he gives her his full attention.

Penny chides us to stop staring, and normally I would take her advice because I hate getting stared at myself. But I can't stop.

There's something about him that compels me to look.

And then Josie joins their group, and I wouldn't be able to tear my gaze away even if I wanted to.

She stands beside Dr. Blackwood, almost coming up to his ears, as he turns to include her. Which is so atypical of what I've seen from him.

But what do I know? I've only known him for a few days.

A couple of seconds into the conversation, Josie cracks up at something he says, her blonde hair swaying with her laughter. I watch for his reaction. I watch to see if he's laughing.

He's not.

He's smiling though. And in all the time that I've known him, this is the biggest he's smiled.

I turn away abruptly and focus on my lunch. It's none of my business how close he was standing to Josie or how big he was smiling.

We eat in silence – as much silence as you can get here – until there's a crash at the far end of the room. It's Annie– Angry Annie – who lives a few doors down and is prone to nightmares. From what I hear, she is known for being a little aggressive.

She's thrown her tray full of food on the floor and is standing, her dark hair tumbling out of her bun.

"I don't wanna eat this fucking food," she declares angrily. "It's fucking disgusting. Makes me wanna kill myself. And I don't want the shiny hotshot doctor either. I want Dr. Martin."

She takes a few steps to her right, but instantly a nurse is on her, trying to calm her down.

"No, don't you come near me. Don't touch me." She's flailing her arms at the nurse, and now techs are on her too, circling around her.

"Keep your filthy hands off me, you animals. I hate you. I fucking hate you all! I don't wanna be here. I don't fucking wanna be here. You killed him, didn't you? You killed Dr. Martin? Like they killed my daddy. You fucking killed him!"

Her fists are shaking and they almost catch one of the techs on his jaw. In the next second, two of them grab her hands, making her thrash against their hold, making her scream.

It's creating a sense of paranoia in the room. People are getting upset, as if waking up from sleep. Looking at their food, at each other. At Angry Annie.

"You killed my daddy. You killed Dr. Martin!" She's sobbing and something clenches in my heart. A tight vise.

Her screams are causing a rush in my blood, a click in my ears. Her jerks, the shakes of her head, her rending voice – everything about her agitated state is getting to me.

This is the very first time I've seen Angry Annie in action. In fact, in my two weeks of being here, this is the very first time I've seen any kind of meltdown, where this manner of assistance is required. Usually, it's empty threats and what now looks like playful jabbing.

For a few seconds, I'm thrown back to the hospital room where I woke up after The Roof Incident. The panic. The weight of what happened.

God, I never want to feel that again.

I never want to be that agitated again. Like I'm losing my grip on reality.

Like Angry Annie.

My vision breaks when I see other staff members pouring into the room, trying to handle the commotion. Suddenly, the row of tables is infiltrated by the navy-blue scrubs. In the middle of all the shouting and chatter, Dr. Blackwood strides over to Angry Annie.

Until then, I've been sitting backed up in my seat, my body all tightened up into a ball. As soon as he starts talking to her, my muscles ease up a little. I don't know why. The more I see his soft lips moving, his jaw working back and forth, the looser I become.

My fists are open. My abdomen isn't contracted. I'm not a rock anymore.

In the periphery I notice a nurse prepping a syringe, though and I'm panicking again.

Oh no.

No, no, no.

Not the needles. Needles are the worst.

They are the fucking worst.

Before I can think it through, I spring up from my chair. It makes a great shrieking noise against the hardwood floor, shocking me, and apparently, shocking the girls too.

"What the fuck are you doing?" Renn asks, alert.

"I've got to stop it. I-I can't let her get stuck with a needle."

Vibrating with a huge amount of energy, I'm rounding the chair when Penny speaks up. "Are you insane? Let them do their job, Willow."

"No."

"Willow! Get back here!" Penny hisses.

"She's not an animal. She shouldn't be made to feel like one," I snap, breathing hard, my heart drumming inside my chest.

"Willow, stop. She doesn't need your help."

I can't tell if that's Renn or Penny, but I don't care. I'm in a trance. A bubble where I can only feel anger and determination.

I have to stop it.

I *need* to stop it.

I need to stop them from making her feel less than human, a freak. Because that's how it feels when they restrain you, dig their claws in your skin. They invade your personal space, get so close to you that you can see the pores of their skin, smell their sweat. You can feel the disgusting heat of their body. Their strong fingers. Their mean, ugly faces. You tell them to back off, but they don't listen. You tell them to let you go, leave you alone, but it hardly registers to them.

You tell them you're not crazy. You don't need to calm down. You need to be listened to. You need to be understood.

But they all think they are smarter than you.

My thoughts are frantic, exactly like my breathing, like I'm living this moment of horror right alongside Angry Annie. Like I'm back at the hospital where people – even my mom – didn't believe me when I told them that The Roof Incident was an accident. Where they stuck me with a needle because they thought I was too agitated, too unhinged.

The big, bad hurricane inside me gets jarred when I crash into someone. It's Hunter.

"I need you to stay calm, all right?" he tells me with a scratchy voice.

"I need to go save her," I tell him.

"You don't need to save her. We've got it handled. She's gonna be fine." He tries to steer me back to the table.

"No, she's not gonna be fine. You can't sedate her. You can't do this to her, okay?" I push against his hold but damn it, I can't.

I can't shake him off.

Tears of frustration well up in my eyes as he tells me that I need to take a calm breath.

I scratch his forearm with my blunt nails. "I don't need to be calm. I —"

I break off when he looks at me, Dr. Blackwood, from across the distance.

His smooth forehead creases up as he scans my face and I don't have the energy to put my mask back on. To not show how this is affecting me. Let him analyze it, if he wants. But I can't let them do this to Angry Annie.

I shake my head once, and then I go rigid and my eyes go wide.

Over Dr. Blackwood's shoulders, I spy the nurse advancing on Angry Annie with a syringe in her hands. But at the last second, he raises a hand, stopping the nurse.

He stopped the nurse.

He raised a hand and stopped the nurse.

He stopped it.

And just like that, Angry Annie loses some of her fight, and so do I.

I watch as Dr. Blackwood continues talking to her. Those soft, thick lips of his moving. Almost like a lullaby. Like hypnosis. Slowly, all my agitated thoughts evaporate, until I feel a jolt. A shock of some sort.

He's touching her.

So far, he hadn't touched her. It was only the techs, but now Dr. Blackwood puts his hand on her shuddering shoulder and bends his head toward her. Angry Annie goes completely lax.

A strand of his perfectly polished hair has flicked down to his furrowed forehead and is almost grazing the top of her head, as they stand there, huddled together.

I swallow but I can't get my throat to work. It's jammed up with so many emotions. Thoughts. Wonderments. So many things.

Most of all, it's jammed up with the urge to know the feel of his touch. I want to know what it feels like to be touched by him, his hands that clearly carry some sort of ancient charm. Healing powers.

Angry Annie is completely still, entranced by him. Apart from a few sniffles, she doesn't make any sounds, and neither do the others. Slowly, the chaos is getting under control. A lull is settling over the room.

I don't protest when Hunter steers me back to my table.

Once Angry Annie goes easily with the techs and sits back

down, Dr. Blackwood turns to face the room. "I'm aware that many of you are not happy with me being here," he begins, and the residual chatter dies down. "And I'm also aware that some of you have been with Dr. Martin for a long time and I know change is difficult."

He sighs, thrusting his hands into his pockets, and in the back of my mind, a voice protests at those healing hands being hidden from view.

"Now, there are two ways we can do this. One, we can fight and argue, but we all know that I'm not going anywhere. At least, not for a little while. Two, if you all promise to behave, I have something that might interest you." He pauses to let it take effect, before continuing, "I'll arrange for you to see Dr. Martin and he'll tell you himself he's doing fine and will be back to work very soon, *if* you promise to cooperate. You'll finish your lunch, take your meds, do the groups and generally, stop giving the staff a hard time." He raises his eyebrows, his hands going to his hips. "Deal?"

"And how you gonna do that?" This comes from Roger.

"Why don't you let me worry about that?" Dr. Blackwood raises an arrogant eyebrow.

"Yeah, right. How do we know you're not bluffing?"

With a slight smile, he dismisses Roger and runs his eyes across the room once again. "Before this day's out, you'll get to talk to Dr. Martin. If not, then one of you can personally..." He shoots a look at Roger. "Bust my balls in front of everyone."

People chuckle, including Roger.

Dr. Blackwood throws out a small nod, but before striding out of the room, his eyes find me again. It's short, momentary. His gaze. He basically flicks his eyes up and down my face, and my body, as if checking for something, as if making sure that I'm okay, as if he's concerned about me. Though, I can't imagine it being… right.

Right?

When he gets his answer, he leaves.

"Oh man, he's good," murmurs Renn in the wake of his departure.

"I like him." Vi smiles.

"I deem him qualified enough to fix me," Penny declares.

Me? I don't say anything. I'm still feeling his perusal. It brought back the little tingling and flutters from this morning when we bumped into each other in the hallway.

All I do is watch him walk away, turn the corner and disappear with his wide shoulders, dark hair and healing hands.

Hands that saved someone from the needle.

Chapter 7

My fear of the needles isn't irrational.

In fact, I didn't have a fear of them until the day after my eighteenth birthday, aka The Roof Incident.

When I woke up in the hospital, the walls were closing in already. When they looked at me like there was something wrong with me, those walls collapsed. I couldn't breathe. My panic was a living thing inside my body. A creature inhabiting me.

I remember screaming, and shouting. So much shouting and all of it was coming from me.

I knocked down the machines. I ripped out the tubing attached to my veins. They wouldn't stop getting closer though. Closer and closer. Descending. The nurses and the orderlies. Like they were going to suck my soul right out of my body. Like they were dementors – the soul-sucking creatures from Harry Potter.

Instead of performing the Dementor's Kiss, however, those creatures stuck me with a needle. It came out of nowhere. Not in a million years would I have imagined ever getting stabbed by a sharp object like that.

It felt like such a betrayal. Such a knife in the back.

Of course, I didn't trust them after that. Of course, I ruined that therapist's charts when she told me that all they were trying to do was help me. Fix me.

I did *not* need fixing. I still don't need it.

My first week at Heartstone, they kept a close eye on me. They would check up on me every twenty minutes, even when I was with a provider. They thought I'd pull another stunt like that and attack someone.

As if.

I'm not an attacker. Well, except for that teeny-tiny urge to throw the paperweight at Dr. Blackwood during our meeting. But I didn't do it, did I? Granted, he took the object away but still.

Anyway, I hate thinking about my time at the state hospital and the first week at Heartstone so I try not to.

But the incident with Angry Annie – actually, let's call her Annie; she's angry for the right reasons because clearly, there's a story about her dad – I've spent the rest of the afternoon thinking about it and feeling a pinch on my hip.

A phantom pinch from the needle two weeks ago.

I've also spent the rest of the afternoon looking for him.

The man with healing hands. Dr. Blackwood.

After his heroic save, I haven't seen him all day. Even when he kept his promise and we did a Skype call with Dr. Martin. He wasn't there. Beth handled it all in the TV room, saying Dr. Black-wood was otherwise occupied.

I mean, I know he's busy. I know that. But I can't ignore

this growing… *something* just under my ribcage. Something like longing but with a sharper edge. More like restlessness.

For some reason, before this day is out, I need to see him.

Irony isn't lost on me. The man I should be running away from is the exact man I'm chasing after.

Twice. In one day.

It's the end of the afternoon and I'm outside, with my book on my lap, alternately feeding the pigeons and watching the sky for the impending storm. Renn and Penny are sprawled on the ground, and Vi is right by me, feeding the birds as well.

I'm contemplating whether to just track him down somehow. The only reason I haven't done it yet is because I shouldn't be doing it. I should be more cautious around him.

But *he saved her.*

That's the only thing I'm thinking about, in a loop, no less.

My dilemma ends when he strides out the front door himself.

Well, there you have it. I can't ignore it now. He practically fell in my lap, so to speak. I spring up from my seat, startling the girls.

Without taking my eyes off him where he stands on the stone steps, I say, "I'll be just a sec."

I don't wait to see their reactions as I walk across the lawn filled with patients and techs. I feel their eyes on me, but I don't care. A staff member might have said something to me too. Maybe asked me a question about how I am and what am I doing. Do I need something?

But I don't answer them. I do need something, but I don't

think they can give it to me.

I'm focused on Dr. Blackwood. He looks at someone beyond me – one of the techs – and dips his chin, probably to say that he's got me.

My lips part at his gesture. So confident and reassuring. So... heroic.

Then his gaze falls on me. He hasn't moved from where he's standing on the top of the steps, tracking my movements with slightly hooded eyes.

Something about his utter stillness and the way he's looking at me brings back the tingling from this morning. It's not obvious, his stare, but I *feel* it. Like the heated sun. The thing that I hate, but I'm not hating it right now.

When I come to a stop at the bottom step, he shoves his hands inside his pockets and begins climbing down.

"You should really fix your book," he murmurs.

I realize I have my book clutched to my chest, and a few loose pages are hanging off the bottom. I shove them back in but the level of irritation I should be feeling at the word *fix* isn't there anymore.

Yet some part of me still wants to cling onto my old ways. "My book is fine. And you guys should really do something about your library. There isn't one Harry Potter book in there."

There's no heat in my words. I know it; he knows it.

But he says, "Noted."

Then I blurt out, "You did a good thing today."

"A good thing."

I nod. "This afternoon."

"You mean that Skype call with Dr. Martin? That was pretty easy to do."

His voice is casual but everything else is curious, alert – his expression, his body. It's not like it was in our meeting the other day. This feels more... personal. Like his gaze back in the dining room right when he was leaving.

"Yeah. That too. But I meant something else."

"What did you mean?"

Now's the moment of truth. Do I tell him about my fear of needles? About that day in the hospital? Am I really willing to volunteer information about myself?

He can do a thousand things with it. He can bring it up in our next meeting. He can use it to ask other questions, questions I don't want to answer.

That phantom itch on my hip flares and I decide to fuck it. I'll cross that bridge when I come to it.

I swallow. "You saved Annie."

"From what?"

"From the needle."

"I didn't know I was doing that."

I swallow again. "Well, you did. She didn't need that. To be sedated like an animal."

The itch on my hip increases and I tighten my hold on the book to stop from scratching it in front of him.

"Is that why you were so upset back there?" he asks.

"If I tell you, will you use it against me?"

He rolls back on his feet, his lips stretching in a lopsided smile. "Is that what you think I do? Use information against my patients?"

"How do I know what you do?" I shrug. "But yes, that's what I think."

Dr. Blackwood takes his hand out of his pocket and scratches his jaw. "You've met some fucked-up doctors, haven't you?" Sighing, he says, "No. I won't use it against you, Willow."

It's great that he said that. I would appreciate it more if I wasn't focused on his hand. The one he's just used to scratch his stubble.

Before I can think about it, I reach out and grab hold of it. His large palm has multiple cuts around the pads of his fingers. One of them is covered in a band-aid. I'm guessing that the cut underneath must be bigger than the others that have been left open.

"What happened?" I gently trace the dark red scratches with my thumb.

God, his hand is so big, large and so fucking warm. My thumb stops moving when I realize that I'm touching him.

I'm touching the ice king.

The heat of his hands. The thrum of his blood. Maybe even his healing power.

I feel his breath, long and hard, almost stirring my bangs, and filling my lungs with his rainy smell. Just as I glance at him, he takes his hand away and puts it back in his pocket. I catch the tail end of his jaw clenching and his nostrils flaring.

"I-I... I was..." I fumble and clutch my book. "What happened to your hand? It looked pretty bad."

"It was an accident." After a pause, he says, "I was fixing the stairs."

"Of your house?"

Another clench of his jaw covered with five o'clock shadow. "Yeah. I just don't live there anymore."

It's very strange but in this moment, I know *exactly* what he's feeling.

I know he didn't like the question, as innocent and without motive as it was. I know that he didn't want to *answer* it. I know the reluctance and tightness he felt. It's similar to when we were talking about his dad, only I was too nervous and stubborn to really appreciate the similarities of our feelings.

Because there are similarities. I've felt the same things.

Only I never thought I'd find someone to share them with and he'd turn out to be the man from the other side of the line.

Sighing, I tell him, "I scared my mom."

He frowns. "When?"

"The day I woke up in the hospital," I whisper, feeling choked up and all alone. "I was so pissed and tired and so scared. I told them… a-about what happened. And they started saying I needed help. Consultations and meds and my mom wouldn't stop crying. I got freaked out. I got…"

My eyes fill with tears. "Everybody was talking at once. They were like, talking and talking and telling me to calm down but they just wouldn't get away from me and… It came out of no-where. The needle. And then, I just felt a little sting and everything went black. I'd only seen it on TV, you know. Like on all those medical shows. They stab you with a needle when you're either dying or acting crazy. I was just trying to make them listen." Sniffling, I wipe my tears. "Tell them that I wasn't crazy."

The restlessness that has been building up all day lessens as I tell him this. How can something that goes against my nature – talking – make me feel at ease?

It occurs to me, then. Maybe it's talking to *him*.

This man who's frowning so hard as he looks down at me. Who's making my heart beat faster and faster with each passing second.

"Do you remember what I told you about the word crazy?" he asks in a low voice.

It's so low and rough that I have to go on my tiptoes to listen to it.

"It's a useless word," I reply, almost like a child, but his authority, his largeness is doing something to me.

"Yeah. Don't forget that."

I bite my lip and his gaze drops to the action before moving away. Quickly. But not quick enough because I felt something exploding on my skin.

Sparks and thunders.

"Thank you for saving her," I say, shrugging; I need him to know that.

That I'm thankful.

"I didn't save her."

I disagree but all I say is, "Okay."

Because I don't want to fight with him. Not right now.

"I made a judgment call," he insists.

Maybe he did. But as I said, I don't want to fight with him. I'm feeling mellow and oddly peaceful right now.

Nodding, I agree with him again, "All right."

His chest heaves like he's angry. "Stop looking at me like that," he rumbles.

I've never heard a sound like that coming out of his mouth. It drips with both authority and intimacy. So much intimacy that it's this thick, potent thing like the smell of the rain in the air.

"Like what?"

"Like I'm some kind of a hero."

"But isn't that a… good thing?" I ask, confused.

"No. Because I'm not a hero." He leans closer. "Using sedatives is the last resort and very rare. It only happens in extenuating circumstances. And it's for both the patients' safety and also for the safety of the personnel who's handling them. I knew I had her, so as I said, I made a judgment call."

In the wake of his speech, a fat drop of water plops on my cheek. Another falls on my head. I look up and see the rain has arrived.

There are squeals and shrieks and suddenly, I hear footsteps all over the place. Everyone's trying to get inside before the rain gets heavier.

And I remember we're not alone. I don't know why I thought we were.

We're never alone in this place. Throughout the day, we get checked on in twenty-minute intervals. Some patients get charted even when they are with a provider because they are considered dangerous. Thank God they are not doing that with me anymore. They don't leave us alone even at nights. On our floor, they do hourly checks through the little windows on our doors. Up on The Batcave, those nightly checks are even more frequent.

So yeah, never alone.

"Do you understand what I just said?" Dr. Blackwood asks, and I look away from the commotion.

Do I understand?

"Yeah."

He nods, satisfied. "Good." Looking up at the sky, he says, "Now get back inside."

I would. If I wasn't staring at the way his throat moves when he talks. And how a raindrop is sliding its way down the side of his neck and disappearing under the collar of his shirt.

Focusing back on me, he says, "Willow."

I shake my head, getting myself out of my stupor. "Right. Yeah. Okay."

I start climbing the steps, but I stop and turn around to find him watching me go.

"Have a good night, Dr. Blackwood." I give him a teeny tiny smile.

Covered in raindrops, he slants me a blank look before striding down the pathway.

As the techs herd us inside and close the front door, I realize I do understand. I understand that he doesn't like to be called a hero. I understand that Dr. Simon Blackwood might be a unicorn of a psychiatrist.

Because not only he makes me want to talk to him and not hate him, but I might even… like him, just a little bit.

***

I have an ache.

It's as old as time. Older than that, maybe.

I'm bruised. A bruise that's destined to remain unhealed forever and ever. Red and swollen and pulsating.

I'm in my bed. The hourly check has just got done. Rain's battering against the window. I see the droplets sluicing down. Thick, wet droplets, and I feel an answering pulse.

Between my legs.

Under my hot blanket, my hand creeps down and presses on my pelvis. I massage it and as much as my fingers are soothing the pain, they are stroking it also. Like when you stroke the soft fur of a wild animal. Sometimes you awaken it, rather than put it to sleep.

I thought they killed it, the meds and doctors. My own brain. I thought they murdered the one thing that makes me normal: my lust.

But no.

It's there. And it's awake tonight. And hungry.

My fingers go under my t-shirt and I drag my blunt, unsatisfying nails across my bare skin in franticness.

I've been kissed before. I've made out, have felt and given inconsequential touches. But the only person who's touched my core is me.

And right now, it's the center of the wound. The eye of my hurricane.

But that's not all. This isn't a random burst of desire. This is designed.

For him. The ice king.

I suck on my finger, getting it wet with my tongue, and slide it inside my pajama bottoms and panties. I find my wet curls and seeping core.

With my other hand, I cup my boobs. They are C cups, plump and hot, my strawberry pink nipples puckered. Using my arms, I push them together, my tits, and rub both my nipples with the fingers of that one hand.

Simultaneously, I rub my clit and nearly come off my bed. I moan; I can't help it. It's not loud but it's a sound I haven't made in a long time. So long.

I feel like I'm making this sound for him. I wish he could hear it. I wish he could see me making it. He'd probably clench his jaw, look at me with a calm, impassive face, gray eyes, and walk away.

Or maybe not.

Maybe he'll stay. Maybe he'll watch me touch myself for him.

Suddenly, I feel his eyes on me. The weight of it. I guess it's all in my head, but it feels so real that I sweat with the heat of his look. It's so real that I want to open my eyes and look at the little window on my door, hoping to see him watching me.

But I won't.

I know he's not there. He can't be. He's home or wherever he lives. And I'm stuck here, lusting after him. Putting on a show for him that he won't even get to see.

I put my finger inside and my pussy feels creamy. Swollen. Juicy. It's gasping like my breath.

I grimace as I go in and out, feeling the burn, the tightness.

My back is bowed with how just a tiny finger is making me stretch, but I don't care.

The burn is so fucking good.

I undulate my hips, hug my wrist with my shaking thighs, as I pinch my nipples, knead my breasts. I move, grind, twitch, and imagine those cloud-colored eyes.

I imagine them not only shimmering with authority, but also with lust. Dark and heavy and piercing. Pulling me apart, analyzing me, caressing me.

And when I break into a thousand pieces and come, I imagine those eyes counting every single piece of me so he can put me back together the right way, like a puzzle.

I turn my face and smother my lips with the pillow so I don't make any noises. Even though I want to. I want to make all the noises, but I can't. Not here.

When I come down from my high, I'm breathing hard. Sweating. And happy. Orgasms make me happy. It's the kind of happiness I chase as often as I can.

"God…" I whisper, biting my lip and smiling through the sting.

But then, my eyes pop open and I look at the little glass window on my door. No one is watching. No one is standing there. As expected.

Of course, I don't want someone to be there. It was just heat of the moment. Feeling pinpricks of embarrassment all over my body, I huddle under the blanket, closing my eyes, hiding from my own thoughts. Illicit desires.

He's not a hero, he said.

Maybe that's why I shattered myself just now. For him. So he could fix me, save me like a hero he says he isn't.

With his medicine in my blood putting me to sleep, I close my eyes to that ridiculous thought. I don't want anyone to save me. I don't need saving. I also don't need a hero.

I definitely don't need a king who builds a castle for the one he loves. The one with the silver hair. And neither do I want that gray-eyed king to call the silver-haired girl, his snow princess.

Days spent on the Inside = 21

Days *left* to spend on the Inside = 21

Days since the ice king showed up = 7

Chapter 8

He's chatting with Josie.

The man of my dreams.

Actually, Dr. Simon Blackwood is the man who *comes* into my dreams. Not sure if it's the same thing. Not sure if I should be dreaming about him at all.

The enemy. But honestly, he doesn't feel like one.

He feels like someone I know but not really. Because I *don't* know him.

All I know is that he doesn't act like any other doctor I've met on the Outside. He hasn't judged me or looked at me with condescension. Like he knows everything about my illness and the things I need, and I know nothing.

I also know that he's fixing a house he doesn't live in and he doesn't like to be called a hero, but he saves people from needles and talks about gluing my book back together.

Other things about him, I've only imagined.

Like his body. All powerful and male.

After that first time when I touched myself thinking that he was watching me, I've thought about him, dreamt about him daily. Every night, I feel like I have eyes on me and I'm putting on a show for him. But of course, no one's there, at my little window.

I am the ballerina with no one to perform for but I do it anyway because my body won't let me stop.

Sitting in the dining hall during lunch, I squirm in my chair, feeling full and achy. I cross my arms across my chest to hide my tightened nipples as I watch him chat with Josie. Not that he's a chatting type, but apparently for her he is.

Suddenly, I've lost my appetite for the food in front of me.

I don't feel like eating my chicken when Josie is close enough to count his eyelashes. Or the fact that he's looking at her like she's a wonder of the world when he hasn't even looked at me once since we talked about needles last week.

Okay, so maybe not a wonder of the world, but something. Something that gives him pleasure. Something that makes his soft lips tip up at the edges.

I look away; I can't watch. Maybe I should interrogate Josie in our session today and ask her about it. Or maybe I can ask him since I'm meeting with him too, at the end of the day.

"You're not gonna believe what I have to tell you." Renn plops down on the seat beside me, her tray laden with food.

Then she looks at me with pity.

"What?" I stab a fork in my chicken.

"Oh, Willow." She presses a hand on her chest. "I love you, but this is gonna hurt."

I sit up straight in my chair. "What? What are you talking

about?"

She sighs dramatically. "I've got some dirt on him. I know you claimed him and so I went digging. People are not talking, which in itself is very weird. But I have my ways."

"What? What ways?" I'm confused now, and fearful of what she has to tell us.

"Can you just tell us and get this over with?" Penny says in a bored voice.

Renn gives me another look of pity before launching into her story. "So, we already know that his dad founded this place, right? But get this..." She looks at us one by one and my heart starts to slam inside my ribcage, more than it was already slamming. "They have been trying to get him to work for them for years. Like, *years*. But he never accepted. Until now. You know why that is? It's because our current Dr. Blackwood didn't leave his job in Boston on his own. He left it because he was fired."

"What?" This comes from Penny.

"Yes. He was fired. Can you believe it? Dr. Blackwood, the excellent doctor, was let go. No one knows for sure though. Official statement is that he quit. But there has been talk that he was *forced* to quit."

Immediately, Penny denies it, but then comes up with all the reasons why he could've been fired. And in their usual way, she and Renn go back and forth.

Forged prescription. Self-medication. Affair.

My heartbeat spikes at the mention of an affair and I want to say *shut up. Stop talking. I can't hear it.*

But all my words have died. I'm stunned. Reeling. Not in a

million years would I have guessed Renn's big news.

He was fired.

Dr. Simon Blackwood, the ice king, the hero, was fired.

Fired for God's sake.

Instantly, I know it's a mistake. It has to be. No one in their right mind would fire him. I've only known him for a week and we've had a handful of conversations, but I know that much.

I believe that much.

"All right. Stop," Renn commands, before turning to me. "I'm sorry I got carried away. Are you okay?"

"I'm fine." I shrug. "Why wouldn't I be?"

"I know you like him –" She raises her hand when Penny protests. "Maybe it's not true, you know."

"I know it's not true."

"You do?"

"Yeah. I mean, I don't believe it. Not everything you hear or even… read is reliable," I say, paraphrasing the man himself.

He gave me the benefit of the doubt. I can definitely do the same for him.

"Well, then, I don't believe it either," Renn says.

Vi smiles at me, nodding. "Me neither."

I smile back and for some reason, it makes me want to cry. This group of girls who have only known me for three weeks have somehow become the best friends I've ever had.

Renn gives me a side hug, which obviously gets noticed by Hunter, who's standing nearby. She blows him a kiss when he tells us to break it up.

"God, you guys," Penny grumbles half-heartedly. "Stop

crushing on the staff. It's not right."

Even though we all laugh, my heart isn't in it. I'm burning up with questions. Questions I don't think I have a right to ask.

But I want to.

I wonder if this is what psychiatrists feel when they are analyzing their patients. I guess not. Why would they? It's all clinical, in the name of medicine.

So I guess, he doesn't feel the same burn when he asks *me* questions. Which is great because it's not like I'm going to answer them anyway.

But why do I want him to feel the same burn that I'm feeling right now?

A second later, that burn takes up a physical form and I feel the heat of someone watching me. I turn around in my seat and my eyes clash with his. He's leaving the dining area with Josie and his gaze is on me.

I sense a strange intensity in them. A strange... passion. An interest. A personal interest. It quickens my breath, makes me sweat under my clothes with the heat.

I'm not sure if I'm making it up or what. But the allure of it is enough for me to keep staring back. Until he looks away, breaking our connection.

My eyes go to the clock in the dining room.

Four hours to go before I meet him again.

Before I'm alone with him.

***

Four very long hours later, it's time for my meeting with him.

Meeting? Session? I don't know what to call it. Here at Heartstone, we majorly spend our time in therapy and only have sporadic meetings with the psychiatrist who oversees things. Which I guess is what Dr. Blackwood is, now that Dr. Martin isn't here.

This is highly unusual but it doesn't mean that I'm not looking forward to it. It almost doesn't make sense, and yet it does.

All I've done for the past four hours is think about the rumors. I still don't believe them, but my burn for answers isn't gone.

Taking a deep breath, I knock on the door and count seconds until it's opened.

Three seconds later, it opens with a click and there he is. Tall and powerful and polished. He is silent as he steps aside and lets me in.

It's dark inside his room. Maybe because the storm has colored the sky black and he only has a small table lamp on. And when he closes the door behind me, the room seems even darker. Quieter, too. More intimate because the ruckus of the rain outside makes the silence on the inside more potent.

"Take a seat," he orders.

I flinch at his voice. It comes from behind me and it sounds exactly like my dreams. Low and commanding. Rough. And just from those three inconsequential words, all of it comes back, that ache. Not that it went anywhere, but still.

I breathe slowly and do as he says.

When I'm settled in my chair, only then, he moves. I hear the sounds. The heels of his shoes carrying him across the room.

The whisper of the wheels against the carpet that surrounds the desk when he rolls his leather chair out. The creak when he sits.

His breaths.

They echo in all the empty spaces inside me. His breaths are making me horny. Even hornier.

"Tell me about him," he says, straightaway. "About your boyfriend."

No small talk. No easing into it.

I look up as I clench my fingers together. Dr. Blackwood's watching me intently. With focus. So much focus. Like I'm his entire world and he's blind to everything else.

I revel in that look. I revel in the fact that in this moment, I might really be his entire world. He wants something from me, doesn't he? Answers to his questions. Even though that should make me apprehensive, I'm not. I'm reveling.

"What about him?" I ask.

"Tell me how you guys met."

I keep staring into his beautiful eyes. "In class. Literature."

"What was the first thing he said to you?"

"'Do you have an extra pen?'"

He keeps staring back. "Did you?"

"Yes. I gave it to him."

"Then what?"

"We started talking. And then, after that he'd always sit beside me, and he'd always ask for a pen."

"He never had a pen of his own."

I detect something in his voice, something scoffing, and I latch on to that like a beggar, thinking that he might be jealous.

Like I was jealous when he was talking to Josie. So jealous.

"He'd forget them on purpose."

"He tell you that?"

"Yes. After we started dating. He said I was so beautiful that he couldn't resist talking to me. And that was his only excuse in the beginning."

I was expecting another round of fire. Another question. But there's only silence.

In the quiet, we watch each other. His stubble usually gets thicker in the afternoon, wilder, untamed. My fingers itch with the need to touch it. See if it's rough and scrape-y like I want it to be.

God, I hope it's scrape-y. I want it to chafe against the soft parts of me.

While I'm rubbing my thighs under the desk, out of his sight, he's probably looking at me for twitches and glitches, to catch me in a lie. But I'll pretend that his deadpan stare is meant to be more than what it is.

"Did you like it when he told you that? Beautiful," he asks, at last.

At this, I have to look away. I have to stop clenching my thighs.

Beautiful.

Did I like it when he called me that?

"Yes. I loved it. I loved that he called me beautiful. No one had ever called me that before," I admit pathetically.

Truthfully.

I couldn't lie. Not about this. Not to him.

Girls like me, they are never called beautiful. I'm too short, too pale, too pudgy.

Too weird.

I wonder if Dr. Blackwood has called anyone beautiful before. I wonder if I was a little prettier, would he call *me* beautiful?

"What else did he call you?" His face is impassive, but his voice sounds roughed up, like a scratchy cloth that rubs along the length of my arms. The side of my neck. The top of my thighs.

And I have no choice but to resume my clenching. This time, I feel moisture ooze out of my core. It's getting wet and swollen. Humid.

"Snow princess," I whisper my lie, and Dr. Blackwood's eyes change.

I see a glimmer in them. A glint.

God, his eyes are so beautiful. So gray. So... rainy and stormy.

They flick back and forth over my face as he asks, "Why?"

"Why what?"

"Why'd he call you that?"

"Because of my hair."

Silver hair, the only thing I'm proud of. The only thing I inherited from my family.

Dr. Blackwood looks at my hair, my overgrown bangs and my loose topknot, and my scalp tingles. The strands oddly feel alive.

"And your skin."

"M-my skin?"

Said skin bursts out in goose bumps at his words. My lips part and I drag in a breath of his rainy smell that seems to have invaded every inch of this room.

He glances away from me, and I notice a random pulse on his jaw that comes and goes so fast I think I've imagined it.

"It's pale. Your skin," he says, straightening up in the chair and picking up his pen.

Even though he isn't looking at me, I still feel like he is. Did he really just say that? Did he really notice my skin?

I mean, of course he would've, but still. To associate it with the name I've given myself in the dark of the night makes me think that he *sees* me. That he thinks about me too.

Jesus, I'm really losing it, aren't I?

"He called me that the first time he kissed me," I whisper, for no reason at all, except to bring his eyes back to me and away from the rainy window. For him to see me.

"When was that?" he asks.

"On our first date."

"He kissed you on the first date."

Again, that scoffing. Again, I tuck it inside my heart, thinking that he's jealous. He doesn't appreciate that my boyfriend kissed me on the first date. He doesn't appreciate my boyfriend kissing me at all.

"Uh-huh." I lick my lips. "We went to the movies."

"And?"

"And well, he kissed me. We were walking back at night. It was raining. Drizzling, actually. My building was like, a block away but he grabbed me."

"He grabbed you."

His eyes are so intense, so heated that I look down at my

lap. I didn't want to.

I wanted to keep staring at him, taking in his reactions, however miniscule they might be. But now that I have his entire focus, I can't do it.

It's too much.

"Yeah. And then, he pulled me into this dark alley. He pushed me against the wall, heaved my legs up around his hips and…" I bite my lip, all the while knowing that he's still watching me. "His hands felt so big. Like they could do anything. They were so warm when he put them on my waist and pressed up against me. I've never felt anything so hard and so… hot. He told me that he was dying to kiss me. He'd been dying to kiss me ever since he saw me."

I can't help it. I clench my thighs together and press my hand on my lower stomach. All hidden. All under the table. Away from his eyes.

"Then what?"

His voice causes a pulse to go through my stomach into my pussy. It's wet and getting sloppy.

"And then he kissed me." I press harder on my belly. "His lips were so soft. Softest thing I'd ever touched. And so different from his rough grip. Different from how hard he was. All over."

I chance a glance at him and find him exactly as when my eyes left him. Stony, intense, watchful.

The ice king.

In fact, he looks colder than ever. Colder than the first time I met him. For a second, I think that maybe he knows the kisser in my head is not my boyfriend. It's him.

Why do I always feel like he can see me, he can read the things inside me?

Then he asks, "How did you feel when he kissed someone else?"

My hand on my stomach stiffens and I drag in a breath.

God, not this again. I'm so totally over The Roof Incident. Fuck.

"Lonely. Depressed. Heartbroken. Like I wanted to die," I reply, sighing.

"Who was the girl again?"

"Zoe. She was in my history class."

"Was she your friend?"

I scoff. "I never had friends. I was too weird for friends."

His fingers around the pen tighten, but his voice is casual – the same – when he asks, "Weird. How so?"

I shrug. "I was the slowest kid in school. I got picked last for everything. I hated birthday parties. I hated parties, period. I hardly laughed. Most of the time I fell asleep in my classes, and then my teachers made someone lend me their notes and I had to stay home all evening to make up for whatever I had missed. So yeah, I wasn't Miss Popular. I was Lazy Lolo. Weird Willow. Wacked Willow. Lunatic Lolo. I can go on if you like."

The color of his knuckles has turned white and I can't help but squirm at the forceful grip he has on his pen. I can't help but think, how would it feel if he gripped me that forcefully?

If he really pushed me into a dark alley.

"Did you confront them?"

Again, there's nothing wrong with his voice. It's as cool as always. But I can't figure out what's going on with his body. It's getting tighter and tighter.

What's happening to him?

I hope he's getting mad on my behalf. I'd really like him to.

I sweep my sweaty bangs off my forehead. "What, those kids?"

"Those kids? Your boyfriend and Zoe? Either?"

"Yeah. I kinda did. At least, the kids. When I was younger. A lot younger, and things they said hurt me. Sometimes I'd push them off the swing at the park when no one was looking. Hid their notebooks or their lunches at school. And sometimes when I was really angry, I'd punch them. Especially boys. In their junk."

The glint in his eyes is admiration; I see it. It warms me.

I actually did do those things. I never admitted to doing them, though. I can't remember if I was ever punished for them. I only know that I denied it to the teachers, to my mom, to everyone. To the point that I forgot I ever did them.

Until now.

Until he asked, and I told him. Just like that.

He's breaking something free inside me. All the locked boxes. All the chained beasts. Simon Blackwood is setting them free and he hasn't even made the effort.

Why is it so effortless? Giving him pieces of me.

I make a fist and show him, repeating his words from last time, "I'm dangerous."

"You are, aren't you? A little warrior," he murmurs, his grip around his pen loosening. "Although that's not how you make a fist."

"It's not?"

He shakes his head.

I open my palm, splaying my fingers. "Will you teach me?"

For a few moments, he doesn't say anything, but then he stands up. The chair squeaks and his shoes click as he rounds the table and approaches me.

I stand too, my heart probably squeezed between the bones of my ribs, trying to fly out.

Stopping a couple of feet before me, he looks down. How is it that even without a single expression on his face, I feel like he's telling me something? Only I don't know what, exactly, but every part of me is listening.

It's crazy. Not the useless kind but the kind that's stealing my breaths.

"Give me your hand," he commands.

"Why?" I ask, even as I obey him.

He takes my hand into his, and I notice all those tiny scratches on his fingers again. I want to ask him about the house, but he speaks over me. "I'm teaching you how to make a proper fist."

My small palm is dwarfed by his big one as he curls my fingers. The last time our touch was over quickly. I couldn't appreciate the heat and the texture of his skin completely.

I do, now. The warmth of his skin seeps into mine as he tucks my thumb down across my index and middle fingers.

"Keep it tight," he instructs, tapping my thumb. "You don't want it to get hurt."

I smile slightly. "Okay."

He's been focused on my hand and the technique of making a proper fist but at my whisper, he glances at my face. There's a dangerous clench in his jaw. I don't know why I think it's dangerous, but it is. Maybe it's because that clench is paired with the look in his eyes. Kind of frosty. Kind of not.

When he lets go of my hand, I don't like it. I don't like the loss of touch, so I lightly punch him on his chest, before he can move away and go back to his chair where he'll psychoanalyze the shit out of me.

And because I've lost all sense of self-preservation, I'll let him.

He stops. Freezes, almost.

I peek up at him through my lashes. "Sorry. I wanted to see if it worked."

"If that's how you punch, I don't think you really taught them their lesson," he rumbles.

"How do you know so much about punching?"

His heart is beating beneath my fist and I want to press down harder, press up on the rhythm that gives him life.

Sighing, he answers, "I've been in fights before."

"Yeah? With whom?"

He shrugs; it's tight. "With kids. At school."

I frown. "Were they assholes to you?"

His lips twitch. "Why? Are you going to use your stellar punching skills on them?"

"Maybe."

My answer makes him chuckle and I feel it reverberating inside his chest. The chest that I'm touching, through the fabric of his shirt.

There's no reason for me to touch it. But I can't not touch it either. Especially when he's not moving away or telling me to back off.

"Is your house fixed?" I whisper.

He swallows; I notice the slow bob of his Adam's apple.

Apart from that grave way he was watching his dad's photo, this is the first reaction I've seen from him or at least, the reaction that he's shown me. That swallow. But before I can really marvel over that, he clips, "No."

Something heavy sits on my chest. It's not my illness. That's where it comes from sometimes. My chest. This is different. This is for him, and for that pained reaction.

"Why are you fixing a house you don't even live in?"

His eyelashes look thick, like a forest around his eyes, as he scans my face. "Because I have to."

I accept his answer with a nod. I *know* his answer. I do a lot of things that I *have* to do, too.

Like lying.

I've lied all my life. For my mom. I've disappointed her a lot. The fact that I struggled with school, with making friends. The fact that I never took much interest in the things that she had an interest in. My cousin took to our store, fashion, cosmetics, jewelry, right from the beginning. My mom wanted that for me too, but I never gave her that.

When I was diagnosed, she was so heartbroken. I saw it in her eyes.

Lying and pretending were the only ways I could keep her

safe. I could keep myself safe from her disappointment.

Until The Roof Incident.

I splay my palm on his chest. "You like fixing things, don't you?"

Kinda like a hero.

He goes all stone-like. The breathing chest under my hand, just... stops. It stops moving. Stops being alive, even. I think he's going to ask me to move my hand. He's going to step back because he hates my touch.

But he simply says, "It's my job."

God, what is it? Why's he so sad?

"Why did you move here? From Massachusetts?" I ask, thinking about the rumors.

Stupid fucking rumors that I don't believe in.

People can be so cruel sometimes. Ask me. I know all about it.

A frown forms in between his brows. A suspicious, almost defensive frown. "Why?"

I shrug, appearing as casual as I can. I'm no threat to him. But I probably look like one because I'm asking the questions.

"I'm just wondering if you'll go back once Dr. Martin is fine and back to work."

The vein on the side of his neck has become taut. "I might."

"Do you miss it? Boston, I mean."

"Not really."

"What about your friends? Colleagues?" Then I add, because I can't stop myself, "Girlfriend?"

It sounded casual, right? I mean, there's no way he can

know I'm fishing for information. About his earlier job, his life before Heartstone.

I hope not.

Dr. Blackwood's frown gets deeper. "Is this your way of fishing for information?"

Damn it.

I purse my lips, and admit, "Yes."

"And what information would that be?"

His smell wafts through my nose as he shoves his hands inside his pockets. There are tons of things I can ask him. Tons of things I want to ask him. But I don't think I can. I don't have the right.

Though there's this question that's burning in the forefront of my mind. In my mind, I see him with Josie. Chatting, smiling.

And I'm jealous, despite the fact that I shouldn't be.

The pads of my fingers dig into his chest, and as I realize his muscles are so toned, so sculpted that there's absolutely no give, I ask, "Do you have someone special, Dr. Blackwood?"

Someone you kiss? Someone you grab and pull into a dark alley and press against walls?

I don't say that but I'm definitely asking that.

It's like he hears the unspoken questions because the heat of his body seems to have doubled. Like his blood is rushing in his veins with an uncanny speed.

With flaring nostrils and a hard jaw, he answers, "No."

"Why not?"

"Because I'm busy."

I want to smile. Actually, I've never wanted to smile this

hard. Ever. His answer calms me but it also makes me restless to move closer to him. I want to trace my palm over the arch of his chest and see if I got it right in my dreams.

But I don't do any of those things. I don't want him to take away this small concession he's given me.

Why is he even giving it to me? I'm not complaining. But still.

"Busy with patients?"

"Busy with my job. Yes," he says, all professional-like.

That's what he is. Professional and distant. Dedicated to his job and fixing people. If Mass General let him go, then they are idiots.

I'm an idiot, too, in this moment.

Instead of backing off, I want to do something. Something that might crack his cool façade. Maybe reaching up and messing up his no-nonsense hair.

What would he do? If I did that? If I grabbed his collar and pushed him against the wall?

And kissed him?

My eyes drop to his lips, his soft, *soft* lips. There's a cleft in the middle of his lower lip. I want to taste that cleft, dig my tongue in it, wet it, suck on it, bite it.

"So you don't have fun at all?"

"No. I'm not a fun guy."

I watch his lips form the words, and every syllable that comes out of his mouth makes my need to shake him, kiss him, mess him up, stronger. Stronger and stronger.

The need is so consuming that I hardly notice when he puts

his hand on my palm and takes it off his body. It's final and smooth, his action. Effortless. As though my touch barely registered to him.

"But I think you have a point. It's after hours and I should go… have fun rather than spending my time with a patient." He steps back then. "I'll see you next week. Same time."

Chapter 9

There's a sun stuck in my head.

It's bright and glaring. It hurts my eyes, my skull, my very bones.

I shove a pillow on my face, trying to shield myself from the rays. Obviously, it doesn't help. Because the sun is inside my head.

Inside. My head.

There are some things people might not know about depression. Like, if you're lucky, you'll see the signs and you'll know it's coming – the episode. But other times, there's no warning. You wake up and it's just there, either sitting on your chest, or shoved inside your head, like a giant light bulb that won't go off.

Depression is also a whore for attention. Just when you think you're okay. Meds are great. There's quiet and peace and maybe, just maybe, a little bit of happiness, it strikes. In a whiny voice, it says, *you didn't forget about me, did you?*

And then it's there. It's real and everything else is fake.

Like the fact that it's a rainy day. I can see the splatter on my window above my bed. And yet, it feels like sun is glaring down at me, leaching away my strength, drying me up, leaving me a mass of heavy bones.

I'm exhausted, and I haven't even opened my eyes yet.

My body feels like it's heavier than yesterday. I know it's not. I know it's impossible – I haven't lost rational thought – but it still feels like it.

In most cases, mental illness is not the absence of rational thought, but the presence of irrational ones, despite all rationality. Well, until you *really* lose it. Then you don't know the difference between anything anymore.

At exactly 6:45AM, the knock on my wall comes. Renn and I have a ritual of talking through our paper-thin wall every morning. But today, I groan and tell her that I can't.

"Willow, you okay?" she asks, concerned.

But I ignore her. I can't do it today. I want her to go away. I wanna sleep.

At exactly 7AM, the knock on my door comes as well, and a nurse tells me that breakfast is in thirty minutes.

"I know," I snap at her from under the pillow.

At my answer, she goes away.

Good.

Of course I know breakfast is in thirty minutes. I've been living here for twenty-four days, haven't I?

Damn it.

I'm not this grumpy, usually.

That's another thing with my episodes. They make me snappy, irritated. Everything bothers me. The crowd, the daily chores, my mom, school, teachers. *Everything*. But I tried my best to hide it on the Outside so I don't seem crazy to anyone.

I toss the pillow away and cover myself from head to toe with my dark blanket. Another knock comes at my door and this time, the nurse's voice is louder. "Willow, get up. Come on. It's way past time."

"Go away," I tell her through my blanket.

"Willow, come on. Is everything okay?"

"Everything's fine. Just please go away," I repeat, hoping she will.

Hoping. Praying.

But when has that ever helped me?

She asks me to get up again, but this time her voice seems to be coming from closer, and I tighten my muscles under my covers.

Is she approaching me? Is she going to touch me?

Because if she does, I swear to God I'll…

I'll fucking scream. I'll scream my heart out.

Because that's what's happening inside of me. Someone's screaming and thrashing and blazing. And I don't have to hide it. I don't have to pretend or lie. Not on the Inside.

I'm already locked up. I'm free to be insane.

A second later, a fist is pulling down my blanket. "What the…."

The nurse is looking at me, both stern and concerned. We've never had a problem before today. In fact, we smile at each other whenever I see her in the hallways or at the nurses' station.

"What's going on?" she asks with suspicion in her voice.

And here I thought we were friends. Or sort of friends. But I guess I'm like any other patient for her. She's nice to me but she can't trust me.

Do it, Willow.

Do it. Do it. Do it.

Do. It.

Scream.

"Go. Away." I grit my teeth.

I'm not sure who I am asking to go away right now, this voice in my head or the nurse. But I just want all of them to leave me alone.

"Willow, I'm asking you nicely. Get up and go to breakfast." She raises a stern eyebrow.

"And I'm telling you I don't wanna get up. Why's that so hard to understand?" I jerk the blanket out of her grip and cover myself again.

"Willow, don't make me call the techs. I don't want to do it."

"Fucking call them." I close my eyes and a breath escapes me when I hear her retreating. It hurts my lungs and I curl up in a ball.

Maybe she'll really bring in techs, security even. And maybe they'll bring a needle. Maybe they'll stick me with it, if I become difficult.

None of that's scaring me. It should; I hate needles. But then, I see him behind my closed eyes.

Dr. Blackwood. The hero.

Maybe he'll come and save me. Like he saved Annie. Yeah, I want him to save me. Just for today.

Please, God. Let him come save me.

I can hear the crowd gathering around my room. Murmurs and voices and footsteps. It's agitating me further. I feel like they are laughing at me, pointing fingers. Don't they get it?

I need to be left alone.

"Willow," Renn calls; she must be in the hallway. "What's going on? You okay?"

I hear Penny's voice too, asking what's going on. Even Violet's talking in louder tones. If this were any other day, I would've talked to them or smiled.

I can't move a muscle today.

Then I hear another set of footsteps and a voice that, despite everything, manages to make it through to me. "Willow."

Dr. Blackwood.

He's here, in my room.

Finally I lower the blanket, but only down to my nose, and take a peek at him.

He's on the threshold, filling the doorway with his massive shoulders, his wingtips half in and half out, staring down at me with a big frown.

Is he here because of the commotion? Or does he really want to see if I'm okay?

"What's going on?"

The nurse fills him in, but he doesn't move his eyes from me, nor I from him. The more I stare at him, the more I want him to come to me and the more I want to cry.

No idea why I want to do the latter. But I feel like I can.

I can cry in front of him and he'll lend me his broad chest, so I can rest my head on it. He'll even let me soak his shirt with my salty tears.

He enters the room, and comes to stand by my bed, towering over me, like he did the very first time I saw him. Shifting the air, making space for himself.

"Get up," he orders.

His voice makes me lose the battle with my tears and they well up in my eyes. "Please make them go away," I whisper thickly.

Again, I'm not sure if I'm talking about the people crowding the hallway or these shadows and thoughts inside my head.

He watches me for a few seconds, roaming his eyes all over my face, with a tic in his jaw. Then he twists his torso to look toward the door. "Can you clear out the hallway, please?" he says to someone behind him. "I've got this."

Slowly, the noises and murmurs die down and the people are taken away. I close my eyes and a tear seeps out, getting into my loose hair.

When I open my grainy lids, Dr. Blackwood is facing me. His chest swells and falls inside the confines of his shirt. "Get up."

I swallow. "Would it matter too much if I just stayed here for a little while?"

"Yes," he clips. "Breakfast's in about fifteen minutes and you need to be there for it."

"I'm not hungry."

"It doesn't work that way."

"How does it work then?"

"There are rules, protocols. They need to be followed."

I know about rules. I've followed them all my life. But then, what has that ever gotten me? This. This illness that never goes away.

Swallowing with difficulty, I take him in, his crisp pants and his polished shoes. I think of his charts. His pen, his glasses. The fact that he's always working. The fact that he doesn't have fun.

Lowering my blanket, I ask him, "Do you always follow the rules?"

He sighs. "Willow, get up."

I would, if I could.

The thing is, I don't think I can stand. And I'm not making this up. Sometimes my limbs don't have the energy. I feel so exhausted and heavy that it seems like my legs won't hold my weight. They shake, making me dizzy.

As always, I've tried to hide it, hide my episodes and bouts, as much as I can.

But in this moment when he's here, I don't want to.

I don't want to hide from him.

Somehow, I move. I gather whatever energy I have in my body and raise my arm to him. Dr. Blackwood glances at it, then at me.

"Can you help me up?" I ask in a small voice.

Not in a million years would I have thought that I'd ask for help. I never have before. Not from anyone. Let alone a doctor. But he's not a doctor, not to me.

And I don't want to be a patient to him, either. I want to be more.

My breaths are choppy, and my hand starts to tremble with its own weight. Only then he comes to my rescue. He grabs hold of my wrist and pulls me up from the bed. Like I don't weigh anything. Like all the heaviness is in my head.

It is.

But God, it's so real.

As real as this gray-eyed man and his rainy smell. As real as this strong chest that I hold onto when I'm standing on my own two unsteady feet.

"Don't go. I-I don't think I can stand." I swallow, my knees buckling.

His chest feels tighter than yesterday when he says, "I'm not going anywhere."

I fist his shirt in gratitude. "Thank you."

Yesterday I was hesitant about my touch. As much as I wanted it, it wasn't necessary to my very survival. Today, it feels like he's the only one who can bear this weight – my weight and the weight of my dark thoughts – with his large body and intense eyes.

So I lean over him, completely, bringing our chests flush together. Or rather, my chest to his ridged abdomen. He lets me, and the breath I take is the lightest one since this morning.

But there's still that lingering heaviness. Something solid and bubbling, at the same time. Something that needs to be purged now that he's here.

Why does he make me feel this way? That he'll make everything better just by his presence.

After a pause, I say, "I went to a funeral once. It was for my mom's friend. I think I was twelve or something. Do you know what I felt, when I looked at the body?"

"What?"

"My mom wouldn't let me go near it, at first. But I snuck up to it when she wasn't looking." I look him in the eye, even though I want to hide my shame. "I was jealous. Of the dead body."

I'm waiting for him to frown or throw me a condescending look even though I know he won't. He's not like that. And maybe that's why I'm telling him.

When he waits for me to talk, staring at me with his calm face and beautiful eyes, I go on. "I thought she had what I wanted. I thought I wanted that. I wanted to *be* that, the dead body. It was something I was aspiring to. I wanted to achieve death. But I couldn't let myself have it. I wouldn't."

"Why not?"

I focus on the pulse of his neck, the triangle of his throat, as I tighten my fist in his shirt.

"Because of my mom. Because I just… I can't bear the thought of leaving her behind." He's blurry through the lens of my tears. "The only reason I don't do it is because I can't take leaving something behind."

A salty drop slides down my cheek before I can stop it. They are like my words today. I can't stop them from slipping out. "Why's it so hard? Why's everything so hard for me? It's not supposed to be this hard, is it? Getting up from the bed. Freshening up. Going to get breakfast. Eating. Saying hi to people. Smiling. Laughing. It shouldn't be this hard. It can't be. It's me. I've got it all wrong somehow. I've got everything wrong."

Wrong. Wrong. Wrong.

That's what I am. I was born wrong. With the wrong kind of blood. In the wrong family.

"If I wasn't born, then my mom wouldn't be so disappointed, you know. She'd have a different daughter. A perfect daughter. She'd throw parties for her. She'd dress her up. And that daughter, she'd appreciate it. I'm not... I don't... appreciate things... I can't..."

My thoughts are breaking up, getting chaotic, but everything screeches to a halt when he puts his hand on me. Or rather just one finger. Thumb on my cheek.

My gaze skitters to his face and the look he gives me is penetrating.

So penetrating that all the glaring brightness inside my head seems to be dimming under the shine of his eyes.

"It's intimidating. It's terrifying to fight every second of every day. To wake up, tired and exhausted, knowing that you have to do it all again. It's easy to give up, isn't it?" he rasps, his thumb sliding along the single stream of tear.

His touch, bare minimum as it is, is dimming every other feeling inside me. My lips part and my heart flutters inside my chest.

The sign that I'm alive. The sign that I can feel his touch.

I nod, brimming with life and yet, so pliable and submissive. "Yes."

"Yeah. It would be so easy to just give up. Not fight." His voice is hypnotizing, so hypnotizing that I want to sleep wrapped around with it. "You know why we don't? At least, mostly? Because we're born fighters. We come into this life, kicking and screaming, bursting with all the energy. There's no shame in having to fight. There's no shame in having to kick and scream. There's no shame in being a warrior. It's the most honorable thing you can do for yourself. Pick up a sword and fight. Just reach out, Willow, and pick it up. That's all you have to do. And if someone makes you feel ashamed just for the fact that you're a fighter, then..." He licks his lips. "Then fuck them."

His words are soft, just as his mouth is, but the intensity in them, the vibration, jolts something inside me. It shifts something.

It's the sun. Maybe it's going behind the clouds.

"You think I'm a warrior?" I whisper, in awe.

"Yes."

"Really?"

"Yeah."

And now, I won't hurt anymore. I won't have to hide anymore.

I can come out.

Maybe I can really come out.

I'm safe. He saved me.

"I must be your dream come true," I whisper to this gray-eyed hero, the fixer. "All broken and cracked."

His thumb flexes over my cheek and I stay still. Still like I'm dead. But the heart inside my chest is beating with probably ten lives.

"I don't dream."

"Why not?"

"Because I have trouble falling asleep, too."

I imagine him in his bed, trying to fall asleep at night. Tossing and turning. What kind of a bed does he have? What color sheets? Does the sleep mess up his hair, thicken his stubble?

My insomnia is medicine-induced. I wonder what his is.

"What keeps you up?"

"Recently, the never-ending repairs."

I shake my head at him, and his eyes shift to my hair. It's loose around my shoulders. Since it's my only asset, I have it long and thick and going down to my waist.

Does he like it? My silvery strands?

"I count sheep," I say instead. "When I couldn't sleep."

But then you fixed it, too.

He looks into my eyes. "Maybe I should try that."

Despite everything, a small smile blooms on my lips. "Did I just cure you? The medicine man?"

He's still tracing his thumb along the apple of my cheek. I don't know if he realizes that. If he realizes that he's still touching me and I'm still fisting his shirt and our chests are moving in sync. When he breathes out, I breathe in. I'm filling my tired lungs with his air.

Does he realize that?

He's in me, now.

He studies my smile. "Maybe you did."

"I –"

"Simon?"

Someone speaks over me and suddenly, all the coziness leaves my body.

Beth's standing at the door, taking us in. Me almost wrapped around Dr. Blackwood. Him tracing his thumb on my cheek.

I'm frozen. Unable to think, unable to do anything.

But he doesn't have that problem, because he steps back from me. The click of his wingtips hitting the floor as he moves away makes me jerk.

"Beth," he says with a polite nod.

He's all calm and composed, when I'm standing here like a frightened animal on shaky, wobbling legs.

Beth moves her eyes from him to me. "Are you feeling okay, Willow?"

"Yes…"

I want to say more but I trail off. What should I even say? I mean, we were a little too close, but it wasn't as if we were doing anything.

Does it look bad? Standing intimately close to your psychiatrist, while he wipes your tears off? Is there no one in this whole wide world who's ever done that?

"Good. Breakfast's under way. You should go join the others." She smiles, albeit with strain. "Simon, can I speak to you for a second?"

"Of course," he murmurs.

With that, they both walk out of the room and I drop down on my bed. I want to sag and dissolve in my sheets but then I realize something.

In my unusual bout of talking, which seems to happen only around him, I basically admitted to another human being… that I've been thinking about killing myself since I was twelve.

The only reason I don't do it is because I can't take leaving something behind.

Medicine

Man

"What were you thinking?" Beth asks, angrily. "Do you have any idea what would've happened if someone else had walked in?"

"Why don't you enlighten me?" I say to her, but I'm focused on the drizzle outside.

I watch it through the window of my office, annoyed, angry. Fucking frustrated.

What wouldn't I give to walk out of here and never look back?

I knew it was a giant mistake when I took this job. And not for the reasons I thought it would be.

From the corner of my eye, I notice Beth moving closer. "Simon, this is a hospital. People are up and moving all the time. It's a miracle no one else saw you."

A gust of wind bends the tree, almost breaking it in half. But it snaps right back up. That tree reminds me of someone. Someone with blue eyes and pale skin.

Abruptly, I turn away from the window. "No one saw me doing what?"

"You know exactly what I mean," she snaps. "Stop making everything difficult. I'm trying to look out for you."

"Look out for me for what reason? I was doing my job. Or is that not why you hired me?"

She shakes her head. "You know what people will say."

I cross my arms across my chest and shoot her a hard look. "I thought you didn't believe what people said."

She purses her lips and I know it's coming. Her platitudes. I fist my hands, feeling the crackle of energy go through my knuckles.

Why doesn't she leave it alone? I'm doing everything I can to fix it. Fucking everything.

"What happened at Mass General, with Claire and the rumors… it was unfortunate. It could've happened to anyone and yes, that includes you too. I know you think you're invincible or a god, maybe. But you're human and you have to be smart, Simon. Joseph has been wanting you here for years. This is your father's legacy and it's yours, if you want it…"

"But?"

She raises her eyebrows. "The board of directors is taking this as a trial run and I don't want you to blow it. This is still a hospital. People talk. We have a zero-tolerance policy, but I can't be there all the time to enforce it. If you are seen hugging a patient, a beautiful, young patient, then there's not much I can do."

"I'm not asking you to do anything."

"I know you asked to meet with her this week. Again."

I narrow my eyes at where she's going with this. "And?"

"I'm glad you're taking an interest in the patients. Joseph has always tried to be involved with them as much as he could. But as you know, sessions and any individual therapy are left up to other trained professionals."

"What's your point?"

"My point is that you can focus on other things. In some in-patient facilities people don't even get to see their psychiatrist. You don't have to be so involved."

"Excuse me?"

"Simon, is there… Is there anything between the two of –"

"Beth," I cut her off, sighing sharply. "Do you really think that I would do something like that with a patient after what I've seen?"

I've known Beth all my life. When I was a kid, she'd bring over casseroles when my mother was going through her episodes. My father made himself scarce during such times, *especially* during such times. And my mother would break just a little more than she already was, every time he wouldn't come home, choosing to spend his time at Heartstone.

Beth has seen all this. She and Joseph, Dr. Martin, have been there every step of the miserable way.

Sadness washes over her face. "Oh, Simon. I –"

I cut her off again because I can't take her pity. I'm not that hungry little kid anymore, and neither am I weak and pathetic like my father.

"Look, I was just doing my job. She's my patient. I know my boundaries. I'm not my father."

I'm better than him.

At the heel of my words though, I feel something. A softness, as if warmth is still pressing up against me in the shape of a tiny body.

Her body. Her long, wavy, moon-like hair.

The only reason I don't do it is because I can't take leaving something behind.

I shove my hands inside my pockets and with them, I shove those nonsensical thoughts away, too.

"Do you blame us? For what happened to your mom?" Beth asks, tears in her eyes.

I don't talk about my mother a lot. The last time I mentioned her was to a twelve-year-old boy, Dean, when I found him at the cemetery.

"The only person I blame is my dad," I say, hoping that she walks away now.

"She was good at pretending, Simon. We all thought she was doing okay. We thought she was in a good place. We had no idea that she was that far gone. We thought we knew her. We did everything to make her happy when your father wasn't around." Tears fall down her cheeks. "But then, maybe we didn't. I don't think I can ever forgive myself for not... doing enough."

That's what I think about too.

Did I do enough? Was I there for her enough? If I was, then why did she do what she did?

Why did she leave me behind?

I spent a lot of time thinking about that. I'd replay all the moments, all the things we did together, my mother and me. How I'd quit everything to be with her, so she never felt alone. How I'd stay up all night if I had to because she couldn't sleep.

I did everything that a good son would do. Everything.

Over the years, I've come to realize that it wasn't me. It was him. *He* killed her. Not her illness. Not the meds.

Him.

And I was left behind.

I wonder if she thought about me in those final moments. If she thought about her son and how she was leaving him behind.

"It wasn't your fault. It was his fault," I say with gritted teeth. "He was the one she wanted, and he wasn't there. He was a fraud, my father. People think he's this legendary doctor, saving everyone, when he couldn't save his wife. He couldn't even stand her and her illness. And my mom knew that. If it weren't for him, she'd still be alive."

"He was a lousy father, Simon," Beth begins after a few moments, wiping her tears off. "A lousy husband. Believe me, I know. You don't have to forgive him. *We* don't have to forgive him. But please, don't throw away something good, something amazing because of him. You can do so much here, at this hospital. Please."

I jerk out a nod, thawing slightly.

"Tell me you'll be careful."

Sighing, I nod again. This one isn't as tight as the first one.

Beth's right. She's looking out for me like she's always done. The least I can do is not make things difficult for her.

But when she leaves, I hear it again.

Willow's voice.

It's soft and scratchy, a little hoarse. The kind of a voice that can get stuck inside a man's head.

The only reason I don't do it is because I can't take leaving something behind.

***

It's raining inside the room.

I watch the droplets hitting the old hardwood floor, forming a small puddle.

Plop. Plop. Plop.

The ceiling in the study is leaking. The discolored patch growing, expanding right in front of my eyes.

Fuck.

This is probably the third time I've seen it happen in the last week alone. No matter how much I fix this house, plaster over the cracks, there's no saving it.

I pinch the bridge of my nose and think about probably getting outside help. Maybe I can hire someone to come do this for me. In fact, I should. I don't have time to fix this house.

I don't even know *why* I'm fixing this piece of crap. I wasn't even supposed to be here tonight. But I took Dean and his sister out for a pizza because apparently, he was in the mood for one. That's what he told me, but I know the truth.

I could guess. His dad was out of town and he was scared. I would be, too. In fact, I *was* that kid.

When I dropped them off, instead of driving away, I walked

inside this house. And instead of walking right back out, I decided to work on the stairs leading down to the basement.

I have no idea why my father let it get this bad, the apparent perfectionist.

Either way, it's not mine, this house. It never was. It never will be. I don't want it. Like I don't want Heartstone or my father's legacy.

I can't wait to get back to Boston. That's my life. But then again, I don't know if I'm going to get it back.

Reaching for my cellphone on the desk, I approach the window and dial the number I've been wanting to. I know it's late at night, but he won't be sleeping.

It rings a couple of times before I hear the click.

"Simon," Greg, my colleague and only friend at Mass General, greets me from the other side.

"Hey," I say, staring at the willow tree in my backyard.

I spent a lot of time under that tree while growing up and ever since I got back, I can't look away from it. That tree has survived a lot. The years of me growing up, my mother's death, my leaving.

That tree is a survivor. A fighter.

Like its namesake.

"I was hoping I wouldn't get this call," he says, thankfully pulling me out of my thoughts.

"Well, you can't always get what you want," I say drily.

"Man, you gotta let it go. It doesn't look good, with the whole lawsuit hanging over your head."

It's not as if I haven't heard the word lawsuit before. But

every time I hear it a jolt goes through my body. Like I've been electrocuted, making me flinch.

I've never paid any attention to these HR things. I never had to. I have an impeccable record. Or had.

"I don't care about the lawsuit. How is she?"

Greg sighs. "She's the same."

I rub my forehead; I feel a headache coming on. I'm trying to remember if I have any sleeping pills lying around or if I'll have to make a run to the drugstore.

"I'm meeting her parents at the end of the week to discuss options."

My fingers halt their movements and a raging ache explodes in my skull. "Fuck options. There is no other option."

"It's been almost two months. Her condition isn't improving, you know that. And I'm sorry to say it's not going to. It's time to let her go. Her parents are tired, too. Their money is running out. The insurance is not gonna cover everything –"

"I told you money is not a problem. I can write you a check right now."

"No, you won't. I'll personally make sure that your check doesn't come through because you've lost your fucking mind."

"You're not pulling the plug." I almost crush the phone in my hand. "You're not killing her."

"She's dead already," Greg snaps.

I clench my eyes shut at the onslaught of pain. It should feel hot, this magnitude of pain. Red and pulsating. But in my experience, my pains have always had a chill to them. A sting. A frostiness.

A partial numbness where all I can feel is the cold, the hard center of it, and nothing else.

"Look," Greg says. "You can't even think about getting yourself involved with Claire any more than you already are, Simon. They're going to see your money, your phone calls as a sign of guilt."

"I told you I don't care about the lawsuit. Her parents can sue me for everything I am, I don't care. I want Claire to come out of this alive. I fucked up, Greg. I shouldn't have but I did. She can't pay the price for it."

"Damn it," he mutters. "Simon –"

"Just give me more time."

He's silent for a moment. Then, "I can give you two weeks."

My head drops in relief and I stare at the puddle of leaking water. "Two weeks. Okay. Yeah."

"But just that. No more. We're pulling the plug after that."

I know that's the right course. I'm aware that patients like Claire don't come back from their coma. But I have some ideas. I have scheduled a phone call with a group working at Berkley. They work with ABI – Acute Brain Injury, and I'm going to present Claire's case to them.

"Okay," I agree, letting it go.

"Good. Now don't call me, I'm busy entertaining and I suggest you do the same."

"Entertain, you mean?"

"Yes."

My lips pull into a smile. "With what? Sausages?"

"Fuck you, man. I've got a good thing going here."

"Who's the lucky lady?"

"A drug rep."

"No kidding. You hate drug reps."

"This one's got a great pair of legs."

I smirk. "Is she aware that you're not going to buy whatever she's selling?"

"Hey, I'm open to whatever she's selling. And as I said, you should do the same. Maybe that'll take your mind off everything. Got any sexy doctors or drug reps or you know? Nurses?"

At his question, my eyes go to the willow tree again. "No, and I'm not interested."

"Whatever. Though you do need to get laid. How long has it been, three months?"

"Didn't know you kept tabs on my sex life."

"Fuck you. Again. All right, I'm out."

We say our goodbyes and then, it's silence. Or actually, not. Because I hear her.

Do you have someone special, Dr. Blackwood?

I hear the words as if she's here, in this room. As if I brought her with me. Inside this shaky debris of a house.

Willow Audrey Taylor, with her silver hair and blue eyes, and a fucking voice that sticks.

I wonder what she'll think of this. The dusty furniture, the leaking roof, broken stairs. The fact that this house is stuck in the past.

You like fixing things, don't you?

I wonder if her pale skin will light up this house, like the moon does.

He called me snow princess. He pulled me into this dark alley...

He pushed me against the wall. His hands felt so big. Like they could do anything.

He was dying to kiss me...

Fucking liar. And fucking Lee Jordan.

She's such a liar. A liar who fights, every single second of every single day and doesn't even know it.

I scrub my hand across my face when I feel something stir inside my gut. Something warm and fucking wrong. Something that makes me think of her skin and soft hair.

Her tiny body.

Just then I hear a noise from upstairs, alerting me to the fact that I'm not alone within these walls. Reminding me that I need to get out of here.

Shaking my head, I turn away from the window and walk out of the room. Walk out of this godforsaken place.

I could take Greg's advice because he's right. It's been three months since I had sex. Random hook-ups are not my style, though. I prefer to know the person and I prefer for them to know that it's strictly physical and nothing else. I don't have time for anything else. I fuck and that's it. It's biology.

But for some elusive reason, I don't want to fuck a nameless woman.

I drive to my hotel, change into my gym clothes and hit the treadmill downstairs. I know even pills won't do the trick.

This is my only option. Work out till exhaustion. Till I overcome this strange, fucking warmth inside my body. The kind

I've never felt before. The kind I don't *want* to feel.

Because I'm not like the man who killed my mother.

I'm not my father.

Chapter 10

My one bad day turns into several bad days.

Every day it's a chore to wake up and face the routine. Every day I almost don't go to breakfast or do my groups. Not to mention, my fucking meds are upping their game where the nausea is concerned. They tell me it's psychological more than physiological. Meaning, it's all in my head. And they can't give me anti-emetics. Although, they finally give me saltines and ginger, probably to shut me up. So there's that.

Every day I want to break down and cry or burst through the front doors and run away, or just dissolve.

But I don't.

Because maybe, just maybe, I'm a fighter. And there's no shame in fighting. There's honor.

He told me that.

Dr. Simon Blackwood.

Simon.

I know I said I won't call him by his name but I'm breaking

my promise. He's not Dr. Blackwood to me, he's Simon.

The man who declared me a warrior. The man who makes me want to *not* die. The man who knows my secret.

He's the only one.

I've never told this to anyone before. Not my mom. Hardly my doctors. But he knows. He knows about The Funeral Incident, where I felt such sharp jealousy, I was willing every bus, every cab, every car to come hit me on our way back home.

A week ago I would've been terrified that he knew that, but not now. Now, I feel peace. Almost like happiness. I know he won't use it against me. I believe that.

I believe him.

Over the next few days, I catch glimpses of him. In the hallways, the rec room, the TV room, on the grounds. But he's always busy. He usually has papers in his hands. He barely stops to chat with people, barely mingles with them.

Although sometimes he chats with Josie. Those times are hard. Harder than any dark days I've seen in the past.

As much as I want to seek him out, I'm afraid that Beth might think there's something between us. I'm afraid that she might take it the wrong way.

She found me the day after she saw us together. She asked me how I was doing and told me that the only thing that should matter to me was to get better. Go Outside with a better understanding of myself and the things I'm battling with.

There was no mention of how she found us, and I decided maybe it's all in my head, like a lot of other things. Maybe she didn't even think there was something there.

For all intents and purposes, I'm his patient and he's my psychiatrist. Well, that is, in fact, the case.

It isn't Dr. Blackwood's fault that his patient thinks about touching him day and night. It isn't his fault that she dreams about him. She rubs her fingers together, trying to feel the fabric of his shirt, trying to remember the coiled strength of his chest. She wants to tell him all her secrets, show him all her dark places, and she isn't even afraid to do that.

It isn't his fault that I'm slowly going insane and it has nothing to do with my illness, and everything to do with him, the man who's supposed to fix me. My medicine man.

In fact, I'm so insane that even though the sleep meds flow in my veins, I've gotten up every night this week in between hourly checks, and written his name on the rainy window: *Medicine man.*

I write his name on the misty glass and watch as the droplets drag the lines of M and N down. Like a single teardrop. When I think about him, I don't think about my illness or hear the noises of the ward or occasional whimpers of the patients. I don't think about how sour my mouth has been all this week.

"What are you thinking so hard about? God, you're gonna burn holes through my book."

Penny's voice gets me out of my trance.

We're at the breakfast table and when I come to, everything looks clear to me. Not dull or burning bright. Just right. The room, the people, the conversation. I'm sitting beside Renn, as usual. Vi and Penny are sitting on the opposite side. The air smells of eggs and strawberries.

Focus.

It's back.

I can focus on these things. I can focus on the trees outside, rather than my imploding thoughts. I can focus on the stray droplets clinging to the window, the damp grounds. It's starting to rain. Things are gray and wet and swollen and promising.

Oh my God, things are *promising*.

"Forget it. She's totally out of it. She probably didn't even hear you," Renn mutters, plucking a strawberry from my bowl and popping it in her mouth.

I look at her. "Hey, stop eating my strawberries."

Her eyes widen in astonishment. Then she goes ahead and plucks another strawberry from my fruit bowl, all the while watching me.

I glare at her and slide my tray out of her reach. "Get your own."

Her lips twitch and then she grins. "Oh my God!"

"What?"

"You're back." She claps her hands and gives me a side hug.

Which obviously gets noticed by one of the techs, who reprimands her. Which obviously gives Renn a perfect excuse to flip the bird.

I chuckle self-consciously. "I've always been here."

"Oh please. I was getting bored out of my mind. Penny was getting so fucking unbearable without your memory flash cards."

"I missed them. They help me keep sharp," Penny reluctantly admits.

I grin at her, feeling warm. I sometimes help her study at the library when she gets anxious about things. I didn't know it meant so much to her.

"We all thought you were gonna be the next Vi," Renn continues, as usual being blunt.

I glance at Vi, ready with an apology on behalf of Renn. But Vi's grinning too. "Well, yeah, we did think that."

That just makes me laugh.

Back on the Outside, my bad days would've horrified me, made me feel ashamed. But not here.

Here, everyone has bad days.

Like Penny, with her anxiety, who talks so fast that you can't understand her. Usually, it takes a staff member to calm her down. And Vi, who goes quiet and won't talk to you even if you begged. There was a day when she didn't say a single word. And Renn, too. Sometimes she gets super snappy, almost as bad as Annie and *you* don't wanna talk to *her*. It happens when she wants to purge but can't.

I look around the room and my gaze falls on a brunette who was admitted at the same time as me. In fact, I remember seeing the same fear, same pale complexion on her face as mine during those first few days, while we were trying to get adjusted to this new place, new meds, new rules, away from the only life we've known. Everyone looked like an enemy then. A threat. The Heartstone Effect.

I smile at her when she catches my eyes. She looks much better now. I wonder if I look better to her as well.

Roger and Annie are huddled in the corner talking like old friends; I think it's a good day for them. A tech is trying to get a patient from The Batcave to eat something. A girl from my floor is simply staring down at her food, looking like she's going to cry. I think she's having a bad day.

Everyone explodes or implodes in this place. That doesn't mean they are crazy. Crazy is a useless word anyway.

They are my friends and I missed them too.

"So, what'd I miss?" I ask, and Renn launches into a lengthy summary of this week's events.

She tells me about all the gossip: A couple of nurses getting into an argument. Annie and Roger might be secretly dating each other. They looked pretty cozy in the TV room last night. Not to mention, right now. Snuggling without snuggling.

"What? That's completely wrong information. Lisa from 2F? She's the one dating Roger. I saw them exchange looks the other day," I point out.

"The other day was last week. Things have changed around here." Renn shrugs, and then she's about to say something else, something super important if her wide eyes and eager expression are anything to go by, but things sort of come to a halt when someone walks in through the doors.

A new guy.

He's not walking in, more like swaggering in, with long, lazy steps. His hands are shoved inside the pockets of his faded jeans as his eyes run across the space. People are watching him openly, but this guy doesn't seem to care. In fact, when he makes eye contact with Roger, he tips his chin in greeting, but Roger only glares at him and looks away. The new guy doesn't mind.

"Who's that?" I ask the table, still watching him as he gets into the breakfast line.

The girl in front of him turns back and checks him out from top to bottom. I can't see what his reaction is, but the lines of his shoulders say that he's relaxed and unbothered.

I guess everyone's getting a little territorial with the arrival of the newcomer.

"Oh, he's the new guy, I think," Penny answers, staring at him as well.

"When'd he arrive?" I ask, thinking how come I missed that too.

"Yesterday," Vi murmurs.

Once the guy's done loading his breakfast on his tray, he makes his way to the empty tables, and decides on the one diagonal to us.

Actually, it's not as if he decides on it by discarding all the other options. It's like this is the place he's been wanting to sit in since he entered the dining hall. Which is curious because, well, he turned to face the room, his eyes going to the empty table he's occupying right now, and then his eyes went to our table. Renn, specifically.

It's curious because Renn wasn't even facing him. She was focused on stabbing her breakfast while this new guy kept his eyes on her, with a very tiny micro-smile as he walked to the chair and plopped down.

"Do you know him?" I ask Renn.

She stiffens, but questions innocently, "Who?"

"You know who. Why's he staring at you?"

She plops a piece of fruit in her mouth and shrugs. "How do I know why he's doing what he's doing?"

I frown at her, completely confused. "What?"

"What?"

I open my mouth and close it, and open it again. "What's going on? Why are you acting weird?"

"I'm not acting weird."

Penny jumps in. "You so are."

Vi nods.

"Shut up. I'm not." Renn shifts in her seat, her eyes planted resolutely away from the new guy whose eyes are pinned firmly *at* her.

"Why aren't you looking back at him? He's handsome." I turn to the girls to get confirmation. "Right?"

Penny nods. "I mean, yeah. If you're into dark hair and dark eyes and good bone structure."

"Exactly." I nod too. "He's got good bone structure. You don't get that often."

Good bone structure and dark hair remind me of someone but I squash that thought because this is about Renn, not me.

"Stop it. I'm trying to eat my breakfast," Renn snaps.

"You hate your breakfast," Vi offers.

"Ohmigod, has the impossible happened?" Penny shuts her book and gives the conversation her full attention. "Are you not interested in a human of the opposite sex?"

"Do you want me to slap you? 'Cause I'm not afraid to slap you," Renn mutters, darkly.

"Hey, quit harassing her," I tell the girls. "Renn doesn't have to like every good-looking guy. She can hate some."

She sits back, waving her hand at me as if acknowledging

my statement. "Thank you."

I smirk. "Yeah, so why do you hate him? Did he do something to you?" I sit up, suddenly getting serious. "Oh my God. What'd he do to you?"

The three of us, apart from Renn, focus on the guy who's sprawled in his seat, popping grapes, watching us, like we're a movie or something. He's still got that little smirk on his mouth. Grudgingly, I admit that he does have good bone structure. Not to mention his hair's all messy, strands falling over his forehead in careless abandon.

Even so, we'll kick his ass if he did something to Renn.

"No way! Renn! You know you can complain, right?" Penny's all charged up now.

"Yes, we can go right now," I say, determined.

I'm ready to stand when Renn almost shouts, "It's nothing, you crazy idiots." At last, she looks at the new guy. "Hey, asshole. Stop staring at me. I told you I'm not interested."

"You *told* him?" Penny's confused.

So am I. "When did this happen? How much have I missed?"

The guy isn't afraid or deterred. His smirk only grows, overcoming his entire mouth. He crosses his arms across his chest, and I see a peek of tattoos circling his biceps, under his black t-shirt.

"Tell me your name and I'll stop," he says in a voice that sounds lazy, just like his demeanor. Careless and reckless and all the less-es.

"My name's none of your business," Renn snaps.

He takes a sip of his juice and leans forward. "Yeah, I

thought that too. But then, last night you came to me and you started stripping. I didn't wanna interrupt you and ask then. That would've been rude," he explains. "And the name I've been calling you in my head is probably turning my mom in her grave. She taught me to never objectify women. So yeah. Tell me your name. That's the least you could do after interrupting my sleep."

To say that we're all shocked is an understatement. The tables around us have gone quiet. Well, they weren't talking much to begin with because mostly everyone has been focused on the new guy. But still. Now, the place has gone completely silent, or rather the pocket in which we're situated has.

Penny's gaping. Vi's pressing her lips together to keep from laughing out loud. And well, I'm the same way. Because the impossible *has* happened. Renn's blushing. She's gone as red as her hair.

That's totally making her angry, though. Because her eyes are flashing. She might have even growled too.

"I never…" She breathes deep. "*Never*, ever came to you, you pig!"

He chuckles. "Right. It was a dream." He spreads his palms as if apologizing charmingly. "Forgot to mention that. But it doesn't change the fact that I've seen you naked. You might as well give up your name."

Renn growls some more.

I can't stop anymore. I laugh and so does Vi. Penny's not far behind. All around, people are chuckling too. The new guy's enjoying himself, I think.

Just to mess with my BFF, I call out, "Renn. Her name's Renn."

Renn whips her eyes to me. "How dare you? You're supposed to be my friend."

"What? He just wanted to know your name." I shrug, chuckling.

Penny raises her hand in the air and I raise mine, and we mime high-fiving each other since we can't exactly do the act.

The new guy tips his chin at me and I nod. For some reason, I like him. Maybe it's the fact that he's so easily and so thoroughly managed to rattle Renn, and he appears more or less harmless.

"I'm Tristan," he says with a satisfied glint in his eyes.

"I don't care," Renn shoots back.

"I wouldn't be too sure about that."

"What's that supposed to mean?"

"It means give it time. I kinda grow on people."

"Why? Are you fungus?"

This makes him chuckle again. "Yeah, I like you, Renn." He runs his fingers through his hair. "You're gonna make my stay very interesting."

She flips him the bird before turning away.

A second later, Vi murmurs, "I wonder what he was calling you in his head."

Penny snorts.

Vi grins.

And I just laugh.

Maybe I don't have magic in my veins and I'm not at Hogwarts. But I'm at Heartstone. I have friends who care about me and who missed me while I was trapped inside my head.

And I have a man who calls me a fighter and saves me all

in the same breath.

So I am in a good place, I think.

Chapter 11

In the afternoon, I hear the worst thing of my life.

Well, okay, not the worst. Because the worst would be if the thing I heard came to pass.

I'm in the TV room, reading the climax of *Harry Potter and the Prisoner of Azkaban*, where they do a wizard version of prison break and fly up to a tower window. I overhear a couple of nurses mentioning something about Simon and my ears perk up.

"...I'll let him know, yeah. I think he's leaving for the day. Josie said they were gonna grab dinner together," says the first nurse.

"Oh! Is it happening? The date?" the second nurse asks with a twinkle in her eyes.

The first nurse shakes her head, handing her a bunch of files. "Maybe. Who knows? I can't wait to ask Josie all about it."

They both laugh as I slowly lose all will to laugh. Ever.

I sit in my plastic chair, deaf and blind, as if I suffered an explosion. I'm not sure if I'm even breathing. But I'm definitely feeling. I'm feeling like I'm going to die. I *want* to die.

Actually, no.

I don't want to die. I want to live.

Yes, I want to live. I want to live because…

Because if I don't live, then I can't stop this. I can't stop them from going on a date. And I need to stop it. I have to.

I spring up, my already-abused-to-the-maximum book falling on the floor in two pieces. I wonder if it's an omen. My book finally cracking in two, right in the middle. With surprisingly steady legs that bend down smoothly, I retrieve the book.

There's no trembling or shaking or any nervous twitch in my body. It's sure. It's completely, absolutely sure and determined to stop this. I can't help but wonder if I'm in a trance. If I'm drugged, or under hypnosis. Or maybe this is a different kind of insanity. A more rational kind.

I'm almost blind to the happenings of the hospital as I walk down the hallway, toward Simon's office. I know people brush past me. I know they are talking. They are working. But I can't see them. My mind's on one thing: the man at the end of the hallway.

The hallway that's not freely accessible to me, a patient. Although, I don't seem to remember this until I'm stopped by a nurse. I tell her I need to see Dr. Blackwood but she says she can help me with whatever I need.

"I just… I need to see him. You can't help me with it," I tell her because that's the truth. She can't help me.

She goes to say something but the man I've been looking for comes out of his office – Thank God – and I call out his name to get his attention.

When he focuses on me, I take a deep breath and ask him,

"C-Can I please talk to you? In your office?"

He frowns but nods. "Sure." To the nurse, "I've got this."

I don't know what it is but every time he says, *I've got this*, something happens to me. Something tingly and warm and all I want to do is wrap myself around his strong, capable body and tuck my face in his neck and never let go.

We walk to his office and he opens the door, gesturing me to get in.

This is the room I never wanted to enter willingly. But now, all I can think about is being here. With him. Smelling his rainy scent and finding ways to touch his hot skin.

I turn around to face him.

He's watching me, studying me, taking me in. "Are you still experiencing nausea?"

I wasn't expecting him to ask that. I didn't even know he knew that. Everyone's been dismissing my ailment as imaginary, so I didn't know if they'd chart it. "No. Not today. Did... did you ask them to give me... saltines?"

"I asked them to give you something to calm your stomach, yes."

There's such a rush of emotions inside me, inside my chest, my belly that I have to take a moment to calm myself.

He saved me from this too, didn't he?

"Is there something I can do for you?" he asks, when I don't say anything for a few moments.

So formal. So authoritative. So fucking sexy.

"Yes."

"And what is that?" He crosses his arms across his chest,

waiting patiently and impatiently at the same time.

"You... I... I haven't seen you in days."

"Excuse me?"

I shake my head. "I-I mean, I wanted to thank you. For, uh, you know, talking to me the other day. Helping me. Thanks for everything."

Oh God, what am I saying?

Although, it's the truth. These past few days have been hard, but his words have kept me going. And saltines.

"I was doing my job," he tells me.

Job.

Yeah.

I know. I know he was doing his job.

But the thing is... I think that I could be his dream come true.

I mean, maybe. If he'll let me.

He's the fixer, isn't he? He likes to fix things. Broken houses. Broken minds. And I'm broken. In the best of ways and the worst of ways.

So this doesn't have to be his job. I don't have to be his job. I could be more to him. Like he's more to me.

"I want you to fix it," I say.

"Fix what?"

"M-my book."

What?

I didn't mean to say that. I meant to say *me. Fix me.* Or rather he can fix me, if he wants to. I can be his willing patient, his playground, his experiment. He can analyze me, feed me meds, dope me up with drugs, whatever. I can be whatever he wants me to be.

"What?" he repeats my thought out loud.

I look down at the book in my hands, which has been broken in two. "Yeah. I mean, I dropped it again and well, it kind of tore in two. Right in the middle. S-so I want you to fix it."

"Right now?"

Damn it.

This is going completely wrong. But I don't know how to backtrack from here. Like, how do I tell him that I want him. That I'm here for him.

How does one *do* that?

"I…" I lick my lips, feeling the first stirrings of unrest. "You know what, yes. It's, uh, it's important."

A frown forms between his brows as he scans my face. I bet he's trying to figure out what I really want. And he'll do it too because apparently I can't hide anything from him.

"From what I understand," he begins, his arms still crossed. "You came to me because your book tore in half and you want me to fix it. Right now."

It sounds insane; I know it. I know he thinks it too. It's in the way he's looking at me. His expression as always is almost blank, but his eyes are so focused, so intense and so *on* me, that a shiver rolls down my spine. My very sweaty spine.

Actually, I'm sweating all over. Drops of sweat move down my body like rain, and I'm both heated and chilled.

"Yes. Because that's what you said to me. In the hallway? When we first met? You said to me that I should fix my book. So here I am. I want you to fix my book. I'm only listening to you."

"As far as I remember, you weren't very receptive to it when I said that."

My first urge is to lie but I don't want to lie. Not to him. Not after everything. "How do you know that?"

He uncrosses his arms and thrusts his hands in his pockets. "You purse the left side of your mouth when you don't like something."

"I-I do?"

He doesn't say anything. Neither does he acknowledge my statement. He simply clenches his jaw slightly.

"I didn't know that. I didn't know that… you noticed. I –"

"I noticed because it's my job," he says again, like he's informing me.

Is it me or did he really emphasize the word *job*?

"Or you noticed because…" I take in a deep breath and jump. "You noticed me."

This time his clench is longer, harder. The slant of his jaw comes alive with it. "Willow, there's a thing called patience. And I'm running out of it. Very quickly. I'm giving you one last chance to tell me exactly what you're doing here, all right? Here goes." His calm voice belies the force of his words. "What the *fuck* are you doing here?"

"Don't go."

There. I said it. The truth.

My heart's pounding. In fact, my entire body is a heart. Every part of me is pulsing and pumping blood. My throat, my stomach, even my toes.

"What?"

I'm probably tattooing my heartbeats onto the spine of my broken book with the way I have it plastered to my chest. "With her."

"With whom?"

"Josie."

I've genuinely baffled him. I've never seen that expression on his face. Well, I've hardly ever seen an expression on him other than either blankness, irritation, or a sort of ingrained arrogance. His brows are creased with confusion and his eyes tell me he has no clue what I'm saying to him.

Does it mean he's not going? Or maybe he's going and it's no big deal.

Oh, fucking hell.

Did I jump the gun?

"I, um," I begin awkwardly. "Are you going out? With Josie?"

"Out, as in?"

I'm melting under his steady gaze. He's destroying me, cell by cell, with the intense way he's looking at me.

Oh God, can I just run away now? Will he notice if I leave in the middle of this very awkward conversation?

He might. Not to mention, he's blocking the fucking door.

"Out, as in…" I trail off.

Actually, fuck it.

Fuck all of it.

I'm not running away. I'm tired of running, feeling like I have to hide. I have to lie. I have to keep the peace because the alternative is unthinkable. It's not.

The truth is that I have feelings for this man in front of me. He's my doctor, my psychiatrist. A lot older than me. But I don't care.

I'm taking a chance.

"Out as in, on a date. Are you going on a date with Josie?"

"Who told you?"

"I overheard a couple of nurses talking."

His expression is unreadable. He's gone from being confused to totally closed off, completely shut, and it hits me like a sharp dart.

"And what if I'm going?"

That dart was poisonous. I can feel it. It's spreading everywhere. My legs, my arms, my chest, my stomach. It burns. Like my veins are on fire.

"I don't want you to go."

"Why?"

Okay, here goes. I can do this.

I can fucking do this.

I blow out a breath, and say, "Because I want you to go with me."

The only reason I'm standing on my own two feet is because he hasn't looked away from me. There's power in his eyes. Maybe even in that beautiful, cold face of his.

"With you." He makes it sound like a flat statement, and it's not helping my confidence. Like, at all. But I've said it now and well, I can't take it back.

I don't want to.

"Yes. When I get out of here. In a little over two weeks."

"Why? Why should I go with you?"

Taking another deep breath, I whisper, "Because I want you to. Because I want *you*. And because I think if you tried, you might want me, too…"

I trail off when I see a muscle jump on his cheek and he breathes deep. His shirt-encased chest rises and falls with it. I don't know what to make of it.

Actually, I do know what to make of it. He's angry.

This was a bad idea. A super fucking bad idea.

What was I thinking? He's never given me any indication that he likes me. At all. He's always been so professional and cool and *what the fuck was I thinking?*

I haven't done anything like this before. I've never had the urge to. Not until him. Not until I heard he was going out with someone else.

Maybe I should backtrack, after all. Maybe I should –

"What about Lee?"

At his words, my thoughts come to a screeching halt. I feel a jolt. In my chest. Like something really heavy fell on me.

"What about the boyfriend you love? What was it he called you again? Right. Snow princess. He calls you that, doesn't he? He called you that when he pulled you into a dark alley, pushed you into a wall and pressed up against you. What about him? I thought you were heartbroken. You were so heartbroken that you jumped from a roof. So, have you moved on, then?"

My vision's filled with him, the line of his broad shoulders, the strands of his rich hair grazing the starched collar of his shirt.

Somewhere in the past few seconds, Simon walked closer to me. So close that I have to crane my neck up to look at his face.

I've never seen him like this before. So angry. More than angry. More than furious even. He's leaning over me, like a thundering cloud, all dark and dangerous.

"What about that love? What happened to that?"

"H-he cheated on me."

"Right. He kissed someone. What was her name again?"

I shake my head but I can't stop my lies from spewing out. "Zoe."

"Yes. Zoe. Tell me Willow, is Zoe real or did you make her up too?"

A few moments ago, I couldn't breathe because there was something heavy sitting on my chest. But now, I can't control the breaths I'm taking. They are wild. Fearful. They are crazy.

Oh God.

"Huh, Willow? Is Zoe real or did you make her up like you did Lee?"

His face is flashing with fury. Heated, scorching. My eyes water. My skin stings. "I-I don't know what you're talking about."

Simon stays silent, but I feel something. I look down and watch him sliding my book out of my grasp. I want to tell him to stop but I can't form the words. His knuckles are leached of any color. They look white, almost like the color of the walls surrounding us, this place. This godawful place.

"Interesting shirt," he murmurs dangerously.

I can't remember what I'm wearing. Something with a Harry Potter quote, I think. His eyes go through the fabric of my shirt.

His intensity is so potent and all I want to do is hide myself.

Always hide myself.

How could I have forgotten that along with being a fighter, I'm a liar, too? I have lied to him so many times. I've made up stories, told him things that weren't true.

I can't believe it was only last week when I spun the story of my boyfriend calling me a snow princess.

How could I have forgotten that?

"A tip for you: if you want to make things up, don't take inspiration from something you're basically an infomercial for. It's easy for people to figure it out."

With the book in his hand, he straightens up and throws it at his desk, making me wince.

"You know my secret," I whisper, tired of this charade.

"That's the problem, isn't it? That it's a secret." A vein is popping on his temple. "That you suffer in silence. That no one knows you're imploding. Not one person knows what you're going through. Not your mom, not your family. Why's that?"

"I don't —"

"Why's that, Willow? Why's it so hard to tell the people you love that you're suffering? That you need help. Do you know how many people just don't say anything? Do you have any idea how many people keep quiet, never ask for help? Do you know what happens to them?"

He grabs my elbow, bringing me flush to his body, making me gasp with how hard he is. How forceful. How the lines around his mouth and eyes are stretched taut.

"They die," he spits out. "They fucking die. Because they

think no one cares about them. Because they think they don't matter. That somehow, it's their fault that they are suffering from a disease, so they should just get it over with. But it doesn't get over with, does it? Because when they die, they don't die alone. They kill people by leaving them behind."

"I'm –"

"You don't want to leave anyone behind, do you, Willow? But you're ready to die, aren't you? You're so fucking ready for your secrets to kill you one day. Isn't that right?"

I shake my head, feeling the pinch of his fingers on my arm. "N-no... I..."

"You think it's your fault. You think your mom should've had another daughter. Why? Because you're ashamed of your illness. You're ashamed of who you are." His chuckle is so harsh, it reverberates inside my own body, inside my own soul.

"You're ashamed that every day you have to fight to stay alive. You're ashamed that you have to fight at all. So you lie. You lie every chance you get. To your family, to your doctors. To yourself. You lie because you're a goddamn fighter. And instead of being proud of yourself, you're fucking ashamed."

Simon's hazy. I guess it's the water leaking from my eyes. It's like I'm watching him through the rainy window of my room. The window where I write his name at night and watch the letters flow like rivers.

My throat is choked up, and I don't think I can breathe for a long time. I don't think I can even stand, my legs are shaking so badly. My entire body is shaking so badly.

He lets me go and steps away from me like he can't stand to

be close to me. Like, he can't stand to touch me.

"No, Willow. I won't go out with you. I will not go out with my patient. And that's what you are. My patient."

As I stand there, I feel like he sucked all the energy off my body and I have none left. Not even a drop.

But somehow, someway, I find the will to blink my eyes and clear my vision. He's there, tall, dark and classically handsome, with eyes the color of my favorite clouds.

Formidable and unapproachable.

And thundering.

***

I don't remember walking out of his room or walking down the hallway. I don't remember splashing cold water on my face and leaning over the sink. But I'm here. In the bathroom and now, I'm staring at my pale, wet face in the mirror.

Oddly, I'm very numb. I'm thinking about the routine ahead of me. I'm thinking I could either go to the library and help Penny with flash cards, or I could watch TV with the others. There's also an option to go to the rec room. Maybe I should ask for more ginger tea because suddenly, I feel nauseated.

A knock comes at the bathroom door. It's a tiny space with black and white retro checkered tiles, and barely any room to stand in.

"Willow, you okay?"

Hunter. I know his sleepy, thick voice.

It must have been close to twenty minutes since I shut myself in here. They probably need to chart my location.

I close the tap and wipe my face and open the door.

"You okay?"

"Yeah."

He studies me carefully. People are always doing that, aren't they? They are always studying me, trying to decide if I'm telling the truth or what?

"You sure? 'Cause it looks like you've been crying."

Hunter manages to sound both angry and concerned, and I chuckle, surprising myself. I didn't think I had it in me. Not right now.

"I have been, yes."

His frown gets bigger. "Did something happen? You want me to tell the docs?"

"No."

My non-answer answers are messing with his patience; I can see that. "Willow, I'm gonna have to ask you –"

"If I want to harm myself? If it's a bad day?"

I don't know why I said that but I did, and it seemed to have surprised him and apparently, me too.

"Well, is it?"

"Yeah. It's a bad day and I do want to harm myself a little," I admit truthfully. "But I'm not gonna do anything about it. Not today."

Days spent on the Inside = 28

Days *left* to spend on the Inside = 14

Days since The Confession Day = 2

Chapter 12

He never touched me.

He could have. But he never did.

The day I hugged him, he didn't hug me back. He didn't even move a muscle except to wipe my lone tear off. Even then, he only used his thumb.

When he grabbed my elbow in his office, calling me a liar, it was only to drive his point home. It was in anger, not in desire.

Simon Blackwood never touched me more than necessary. More than what was required.

Touch.

All the other senses can satisfy only so much. You want to touch. With your hands, your mouth, your tongue. It's like an itch, very similar to my symptoms. You constantly think about him. You constantly think about touching him, his skin, his hands, his hair, the stubble on his jaw, his strong chest, the grooves of his stomach, his tree-trunk thighs.

You touch *yourself* in frustration, in desperation, in lust because you can't touch him.

Touch is everything. Touch is the litmus test of attraction.

Simon never touched me. Not that there was any other indication that he liked me back but I just like to torture myself with re-thinking, re-analyzing. Re-everything.

"Willow?"

Someone calls my name and I look up. I've been toying with my nails. I trimmed them this morning under the watchful eyes of a nurse. Sharp objects. You can't have them. Not on the Inside.

I'm in the reflections group right now. It happens at the end of the day where we discuss if we stuck to our goals – the ones we set for ourselves at the beginning of each day. It's basically to keep track of the things we're doing every day to be able to lead a functioning and stable life when we leave here to go Outside.

"Would you like to contribute? What was the goal that you'd set for today?" Ellen, the therapist who conducts these meetings, asks.

We're in a big circle, about twenty of us, and Ellen is the focal point. I want to go with something simple, straightforward like, I tried a new yoga pose today – only because Renn's been on my back to do some exercise – or I read a few chapters of this self-help book. I lost my Harry Potter on The Confession Day and I have no plans to go retrieve it. Or I can say something about my art therapy project that I tried to finish.

Clearing my throat, I sit up. "I, uh, my goal was to…" I clear my throat again. "To live. When I woke up this morning, I decided to live. And not give in."

I'm looking at Ellen but I'm not really looking at her. My eyes are unfocused. I always thought that if I said these words out loud, something would happen. Something drastic. Horrible. Something life-altering. I thought people would look at me like I'm a ticking timebomb. Like I'm thinking of killing myself right this second. Like I'm not fighting with every breath that passes my lips.

But nothing happens at all.

Nothing outward, at least. Whatever's happening is happening inside of me.

"That's basically my goal every day," I continue. "I mean, mostly. Sometimes I'm okay. I think of coffee or my classes, you know, when I was Outside. Or the new Harry Potter t-shirt I wanna buy. There's this online store that I absolutely love. They have great stuff."

I lick my lips and collect my wayward thoughts. "But some days it's hard to think about anything else other than… dying. Disappearing. Dissolving. For as long as I can remember, I was always that weird kid who people talked about. Nobody wanted to be friends with me. It hurt, and I retaliated in my own ways, but it was okay. My family's great. They all love me. Very much. Especially my mom. She brought me up by herself. And because I'm the baby of my family, they worry a lot. Maybe too much. And I always wanted to not make them worry."

The Funeral Incident was the first time I ever *really* realized that something was wrong with me. Something terribly, horribly wrong. Before that death was an abstract concept, but after the funeral, death became so real. Like, a dream. A vision.

In my visions, I'm always wearing a long white, sleeveless dress that gets stuck to my body during my fall, outlining my breasts, my stomach, and my thighs. I see my mouth falling open but not to scream but to absorb the air, the sky. My arms are always wide open too like wings, but they are not there to keep me flying, they are embracing the glory of the fall.

Wiping my nose with the back of my hand, I keep going, still unseeing, focused on something inside me. "I was diagnosed with clinical depression at the age of fourteen. My mom was so shocked. Heartbroken. I was too. I mean, it's not pretty listening to the doctor analyzing you and giving you meds and whatnot. But it was okay because I knew. I knew the reason behind my weirdness. I remember my mom taking some time off from the store to be with me. I guess, she thought I needed the support. I have a feeling she needed it more than me.

"I always thought it wasn't her fault that I was this way. Nobody wants their baby to be born this way, you know. Everybody prays for a healthy baby. A happy baby. It's not her fault that I'm ill. That I've never been happy. I mean, I've been happy, of course. But it just never lasts. So yeah, I always thought it's not her fault that I'm fighting this battle. She's given me everything. All the love, all the comforts. It's me. Things are wrong with me. She shouldn't get the brunt of it. So I hid. I always pretended to be okay. I never talked about all the stuff inside me. I never thought it could help. I mean, they can't magically cure depression, right? I always thought my mom was already going through the effects of my diagnosis. I didn't want to add to that."

There's silence. No one's saying anything. I feel like I'm

talking extremely loud, but I can't stop. I have to get all of it out now.

"I've been lying for a long time. Sometimes I think that's all I know. Lying, hiding, pretending. Six weeks ago, I attempted to kill myself. I jumped off the roof of our summer house in the Hamptons. It was my birthday. Birthdays have always been hard for me. It makes me the focus of attention. It requires a lot of pretending. There's, uh, a lot of laughter and noise and just happiness. I've always had trouble with them. Anyway, on this birthday I don't know what happened. It became too much. I couldn't stop myself. I'd been feeling low, very low for weeks. Maybe the whole pretending became too much? Maybe it was the big birthday, the milestone, eighteen? I don't know what it was but I just couldn't do it anymore. In fact, the party was supposed to be a double celebration. I'd gotten an acceptance letter from Columbia. They gave me a scholarship too. Everything was perfect. Except me. My mind."

I see the roof in my head. The edge. The perfect summer night with all the stars. I resembled the pale moon. Even so, its meager light irritated me. The breeze scraped against my body. God, I wanted relief. My head was exploding. My world was ending. Or at least it felt that way.

I wore a dress that day, a summer red dress. My cousin had insisted. She told me to stop dressing like a kid. I was eighteen. I was officially an adult. A woman. She even put red lipstick on me.

"But I didn't die, obviously." A few people chuckle, and I finally smile. "When I woke up in the hospital, I was terrified. I thought my secret was going to be out. My mom... I've never seen her that way. She was devastated. She didn't even look like my mom. She looked dead. Like, I'd killed her. She didn't know what she'd done wrong. It petrified me. It fucking scared me that I'd hurt her. That my defective brain fucked everything up. I did what I always do: I lied."

I sigh and bite my lip. "I made up a story. I told her that I had a boyfriend and that I was keeping it a secret and well, he cheated on me. I told them I was heartbroken and a little tipsy and jumping seemed like a good idea at the time. I thought if I lied, my mom wouldn't blame herself, for not doing enough, for missing the signs, whatever. And I think I also lied because... because I wasn't ready to accept that there was something wrong with me. That I needed help. Serious help. I always thought that if I took the meds, went to see my psychiatrist for regular check-ups, pretended everything was okay, everything would be okay. The power of the mind or something, I don't know. But my mind is a little broken so there you go. I just wasn't counting on her sending me to therapy. So my plan kinda backfired." I chuckle, and people follow suit.

For this part, I fist my hands in my lap. "Lee Jordan. My imaginary boyfriend. He is not real, of course. I don't know any Lee Jordan. I made him up based on one of my favorite books, Harry Potter. The girl he cheated on me with, Zoe? She's real, though. She was one of the girls who always hated me. It was fun to make her into a villain."

Finally, I come to.

I look at Ellen. She's got a smile on her face. A sympathetic smile. A sad smile. I know about sad smiles. They taste like tears. Salty and a little sour. I'm tasting that smile right now.

"What made you tell us today, Willow?" she asks.

"Because the thing is that it's not my fault either. That I was born this way. It's not my fault that sometimes things get just a little bit harder. It's not my fault that every day I fight a silent battle. I implode. I don't make a sound. I don't say a word. I don't let anyone know what I'm going through. It's like I'm blaming myself. And I don't want to do that anymore. I told you because it's not my fault. It's not my fault that some days my goal is just to make it through the day. While others make plans to ace an interview or a test or go see a movie or for a walk, I make plans to just get through the day. It's not my fault. It's my achievement. It's my strength that I fight. Someone told me that I'm a warrior, and that I'm ashamed of it. So this is me..." I nod, unfisting my hands. "Not being ashamed. This is me asking for help."

I don't know what I'm expecting after everything I said but getting wrapped up in a giant hug wasn't what I was thinking of.

A startled yelp escapes me as Renn basically crashes her entire body into mine. Rules be damned. I hug her back. As hard as I can. I hug her as hard as I've always imagined being hugged. Maybe ever since I was born with more than blood in my veins.

Renn's voice sounds teary and broken when she whispers, "I fucking love you, you know that? I always knew we'd end up being BFFs."

Chuckling and crying, I tell her, "Thanks for talking to me that day when I first came here."

"Eh, I couldn't be so cruel as to not give you the pleasure of knowing me."

I laugh. "I fucking love you too."

Ellen says that it's enough, and we should break up. But

we don't listen. People are getting up from their chairs, filling the room with scratching noises and murmurs. And suddenly, I'm being hugged by Penny, and then Vi, followed by Roger, even Annie and Lisa, and a bunch of other people I've never talked to.

I'm laughing like I've never laughed in my life.

Amidst all the smiling and high-fiving and Ellen and a couple of techs trying to get everyone settled, my gaze catches someone.

He's standing by the door, among a few nurses and Josie, with his eyes on me. I don't know how long he's been standing here. If he listened to any of what I said.

This is the first time I've seen him since The Confession Day, two days ago. I want to look away, embarrassed. Again, what was I thinking? I don't know what came over me. But there was this urgency that I couldn't ignore.

I wanted him to know. I wanted him to know what I feel for him. I wanted him to know the truth. Maybe because my feelings for him – crush, fascination, whatever – isn't like my illness. It's one pure thing, and I didn't want to hide it. I'm not ashamed of it.

And I shouldn't be ashamed of my illness either; he was right. This was my first step toward it: admittance.

I don't know why he isn't looking away. Or why he's still standing there, staring at me when there's so many other things to look at.

But he was right about this other thing too.

He's my psychiatrist and I'm his patient.

Just the thought of having anything between us other than

medicine is foolish. Besides, I don't even like doctors, right? I hated them. I mean, I still hate them.

Too bad he doesn't feel like a doctor and too bad my heart-sick soul doesn't know the meaning of foolish.

So I don't look away until he does.

Chapter 13

I'm summoned by the ice king. Again.

My appointment with him isn't until tomorrow so this must mean that it has something to do with The Confession.

Great.

It'll haunt me forever, won't it? Like The Roof Incident.

Maybe when I get out of here, I can laugh about it like I laughed about my illness yesterday. A woman in her mid-thirties, Karen, came up to me and told me about her own struggles with depression, and how it took her years to get help. I'd seen her around on my floor but we'd never chatted. I'm glad I did.

I also talked with the brunette who was admitted at the same time as me. Her name is Tina and she's bulimic. We swapped stories about our first week and how she couldn't sleep with all the noises and the smell. And how lime jello makes her break out in sweat.

We cried about things and then, we laughed.

Yeah, there was a lot of laughing. But somehow, I doubt that I'd laugh about The Confession.

My illness might come with a prescription, but there's no pill for heartsickness.

On top of that the problem is that I don't have a lot of experience with crushes. I mean, I've had them. Obviously. But I've always admired those guys from afar. I've never approached them. They would've died, or at least passed out. Being approached by Weird Willow, who hung out in the back with her book and her Harry Potter t-shirts.

In my entire eighteen years, I've had only one boyfriend and that was because he wanted to get close to me and ask about all my symptoms; he wanted to be a doctor. When I found out about it, I dumped him. Thank God, I never told my mom about him. She would've murdered him for breaking my heart.

Anyway, I have zero experience with crushes, confessions, and rejections. All I know is that I'm supposed to act cool and calm. Not sure if I'm the right person for that but we'll see.

I knock on his door, my palms sweaty. "You can do this, Willow. You're a fighter. You can fucking do this –"

The door opens, and my words get lost in my head.

Is it me or has he grown even more handsome overnight?

His hair's a little longer than before and the strands curl at the ends. Maybe it grew out in the two weeks he's been here. Seems like a lifetime since I first came into this room, thinking he was the enemy.

My world turned upside down in the last two weeks and his has remained the same.

Life's a fucking biatch, isn't it?

He's staring at me with the same intense eyes as he was yesterday afternoon. As if he never stopped looking at me at all. As if the few hours in between don't matter and he's picking up where he left off.

It's making me nervous.

"Can I come in?"

"Were you talking to someone?" he asks, his hands inside his pockets, only his wristwatch peeking out.

"Yes."

"With whom?"

"Myself."

He throws me a lopsided smile and steps aside so I can enter. Though he hasn't given me a lot of space to work with like he usually does. Meaning my arm grazes the ridge of his stomach when I pass him by and every nerve ending in my body stands taut.

How is it that I can feel this explosion of sensation all over my body and he doesn't have a single hint of it?

It's so unfair.

"How are you?" he asks from behind me and I turn around to face him.

He's standing by the door, leaning against it, actually, like he has no plans to sit down. The toes inside my bunny slippers curl, for some reason.

"I'm okay."

"How do you feel? After the group yesterday?"

I nod. "I feel good."

"It was…" He seems to be choosing his words carefully,

slowly, while being completely focused on me. "Commendable and brave. What you did yesterday. Very few people can admit their flaws even to themselves, let alone to a room full of people."

Mesmerized.

He kind of looks mesmerized by me. Which is so, *so* ridiculous that I feel like maybe I'm seeing things.

"Uh, well, thanks," I say, unsurely.

He goes silent for a few seconds and I'm waiting for the bomb to drop. He's going to say something about The Confession Day; I know it. I can feel it. It's coming. I tighten my body and make fists out of my hands.

You can do this, Willow. Just don't blush too much.

"I was harsh with you," he says finally, and I see a flicker of regret flash through his eyes.

Okay, I was totally not expecting that. I thought he was going to talk about my conduct as a patient or something.

My mouth parts as I take in a breath. A shaky breath. The truth is that yes, he was harsh, and as usual, I've thought about that.

The thing is that Dr. Simon Blackwood isn't harsh. Not usually. He's blunt and truthful, but he isn't an asshole.

Assholes are immature. Boys trapped inside a man's body who don't know what to do with it. So they make everyone around them miserable, instead of just sucking it up and dealing with their problems.

This man in front of me, in his crisp shirt and wingtips, is anything but immature. He's a *man*. Through and through. Mature, masculine, commanding.

Sexy.

But I'm not thinking about that right now.

"You were." I nod. "Why?"

Exactly. Why?

Why the fuck was he so ticked off when I asked him out? I mean, it could be that he really hates me and was totally disgusted by the idea of going on a date with me. But this isn't high school, and I've already established that he isn't immature.

So there has to be something else. His anger has to have come from somewhere else.

At last, he leans away from the door and stands up straight.

"Because there are moral and ethical concerns involved. I'm your doctor. You're my responsibility. You're under my care. There are lines that can't be crossed. Your health depends on it," he says in a low, severe tone.

Almost passionate.

He's so passionate about taking care of me. About my mental health. Well, about his job.

But as twisted as I am, it almost makes me feel special. His passion inflames *my* passion, a quickening in my belly.

Taking a deep breath, I try to get my misplaced reactions under control. This is not the time. *So* not the time. My lust can roam free when I'm alone in my room at night. Not here.

Besides, I need to know something. Something about what he said on The Confession Day.

When they die, they don't die alone. They kill people by leaving them behind.

"Do you know a lot of people like that? Who give up?

Who… die?"

His expression remains the same, severe. So I don't know if he heard me. But this is the only conclusion I came up with – that he might have some experience with people like me. Obviously. He's a psychiatrist. But I think this is personal.

Something that makes him go dark and devastated at the same time.

Then he jerks out a nod. "Yes."

It's said in a small voice. Not in intensity but in volume. As though he didn't want me to hear it. As though it came from somewhere deep inside of him.

My heart clenches; I was right.

He does have personal experience with it. He does know someone who's given up. I wish I could ask him. I know he won't tell me, even if I did.

It's not my business, anyway. It shouldn't be. My chest shouldn't ache for him. I shouldn't want to wrap my arms around him and give him a hug. Because he looks like he could use one. He's just too hard and closed up.

It's not going to be me, though. That much I know.

But I can always use my words. "I… Whoever they are, I maybe understand what they were going through. And I just wish they hadn't given up." I stare into his eyes, so he knows I'm giving this to him. My words are for him, even though I don't know why he needs them, what his involvement is.

"I wish they hadn't left their life and the people in it be-hind. Maybe they would've found a reason to live. A reason to be happy."

I sigh and lower my eyes, looking down at my slippers. Blinking, I get rid of the moisture. I can cry once I'm out of this room. I can cry when the man I'm crying for doesn't know I'm shedding my tears for him.

Is it creepy to cry for the crush who doesn't want you back? Maybe. But then, I've always been a little weird. So there.

Wiping my hands on my yoga pants, I look up and my breath evaporates. Because he's staring at me like he's never stared at me before. And that's not even the part I'm focusing on.

It's the fact that he looks so... open and angry and tortured, even.

His cheekbones have sharpened and there's a flush covering them. A dark hue that wasn't there before. He seems to have sprawled, even though he hasn't moved an inch. His shoulders cover the entire breadth of the door.

God, he's so big.

No, actually. Big is the wrong word. He's large. In body, in presence.

I don't know what makes me move, what makes me approach him, but I do. I keep putting one foot in front of the other, until I'm standing close to him, tilting my neck up like I'm looking at the cloudy sky.

"I... Can I go now?" I whisper.

He bends toward me. Not like he did yesterday when he was all shaken up and furious. This leaning is slow and filled with a different kind of intensity.

"No."

I swallow, looking into his eyes, which have moved down

to my lips. Has he ever looked at my mouth before? I can't remember. He's always been so professional and distant that just one look of his seems exaggerated, almost too much to handle.

"W-why not?"

"Because I'm curious about something."

I lick my lower lip. I swear it's not meant to be provocative. It's just that his stare is making them tingle and dry out. I didn't know that a body part could be shy until this man focused on it like this.

"About what?"

Again, I'm expecting one thing but something entirely different happens. Instead of answering with his words, he touches me. Of his own volition.

His hands wrap around my neck, his fingers spanning the entire length of my throat, tilting my face up. My eyes are wide; I can feel it. I can feel them popping out. I can feel my heart popping out too, bursting with too many beats.

He's touching me.

Touching. The litmus test of attraction.

"I'm curious about," he whispers, his breath wafting over my nose, drugging my senses. "Why the fuck do I want to kiss you?"

"What?"

My hands reach up and hold his wrists. I feel like my world just went unsteady and I can't stand up straight without his help.

Did he just… Did he say he wants to kiss me?

There's a slight frown on his forehead, as if he's genuinely perplexed. As if I'm a riddle and so is his desire to kiss me.

"It doesn't make sense." His gray, almost black, gaze flicks back and forth. "You're my patient. You're my responsibility. I'm supposed to fix you, not think about your lips. I'm not supposed to think about your mouth or the taste of your tongue. If you really taste like you smell."

"How... How do I smell?"

His chuckle is short and harsh as he moves his hand and grabs my face. "Like lemons. Like you've been sucking on lemon wedges all day long with that pink mouth of yours."

I feel the heat of his hand on my flesh. He's burning up, slowly boiling over. "I-I... It's the lime jello," I reply, as if that's the most important thing in the world right now. Explaining the source of my smell and possibly my taste too.

His grip on my cheeks increases. "That was for me, wasn't it? That whole lie about getting kissed in a dark alley."

Oh God. Why'd he have to bring that up?

Again, I don't know what I was thinking. I was so overcome by this urge to show off. To tell him without telling him that I've been thinking about him. Dreaming about him. And that I'm not ashamed of any of it.

My cheeks are possibly the same temperature as his fingers now, all heated up with embarrassment and lust. Even though I want to look away, I don't. I stare into his passionate gray-black eyes and nod. "Yes."

He shakes his head once. "Is that how you want to be kissed, Willow? In a dark alley, pressed up against a wall?"

I know I'm panting. Probably even salivating right now. My thighs are trembling. There's a buzzing inside my stomach because yes, I do want to be kissed like that. I do want to be devoured, eaten up, swallowed in.

By him.

"Yes. Like that."

"That's what you want, don't you? For a man to go so fucking crazy for you that he can't afford to be a gentleman. That instead of dropping you off at your front door and walking away with a chaste goodnight kiss, he pushes you against it and fucking kisses the breath out of you."

Yes. So much yes.

He's gotten closer to me with every word out of his beautiful lips and I go on my tiptoes to bring our mouths even closer. "No. Not just any man. You. I want you, Simon."

A shudder ripples through him, like a shock wave. It ripples through me, as well. Why did I wait so long to say his name? It was stupid. I'm not going to be so stupid anymore.

Well, aside from what we're doing right now. It doesn't feel stupid, even though it should, for all intents and purposes. Especially after his whole moral and ethical argument.

"You're not my type," he growls, pushing his forehead against mine.

"I'm sorry?"

"You're young. You're reckless. Inexperienced. You believe in happy endings, don't you? Fairy tales and fucking magic."

His breaths are wild, frustrated. Like believing in good things is a bad habit. Believing in something bigger than you is silly.

I frown, pressing harder against his forehead. "Of course

I do. If someone like me doesn't believe in magic, then there's no hope for anyone else. There's no hope for me. And it's not a bad thing, you know. It's not a bad thing to believe in something. In fact, it shows that you're brave and –"

His mouth pulls into a humorless smile. "And you don't know when to shut the fuck up."

"Hey –"

"Willow."

He flattens my cheeks with his hands, asserting all his stupid authority over me. Too bad it only makes me hornier and I have to clench my thighs against the shivers running through my lower body.

"What?" I somehow manage to squeak.

"Shut the fuck up."

I gasp; how dare he?

But it gets swallowed up by his mouth.

I freeze. It's happening.

He's kissing me.

Simon Blackwood, the ice king, my psychiatrist, is kissing me. His lips are on mine and they are moving. Slowly, thoroughly. They are so warm and alive and wet.

So wet. Maybe as wet as I am, down there. In my pussy.

Clutching his wrists harder, I lean against him, both restless and in relief. I've been dying all this time. To feel him like this. For him to cross the line that I've already crossed ages ago.

Moaning, I press harder against him, plastering my body over his, almost draping it, and he groans into my mouth.

"You do taste like lemons," he rasps, licking the seam of my lower lip.

My hands sink into his hair, then. All soft and velvety and dark. They make me smile. "It's the lime jello," I repeat, looking into his hooded eyes.

"Fucking hate lime jello."

"Me too." I lick my lips and his nostrils flare. "B-but you should try the ones here. They taste good. Like, so good."

His fingers move from my face to my hair, undoing my loose topknot. "Yeah." Burying his hands in the strands, he whispers not to me, but to my lips, "And that's the problem, isn't it?"

I don't get what he means, but I don't have the time to think over it before he covers my mouth again. This time his rhythm is not as slow. It's thorough though. So thorough that I feel his lips all over my body. I feel them on my throat, the back of my neck, my stomach, my thighs.

I have a feeling the earlier soft and slow kiss was only the beginning. He was sampling my lips, getting a taste of them. Warming them up. So he can do more. So much more.

And he does.

He thrusts his tongue inside my mouth, taking me by surprise, and I fist his hair, going up on my tiptoes. My lips open wide as I take him in, as I take a part of his body inside mine, and something clicks into place.

I feel like I needed that, his tongue inside my mouth, tasting, sweeping, licking. Hungry. I needed to be his food, his sustenance, like he's become mine.

Latching on to his tongue, I suck on it like my life depends on getting his flavor, filling my belly with it. It makes him go wild.

It makes him growl inside my mouth like he's more than a man. He's an animal. A carnivore.

Simon maneuvers my face so he can go deeper, and so I open my mouth wider. Like a receptacle of some sort. For him. For his rainy, fresh taste. For his tongue.

Even his teeth.

They nip at the seam of my lips, sending sparks down to my pussy that's just getting sloppier and sloppier with every second.

Drenched. That's what my core is. Like the grounds outside. It's a stormy day and the rain is coming down hard, like Simon's mouth on mine.

Grunting, he's slamming it over and over, his fingers fisted in my hair. He's feeding on my mouth like I'm feeding on him. I'm sucking and swallowing, eating him up.

But his sucks and pulls and tugs have a purpose. They are selfless, unlike my selfish ones. They are curing me.

Yes, my medicine man is curing me, purifying my blood, vacuuming the illness out of me.

With his mouth, his kisses, he's drinking down all my poison. That thing inside me that gives me blue eyes. He's making me cleaner, healthier. He's purging me.

He's making me happy.

The thing that's as elusive to me as love.

I feel myself getting lighter, more pliable, until all I can feel is him and his ridged, sculpted body. I arch my spine. I push my breasts – restless and heavy with engorged nipples – into his chest and clutch his shoulders.

"Simon…" I whimper when he lets me come up for air.

"Don't talk," he orders and resumes kissing me.

Jesus.

His authority will kill me. I'm so fucking wet right now. I moan with how swollen I am. I'm almost tempted to let go of him and rub my pussy. Shamelessly masturbate as he cures me.

Or better yet, have him do it. I want to shove his hand between my legs and ask him to touch me there.

I can almost see it.

I can almost feel his big hand between my legs, his fingers pinching my clit, grabbing my cunt. I can almost see myself riding his fingers, humping it like I do my pillow. I'll drench his wrist; I know that. I'll cream his palm like I'm creaming my panties and he'll watch me do it.

But how can I be selfish and ask him to rub my pussy when he's making me feel so good? I need to make him feel good, too. I need to give him something. And then, I know how. I feel him. On my stomach.

His cock. His thick, hard arousal pressing into my flesh.

And he is *hard*. And hot. And so big. Like a pipe or something. It makes me feel so small, smaller and more feminine than I've ever felt.

So I undulate against him.

I rub my stomach up and down his hard length as I clench my thighs for about the thousandth time since he started kissing me. It causes his dick to throb. It pulses. Like it's alive too, just like my pussy.

I haven't seen a dick before, not in real life. I've touched one, sure. But that was when I was a sophomore and my boyfriend was just a boy.

Simon is a man and his cock has to be the most masculine thing I've ever experienced. And I have only touched it through the layers of clothing and on my stomach. I still move up and down, almost touching him with the valley of my breasts.

Simon growls in my mouth.

It's like I'm jacking him off with my body. With my soft stomach and heavy breasts. I've always hated them, but if my pudgy body can bring him pleasure, I'm all for it.

I wonder if I can make him come like this.

I want to make him come. Orgasms always make me happy. They must make him happy too.

So yeah, I want him to come and be happy. Like I am.

Be happy for me, Simon.

But then he rips his mouth away and my eyes snap open. Don't know when I closed them.

A whine forms at the base of my throat and I want to ask him what happened. Didn't he like it? I was trying to make him feel good.

I open my mouth to ask him when I hear voices. Footsteps and giggles. Someone's saying they are going to see if Dr. Blackwood is in or not.

My eyes widen as I stare up at him. He's rigid. Flushed. His hair's a mess. His shirt is in disarray and his lips are red and swollen. Glistening with my kisses.

It's like he's marked and I realize with the throbbing of my lips that I'm marked as well. We both marked each other with our lust and now people are going to find out.

"Simon…"

I trail off when he grabs my hand and pushes me to the side. My back goes against the wall, by the door and I stare at him fearfully just when the knock comes.

With a clenched jaw, he says to whoever is knocking, "Just a sec."

His voice sounded calm but his chest is still breathing with franticness. His eyes are still wild and on me.

"I'm –"

I don't know what I was going to say but Simon doesn't wait to hear it. He lets go of my arm and spins on his heel. I see his massive back going up and down with huge breaths, his fingers running through his hair, before straightening his shirt.

At last, he steps toward the door, opening it with a click.

"Oops, sorry. Did I interrupt something?" a nurse asks.

"No. I was just on the phone," he says.

I can't see him. He's blocked by the door, but he sounds as he always does. Patient and calm. Me, on the other hand? I'm freaking out.

My heart won't stop jackhammering, and some of their words get jumbled when they reach me. All I can gather is that she wants him to sign off on something, but he in turn suggests that he'll take a look at the inventory first. Whatever that means.

And then they're gone. Simon walks out, closing the door behind him, taking the nurse with him.

I breathe out a sigh of relief. Although I'm so high on adrenaline and on the kiss and on everything Simon Blackwood that the sigh is more like a panted breath.

I know why he left with the nurse. He was giving me a chance to escape, without being found out.

Biting my lip, I do just that. I walk quietly to the door and open it to peek outside. The hallway is empty and the nurses' station at the end only has a couple of people who aren't looking this way.

Thank God.

Quickly, I step out of the room and walk away from his office.

What were we thinking? It was stupid. So fucking stupid to do that.

God.

But for some reason, I can't stop my beating heart and the smile on my lips.

Chapter 14

"God, I'm not made for this," I almost whimper, my body contorted in ways I didn't think possible.

"Shut up. Everybody's made for yoga," says Renn, bent in the exact same way, facing me. On her though, the pose looks effortless.

"Not me. What is this?" I heave, trying to find my balance before my back gives out on me. "Why am I on my hands and toes? Why am I…" I lose my breath for a second. "Upside down? It's not natural. Oh God, I feel my lime jello in the back of my throat."

"You're such a drama queen. It's called downward dog." Renn rolls her eyes. "It's like, the most basic yoga pose. Kids could do this."

"Do I look like a kid to you?" I swallow but gravity is working against me. "I can't believe I let you pull me into this."

"Exercise is good. It's healthy, okay? We're being healthy. We're being productive with our day."

I clench my eyes shut, the muscles in my calves probably

starting to erupt in flames. "Shut up. You're only doing this because you think you're putting on weight."

It's true. This morning, Renn knocked at my wall to tell me her favorite top is fitting her tight around the tits. She called it the underarm/bust fat.

"My clothes don't fit," she practically shrieks. "It's a disaster, Willow. I get anxious when my clothes don't fit. So shut up. We're doing this."

My throat's drying up and I feel like I'm going to pass out on the ground. The sun's not helping. I fucking hate the sun. *Hate* it. The rays are piercing me like needles, making me prickle and sweat.

"I can't… I can't breathe." I heave again and blow at my bangs.

"You just did, you moron. Just hold the pose for a few seconds. Don't you like the burn in your muscles? Your ankles. Feel the burn in your ankles."

"I don't care about my stupid ankles." I grit my teeth, sweat going into my eyes. "I'm dying. *Dying.*"

Renn blows a puff of air, dismissing my concern. "You wish."

I snort. "God, I hate you right now."

I do. I *so* do.

Why am I not reading like Penny or feeding the birds like Vi? Or why am I not at the library, reading a dozen new Harry Potter books? Yes. They finally listened to me, and now the library has the entire series of Harry Potter. Isn't that wonderful?

But instead of petting those paperbacks and smelling their

pages, I'm here. Why? I have no clue. I don't even know how I got roped into this. Except Renn said something to me at breakfast and I said yes without listening since I was lost in my own head. So here I am. *Standing* on my head.

All because Simon Blackwood kissed me.

And then he ran away.

Well, he gave me time to escape without being seen but still. What does it mean that he kissed me? Does it mean that he likes me now? Has he always liked me? Why did he say no to the date, then?

What happened between us?

Damn it.

All of these questions are making me dizzy and this stupid yoga is not helping. I keep replaying it in my head. He kissed me. We kissed each other. I tasted him. He tasted me. I touched him. He touched me. I felt his arousal. I almost jacked him off with my stomach.

He cured me with his mouth.

I can't stop thinking about particularly that. How his lips made me feel happier than I've ever been in my life. His kiss was a massive dose of lithium, lighting up the dark places in my brain.

That's what I dreamed about when I fell asleep in my bed last night. Him lighting me up, chasing away the darkness by just being him.

My personal hero. Designed just for me.

I woke up this morning, my hands stuck between my legs and my panties shoved to the side, thinking about him.

But then, we almost got caught.

Oh gosh, my heart still jumps thinking about that. That knock is the kind of sound I'll never forget.

I haven't seen him since then, though, and I don't know what it means. Do I hunt him down so we can talk about this? So we can figure this out? Or do I go see him for our appointment this evening?

What am I supposed to do?

My thoughts come to a halt when I see wingtips in my line of vision. Instantly, I spring up from my contorted position, but I forgot about the dizziness and I get a wicked head rush, almost toppling me over.

But a hand on my wrist stops me from falling.

"You okay?" Simon asks, pulling me upright.

I blink, adjusting my eyes to the sun, even though I've been under it for almost an hour now. Blowing on my bangs, I nod. "Yes. Thank you."

He studies me for a few seconds, probably making sure that I'm really okay before letting me go. He doesn't look away from me, however. He watches me like he was doing yesterday in his office, only today, his stare feels like a weight.

A physical thing. It's as if that's all he can do: watch. And nothing else. So, he's pouring all his intensity into it.

"Hi," I say, waving my hand lamely, hoping he'll say something, praying it doesn't look like I'm staring at his lips.

Because I am. In the direct sunlight, his lips are shining. They look even softer. Did I really have them on mine yesterday? Did he really kiss me? I lick my own lips as if his flavor still lingers there.

His gaze shifts to my action and he takes a step back, clip-
ping, "Can we talk for a second?"

I bite my lip then, feeling apprehensive, and his nostrils
flare. Almost angrily, he marches a few steps ahead, without waiting for my answer.

Well, that was rude. I almost don't want to follow him but
who am I kidding?

I'm obviously going to follow him. I'll always follow him.

And I do. We're away from Renn and the crowd, standing
under the tree, but the relief I should feel after getting out from
under the sun isn't there.

I'm uneasy. As in, extremely uneasy.

"I have something for you," he says, all somber.

"For me?"

"Here." He offers me my old Harry Potter book that I'd left
in his office on The Confession Day. "I fixed it for you."

I look at him, his smooth, expressionless face, and then at
the book. I wasn't even thinking about it. I haven't been thinking
about it at all. I should be filled with gratitude that he thought
about me and this book, and I am.

But I'm also a little nervous. A lot nervous, actually.

Taking it from him, I clutch it to my chest, hugging it.
"Thank you. You didn't have to do that."

He tracks my movements, eyeing me as I hug myself with
my arms, and shoves his hands down into his pockets. The hands
that he put on me yesterday, of his own volition.

I can feel them over my pulse on the side of my neck. I can
feel them in my hair too, fisting the strands. My heartbeat jacks up

as my scalp tingles. Why is every part of my body already used to him when he's only touched me once?

It's magic. It's fucking torture.

"It was a mistake."

He doesn't have to define what 'it' is. I know what he's referring to. And I hate that. I hate that I immediately know what he means. I don't even get the delay-time of comprehension. I can't ease into the knowledge. I already *have* it.

"Was it?" I ask, my body feeling all cold and sweaty at the same time.

"Yes." The angles of his face are sharp and defined, unforgiving. "It was a major failure on my part. It never should've happened. I was less than professional. It's a line I never intended to cross."

"But you did."

Remorse flickers through his features, right alongside something else. Something like anger. At himself?

"Yes. And for that I'm deeply sorry."

"You're sorry?"

"I would understand if you wanted to take this to Beth."

"You would?"

I'm aware that I sound like a parrot. A dumb parrot, at that. But I don't know what else to say. What else to think other than this deep sense of betrayal.

"Yes. I made a mistake, and I'm ready to face the consequences, if I have to."

I'm so pissed off.

God.

So fucking pissed off. While I was dreaming about his kiss, he was thinking about how much of a mistake it was. He was thinking how best to approach me and tell me that he's sorry.

"Is this your way of apologizing?" I wave the book, the book he fixed for me.

He nods, appearing grim.

"Did you stay up at night, fixing it?"

"Yes."

I shake my head, lowering the stupid book. I hate this stupid book. I want to take it and tear it apart. Ruin all his hard work.

"Why'd you kiss me?" I ask, gritting my teeth.

Simon doesn't like this question. His gray eyes glint with anger, agitation almost. Tough luck. He's asked me a ton of questions that I haven't liked. But I answered every one of them. I wanna see if he'll tell me the truth or if he'll lie.

Come on, Dr. Blackwood.

"Temporary insanity," he replies. "It was a slip-up. A momentary lapse of judgment."

"Right."

Kissing me was temporary insanity.

Great.

Wonderful.

It flares my anger. It flares it to the point where all I can do is smile tightly and nod. And make claws out of my fingers and dig them into the book. Stupid fucking blunt nails.

Stupid fucking book.

"What would happen if I told Beth? Would you get fired?"

Did you get fired from your last job for something like this, too?

I don't ask that. But it runs through my mind.

And I do have the right to think that because let's face it, I hardly know anything about him. Whatever I know is based on my feelings, not facts. I still feel guilty though. I feel disgusted at even having that doubt about him.

God, I'm a mess. And he's a jerk.

"There'd be an investigation, if you pressed formal charges. The board would have to get involved."

I'm trying to read his face. The sun is so bright that every nuance of it is visible. The curve of his lip, the corner of his eyes, the lines around his mouth. I'm trying to see if any of those would betray the man they belong to.

But no. Nothing. I'm still clueless about what happened to him at his previous job.

I'm still clueless about him.

"Well, then I absolve you. It was temporary insanity, wasn't it? Everybody makes mistakes. It doesn't mean you have to sit through an investigation for just a kiss."

His hooded eyes and his clamped jaw are the last things I see of him as I walk away.

I take it back.

Simon Blackwood *is* a fucking asshole.

***

I used to have a pet goldfish.

Her name was Hedwig, after the pet snow owl of Harry Potter. My mom got it for me for my twelfth birthday, and I loved Hedwig to pieces.

In fact, for the longest time she was my only friend, aside from my mom. One night I couldn't sleep, and so I kept chatting with Hedwig, telling her about all the things I'd like to do but couldn't ever find the energy to. And suddenly, it hit me.

She never talked back. She simply circled the glass tank over and over, blinking her eyes and gaping her mouth. I thought maybe that was her way of communicating and I wasn't capable of understanding it. Just like she wasn't capable of understanding me.

What the hell was I doing with her, then?

Next morning, I decided to set her free so she could find her friends. It wasn't fair that I kept her for myself when she could have a chance to meet people like her. At least one of us should be happy.

I'm missing Hedwig tonight.

I wonder what happened to her. Is she alive? How many years do goldfish live, anyway?

I hope she found her friends. I wanna tell her that I did too. I finally found my friends. My kind of people. I finally found a man, as well. He's kind and sexy and so fucking handsome. He looks like a king and kisses like a beast.

But he thinks our kiss was a mistake.

I'm watching the rain from my bed, my knees drawn up and my back propped against the wall. The book he fixed for me is in my lap and I'm hugging it, like I would hug him. The night shift nurse who does hourly checks just left. She saw me through the square window on the door and found me awake so she stopped by for a little chat. I'm pretty sure she'll put on her report that I wasn't sleeping even though I'm on sleep meds, and a certain someone will hear about it.

Whatever. I don't care.

I'm drawing shapes on the misty window with my finger. I refuse to write his name, even though that's what I want to do. I refuse to be that pathetic. At least, tonight. I figure there's going to be a lot of lonely nights for me in the future. I'm saving pitifulness for later.

I watch the rain pouring down on the screen in rivulets. There's a storm out tonight, thick and loud.

Even though the sounds on the inside are drowned by the sounds on the outside, I still hear the door of my room opening. The air inside the four walls changes and I whip my eyes to see who it is, terrified.

The shape standing at my door is tall and large. It's almost blocking the dim lighting of the hallway, causing my small room to plunge mostly into darkness.

Even so, I can tell who it is. I'm pathetic after all, because I've memorized the outline of his body and his rainy-weather smell.

Simon Blackwood.

What the... Am I dreaming? Did I conjure him up?

I'm huddled by the wall, gripping my knees, trying to breathe, or rather, *not* breathe this fast. If I'm dreaming, then this has to be a nightmare. Why else would he come here, if not to torture me, torment me, and break me down?

Without turning around, he closes the door behind him. The soft click of it is a jarring force I need to realize that this is real life.

He really is here. Inside my room. In the middle of the

night.

"What are you doing here?" I whisper-hiss, throwing the book aside, springing up from the bed.

"You didn't show up for our meeting tonight," he says in a low voice.

A voice that makes me jump.

Even though the rain outside is chaotic, his voice seems louder. His voice seems like a declaration of some sort.

A proclamation that he's here.

Holy fucking shit.

"What the hell are you doing here?" I repeat my question, although on a whisper, ignoring his statement. "Who said you could come into my room?"

Technically, this isn't the first time he's been here. Last time was in broad daylight and everyone knew he was in my room. Doesn't he remember though? Beth saw us. Not to mention, we almost got caught kissing in his office.

Stupid, fucking phenomenal kiss.

Simon takes a step toward me and my eyes jump to the little window on my door. I'm half-expecting to see an outraged night nurse or even Beth standing there, peeking inside, drawing all the conclusions – *wrong* conclusions – about his unexpected visit.

"I was waiting for you."

"What?"

"Why didn't you show up?"

"What does... I don't..." He walks closer to me and this time I hear a creak that makes me jump. "Oh my God. Stop. What are you doing? Don't move. This fucking hospital is falling apart, okay? Just don't move."

Of course, he doesn't listen.

Of course, he wants to kill me. This is what it is.

He's here to kill me. He's a murderer. I wouldn't put it past him because he is already stealing my breath away. He is already a thief. There's a high likelihood that he's a cold-hearted killer, too.

He keeps walking closer until I feel the heat radiating out of his body.

God, he's hot. In temperature and in other ways. But I'm not thinking about the other ways right now.

I won't.

"Do you think this is a game?" he snaps.

"What?"

I squint at him, trying to discern his expression. There's no moonlight tonight; the rain is covering every inch of the ground and the sky. And the hallway light is dim, not to mention, this reckless man in my room is blocking it with his giant shoulders. So I can't really see anything, other than his shining dark eyes and the shadowed lines of his face.

"Answer me, Willow," he commands. "Do you think this is a game? Do you think your health is a game?"

"Of course not."

"Then why the fuck didn't you show up for the meeting?"

Is he really asking me that? After he pulled a 'temporary insanity' clause on me?

"Because I didn't wanna see you," I snap back. "Can you go now?"

I swear I see a pulse on his jaw, as if he's angry. Then he

shakes his head, sighs sharply and asks, "Why were you crying?"

"What?"

"I saw you through the window."

"You've been spying on me through the window?" I hiss, trying to keep it down, wiping the tears that I didn't know I was shedding in the first place.

"Spying is a strong word. I was trying to check up on you."

I raise my hand in a *stop-right-there* gesture, blowing at my bangs. "I don't even wanna address the fact that this is a gross invasion of privacy. Because something much more drastic is at stake right now. Remember what happened yesterday back at your office? And before that? Beth saw us. There're eyes everywhere."

"Beth's not here."

"What?" I shake my head at his casual comment. "We have hourly checks, in case you've forgotten."

"The nurse thinks I'm in the supply closet and the check isn't for another fifty-six minutes."

"You've been counting?"

He completely ignores me and instead says, "You didn't answer my question. Why were you crying?"

I sigh, tired, but so charged up at the same time. I know I won't be able to sleep tonight. Actually, I'm not even thinking that far out. I'm only thinking of now. Like there's nothing beyond him and this moment.

"What does it matter to you?"

He leans closer then, and at last, I can see his features a little better. Like he's come out of the shadows. His brow is furrowed and his hair's sticking up on the sides making me think that he's been plowing his fingers through it.

I'm almost shocked to see him this way, ruffled and bothered. Nothing bothers him, not from what I've seen. He's a block of ice but not right now.

Tonight, he looks like a man who's tired, exhausted, imperfect, and so fucking glorious.

"It matters to me because you're my patient and you missed your meeting, and now you're awake at night, crying." His eyes glint, troubled. "Which is why I'm asking you again. Why were you crying, Willow? Why are you even awake? With Trazadone you should be fast asleep."

I'm such a sucker that I can't see him like this. I can't see him upset. I should tell him I'm crying because of him. I can't sleep because of him. Because he kissed me and then pled temporary insanity.

But as I said, I'm a sucker so I look away from him and tell him the other truth, "It's not the meds, okay? I miss home."

"What about home?"

"Hedwig."

"You had a pet owl?"

There he goes again, stealing my breath. How fucking unfair is it that I've finally found a man who knows Harry Potter like I do, but he isn't into me. "Goldfish. I set it free when I was twelve. Well, gave it back to the store and asked *them* to set it free. Right after The Funeral Incident…"

Okay, stop, Willow. Stop talking.

I thought I hated talking. But something about him makes me want to talk and spill and bare my soul.

I'm so stupid.

"Why?"

I can't believe we're having this conversation. I can't *believe* he's here.

How is this my life?

I glance at the little window on the door again before focusing on him. "Because I thought she was alone and she needed friends."

I want to say more but I grit my teeth. Enough. I've already told him so many things about me, while I know nothing about him. Not that I'm interested.

I'm *not*.

"What about you?"

"What *about* me?"

"Didn't you need friends?"

Fisting my hands, I say, "I was okay. I was handling it."

Thunder cracks and reverberates through the room, throwing the light of the sky on him. My intruder. The face sculpted by the gods. It has to be. And those eyes. They were probably drenched in the rain clouds to get that rich, gray color.

Everything about him is so poetic. And everything about his poetry is fucking tragic. For me.

"That's what you do, don't you?" He scans my face in the darkness. "You handle things. All alone. You fight for them. Every time. All the time. You fight."

My eyes feel heavy, grainy. "Yes. I'm a warrior. Maybe I should tattoo that. Warrior Willow or something."

"Yeah," he murmurs. "Maybe you should."

"Okay, now can you go?"

I blow at my bangs again and I see his eyes roving to my loose hair, and I'm racked with such longing. It grips every part of me. My lips, my fingers, even the roots of my silver strands.

Will he never fist them? Will he never kiss me again, taste me, cure me, let me taste him?

There's so much to do, so much to discover. I didn't get to touch him last time the way I wanted to.

God, please. I want him to touch me.

Perhaps his thoughts are the same as mine because instead of going away like I asked him to, he puts his hand on me. Again.

And I squeak. His fingers circle my throat, his thumb pressing on the fluttering pulse on the side of my neck, like he did yesterday. As if he wants to feel the life inside me, my essence.

My vitality.

My eyes are wide and shocked. "Wh-what are you doing?"

His eyes are on his fingers, as if he can't believe they are there. He puts pressure around my neck, and it arches and so does my back. He isn't hurting me. There isn't even discomfort. It's just that he's touching me, holding my throat in such a possessive way that I can't help but make room for him. Or rather my body can't help rearranging and shifting.

"S-Simon…"

Without answering me, he bends down, like really down, his hand leaving my throat so his arms can go under my ass.

Then, he does something that I never, not in a million years, expected him to do.

He lifts me in his arms.

Chapter 15

Oh my God.

I'm in his arms. He's carrying me in his arms.

Like I weigh nothing.

"Simon..." I squeak, a little too loudly for my comfort. "What are you doing?"

His large palms are under my ass, and my thighs and arms are wound around his big body as he carries me to the wall, by the bed, the wall that I share with Renn. He props me against it, his arms secured around my waist.

I'm panting as if I've been running or doing yoga. "What the..."

Simon adjusts himself, his body shifting between my legs. Like a big mountain.

My night pajamas are short, covering only the tops of my thighs, and I didn't even realize that my legs have been bare all this time, until they scraped against his clothes. The sensation makes me squeeze them, and all I feel is miles and miles of sculpted muscle. A terrain of muscles.

"Do you live at the gym?" I blurt out the first asinine thing in my head.

God, why am I so lame?

He doesn't answer me. He doesn't even acknowledge my question. He simply moves closer when he's happy with the way he's situated me.

His forehead grazes mine and his torso presses into the juncture of my thighs, making me squirm. "I want you to promise me something."

I fist his shirt on his shoulders. "What?"

Simon grabs my face then, forcing me to focus only on him. Like I wasn't already. Doesn't he know? I can't focus on anything but him when he's close.

"You won't miss an appointment again," he rasps. "Ever. With me or with your therapist. Your group session, your meds. You won't miss any of it. You won't jeopardize your health in any way or fashion. Promise me."

"Simon—"

"Promise me, Willow. Your health is the most important thing to me. It's not a joke. Do you understand? You won't let anything affect it. *Anything*. Least of all a man like me. Tell me you understand."

His voice is so dark and heavy, laden with things I have no clue about. All I know is that it's imperative for him that I say yes. The way he's looking at me like I hold all the answers to his problems, like his life depends on me, I can't deny him anything.

So, I nod. "I-I do."

His chest expands with his long breath. "Good."

"What do you mean, a man like you?" I ask, my hands traveling up to his hair. I sink my fingers into the strands, feeling the rich softness.

Simon doesn't answer me for a few heartbreaking seconds and I want to hug him so badly. Because I know something is bothering him but he won't tell me what.

"A man prone to mistakes," he says, at last, in a ragged whisper, his eyes on me. In fact, his eyes are roving all over my face. Back and forth. Up and down. Fast and slow. All at the same time.

It's like he'll never see me again, and it scares me.

"What kind of mistakes?" I ask, massaging his scalp, scraping my fingers through his hair.

He groans, his eyes almost dropping shut with pleasure.

Despite everything, I smile. I smile because I'm giving him pleasure. Me. Somehow, Weird Willow is making this man groan.

It makes me happy. It makes me horny, and I rock, rubbing my core against his torso.

His eyes open, shining and black, his hands going to my hair, his thumb grazing my jaw. He's touching me on the face, but strangely, it resonates in my stomach, pooling and swirling like liquid lust.

"Do you know I watch you?"

"What?"

His nostrils flare. "Yeah. I watch you. In fact, I can't stop watching you."

"Y-you watch me?"

"Yes." His reply is so guttural, so full of loathing that I don't know what to think or do except tighten my thighs around him.

And blurt some words that I don't think make much sense. "I didn't... You..."

"You didn't know, did you?"

I shake my head.

It makes him chuckle, my ignorance. But there's hardly any humor in it.

"You love strawberries, but you hate blueberries," he murmurs. "You always leave them out of your fruit salad. You always like to sit on the bench closest to the gate while feeding your pigeons, like you're planning to make a run for it. You blow on your bangs when you're nervous or agitated. You've started to laugh more ever since you talked in the group. And you know what else?"

I don't think I can talk right now. I don't know any words. I don't know any sensations and emotions, except him. He's all I know in this moment.

My ice king.

Good thing he doesn't seem to need an answer because he goes on, his fingers flexing in my hair, as if his body is flooded with all the electric energy. "I fucking hated it when you laughed at him."

"At who?"

"At the new guy. Tristan. You were playing cards and he was teaching you and I fucking hated it. If a nurse hadn't called me away, I would've done something... regretful."

I vaguely remember it, playing poker with Tristan and a few other people. Mostly I wanted to piss Renn off, because she starts blushing whenever he's around and it's fun to watch. But I didn't... I didn't know...

He was watching me.

Oh God, he's been watching me all along.

My lips part as I stare at him with wide eyes. My skin flutters, raises itself in goose bumps. There's a buzzing in my stomach, my pussy. My soul. It's like every single molecule, every atom I'm made of is excited.

"Simon, I –"

"Stop looking at me like that," he spits out, cutting me off.

"Like what?" I wiggle in his lap, his authoritative voice making me hotter and hornier.

His one hand goes to my waist to stop me from moving, plastering my spine to the wall. "Like I'm some kind of a hero. Like this is a fucking fairy tale." Grabbing the back of my neck with his other hand, he pulls me closer, bringing me flush to his chest, almost flattening my breasts.

"I told you, Willow. I'm not supposed to think of you in any other terms but as my patient. Do you know how unethical this is? Me coming into your room in the middle of the night? Do you know what kind of men do things like this? Weak men. Men who fail. Men who can't control themselves. You don't want anything to do with men like that, Willow. You need to be smart. You need to stay away from men like me."

I want to tell him that smartness, playing by the rules, being good... all of this is over-rated. And then I want to grab the back of his neck too and plaster my mouth over his because *Jesus Christ*.

He's been watching me, and he wants me. But he hates

that. His strange protective instincts are turning me on so much. And if it's wrong, him watching me like a stalker or like I'm prey, then fuck it. I don't care.

I love it.

I cup his hard jaw, feeling his rough stubble and hardly controlling myself from moaning out loud. "Simon, you don't –"

"My only solace is that I don't give in. When the thought of you becomes too much and I want to touch you or see you or jack myself off, I don't. I run. I work out. I fix that house. But I don't give in." His breaths are choppy, coming in short bursts, waves. "I can't give in. I can't fail."

Lightning streaks across the sky again, illuminating his severe features and mussed up hair. Illuminating Simon. My Simon.

He's telling this to himself, reminding himself that he can't fail. Why? Why is it so important for him not to fail?

Why is it a failure to begin with? Wanting me? Wanting *this*?

"But I do," I whisper, my eyes on the verge of leaking water, trying to tell him that he isn't alone.

He focuses on me then, like he's seeing me after quite a while. "You do what?"

"Touch myself." I lick my lips and he homes in on the tiny movement, as I continue, "At night, when I can't sleep, I touch myself. My breasts, they become so heavy and they hurt me so much. And my nipples poke through my t-shirt and I have to pinch them. A-and I imagine that you're doing it to me. But your hands are so big and large, and I always end up being disappointed with my own fingers. So, then I…"

"You what?"

I flinch at his words and without meaning to, I rub up against him, going up and down. My breasts scraping against his chest and my pelvis hitting his stomach. His dick.

It's hard and lodged between us. In fact, it's lodged right where it should be. Between the lips of my pussy.

"You what, Willow?" he asks again, and I bite my lip, watching him through my lashes as I writhe against his hard pole.

He shudders – shakes – at my movements and his eyes turn even darker, if possible.

"So then, I-I put my hand under my shirt and cup them. I try to… I try to push them together, and then I close my eyes and I think about you sliding your dick in between them, like you're – you're fucking me. But then, I get so self-conscious, you know. I d-don't know if my breasts are big enough for you. If you'll be able to fuck them. I…"

He pushes back, his cock almost bursting out of his pants, poking into my tiny hole. "You what? What do you do?"

My neck can't support the weight of my head anymore. So it drops down against the wall. The dark ceiling is flashing in and out of my vision; I'm so turned on. "I play with myself, then. I touch my clit and put my finger inside me. But j-just one finger."

I feel him grazing the column of my throat with his nose as he grinds his erection into my core.

"Yeah? Why just one?" he growls.

His question coats me in embarrassment and I shut my eyes, biting my lip and shaking my head. Simon doesn't let me escape though. His hand in my hair moves to my chin and he forces me to look at him.

"Why?" he asks, again.

Swallowing, I tell him, a flush covering every inch of my body. "B-because I don't want to stretch it out. I want to keep it tight and small for you."

In this moment, I'm so aware of him and how old he is. How experienced and mature and commanding. Whereas me? I'm so young. Hardly been kissed once or twice.

I wonder if he thinks I'm too childish.

It's the truth though. I've never put more than one finger inside me. I've been terrified to. Maybe this is why. For him.

Maybe it wasn't random. Nothing about me and nothing about him is random.

"Have you been…" I clutch the collar of his shirt. "With a lot of women?"

His jaw ticks. "Why?"

"I know you said you don't have anyone special but…" I shake my head, wanting to look away from him, but I can't. Wanting to sound more mature than this, but I'm so wracked by jealousy, all of a sudden. So wracked with the unfairness of the fact that I met him so late in his life.

"But what?"

"Did you go on a date with her? With Josie?"

He studies me, his lips parted like mine. Maybe he's remembering that day like I am. When I told him to not go. When I asked him out. It seems so long ago right now.

"No," he replies.

It makes me smile but it makes him angry, my smile, and

his grip on my chin tightens. An expression flashes like lightning across his face and he asks, "Is it? All nice and tight?"

I blush at his words. "Y-yes."

"Fuck." His hips jerk, his shaft hitting my clit. "*Fuck...*"

His curses make me moan, make me move against him, against that hard part of him.

"Listen to me, Willow," he says in an abrading voice. "It's going to stay that way, your pussy. Do you understand? It's going to stay all tight and small. No one is going to touch it, including me. This is wrong. The things I feel about you and the things you feel about me. It's wrong. It's unethical. We should know better. *I* should know better. This isn't happening, okay?"

Despite his words, he grinds his hips into my pelvis, making me push back.

"I want it," I moan, writhing and squirming.

"No."

I jerk, almost jump over him, over his hot dick. "Please."

"Willow, whatever this is, it isn't real. All of this. It's co-dependency. You think I'm saving you and I think I'm the only one who can save you. It's all fucked up, all right? We can't do this."

"But you're forgetting something," I whisper, knowing it in the depths of my soul.

As much as I enjoy the fantasy of him curing me, of him being my medicine man, I know he can't. I know in this life, the only person who can save you is yourself. I've been fighting to save my life ever since I was born.

I don't need him to save me. I need him to kiss me right now. And touch me, possibly fuck me.

Oh God, yes, I want him to fuck me.

"What?"

"I'm the Warrior Willow. I can save myself."

"Willow —"

I cut him off by smacking a hard kiss on his mouth, surprising him. "Shut up and kiss me."

Smirking, I undulate against him and he growls, claiming my lips in a kiss. But I want more. So much more than a kiss, so I sneak my hand down and cup his erection through his pants, making him rip his mouth off mine and hiss.

I squeeze his length, feeling it throb in his pants. Maybe it's oozing pre-cum, too. Like I'm oozing out my cream.

Maybe he's hard but wet like I'm soft and drenched.

"What, are you going to jack me off?" he asks, all still and rigid, while his eyes are glittering dangerously.

"Maybe."

He cocks an arrogant eyebrow. "I doubt your little girl hands will fit around my dick."

I offer him a sweet smile as I get to his belt buckle. "Why don't we find out?"

A muscle jumps on his cheek and I'm waiting for him to stop me. I'm waiting for him to grab my wrist and halt my movements. When he doesn't do anything, only stands there, watching me, I get to work.

I've never opened a belt buckle before but how hard can it be? It looks pretty easy on TV. But paired with darkness and my over-eagerness, I fumble. A lot. And he doesn't come to my rescue.

"You could help me," I mutter, keeping my eyes glued to

that stupid accessory.

"I think you can handle it."

I look up at his dry but rough tone. "You don't think I can do it."

His gaze is hooded as he whispers, "I think it's magnificent to watch you fight for it."

His face is slashed with lust, painted, almost. I lose my breath at the sight of his sheer need. I lose my breath at the passion in his voice.

Simon Blackwood is such a contradiction.

He wants to save me, but he also wants me to save myself. He wants me to fight, and at the same time, he wants to protect me.

A unicorn.

He's a unicorn.

Biting my lip and gathering all my strength against a rapidly falling heart, I focus on the task. Surprisingly, his scrutiny doesn't make me nervous and within seconds, his buckle is open and his zip is undone.

My lips part as I reach in, under his boxers – why is it so sexy that he wears boxers? – and make contact with that hard flesh. It's not difficult to find it; it's there, sprung up and straight and so fucking hot.

I whimper as I palm the hottest, softest and hardest thing in the world: his bare cock. My whimpers are answered by his groan.

Both of our sounds are low and rough, and they reverberate through our bodies, somehow settling between us where my hand is touching his cock. There are flutters and tingles and heated pinpricks, and I grip him tight, making him shudder.

Simon leans forward, almost falling on me, and his head bumps against the wall, his mouth parted just under my ear. He grinds his forehead into the wood, and I rub my cheek against his stubble, trying to soothe him.

My eyes go to the rain-drenched window, the thunder, the chaos outside. The storm. But it has nothing on the storm on the inside.

He was right. My little girl hand can't fit around his entire length. So I use both of them. I grip the base of his cock, thread my fingers around it, start pumping. Slow, erratic pumps. Unpracticed but I don't think he minds.

"Fuck…" Simon curses, again.

His puffs of breaths under my ear, on my throat, are making me achy, achier than ever. It's making me sweaty as well. A drop of perspiration slides down the side of my cheeks. But I don't know if it belongs to him or to me. Our sweat, our skin seems the same, in the near darkness.

Even though I can't see his erection clearly to gather its nuances, I still know that the top of his dick is rounded and hot. And so smooth. It's wet too. There's a line bifurcating it and the more I thumb that delicate spot, the wetter it gets.

"You're leaking too. Like me," I whisper and to show him what I mean, I bring his erection to my core and rub it along my pajama-covered slit. I moan at the sensation of his naked shaft rubbing against my clothed pussy. It's hitting my clit in just the right way. I think I can come like this, moving over him, jacking him off.

His shuddering chest hollows out and I'm afraid he's

stopped breathing. But then, he pushes out a large breath, fluttering the stray hair stuck to the line of my neck. "Use it to lube me up."

I stop, my fingers flexing around his cock. "What?"

He raises his head, his eye so close to me that if it were day, I would see myself reflected in the depths of his gaze.

"You want to jerk me off. Then I want you to lube me up with your cream."

Before I can comprehend what he means, he uses one hand to heave me up against the wall, securing me, and with the other, he shoves the crotch of my pajamas to one side, taking my drenched panties along, and baring my pussy.

"Wh-what are you doing?"

"Taking what you made for me." He nips at my lower lip as his fingers swipe along the seam of my core.

"Oh God." I shiver, my eyes clenching shut, my hips twisting.

He's touching my pussy with his finger, slanting up and down my wetness. Almost slipping, actually, with how soaked I am.

I'm embarrassed.

God, I'm so fucking embarrassed at the fact that I haven't shaved down there in ages. They don't let us. Either you have to do it under supervision or you don't do it at all. I chose the latter and it's only hitting me now, as his fingers flick through my damp curls.

"Christ," he curses, thumbing my clit, sending shooting sparks through my blood. "It's making me insane how soft you are. You're the softest thing I've ever touched. All innocent and pure."

My embarrassment melts away at his words. I might even be smiling in the darkness; I can't be sure.

My own fingers slip around his dick as it throbs and a drop of pre-cum slides down. Then I stumble upon loose skin around the head of his cock. I gasp as I touch it. It has to be the most delicate thing in the world. Like a bundle of silken threads.

"You are so soft, too."

He chuckles. "There's nothing soft about me, Willow." Then, "Wrap your hands around my cock. Tight." He waits for me to obey him. "And smack it against your pussy."

"I'm sorry?"

"Do it," he commands.

I do, albeit awkwardly. I tap it against my bare cunt once. Twice. Moaning.

"Harder," he grunts.

I do it harder, writhing my hips every time it hits my clit. "Oh God…"

"Good," he praises. "Now, put it in the middle of your tiny slit."

I look up to find him watching my hands between us. I place him so that the lips of my core are hugging his girth. It makes him twitch and press his thumb on my clit.

"L-like this?"

His hips pump, slicing his dick through my slit like it belongs there. "Yeah. Just like that."

"God. Simon… this is…" I moan as I begin to move as well, my wet, sticky hands coming off his dick and gripping the side of his shirt.

We both rock against each other, my cunt stretched around his cock so tightly. I whimper, my eyes clenching shut. I wish I could keep them open and see it. I wish I could watch as he thrusts his hips in a rhythm, pumping, the head of his dick hitting my clit.

My pussy is clenching, fluttering with every slide. It's juicing up, probably preparing itself for that massive shaft that keeps working it. My pussy is hungry. I'm hungry.

He's so close. That part of him is so fucking close and yet, it's so far. I wish he would put me out of my misery.

I wish he would put it in.

He's right there. Right *there*. The head of his erection could so easily slip inside my hole. I know he won't though. I know it.

I somehow know *him*, even without knowing anything about him.

But one day. One day I'm going to make it happen. One day I'm going to make him fuck me.

For now, this has to be enough.

I'm buzzing with the way his dick is moving up and down, pumping. It's both shocking and electrifying, his bare, most intimate skin rubbing into mine. My nails dig into his sides as I hold on to him and twist in a perfect rhythm.

Grind, grind, grind.

It's so sticky and messy, the way we are thrusting against each other. My night shirt has ridden up and is bunched around my waist. His clothes hang haphazardly from his body.

If it were not for our raging breaths and the rain outside, we would hear the sounds of our own slippery arousal. As it is, I can feel his pre-cum dripping over my pussy, my bare lower stomach, and I feel myself making a mess of the tails of his shirt and pants.

The musky smell rises around us. A mix of him and me. Just the fact that we're so entwined right now and hot and brimming with life and lust and all these feelings that I don't know what to do with, makes me come.

My moan gets swallowed up by Simon.

Although he curbs my sounds, he can't curb my shivers. My shakes. The earthquake inside me. My sweaty, buzzing limbs are trembling with a power I haven't felt before. It feels like this is my first orgasm.

And it is. With a man. With Simon.

It goes on and on and it would scare me if not for him, holding me, placing tiny kisses on my lips. As I come to, I kiss him back. Our tongues mate and our teeth clack. I suck on his mouth like he was sucking on mine that day, trying to cure me. I do the same to him. I try to suck off all his demons and set him free.

Maybe I'm doing it, releasing him, because a second later, he comes too.

Simon lurches, and I can feel the beginnings of a pained moan in his chest. Actually, it starts up in his tight, spasming stomach and I think he's going to roar. The sound of his orgasm is going to be super loud, louder than the rain outside.

So I keep kissing him. I keep sucking on his mouth and absorbing his explosion on my tongue. It's like being struck by lightning, and I spasm right alongside him.

He's tight but shaking. His cum is flying everywhere, getting on my stomach, spraying on his shirt.

When it's over, we pant against each other's mouths. Simon

doesn't let me go, however. He puts back my pajamas, covers my shuddering pussy with such tenderness that I want to cry. Though you wouldn't find the evidence of that softness on his face.

It looks grim.

"Simon —"

"Don't," he clips.

He balances me with one arm and with the other, jerks his pants up and closes his zipper, leaving his belt hanging around his waist limply. Then he gathers me in his arms and carries me back to bed.

He bends and lays me down as I stare at him but he doesn't return my regard.

Simon is ready to turn away and leave, and I grab hold of his wrist. "Kiss me goodnight?"

He works his jaw back and forth. "Go to sleep, Willow."

"Please?"

Sighing sharply, he leans over me and kisses me on my forehead. My entire body smiles at his tender lips. Before he can move away, I grab his collar and stop him. "You can't be perfect all the time, Simon. Perfect is super boring and a lot of pressure. It's okay to give in."

When he goes to say something, I kiss him hard. "Good night. Hope you sleep well."

I let him go, then.

But as he's about to open the door, I can't resist adding, "You can jack yourself off, if you want. But promise me you'll say my name when you come."

His back goes all rigid and he bows his head. A second later, he mutters, "Just fucking go to sleep."

I go to sleep, smiling.

Days spent on the Inside = 35

Days *left* to spend on the Inside = 7

Days in which to woo the ice king = 7

Chapter 16

I'm going to woo Simon Blackwood.

Yes. I'm going to woo the ice king. Me, the snow princess.

I smile, staring at the ceiling in the early hours of the morning. Who said only kings can woo? A princess can woo a king, too.

I'm going to woo my king. Well, because he won't do it himself. Something is holding him hostage. A demon or a dragon. Something that runs in his veins right alongside his blood, like my illness runs in mine. Only his demon isn't a diagnosis.

So I'm going to slay it, whatever it is. I'm determined.

And happy.

The thing is that I hardly ever wake up with this much energy. This will to smile.

Knock, knock, knock.

I stop smiling and look at the wall. Flimsy and thin. The wall that carries all the sounds across.

"Hey," I say, turning on my side, watching the white plaster with apprehension.

"Hey." Renn's voice floats through.

Okay, so I know that what happened last night was risky as hell. I know that. Those fifty-six minutes between hourly checks weren't foolproof. Anyone could've walked in. Anyone could have walked down the hallway, taken a peek through the small window of my room and would've found Simon and me, rubbing up against each other.

I know that. I know we got lucky.

I also know that the wall separating me from my neighbor is thin, wooden. As in, so thin and wooden that even whispers carry across. Thank God I've got the corner room with the stairs on the other side, so I only have one neighbor to contend with. And even though it was raining and storming last night, there's every chance Renn has heard something.

But she would never say anything. I've only known her for thirty-five days and still, I know it. I know she's my BFF. And when I leave here in seven days, I'll take all these memories and friendships with me.

"Sleep well last night?" she asks casually.

Even so, I'm a little apprehensive. Not of the fact that she might tell someone but of the fact that she might think less of me.

I clear my throat. "Yes. You?"

"Pretty amazing." She turns on her side, as evident by the rustling. "So it was crazy last night, wasn't it? With the rain."

My heart's racing now. God, I can't tell from her voice what she's thinking.

Please don't let her judge me.

"Yes. Super crazy." I grimace in the quiet.

"So?"

"So…"

"Are you really gonna make me say it?"

"Say what?"

"Willow."

"Renn."

She growls. "Jesus. I know, okay? I heard. And if you think that I didn't, then you're stupider than I thought."

"Hey, there's no need to be rude."

I hear a huff. "Fine. I'm sorry. But what the hell were you thinking, Willow?"

"I… don't… I wasn't planning on it."

"I can't believe it happened. Anyone, and I mean any of the night shift nurses, could've walked in on you."

"I know." I clutch the blanket and hide my face under it before mumbling, "I can't believe it happened, either."

"How did it even happen? Like, what? How… I don't…"

I lower the blanket. "Actually, I kind of asked him out on a date a few days ago."

"What?"

"Lower your voice, you idiot!"

"Oh, I'm the idiot between the two of us? Me? And you're so fucking smart asking him out, right?"

"Fine. Be that way. I'm not telling you anything." I flop down on my back and cross my arms across my chest, hoping she doesn't call my bluff.

Because I'm dying to tell someone.

This talking thing is very addictive. Now I know why girls

at my school always traveled in packs. They wanted to gossip. Not that what happened last night is an inconsequential topic or gossip, but still. I need a friend right now.

Renn sighs. "I'm sorry."

"You mean that?"

"Yes. But you can't blame me for reacting pretty strongly to this piece of information. You never told me." More rustling. "How come you never told me?"

I sigh too and turn to face the wall again. "I didn't know what to say. He obviously said no. He told me he didn't have feelings for me. So that was that."

"But then, how was he here last night?"

Something flips in my stomach as I remember all the things he said to me. All the things he's been thinking about. I thought he didn't even look at me. I thought nothing about me appealed to him. I thought he was objective, cold, impersonal.

He wasn't.

He watched me. He's *been* watching me. He wants me too.

Isn't that the most miraculous thing in the world? It's more miraculous than magic. Who needs magic if you have that?

Him. Wanting me like I want him.

"But then, he told me that he wanted me too. But he didn't want to give in because of what we are."

"What changed?"

I try to remember what happened leading up to the kiss. I talked in group, and then he called me into his office, and I asked him if he knew someone who'd given up.

Yes.

That's what he said in such a heartbreaking voice that I felt my own heart break.

"I-I'm not sure. There's something. Something in his life that's bothering him. But I don't know what."

"Do you think it's his previous job?"

I sigh. "Maybe. I can't say. But it feels personal. Maybe it's both."

"Do you want me to find out?"

"What do you mean?"

"So you know my dad is on the board of directors, right? My dad's assistant is pretty resourceful. He's the one who calls every week to check up on me. I can't promise the personal details, but I can tell him to ask around and maybe we'll find out something about his job."

It's tempting. So fucking tempting. I can find out what's holding him back, and then I can tell him that it doesn't matter.

Nothing matters because I want him. I want him more than I've wanted anything in this world.

But then, I know a thing or two about secrets. I had a few of my own, and I can't do that to him. I'll wait. I'll wait for him to tell me. Wait for him to trust me like I trust him.

"No. It's an invasion of privacy. Whatever it is, it doesn't matter."

Renn protests but lets it go when I insist.

"Was it good?" she asks a few moments later.

I chuckle. Only Renn would ask that.

It doesn't feel like it happened to me. It doesn't feel like my lips were the ones he kissed, and my skin was the one he touched.

It doesn't feel like he made me come on his cock and in turn, he came on me. His cum splattering all over my stomach and pussy. It feels surreal, like a dark, lust-filled dream.

But it wasn't a dream because I can still feel him. Still feel the weight of his hot dick, slicing up and down my slit. It's throbbing, you see. My clit, my tight channel. And it's so wet. Still.

"Yeah. It was pretty fucking good," I reply.

"Oh man. I knew it. I knew he'd be good in the sack. He just has that look, you know." Her sigh is one of longing.

Mine is, too.

I fold my hands beneath my cheek. "Tristan has that look, too, actually."

Renn goes all quiet.

I poke my finger at the wooden wall, as if she'll be able to feel it. "Why don't you like him?"

No answer.

"Renn."

"Willow."

"Tell me."

She huffs softly. "Because I think he's dangerous."

I'm instantly on alert. "What? You mean, like, *dangerous* dangerous?"

"Dangerous to me," she clarifies. "Guys like him, they pretend to be all charming and irreverent and, you know, harmless. But he's not. He's fucking dangerous to girls like me."

Finally, I understand. I get it.

"You like him," I say in an awed voice. "You're just afraid he'll break your heart."

"I'm always afraid of that, Willow. I don't believe in love. I know I *can* love but I also know that love's mostly just bullshit. It's a shot of dopamine. And trust me, I like getting high but dopamine ain't the way to do it. I'd take crystal meth over fucking hormones, any day."

"Okay, so, there's a lot of objectionable content in there that I'm not going to address right now." I smile sadly. "You sound like Penny."

"Well, I know my chemistry, so."

I nod, thinking about what to say. I finally settle on, "I don't think you should be afraid. To fall, I mean."

"Yeah? Based on what? Your midnight visitor?"

I think about her question, drawing random shapes on the wall.

Oh, who am I kidding?

I'm writing his name in invisible ink. Good thing they don't give us pens without supervision – sharp object. I'd be writing his name all over the walls. I'd fill this entire fucking hospital with his name, on every wall, in every corner.

"I've never been afraid to fall. In fact, that's what I do. I fall. But I always wanted to do it because my illness made me do it. I don't really know myself sometimes, you know. My thoughts aren't my own. They are so overpowered by my illness. By what I have. Sometimes I don't know if dying is what I want, or if it's something my depression is making me want." I swallow. "But this time I want to fall because *I* want it. I want him. It's me. It's completely me. It's like I know myself. *He* makes me know myself. He made me realize that I'm strong. I'm a fighter. He sees me, somehow. Beyond everything. I feel like we're so buried under our issues, Renn. We've got so much baggage and a lot of it is not in our control. But he sees beyond that. I can't hide from him. He sees the real me."

I hear sniffling and I realize Renn's crying. I'm crying, too.

"I didn't mean to make you cry," I whisper.

"Too late."

I chuckle sadly. "I'm sorry. Don't cry."

"How can I not cry, Willow? This is a disaster."

"What is?"

"Me. You. Him. But, you and him more than me. Oh my God, Willow. You love him."

"I don't," I say but I know I'm lying.

I know my heart's racing in my chest and my skin has broken out in goose bumps. There's a weird sensation in my stomach, a buzz. An electric buzz.

I mean, I know it looks stupid. Falling in love with a man I don't know much about. We've been together once and it wasn't even sex.

Maybe I'm being completely naïve and young and immature but what I feel for him, the way he has affected me since the beginning, even before I saw his face, the way I spilled all my secrets to him… Maybe I was always heading this way.

I was always going to be lovesick. Heartsick. Just sick.

"You so do, Willow," Renn says. "Do you know how crazy it is? I don't even know what to say right now. What if he's not what you think he is? Do you really know him?"

"I think I do. Where it counts."

"What if you guys get caught? What then?"

"I… I hope we don't."

That's such a lame answer. But the truth is I really hope that we don't. I only have seven more days here. Once I'm out, it doesn't matter what we're doing, right?

Who cares?

We only have to be careful for the next seven days.

"Willow, I have a bad feeling about this, okay? He could lose his job. You could, I don't know, undo all the progress you've made. You said it yourself. We're buried under our issues. You don't need this. You don't need another issue in your life. Please, tell me you'll be careful. Just please."

"I promise," I reply, blinking back my tears, love rushing for my BFF.

Who knew I'd find my Best Friend Forever on the Inside?

"Do you judge me?" I can't resist asking.

"What? No," Renn insists. "I just want you to be careful. And I don't mean be careful around the hospital. Be careful with him. Because people like him and people like us… we've got a line between us, Willow. There's a big, huge divide. There's a reason why they wear lab coats and navy-blue scrubs and diagnose us. And there's a reason why we're here, away from the real world, our lives interrupted. It's not something to be ashamed of but it's also not something to be taken lightly."

He said the same thing to me, when he made me promise that I won't let anything come between me and my treatment.

And I won't.

My feelings for him have nothing to do with my illness. They are independent, separate. They are mine. They are not a result of a deficiency or a faulty gene.

My feelings for him are me.

Not a lot of people will get it, in fact.

They'll think I'm crazy to fall for a man like him. My psychiatrist. The cold and distant ice king. They'll think it's anything but love. They'll think I'm a statistic. An insane girl falling for the man who's trying to save her. It's a doomed love. A love born to die.

A broken girl falling for her fixer.

But what they don't know is that my fixer might be a little bit broken too. There's something haunting him and it's more than the fact that I'm his patient and he's my psychiatrist.

And I have seven days to convince him that it doesn't matter who we are or what we are, we're made for each other.

***

Thirty minutes later, I climb down the stairs to go to breakfast and find him in the hallway. We look at each other across the space, his eyes pinned on me in a way that I now understand.

I begin walking toward him and he does the same. A few patients flutter past me. A tech carrying a file throws me a nod. A few nurses greet him. We do what we're required to do. We smile, nod back, all the while gravitating toward each other.

Or at least, it feels like gravitating. Because in this moment, there's nowhere I'd rather be going than toward him.

We come to stop in front of each other, a little further down the dining room.

"Dr. Blackwood." I nod at him.

"Willow." He doesn't nod back; he simply eyes me, my

face, and my t-shirt.

My nipples wake up, as if he's touching them, not with his eyes but with his hands.

Oh God, his hands.

He shoves them in his pockets as he stares, and I have to ask, "Why do you always have your hands in your pockets?"

"To control myself," he rumbles, his voice thick and syrupy, like his eyes.

My heartbeat jacks up. "From what?"

He looks up, his gaze dark, as dark as last night. "From doing the things they shouldn't be doing."

I swallow, my heart in my throat, preventing me from saying anything to that. Although I want to say things. So many things.

"Interesting shirt," he murmurs.

My nipples become engorged, painful. So fucking painful. And so do my breasts. There's a tingling in them that only ever comes when I'm on the verge of losing myself to an orgasm. Too bad I'm standing in the middle of a hallway, with the morning bustle of a hospital.

"Thank you. It's, uh, Harry Potter," I say lamely, like I did the first time I chatted with him in the hallway. As if I want to talk about fiction and magic, instead of begging him to ease the pain in my tits.

He knows what I'm thinking. He has to. Something flashes on his face. Something carnal, and I have to cross my arms at my back so I don't touch him. I wish I had pockets too.

"I know."

I bite my lip. "I slept well. Last night, I mean. Like a baby."

"I'm glad meds are doing their job. Besides, you *are* a baby." His voice is filled with barely leashed frustration.

I'm not a baby. Or a little child. Or his responsibility. Though weirdly, it makes me all horny that he thinks so. What he doesn't know is that this *baby* is really a snow princess who's going to slay his dragons.

Deciding to let it go, I narrow my eyes at him. "Last night was risky."

His nostrils flare. "That's why it won't happen again."

Boom, boom, boom.

That's my heart, matching the thunder last night.

"It shouldn't," I agree with him. "There's a line between us."

"There is."

"I'm... kind of defective and you're kind of not."

He takes a step closer to me and it's very hard for me to simply stand there and not take a step closer to *him*. He leans his head toward me and I become hyperaware of the surroundings. Is it intimate-looking, the way he's paying me all this attention?

But for the life of me, I can't move away from him. I can't bear to sever this connection, even if it's in the light of day and people surround us on all sides.

"Let's get one thing very clear," he says in a low but intense voice. "There's a line between us, Willow. But it has nothing to do with your supposed defectiveness. You got that? There is *nothing* defective about you. Am I clear?"

My legs tremble, shake.

They shake like I'm in the middle of an earthquake. Like

the one I had last night in his arms. I feel a flood of emotions, so many jumbled emotions that I don't know what to do with.

The only thing that makes sense to me right now is the fact that I love him.

I love this man.

I look at the sculpted line of his jaw, wanting to kiss his stubble, but knowing that I can't. "Yes."

"Good." He takes a step back. "I want you to focus on your treatment and nothing else."

"And will you focus on treating me?"

"That's my job, yes."

"I don't want you to lose it. If..." I trail off, since we're out here and I can't really say what I want to say.

His face becomes blank. "Why don't you let me worry about it? Besides, there's no if. Because as I said, it won't happen again."

I stare into his eyes, trying to read if he means it. Logically, rationally, he should mean it. If we get caught, things could end very badly. For him. I don't want him to lose something he's so passionate about.

It could end badly for me, too. Although I don't care about myself as much. I wouldn't care if they locked me up and put me in chains, for wanting something I shouldn't want.

It's startling, that revelation.

I've hated being sent here. *Hated*. And now, I wouldn't mind living here, in captivity, as long as he wants me back.

Nodding, I say, "Okay."

"I'm glad we're on the same page."

We are. His eyes say so. But why does it feel like the page we're on is not the page we're supposed to be on?

I should go have breakfast now. I see everyone going into the room, throwing us glances. But I can't make myself move. Not when he's watching me like this. Like he'll stand here for as long as I will.

Like what happened last night is going to happen again.

"It's a good day, don't you think?" I murmur.

He looks at me suspiciously. "A good day for what?"

I can't stop myself from smiling then. "Poker."

The look he gives me is scorching. I see him tightening his fists inside his pockets. "Poker."

"Uh-huh." I nod, tightening my own arms at my back because I so want to ruffle his hair right now. Or maybe crease his neatly-pressed shirt. "You should come play with us, Dr. Blackwood."

"Who's us?"

Sometime last night, I dreamed of Simon being jealous of every other man I come in contact with. It was weird and exaggerated. I mean, he won't be jealous of *every* man, will he?

Looking at him, I can't say for sure. "Uh, a bunch of people. Renn and the girls. Tristan."

"Right." His mouth tips up in a hard, lopsided smile. "You know, I'd be very careful about who you play with."

"Why's that?"

"It might piss me off."

"Then come play with us. Or you know, just watch."

His eyes flare dangerously, and my breath hiccups. I still

can't believe that he's been watching me. Like a beast roaming inside the castle. My lonely ice king.

"You shouldn't be so uptight, you know. And perfect. In fact," I say, my voice all breathy and my chest almost heaving with all the sensations. "I think you'll like how free the people are on the other side."

"What side is that?" he asks at last, in a soft voice and awareness in his eyes.

"The side where craziness lives. And I'm not talking about the useless kind."

Simon studies me with a clamped jaw before nodding and stepping back. "Well, you have a good day, and for your sake, I hope you don't play poker."

Chapter 17

I played poker.

But I'm not very good at it. So, I kinda lost. I'm up to about twelve thousand in debt, that I have to pay when I get out of here next week. We're all very heavy betters here at Heartstone.

I'm in my bed, sitting in the exact same position, drawing shapes on the window. It's raining again. Heavy and loud, masking every other sound but the sound of the sky falling.

The night nurse just peeked in through the window and I was pretending to be asleep. It's midnight and there's exactly fifty-three minutes till another hourly check. He's three minutes later than yesterday.

Like last night, I sense when the door of my room opens and he enters.

Immediately, I'm up on my feet. The floorboards creak, but tonight, I'm a little calmer about it. I shouldn't be, though. It's dangerous.

"You're late," I whisper as I take in his form, dark and tall.

Kind of menacing, but kind of not.

Tonight, the darkness doesn't seem so dark. I'm more adjusted to it. I can see the messed-up strands of his hair, the look in his eyes and the wet splotches on his shirt as he walks closer to me.

"You should be sleeping right now," he says, gruffly.

"You should be too."

"Insomnia can exacerbate your condition, Willow," he informs me.

I almost pout. "As far as I know, you also have trouble falling asleep."

"We're not talking about me. And I'm not the one with a Major Depressive Disorder."

Okay, enough.

I don't want to fight when there are other issues at stake.

"Why are you wet?" I reach out and catch the stray droplets on his throat with my finger.

I feel him swallow. "I almost went back to my hotel."

Halting my movements, I eye him. "Why?"

His jaw moves but he doesn't say anything. I guess that's my answer – he didn't want to come. My heart clenches as I ask, "How far did you make it?"

He puts his wet hands on my waist, making me gasp from the chill. "Halfway to the hospital gates."

"What changed your mind?"

"You were laughing too much. With him."

I clench my thighs at his tone. All roughed up and angry.

I know I shouldn't have. I know he was aware of it, me playing poker. We were in the rec room and he was by the door.

There was a chart in his hands and he was staring down at it. But I knew that he was attuned to my every move. It's a thing he does, where he watches me without being obvious, without even directly looking at me.

It's unnerving and so fucking arousing. It's like whatever I do, however I move, he takes it all in. It's heady to be this much at the center of someone's attention. It messes with all my control. My rationality. It drives me insane.

It makes me fall for him with open arms, and in a white dress.

My hands slide over to his shoulders and I feel his roped muscles under my palms. "I'm not interested in him."

I'm interested in you.

He tugs me closer until I go flush with his damp body. "Good. He's not the guy for you."

I cup his hard jaw, wiping off droplets, feeling the texture of his stubble. "Are you the guy for me, then?"

"No."

It might take me an eternity to convince him that yes, he is the guy for me. He's the only guy for me. But I only have seven days to fit in an eternity worth of wooing.

And tonight is the night.

I'm going to give him something. A gift. My trust in the form of my body. My virginity.

Yes, I'm aware that it might be silly to have sex and then magically expect him to fall in love with me.

But the thing is this is all I have. My body, my desire, my lust. This is the purest part of me. My need for him is unpolluted, the one thing I own, and I'll give him that. I'll give him my trust.

If it's stupid, then so be it.

I watch the moisture dripping along the line of his sculpted cheeks. "What does the nurse think tonight? About where you are?"

"Supply closet. She thinks I'm the best doctor she's ever worked with because I'm helping her with the inventory. Better than even my father." He scoffs, "But I'm not better, am I? I'm only pretending to help her, so I can come see you. I'm like him."

It's important for him. To be better than his dad. It shows in every part of his large body. I remember from our first meeting when we talked about his dad and he clammed up.

I wonder why. Why is there such a rivalry between them?

I can't ask him though, can I? I can't ask all these burning questions inside me because I know first-hand how it feels to be asked.

But I can show him. I can show him that I'm not afraid of whatever it is that's haunting him.

I meet his eyes. "I think you're exactly who and where you're supposed to be."

Mine and with me.

One day I'm going to say it out loud to him. One day we won't have to meet in the dark like we're thieves. Like what we have is something to be ashamed of.

He looms over me, the drops of water plopping onto my cheeks, and I arch into him. "Yeah?"

I go on my tiptoes and place a soft kiss on his lips, and whisper, "Yes. Because I want you to do something for me."

He presses a hard kiss on my mouth, like he can't resist having a taste. "What?"

I can't resist a taste either. So I go in for a soft kiss on his stubborn chin and lick his stubble. The rough texture of it on my tongue is so fucking sexy that I get distracted and keep kissing and licking him, like an eager puppy.

Groaning, he presses our lower bodies together and I feel the hardness of his arousal against my stomach. "What do you want me to do, Willow?"

I move my tummy against his cock, hoping it finds its home tonight, inside of me. "Help me up first."

Without giving him time to think, I push on his shoulders for balance as I heave myself up and wind my legs around his waist. His arms drop to my ass and he gives me a boost and just like that, I'm wrapped around him. Tightly and effortlessly.

Simon is frowning, though. His body is tight, and I squeeze my thighs around him, grinning. His frown increases in intensity when he sees me beam.

I kiss his nose, making him slide his hands inside my pajama shorts and knead the flesh of my bare ass. "Okay, so don't be mad, all right?"

The way he's watching me, all alert and almost apprehensive makes me think he already knows what I'm going to ask, and he's going to be mad, no matter what.

With my hands around his neck, I boost myself even more, going up on his body so I look down at him for a change. "I want you to take my virginity."

His nostrils flare; even looking up at me, his neck at an

angle, he hardly appears any less intimidating. "Excuse me?"

I bite my lip. "Please. It'll be like a huge favor."

"Favor being taking your virginity."

His dry, tight tone makes sparks shoot down to my core. Why am I so attracted to his commanding voice? His authority. The fact that he's so much older than me and so much more experienced.

I peek at him through my lashes. "Yes."

"How's that a favor?"

Simon's watching my mouth as if he needs to *see* the words coming out of it. I know the reason I'm going to give him is outrageous but it's his fault. He won't take the gift I'm offering. So I'm going to trick him.

"Because if you don't, then someone else will take it."

"What the fuck?"

It's like I'm hugging a rock. A hard, unforgiving but breathing rock.

"Before coming here, I had this plan. I wanted to, uh, not be a virgin when I go to college. So, I was going to give it to someone."

This much is true. I was going to go out with my cousin and find someone to hook up with. Actually, my cousin was going to make me go out with her, so she could find me a guy. I said yes to appease her. But I know if it really came down to it, I would've made some excuse.

It's not as if I didn't want to get laid, but I didn't want to get laid like that.

"What is it? A fucking t-shirt that you were going to *give it* to someone?" he growls angrily, pressing my lower body to his stomach.

I flinch at his tone, but I'm determined to see this façade through. "Hey! I wanted to experience life, okay? I've been too ashamed of myself and everything wrong about me that I never really stepped out. I only ever had one boyfriend who turned out to be crap. So my cousin came up with a plan. She was gonna get me a fake ID and she was going to take me to a bar. And she was going to find me a guy."

Again, truth. But he doesn't need to know that I was completely against the fake ID plan. I'm not an idiot. I know how dangerous it can be, going out like that.

"No." He almost squeezes the breath out of me with his hold.

"That's all you ever say," I snap, and then try to imitate his low, growly voice. "No."

I probably sound bratty right now. Bratty and horny. But it's just what he makes me. He's so stubborn and good and noble and God, I just want him to fuck me.

Why won't he fuck me?

Simon gives me another squeeze to let me know that he isn't happy with me. "First of all, your cousin is fucking stupid. Do you know how dangerous it is to hook up with random men? You have no idea who they are. Who they've been with. If they're safe or sanitary. That's how you end up in a ditch in a body bag. Or with an STD." Like last night, he grabs the back of my neck and brings my face down to his. "And second of all, you're not giving *anything* to anyone. All right?"

I breathe through my nose and stare into his eyes. Of course, I know that. And I don't want to give *anything* to anyone, anyway.

"Then why don't you take it?"

With a clenched jaw, he replies, "I told you, Willow. As long as you're under my watch, you're going to stay a virgin."

"But I'm not gonna be under your watch for much longer."

His grip flexes, as if it hasn't occurred to him that I'm leaving in seven days. My incarceration is over. I'm free. Or I will be.

But I don't want to be free.

I don't want to go Outside. I don't want my life back.

I want him.

If being with him means living in this bland, white, moldy-smelling hospital, with a no-touching rule, and no-going-outside rule, I'm okay. I can take it. I can sleep in this lumpy twin bed, talk through walls, read the same books over and over. I can get startled awake by the whimpering and nightmares and noises of purging. I can take the humiliation of opening my mouth, showing them if I've really swallowed the meds or if I'm faking.

I'll take all the pills they will give me. Nausea, insomnia, night sweats and chills – I'll take it all as long as I get to be with him.

"Please, Simon," I beg, grazing our lips against each other. "If you don't, someone else will. And it'll hurt."

He closes his eyes and breathes deep.

I place soft kisses all over his jaw, his face, his eyelids. "Please. He'll make it hurt and I don't want to hurt, Simon."

"Willow."

My name on his lips is a growl. A thick, tortured growl and I just want to swallow it up. I want to swallow *him* up.

"Please don't say no. Please, Simon. What if he isn't careful with me? I told you my pussy is so tight. It's so small." I'm at his neck right now, drinking the leftover drops of rain, licking his salty skin.

He fists my hair and moves me away from him. "Willow, now's the time to shut the fuck up, all right?"

Even though I don't have access to his skin with my lips, I rock against his pelvis, all the while hating the fact that we're wearing clothes. If we weren't, I'd show him, I'd make him feel how wet I am. How I'm almost gushing for him.

"It is," I insist, ignoring his command to shut up. "I promise. I'm not lying. You c-can put your finger inside me and see for yourself. It's tiny."

"I'm warning you, Willow."

In any other situation, his growls would probably scare me. But not right now. Nothing scares me. Least of all him. I don't have any space in my mind, my heart, my body for fear. It's all desire and urgency.

I'm all need for him. I'm all me. Not a single drop of my illness.

I slide my fingers inside the open collar and touch his warm, smooth skin. "I know you'll be careful with it. I know you'll take care of me. Please."

I feel his chest vibrating, and he tightens his grip on my hair. "Have you been thinking about it all day? How to manipulate me into fucking you?"

"Yes," I say truthfully.

My answer makes him widen his stance like he won't budge no matter how much I push him. "I'm *not* fucking you. You don't want to get fucked."

I undo the top button of his shirt and slide my hand even lower. But he stops me. He puts his palm flat on mine and doesn't let me go anywhere. I look into his eyes, hard and dark and swimming with lust.

My heart squeezes in my chest. And again, I want to ask him. I want to ask him about the things he's been hiding. About why he won't let himself have me.

He's so magnificent. Why can't he see that?

"You make me happy, Simon. No one's ever made me happy before," I tell him, ironically with tears in my eyes.

For him. For myself. For all the things he isn't telling me.

It's the truth.

Simon Blackwood makes me happy. He makes me warm. He makes me want to fight for him.

His face is pulsing with something and before I can make sense of it all, he slams his mouth over mine and kisses off all my words.

It's a relief, this kiss. His tongue. His flavor. His smell. The swallows and the sucks of his mouth. I don't know what his intention is but I'm not letting him go. I wind my arms around him and hook my legs at the small of his back.

I'm not letting him refuse me any longer. I can't do it. I want him to give in.

Then suddenly, his mouth isn't on me and I'm moaning

with frustration. "Simon…"

"Listen to me, Willow." He grabs my face and demands my attention. "Listen to me very carefully, it will be just once. Just one time. Just tonight. And it will be because you want it. *You*. You want me to do this."

I wanna say something more but he doesn't let me. "And, Willow, you won't fight me on this. Because I swear to fucking God I'm this close to losing it and you don't want to see me lose it. So, you won't make this difficult. Do I have your word?"

My heart's racing. It's racing, racing, racing. It's *flying*. My eyes are wide, and I can't catch my breath. Did he really say what I think he said?

"Did you…" I lick my lips and blurt out my thoughts, "Did you really say what I think you said?"

He shakes his head once as if exasperated, and mutters to himself, "I'm already regretting this." To me, "Willow, do I have your word or not? Just this once. Then no more poker or whatever fucked up plan you come up with."

I'm so relieved and so fucking happy that I don't have it in me to even take offense at his tone.

I nod. "You have my word."

Not.

His eyes flash with something. All his desire. Everything unchained and saturated and dark. It makes my pulse skitter and pores sweat. It's like the air suddenly turned all dirty and humid. Heavy and swollen like I am. Filled to the brim with drops of lust.

Then he moves.

We've been standing in the middle of the room all this time

and when he comes unglued from his spot, the floorboards creak, and the thunder crackles. He only has to take a couple of steps before he reaches my bed and tries to lower me onto it.

I don't let him. "We can't. The bed, it creaks."

I can literally see him shaking. His teeth clenched so hard that I know he must be hurting. "Tell me this is a joke."

"No." I shake my head. "No joke."

He releases a short laugh. Though it lacks humor. "Where do you propose we do this?"

I swirl my finger in his damp hair. "Against the wall."

His frown is the biggest one yet. "You want me to take your virginity against the wall."

"Yes." I point to the wall I want. "That one. It's by the door so it isn't in the direct line of sight from the little window on my door."

Again a burst of a laugh, angry, incredulous. "You've thought about everything, haven't you?"

I nod. "Yes."

"But you forgot something."

"Wh-what?"

"You forgot how big I am," he says with gritted teeth. "I'm pretty fucking big and you're tiny, aren't you, Willow? So fucking tiny and snug that you were worried someone might hurt you. Do you know what happens when a man fucks you standing up? Do you know what will happen if I do?"

Swallowing, I shake my head, twisting in his lap. All this big and tiny talk is messing with my lust, dialing it up several notches.

"I'll have to jam my way in. I'll have to fucking shove my

cock inside your cunt, and every time I pull out, the gravity will pull you down. Do you know where you'll feel me, Willow?" He doesn't wait for my answer, all big and brooding and stationary. "In your fucking stomach. You'll feel me in your soft stomach. I'll be so deep inside of you that you won't ever get me out. Do you want that, Willow? Do you want to feel that? Because even I can't save you from that hurt."

I should be nervous, I know. He's not exactly painting a very pretty picture. I don't want to feel anything in my stomach.

But then again, if it's him, I don't mind.

Except...

"Have you done this before?" I ask, disgruntled.

Something about that makes his lips twitch. "Not with a virgin, no."

The way he says the V word, like it's a curse, makes me want to smack him in the head. What does he think virgins are? A different species, from another planet? Born and bred in captivity?

I wiggle over him, accidentally rubbing his dick over my pussy. Or maybe not so accidentally. Maybe I did it on purpose because I'm so fucking horny.

"I asked you for it, didn't I? I can handle it." I hover over his lips and whisper, "You being in my stomach. I'll be as good as any other woman you've fucked."

He's silent for a beat before finally, *finally* pushing back against me.

"You won't be."

Chapter 18

My heart breaks a little at his statement.

At his confidence.

But I don't get to voice it because he changes direction and goes to the wall. The wall I pointed out to him.

My back hits the brick just as he mutters, lowering me to the ground, "You'll be better and that's the whole fucking problem."

At first, I can't believe he said that, but then I can't help it; I smile.

He growls, though. "Stop making things difficult, Willow. Or I'll leave right now."

I shake my head. "Sorry."

He goes down on his knees then, taking my pajamas and my panties with him. That was so sudden that I don't have the time to prepare or do anything but gasp.

"Simon, I don't —"

My speech cuts off when he snaps his eyes up. "You asked for it, didn't you?" At my small nod, he swallows. "So, I'm doing it. But that's it. From here on out, it's my show. You'll do as I say. Because if I get even a little bit of indication that this is hurting you in any way, I'm going to stop."

I fist his hair. "No, okay. I won't say anything."

"Good."

I bite my lip and my stomach clenches at the sight of him on his knees. The top of his dark, messy-haired head reaches my heaving breasts. But his face is bowed; he's looking at my pussy and

I curl my toes at his intense stare.

Simon pushes my top up, dragging it across my trembling stomach with his splayed palms. His touch is so possessive, so rough and so tender at the same time, and I breathe really slowly, really carefully to absorb everything.

"The first time I saw you, you were on your knees, picking up the pages of your book," he whispers, his eyes on his own hands as he watches them tug my nightshirt up.

I remember that. I remember that so well. I hated the idea of him. Another jerk of a doctor. Another man with a God complex who would mess with my life.

He did mess with my life. He still is. But in a very good way. A very, very good way.

"I couldn't see you that way. I have no idea why. I didn't even know your name. I hadn't even seen your face. I just…" He watches my stomach as it slowly comes into view. "I just knew. That you didn't belong there. On your knees."

I press my lips together, trying to keep my tears at bay. They are happy tears though. So happy.

Such a strong longing grips me. It's almost like panic. What if this doesn't work? What if he can never lose his demons? What if after seven days all of this is over?

I can't believe I'm freaking out like this. When I'm half naked in front of him and he's about to do things to me. Delicious things.

But then Simon presses a soft kiss on my trembling stomach and all my negative thoughts go poof. He sucks in the flesh, nipping it with his teeth, making me moan.

He lets the spot go and looks up, at last, his hands under my heaving breasts. His breaths are wild, and every inch of his expression has been washed over by lust. "You really are a snow princess."

His thumbs caress the undersides of my tits and my hips roll off the wall, trying to get closer to him, to his touch. My nipples are sore, poking through my shirt.

"Right now, I don't feel like a snow princess," I admit shakily.

"Yeah, what do you feel like?"

"All hot and burning up."

With a lopsided smile, he pushes my top up even higher, exposing my breasts to the night. My back bows and my hands find his neck, latching on.

"Where?" he asks. "Where do you feel hot, Willow?"

"M-my breasts."

He covers them – my heavy, horny, achy tits – with his hands. "Does that make it better?"

As much as I love his touch, it's making everything worse. It's making me even hotter. "No."

Simon kneads the flesh, before rolling my turgid nipples between his fingers. "How about this?"

I swallow, clawing at his neck. Good thing I don't have sharp nails right now or I'd draw blood with how tightly I'm holding him. "More. Please, more."

His puff of warm breath is a chuckle and I arch my hips again. I want something. I want him. My channel is pulsating with so much need. It's like a fever.

"Maybe I should do this." Letting go of my nipples, he gathers my mounds, massaging them, making me hiss and grit my teeth. It's like he's touching all my pleasure points at once and it's so good that I can't even take it. My body is short-circuiting.

Then he presses my achy flesh together, making a valley.

"Isn't that what you do, Willow? In your bed? When you think about me? You press your tits like this and imagine me fucking them?"

He brings my breasts together, only to pull them apart. Over and over. Slowly, methodically. Every push and pull sends sparks down to my core. There's a heaviness that's growing inside my stomach.

I tip my face up to the ceiling. "Yes."

Then I feel something that makes me moan and steals my breath all at the same time. I whip my gaze down and find Simon at my breasts. His mouth is puckered and latched on to the underside of it. He's sucking the skin as he would suck on a nipple and I whimper out his name.

He looks up, smirking, all the while making a meal of my breast.

"Tastes like your mouth. Tart and sweet," he growls when he's done.

But turns out he's *not* done, because he takes a swipe of my nipple with the flat of his tongue.

Swipe, swipe, swipe. Suck.

God, he's sucking my nipple so good.

"Simon…"

I feel his shirt against my bare stomach, my naked thighs. I want to grind against the cloth, so he knows how wet I am for him. So fucking wet and creamy.

Slowly, Simon makes his way down, pressing soft kisses on the center of my chest and my belly.

My entire body tightens when he reaches the top of my core. He grasps my thighs with his hands, forcing me to keep them open, like he knew I'd try to close them.

I wouldn't, though; I'm shaking with nervous energy. And I can't deny that I'm a teeny, tiny bit freaking out with him so close to my nether parts.

No man has ever been this close to them.

"Simon, please. I think... I –"

He's looking at my pussy, bared and unshaved, as he asks, "You want me to stop?"

"No."

"Then shut up."

The words are a relief more than a command. Like he didn't want me to say no. Despite my nervousness, warmth pools in my chest.

Simon noses the top of my cunt, smelling my damp curls, and I have to shut my eyes now. I can't... I can't look. It's too erotic. Too out there.

Although I can feel, and I can definitely hear.

His chest shudders with a groan. He's cursing. It's like a chant as he rubs his nose, his parted lips on my skin. He hasn't even gotten to the main part yet and I'm already on the verge of falling.

My thighs are damp with both sweat and my cream. My pussy won't stop leaking. I'm making more and more of it and I would've pushed him away if I were able.

I'm not.

I'm not able to push him away at all. All I can do is bring him closer. Put my hand on his shoulder, fist his shirt and tug him ever so close.

"You're breaking your word already, Willow," he groans.

I open my eyes and the dark ceiling comes into view. Somehow, I lower my head and look at him.

What does he mean? My word about not making things difficult? How did I break it?

"H-how?" I ask his head. "What did I do?"

"You don't have to do anything," he mutters.

My heart's in my stomach. Actually, my heart is where he's looking at me and it fucking skips a beat when I feel his breath, hot. Right in the center of my core.

I jump so much that he has to band an arm on my lower stomach to keep me in place. With his other hand, he opens my pussy. I feel his fingers parting my lips in the shape of a V and I would've have said something about it because frankly, that's just so strange and new and dirty, if he hadn't gone and taken a lick of my exposed flesh.

"Oh…"

He does it again and again, until he's swirling his tongue at my entrance. He sucks in my clit, swallowing it, and I almost dislodge his arm from my jerky movements.

Moans are threatening to burst out of my throat, but I know I can't. I know I can't make a sound. As it is, my heavy breaths are echoing around the room, along with his low grunts.

So I push the fabric of my nightshirt inside my mouth and bite down on it, trying to tame my wild sounds, against the electric shocks he's delivering me with his tongue.

Simon doesn't notice any of this. He doesn't notice how I'm trying to contain myself. He's busy eating me the fuck out. Making me go crazy with want and hunger.

I go on my tiptoes, my calves and thighs completely clenched, when he takes his arms off from over my stomach and lifts me up with his palms under my ass. His mouth gets buried in my cunt and I grip the back of his head, biting the fabric of my nightshirt harder.

His tongue is hot and vicious as it slaps against my clit and my tight little hole. With each breath he growls, sending puffs of hot air into my channel, making it clench.

The day he kissed me, it felt like he was sucking off my illness through my mouth. Tonight, it feels like he's doing it through my hole. He's making me better by eating out my cunt.

Then his tongue enters inside me and I'm done.

I come like I've never come before. I've completely left the ground, arching against his working, sucking mouth as I clutch him to me. My face is upturned, and my neglected breasts are throbbing like my climaxing pussy.

I want to scream. I want to shout. But my detonation has to be silent because we can't get caught.

In the midst of my world getting flipped, Simon lets go of my tender, swollen flesh, and comes up to his feet.

I don't have time to catch my breath or stop shaking when I'm heaved up again, my spine sliding up on the wall, and Simon's breathing over my mouth, smelling like the rain.

Smelling like me.

"I'm sorry," he whispers thickly, and then I feel like someone has stabbed me with a knife, and I stop breathing.

I think I've died.

And I'm not happy about it. Not at all.

I didn't want to die tonight. I wasn't even thinking about it. I was only thinking about him. About the fact that I'll finally feel it. I'll have finally given myself to a man I was born for. Never mind that it's happening at a psych ward and he's my doctor. Never mind that we can get caught and so far, we've been very lucky.

Never mind all of that.

But now I'm dead and I can't breathe; there's so much pain. Or maybe it's all in my head.

Because I feel it. I feel him inside me. I feel the fullness. I feel him inside my stomach, and I feel him over my mouth.

I'm alive. I can *feel* things.

His mouth is locked with mine in a kiss. He's kissing me. Hotly, slowly. His taste is on my tongue, mixed in with my tart juices. Cocktail of rain and lime and musk. I have to admit I like this cocktail much better than the one made of Prozac and lithium.

Simon breaks off from my mouth and I notice his lips and his jaw glistening. "You okay?"

I swallow, thinking, hoping that I look the same, all wet and shiny. "Y-yes."

"This was the only way. Like ripping off a band-aid."

I'm panting, sting laced in with my every breath. "O-okay."

He shuts his eyes for a second and through the fog of pain,

I see his strained features. The sweat rolling down his forehead, his sharpened cheekbones. The taut tendons of his neck. I feel him throb inside me. Maybe his heart fell too, like mine did when he entered me and now it's beating where we are joined.

I wipe the sweat off his forehead and he opens his eyes. There's a war in there. War between lust and restraint.

"I feel it," I whisper.

"What?"

"You. In my stomach."

He jerks slightly at my words and so do I. The pain flares for a beat before dulling to a throb.

"Does it hurt too much?"

"A l-little."

He grits his teeth. In anger. In remorse.

And then, he goes to fix the pain. He thumbs my clit, playing with it, juicing up my pussy.

Moaning, I ask, "Am I tight?"

"Yes."

His thumb is making me restless. "Tighter than all the other women you've had?"

At this, anger flashes through his features. His body shudders and he widens his stance, all the while trying to keep still inside me, all the while making my channel cream for him. I get the feeling that he wants to move, only so he could punish me for this question.

But obviously, he won't.

He's him.

A drop of sweat rolls down the side of his cheek. "We're not talking about this."

I wipe it off, raking my fingers down his scalp, making him groan in pleasure. Then, I begin to unbutton his shirt and he shoots me a dark look, his hand on my clit goes still.

"Why not?" I ask.

"Because it's irrelevant."

I'm down to his fourth button when I look up, moving slightly on his dick, making him hiss. "Then why were you with them in the first place?"

He growls when I circle my palms over his chest. God, he's sweaty and hot and his muscles bunch up under my touch. It's like I control them. His heart is booming, and I can feel it. It's like I control it too.

"Biology," he clips as I trace my fingers up and down, trying to memorize him.

I sink my hands in his dark chest hair. "This isn't biology?"

"This is fucking madness."

This time I definitely feel the shakes roaring through his body. His restraint is turning me on.

Fuck pain. Fuck everything. I want him to move.

I peek up at him through my eyelashes, feeling all kinds of reckless. "Am I so tight that you wanna move?"

His dick throbs again and the feeling of fullness increases.

"Yes."

"Then move." I rock against him and he groans.

"Stop. You're gonna hurt yourself." His arms almost vibrate with his control and he grips my ass tightly, trying to keep me still.

"I won't. You made it all better when you were playing with

my clit." I shake my head, undulating against him again. "I want you to move, Simon."

He drops his forehead over mine. "I'm trying to give you time to adjust to my size."

"I'm totally adjusted."

He chuckles lightly, and I feel his stomach clenching. I'm about to say something else to convince him when I hear the noises.

And laughter.

I freeze and so does he.

The sounds are walking closer. Footsteps and a muted conversation.

I press my palm over his heart as my breathing quickens. Someone is walking down the hallway. Someone is walking toward us, toward my room.

Simon's staring into my eyes, his arms bunched up under my butt, keeping my trembling body from falling off. But his breaths aren't erratic and choppy like mine. They are calm. I don't understand it.

How can he be calm?

I clutch him tighter, winding my arm around his neck and grasping the collar of his half-opened shirt.

What if they take a peek inside my room through the window on the door and catch us together? I know we aren't in their direct line of vision; that's why I chose this wall but still.

What if they take me away from him? I'll fucking scream this place down. I'll claw and scratch at anyone who dares to take me away from him.

Not now. Not when I've felt him inside me. When he's still throbbing and my restlessness is still there. I still want him to move. *I* still want to move.

My eyes are filling with water, the closer they get to my room. I bite my lip and keep staring at him, all still and silent and afraid and horny.

But then he moves, making me jerk.

I widen my eyes at him. His face is unforgiving and harsh as he moves again, flaring my lust even more.

"No, Simon," I protest in the barest of whispers, shaking my head.

"Why not?" he says, slowly starting a rhythm, keeping me locked between the wall and him. "You said you were adjusted."

"P-please." I clench my eyes shut. "We can't make a noise."

He shifts on his feet and I hear a creak. It's as loud as a siren and my heart is in my throat. I'm so terrified. But even my fear can't mask the pleasure. It's slowly spreading through my limbs as he pumps in and out lazily.

"Maybe we should." He kisses the side of my mouth. "Maybe we should call them, yeah? They'll stop this madness."

"No. Please."

My face is buried in his neck as I rock back against him. I can't help it.

Even though they're coming closer and closer and my heart's beating like it might give out any second, I can't stop this. I can't stop the goose bumps, the fullness. The friction.

God, when he slides out and comes back in, I see stars. I feel the spark.

I've never felt this way before. Everything is heightened. My sense of smell. My ears. My sense of touch, taste. His skin tastes salty with sweat and probably lust and I can't help but lick the side of his neck, his taut vein.

He does the same. He licks my throat, smells my skin just under my ear, as he keeps stroking me with his dick, grinding against my clit.

I'm burying all my moans in his flesh, and it's a good thing because just then, we hear the loudest laugh.

They are here. They've come. Why else would they be walking this further down the hallway if not to come into my room? Mine's the last one on this floor, located in a corner.

A tear rolls down my cheek and I hug him with everything I am.

Strangely, he hugs me back.

It makes me cry even more. It makes me move against him even more. He does the same. His strokes are faster than before. Like he wants to get his fill of me, use me up before they take me away. My pleasure shoots sky-high and so does my need to moan, make a sound.

God, please. Please, don't let this be the end.

I suck on his neck, drink down his flavor. Even though my eyes are shut tight – I can't look – my ears are on alert and my pussy is juicing up over his cock.

Any second, I expect them to open the door.

Any second now…

It doesn't happen.

Nothing happens.

They keep walking, whoever they are. They laugh and talk, and their footsteps recede. They were just passing by. That's when I remember the stairs by my room. They were probably headed to them. Not to me.

For a second, I can't believe it. I can't believe we've been given a reprieve. That we got lucky again. It's okay. We're safe.

We can do this.

He can fuck me, and I can fuck him, and no one has to know. Not tonight. Not right now.

Through my tears, I'm beginning to smile when Simon moves away from me. The pressure of his heavy chest easing off my breasts makes me hiss. It makes my nipples tingle.

Unlike me, Simon isn't happy. He's mad and he palms my ass and heaves my thighs over his waist. That shock of a movement makes me lose my breath. It also makes me grind my clit on his pelvis.

"This is fucking insane," he thunders, and letting go of my butt, he clutches my face. "Do you know what would've happened if we'd gotten caught?"

I grab his wrists, tears still streaming down my face. "I would've taken all the blame."

He pumps his cock into me, jerking me up the wall, and my mouth falls open on a silent moan. "No. I'm to blame. Me. I'm fucking you, aren't I?" Another vicious jolt of his hips. "It's me inside you."

"Yes. B-but I… I can't… If they…" I sob, almost bursting with pleasure and all these pent-up emotions and adrenaline.

It's embarrassing. The way I'm crying and moaning. But

I can't help myself. It's like I'm jam-packed with every little thing that I can feel. Every little thing a girl can possibly feel during her first time, and I don't know what to do about that other than expel it through my sounds and the water in my eyes.

He gets it, this man. Who's claiming every inch of me with his dick.

"Shh… it's okay. It's okay. I'm here…"

Simon breathes over my mouth, shushing me, all the while grinding his hips into my clit as if digging out my juices from the furthest corners of my body, my soul. He drinks down my tears, licks them up as he pumps into me, slowly replacing my bursting emotions with himself, his reassurances, his presence, his cock.

My body goes loose, my thighs slipping off his waist as my heart hammers in my chest, but he pulls me up. He doesn't let me fall and he doesn't stop fucking me.

His deep, *deep* thrusts make my body jiggle. My tits bounce and I'm getting closer and closer to climaxing. His legs are bent, and his thighs hit my ass with every thrust. I hear a slight slapping sound every time he bottoms out, and even though it's loud, I can't fault him for that.

Those sounds let me know that a part of him is inside me. Those sounds let me know that he's fucking me like I wanted him to and we're shaking this entire castle – this psych ward slash the Victorian monument of love – with our passion, our lust.

Simon catches my mouth in a kiss. And it's as if I was waiting for exactly this because I fall apart. Once again. Though this time he's inside me and I feel my channel clenching over his rod. I feel his chest breathing against mine. I feel his heartbeat.

And then I feel him come.

I feel him pulsating for a second before he pulls out and comes on my pussy. He paints my curls with his cream and that makes me come some more, slumped against him.

His stomach clenches with every splatter of his cock and he groans, gripping the base of it, slapping it against my slit, making me writhe with the residual tingles.

When the storm passes and he stops coming, I hug him like he'll disappear.

"Please, please don't say it," I whisper in his ear.

"Don't say what?"

His whispers sound tired and lazy, making me want to shower him with kisses. "Don't say it was a mistake. Please."

He goes all tight and stiff and I'm sure he's going to say it nonetheless, breaking my overly-emotional heart. But all that comes out of his mouth is, "I won't."

I thought that would be a relief, but it isn't. It only means that he won't say it, but he'll think it. My heart squeezes painfully, as he moves and carries me to the bed.

He lays me down like he did yesterday. But unlike last night, there's a lot more damage that we've done. His shirt is half undone; I can see the outline of his muscular chest, those springy dark hairs that make me bite my lip. His cock is half-mast and peeking through the zipper of his pants.

Something about that is just so sexy.

I get a sudden flash of him in his house, all naked and sweaty, post-sex with someone. With me. I can't imagine him with anyone else. Didn't he say other women were irrelevant?

I so, *so* want that flash of a vision to come true. Maybe it will. Maybe next week, when I'm Outside, I can go to his house. We'll make love on a bed and we'll be as loud as we can be. He'll pick up my shorts from the floor and the boards won't creak. He'll slide them up my legs like he's doing right now and put his blanket on my body, instead of the one I have here.

I want it so much that my stomach clenches with longing.

I watch him straighten his clothes with watery eyes. And then I watch him getting closer, leaning over me.

"Go to sleep," he whispers, kissing my forehead.

"Seven days."

He stares at me. "You've been waiting for it. What was it you said to me exactly?" He thinks about it. "If I were half as good as they say I am, I'd see the error of my ways and let you go."

I did say that to him and I feel like such a fool now. For so many reasons. "I was an idiot."

"No, you're not. But it's good." He swallows. "That it's almost here."

"Yeah. I'll miss this place, though."

I'll miss you.

"I don't want you to."

"You don't?" I hate how small my voice sounds. How lonely.

He studies my face and I try to keep it blank. I might be failing, though. "No, I want you to get out of here and never come back. I want you to live your life and I want you to fight. Because you're a fighter, Willow. A warrior." Then, "And don't ever go to a fucking bar to pick up guys."

"So where do I go to get them?"

He hates my question, or at least that's what I think it means, his flared nostrils and the vein on his temple.

I'm waiting for his answer with bated breath. Even my heartbeats are suspended. Maybe he'll say it now. Say something, *anything* that will give me an indication of what the future holds for us.

"Nowhere," he says, and I widen my eyes. "They'll flock all around you once you go to college."

Simon leaves then, and I smother my face in the pillow and cry.

Chapter 19

"Are you looking forward to getting out?" Josie asks in our session next morning.

Not really.

"Um, yeah. But, well, I'm going to miss you guys," I say, shifting in my chair and feeling a twinge of discomfort between my thighs.

I look at my lap, covering my face with my loose hair. I'm pretty sure I'm blushing. I'm definitely throbbing. Between my legs, in my chest, in my stomach.

It's like he's still in there. Stroking, pumping, making me his.

"Aww. We're going to miss you too. But you know, you've made such progress, Willow. I'm so happy to see that. I think you're ready. Just always remember, you're not alone. That's the key."

I meet her eyes at this and clench my fingers together. "But I'll always have bad days, right?"

Her smile is sad. "Yes. I want to sugarcoat it but I'm not going to. Unfortunately, therapy or meds, they don't cure depression. Nothing will cure it. But they can help ease your burden. That's the best you can hope for. That's the best anyone can hope for, Willow. Life is…"

She shakes her head, searching for words, I think. "Life is long. I know people say life is short, and in some ways, it is. But it is too long if you're living it alone. Don't hesitate to ask for help. Don't think that you're weak just because you stumble. Everyone stumbles. Don't isolate yourself just because you have to take a pill every day. You'd be doing yourself a disservice. Live your life the best you can and ask for help. People aren't made to live their lives alone."

I nod, blinking back tears. I agree with her. We aren't made to live our lives alone. Not me.

And not him, either.

It makes me want to tell him. I want to tell him what I feel. Maybe it will give him courage to say the same. Or at least spill his secrets.

Or maybe it will make him push me away. Which I really can't risk because I only have six days with him.

Gah. Why does he have to be so complicated?

We spend the rest of our session talking about all the things I'll be doing once I'm Outside. We talk about Columbia and my scholarship and how afraid I am of losing it, of failing at college. Studies have always been hard for me but somehow, I managed to snag that scholarship award. But now I'm afraid. Again, she tells me that I can always ask for help with my courses and it's okay if I struggle. She believes in me. She knows I'll pull through.

When I'm done, I make my way to the rec room and try to focus on reading. But I still feel him.

In fact, I feel him so much that I don't feel anything else. Not when Hunter comes to me with the meds. Not when Roger and Annie say hi to me as they pass me by.

It becomes so bad, my absent-mindedness and my need for him, that I almost go searching for him.

But I won't.

First of all, I overheard one of the nurses say that he's on a conference call. And second of all, I don't want to hunt him down. I want him to hunt *me* down. I want to see if *he'll* find ways to see me.

If he'll come for me.

I'm praying for it. Because if he does, then maybe he does feel something for me. There's a teeny tiny light at the end of this dark tunnel.

A moment later, I see it. The light.

It comes in the form of a tall man, with polished wingtips and hands thrust inside the pockets of his dress pants. My eyes travel up and up, until I reach his face. His beautiful, carved face.

As much as I have come to love the cloak of darkness, I find that I love the day more.

I see his features clearly. I see the strength of his shoulders. The softness of his mouth he has been kissing me with, or rather driving me insane with. I see his tapering waist that I've been wrapping my legs around. It looks and feels like a slab of rock.

"Willow," he murmurs, tipping his chin at me.

His eyes flick up and down my face, as he takes me in and

my loose hair, like he's doing the same thing, absorbing me in the daylight. He lingers a little bit on my chest, probably reading my t-shirt. Today, it says: *"Beware of the love child of a Disney Princess and Hermione."*

"Dr. Blackwood." I nod, trying to keep my voice less breathy and more unaffected. Not sure if I managed it, though. Swallowing, I try again. "Is your meeting done?"

"Have you been spying on me?"

I can't help the slight smile that overcomes my face. "No. The nurses were talking."

He accepts the answer with a nod. "Yes. Just."

So he did come looking for me as soon as it was over.

Thank you, God.

"I see you're not playing poker," he comments in a casual voice.

I glance at the table across the room where the whole gang is playing poker – the girls, Tristan, Roger, Annie, and Lisa. Despite looking pale and gaunt due to The Heartstone Effect, Tristan is shooting his signature smirk at Renn and she's ignoring him, blushing like crazy. They asked me to play too, but I refused.

"I'm not interested in poker anymore," I say, looking back at him. "Besides, I wasn't very good. I always lost."

He frowns, albeit slightly. "That's because you weren't taught well. There's no magic to poker. It's all very scientific."

At this, my smile becomes a grin. Gosh, how much have I smiled ever since I came out here to Heartstone. Ever since I met him. Probably a million times.

He's still jealous.

"Maybe you should be the one to teach me, you know. All the ways of poker and…" I trail off, throwing him a smirk of my own. "Other worldly things."

He stares into my eyes for a few beats, his gaze intense and full of something secret and crackling. When he's done with his perusal and making me squirm in my seat and waking up all the sore muscles, he says, "Can I see you in my office for a second?"

I sit up, alert. "Uh, right now?"

The look he gives me hits me right in my belly and the sore muscles of my thighs and ass. "Yes."

And then he steps back and leaves, or rather strides out of there. How does he do that? Pack so much sexual energy and authority into one word: yes.

I watch him go. He's probably expecting me to follow him right away.

And I will.

I know I will follow him. There's no other choice.

Be cool. Be cool. Be cool.

It's dangerous and reckless to see him in his office in broad daylight. It's practically setting ourselves to be caught.

I stand up from my seat, nonetheless.

He was right. It *is* madness. But madness is us. The rest of everything is inconsequential. Besides, I only have six days.

As I walk toward the door, my eyes catch on someone. Beth. She's on the other side of the room and I have a feeling that she's watched our conversation, Simon's and mine. She saw that we were talking to each other. I wonder if she saw the intimacy there. The familiarity.

Is there any familiarity, though? Did we change in ways we don't even know about?

My heart pounds and I expect her to walk over to me. Stop me, maybe. But she throws me a smile before going back to the nurse she was talking to, or rather, supposed to be talking to.

Feeling an immense amount of relief, I leave, and a minute later, I'm at his door, knocking on it.

He opens it before I can even finish that knock and I almost barge in. The room appears dark, darker than usual. And I realize it's the windows. The blinds on them are closed, cutting off the daylight, throwing the room into shadow.

It ratchets up my heartbeat.

He closes the door and I hear two clicks, instead of the usual one. One of the door closing and the other of it being locked.

Locked doors. Such a luxury in a place like this.

Our rooms don't have locks. We don't get the privilege of it. I know it's for our own safety but still. It doesn't make it any easier.

No sharp objects. No privacy. Life interrupted.

So then, how did my life start in a place like this where all lives go on pause? How did it happen that I found everything I've been looking for on the Outside, here on the Inside?

It's him.

This man with gray eyes and dark hair, who just locked the door and who also closed the blinds before I got here. Who came for me as soon as he was done with his meeting. Who found ways to find *me*. And who's staring at me with such frustration and desire that all my thoughts are about one thing.

I want to kiss him.

Yes, I want to kiss *it* out of him. His lust and his agitation. I want to taste it. Taste the flavor of it, of him on my tongue.

I want to suck him off.

My gaze falls below his belt.

"Stop staring at my cock, Willow," he warns.

And of course, I do the opposite. Doesn't he know me by now? I glance at it again, and I swear I see it lurch inside the confines of his pants.

"Your pants are too tight," I tell him sweetly, trying to act like it's not a big deal. "I thought so the first day I saw you. They show off way too much. And I think I just saw *it* move. You know, FYI."

My comment makes his eyes smolder, and he begins walking over to me in slow, predatory steps.

Bad move.

Such a bad move on his part if he doesn't want me to stare at his dick.

I can't help it. When he walks, his pants stretch against his muscles and my eyes automatically go to his thighs. His powerful, *powerful* thighs, and well, his powerful cock.

The reason for all my dreams and discomfort.

Simon comes to stand in front of me. "Maybe the *it* is too big for my pants. You ever thought of that?"

Smirking, I shake my head. "Maybe the *ego* is too big for your head."

He bends down, all menacing-like. "Are you done making inconsequential comments?"

"Maybe."

He smiles slightly, which makes me tingle a little bit. He reaches out and takes my book from my hands. And before I can protest, he throws it at the leather couch we've been standing by.

"What –?"

"Are you experiencing any discomfort? Any soreness?"

I shiver at his question. Every sore spot, every ache flares to life. Just by him asking about it in such a frank, almost clinical manner. Just by him looking at me like that. From top to bottom. His eyes lingering everywhere. On my lips, my throat, my chest, stomach, the juncture of my thighs. He travels down and pauses at every curve and every valley.

I might as well be not wearing any clothes. He might as well be touching me with his hands.

"Wh-where?"

It's a legit question. I'm actually sore everywhere below the waist.

"Anywhere. Everywhere."

"Well, a little. I mean, in my thighs and butt." I'm compelled to explain, "I'm not very athletic."

"I'm aware."

I frown at him. "How?"

"I've seen you trying to touch your feet. Or was it the ground?" His lips twitch. "It was quite informative."

I gasp and slap his chest, remembering that day outside when Renn roped me into doing stupid yoga stuff with her. It was also the day he kissed me.

Still, I say in my snottiest voice, "It's called downward dog. And it happens to be very difficult. One of the more advanced yoga moves."

"Is that so?"

No, I'm lying. But whatever.

I sniff. "Yes."

Simon throws me a lopsided smile, before tipping his chin to one of the chairs. "Sit."

I narrow my eyes at him, trying to figure out what he wants. But of course, I can't.

Slowly I amble to the chair, but at the last minute, I change my mind and boost myself up on his desk. I sit at the edge, my eyebrows up in a challenge, my legs swinging back and forth.

His gaze is challenging too as he approaches me and fits himself between my legs. Then he leans over me and my back arches at his proximity. Still eyeing me, he picks something up from the desk.

"Here."

I look down at his hand. There are two pills sitting in the middle of it. Both white, both tiny.

My heart starts racing at the sight of them. Is he giving them to me?

Meds are not what I'd call my friends. Well, for obvious reasons.

I hate everything about them.

Everything.

Still, I take them from his hands. I do it.

My fingers might be trembling, and I might be apprehensive but I transfer them onto my palm, whispering, "Can I have some water, please?"

His eyes turn harsh at my question. "Aren't you going to ask what they're for?"

I should. I really should.

But I won't.

As much as I hate the meds, I love the man giving them to me. And I trust him. Last night was just the beginning. I'm going to show my faith in him every chance I get.

I'm going to show him that he's perfect exactly the way he is.

I keep staring into his eyes as I shake my head. "No."

Simon gnashes his teeth. A vein pops at his temple and I feel like he's going to explode. But he releases a breath and pinches the bridge of his nose.

"Damn it, Willow," he curses, exasperated. "You're supposed to ask."

"Why?"

"Because it's the smart thing to do. What if someone gives you something that could harm you? You're on all kinds of drugs. What if these hurt you? What if these cause an Adverse Drug Reaction in your system? What then? Do you know how stupid it is to take something – meds, no less – from a man you don't know?"

"I know it's stupid. But it's you. I do know you."

Scoffing, he shakes his head. "You don't."

Why don't you tell me?

"I know you won't hurt me."

Simon breathes out a long breath again, his chest puffing out in his crisp blue shirt. It goes so well with his eyes. He snatches those white monsters from my hand and holds one up. "This. Is for your pain. It's Tylenol. It won't react to any of the drugs you're taking."

Oh.

Oh God.

Why? Why did he have to go and do that?

He's stupid, isn't he? He has to be. He's completely sealed his fate. He got me pills because he thought I was in pain.

How the fuck can I let him go now? And then, to grow all tight when I say I trust him? How can I *not* trust him?

Idiot. He's a major idiot.

An idiot I'm irrevocably in love with.

He tries to give the pill back to me, but I don't take it. Instead, I open my mouth and peek my tongue out. I want him to feed it to me.

His cheekbones turn dark with a flush that I find so fascinating, so alluring that I want to touch it. But I won't. Not yet. I want him to fix my pain first. I know it'll soothe him; he's big on consequences.

When he places the pill on my tongue, I close my lips around his fingers and suck on them. Like I would suck on his cock. As soon as this pill business is over.

His gray eyes turn almost black, like a storm is coming and I'll have to batten down the hatches. The poor man doesn't know that I love the storms. They don't scare me. And neither does he.

I let go of his fingers and he offers me a glass of water. "Drink."

His voice is rough, and as I take a sip of water and swallow the medicine, I glance at his pants. Yup, he's turned on. Hard and ripe for me.

When I'm done, I give him back the glass and swing my legs back and forth, biting my lip.

His puff of breath is both frustrated and turned on. Then he picks up the other pill. "And this… you know what this is for?"

I shake my head.

My ignorance doesn't help with the tightness of his features and body. I wish I could take away his frustration with my touch but he clearly has something to say and a point to make. So I'm being good and listening to him.

"This is the morning-after pill," he almost snaps.

And my breath hitches. I stop swinging my legs.

Finally, he's happy with my reaction. I can see that. His eyes look satisfied with that fearful hiccup in my breath. "You know why you have to take this?"

I grab the end of the table to keep myself from sagging. The fullness that I've been feeling ever since I got up in the morning acts up now. It's much worse, much more potent, alive, as I relive those moments from last night.

I'm reliving every stroke, every ridge and groove of his cock as it slid in and out of my snug channel. He was bare inside me.

"B-because we didn't… I…"

Finally, he touches me. He puts both his hands on my waist and hauls me even closer. "Because you drive me so crazy, you tempt me so fucking much that I forgot the condom. I didn't even think about it."

I see him coming on my untamed curls and my stomach, and I swear I can still feel his cum on there.

"But you came on my... You came outside."

Groaning, he fists the fabric of my t-shirt. "Yeah. And that's because I'm sick. I wanted to see my cum spray on your cunt. I wanted to brand you."

His words make me arch my back and show off my heavy, engorged tits to him. "Oh. I d-didn't..."

"Do you know when I realized I fucked up?" He swallows. "When I woke up with your blood on my cock."

A tiny whimper escapes me, and I grip his biceps. "I woke up with blood on my thighs too. And your cum. Dried up on my tummy."

His forehead is resting on mine and I can feel his words on my mouth when he says, "Do you know what happens when a man comes inside you, Willow? Do you know what will happen if I fill your pussy with my cum?"

I jerk out a nod. "Yes."

"Yeah? Tell me."

My fingers dig into his arms at his tone. Like he thinks I really *am* naïve. He thinks I don't know anything about the world and it's his job to educate me. He's really teaching me worldly things.

I don't know why this turns me on so much. But it does.

Gasping, I begin, "If y-you come inside me and fill me up with your cum, I can get pregnant."

The P word makes me both horny and scared. I'm so confused by my reaction. The only thing I should be feeling is fear. I should be scared of getting pregnant. I shouldn't be getting wet.

Simon brings his hand to cup my cheek. "Do you want

that? Do you want to get pregnant, Willow?"

At last, I feel the right emotion. Fear.

My eyes widen, and I shake my head, almost violently. "No. Never. I don't…"

Simon frowns, his sexual haze leaching out of his eyes as he studies my reaction. "You don't what?"

Swallowing, I grip his shirt. "I don't ever want to get pregnant. Not ever."

He moves away, causing me to let go of him. He's all serious now as he scrutinizes me. "Explain."

I huff, blowing at my bangs.

What just happened?

I'm hot and horny and so fucking afraid at the same time. I huff again.

I've never really thought about getting pregnant. I mean, come on. I've only had one boyfriend and until last night, I never even had sex.

Unlike other girls, I daydream about death, not giving birth to new life.

But as soon as Simon uttered the word pregnant, I knew. I knew it in my heart that I'll never have babies. I can never have them.

"Look at me, Simon. Look at where I am. I have to take meds, do therapy to be normal. Not that I'm ashamed of it. I mean, I'm trying not to be. I'm learning. But I can't have babies. Ever. What if my baby turns out like me? What if I curse her with my illness." I sweep my bangs off my face. "I can't do that to her. I –"

"Willow," he cuts me off with a black frown. "Shut the fuck

up."

And I do.

Simon crosses his arms across his chest. "You'll have babies."

"What?"

"Not now but when the time is right. And you won't think about cursing them because it's bullshit. There's nothing wrong with you. I've said it a hundred times before and I'm saying it again, you're a fighter. There's nothing wrong with being a fighter. You're not less than anyone. If anything, you'll teach them to be like you. You'll teach them to fight. Am I clear?"

My eyes have welled up and my throat is full of one and only one emotion: love. For him.

As if the pills weren't enough? He has to go and do this.

Seriously. If I wasn't in love with him, I would think he's being cruel by being so... *nice.*

I nod wordlessly.

"Excellent," he clips and produces the pill in front of me from out of nowhere. "Even though, I didn't come inside you. We're not taking any chances."

Dutifully, I open my mouth and he puts it on my tongue before giving me a drink of water. Then he sets the glass aside and flicks the bangs out of my eyes, wiping the tears that have escaped off my cheeks.

God, I'm such a mess. Such a giant, sniffling mess.

"I'm sorry," I whisper.

"For what?"

"For ruining your plans."

He eyes me, still tucking my wayward hair behind my ears. "My plans."

I nod, clutching his shirt and bringing him in for a hug. I put my head on his chest and swing my legs to and fro. "You wanted to have sex with me, but I ruined it by crying."

His laugh vibrates his chest. "What makes you think I wanted to have sex with you?"

Shifting away, I look up at his smiling face. "Why did you close the blinds?"

"There's too much sun."

"There's not. You locked the door, too."

"Too much noise."

"That's such a lame answer."

I glance down at his dick again. It's straining against his pants. I wouldn't call it all hard but it's half-mast, making a liar out of him.

"Your dick is getting hard," I tell him, squirming on his desk, watching his erection getting to its full height.

"It's biology. If you keep staring at it with your bratty eyes, it will get that way."

I give him those bratty eyes. "I wanna suck it." He flinches at my declaration and I keep going. "But I won't ask you for that. And you know what else? I won't be begging you to fuck me, either."

"You won't?"

I pout. "No. Because if someone wants to fuck me, then he should have the courtesy to tell me that himself. I have pride, you know."

Finally, he stops smoothing down my hair and starts playing with the seam of my lips. "That's good, Willow. Pride is good. One of us should have that." I try to press my thighs together but can't. Because he's between them. I end up squeezing his hips.

"You don't have it anymore?" I ask, puffing out those words on the pad of his thumb.

"No."

"Why not?"

"I don't have my pride, Willow, because I feel like a man on death row. Begging for life. Begging to live one more day. Begging to fuck you one more time."

Winding my arms around his neck, I arch my spine. "What'd you do to get on death row?"

"Took your virginity. Made you sore. Made you bleed."

He looks like he's imagining it, making me bleed. I'm imagining it too.

Maybe it wasn't the ideal situation or the place to have sex for the first time. But it was perfect for us.

This is where we met, at Heartstone. This is where I accepted myself and this is where I gave myself to him. I wouldn't change a thing about last night or any of it.

I place a soft kiss on his lips. "Yeah. You did make a mess on me."

Growling, he smacks a hard kiss on my lips, his fingers getting buried in my hair. "Then there's no hope for me, is there? I should be fucking hanged for dirtying up the snow princess."

I shrug. "Maybe you can live one more day. Maybe you can

make it up to me, for making me all dirty and sore, so you can fuck me again."

As soon as I say the words, he slides me off the desk and carries me in his arms. It makes me realize once again how small I am compared to him. How tiny and delicate, and how he can pick me up and put me wherever he wants me.

In this case, it's the brown leather armchair.

He makes me put my knees up there and grab the arm with my sweaty palms, leather sagging under my weight.

I twist and look back. "Simon, I –"

He's behind me, large and looming. His shoulders are jerking up and down with his ragged breaths as he looks up. "I know what you need."

He goes to work on my yoga pants. He pushes them down and down, until they band around mid-thigh, leaving my ass bare and exposed. Despite the embarrassment that he can see everything in the daylight, my entire behind, I breathe in the first sigh of relief. If he's rearranging my clothes, that means I'm one step closer to getting fucked.

And that's all I care about right now.

Simon goes down to his haunches and I feel him sliding something on my feet. My toes wiggle and I realize it's my bunny slippers. I must have lost them somewhere along the five feet to the armchair.

"Keep them on your princess feet. Don't fucking lose them," he commands before putting his mouth directly on my pussy and making all words die on my tongue.

I don't even get the time to appreciate the whole kinkiness

of him putting on my bunny slippers and calling me a princess again. The whole wrongness and rightness of it.

I arch my back as he takes a swipe of my core, trying to move away from his hot tongue because I'm so sensitive and sore. But he grabs hold of my bare ass cheeks and keeps me in place. His mouth stings my swollen and bruised parts, but he's also managing to soothe them.

He's lapping and licking, breathing on my most sensitive part, which is rendered tight because of the lack of space on the chair and the fact that my thighs are almost squished together due to the waistband around them.

When his fingers dig into my ass and he grabs a fistful of flesh, pulling it apart, I bite down on the leather. Its sour taste hits my tongue as Simon digs deeper into my channel. He's licking my hole, going around and around, and I'm leaving indentations of my teeth on the leather writhing against his tongue.

Soon, Simon makes me come with his mouth and the leather absorbs my sobs.

Quitting my pussy, Simon stands up and somehow, I manage to turn around and look at him. Watching my half-nakedness, he unbuttons his pants and lowers them, along with his underwear and gets his cock out. This is the first time I've seen it in daylight.

Jesus, it's big. And swollen.

No wonder I had to jack him off with two hands. The head of it seems purple in color, darker than the rest of the length. And he's oozing out pre-cum. A white, pearly drop that makes me think of white, pearly gates.

Keeper of the black gates of Heartstone has a dick that

makes me think of the white gates of heaven.

God, I want to suck it.

It's like he knows what I'm thinking. "Don't look at me like that."

"Like what?"

"Like you want to hero-worship my cock."

I blush. "I want to."

"Not happening," he growls. "I told you. You don't belong on your knees."

In front of you, I do.

Instead of telling him that, I keep my mouth shut. One day I'll suck his cock no matter what.

I watch him fish out a condom from his lowered pants and something warm overcomes me. This is the final piece. Him taking care of me. Him thinking about fucking me and planning for it.

I rub my thighs together, anticipating the fullness.

Putting the latex on his length, Simon whips his eyes up to mine. "My princess wants to get fucked, doesn't she?"

I nod, biting my lip. "Yes."

The smirk he gives me makes me spill out a drop of my cum. I fucking feel it making its way down my thigh. I've never, not ever, been this turned on.

Once he's done, he puts his hand on my waist, arching me up further. "Good. Because that's what I'm going to do. I'm going to fuck my princess like I'm a goddamn criminal on death row."

With that, he slides his cock into me and I have to bite on to the leather again to keep from screaming.

Simon curses as he bottoms out and I feel like he's gone

further than my stomach. Maybe he's touching my soul in this position, chipping away at it so he can make a permanent place for himself.

God, if that isn't cruelty, a wicked game of sorts, I don't know what is. Making his home inside of me when I don't know what's going to happen in six days.

But I'm not going to think about that when he has begun a rhythm, his hands around my hips.

Actually, I can't even call it a rhythm. It's super unsteady and choppy. He rotates between lazy, long strokes that curl my toes in my soft slippers, and short and fast thrusts that make my breasts shake.

Eventually after probably his tenth stroke or maybe hundredth, I let go of the chair and grab hold of my jiggling tits. I plump and squeeze them as the sound of our slapping flesh fills the room.

I feel like it's too loud, the noises we're making. It's too dangerous. We're tempting fate.

Simon should slow down his thrusts. He shouldn't be driving into me this fast – no matter how good it feels. He shouldn't be bouncing against my ass this way.

Instead of asking him to stop though, I push back. I don't know what I'm thinking or why I'm doing this, but I just can't stop. I have to fuck him back.

Then he changes the angle. He lets go of my hips and buries his hand in my hair, bending over me. His chest and stomach, all corded and tight, scrape against my sweaty spine. His stubbled jaw grazes the side of my cheek as he fucks into me.

This way his hips grind and he's delivering short, deep jabs that I feel in the center of my being.

"Does my princess like it?" he rasps in my ear, his hand grabbing the back of my neck in a possessive hold while his lips place soft kisses in my hair.

I buck again at the word *princess*. If he decides to make a habit of calling me that, I might never come down from this high. I might always be falling. Flying.

I look at him with foggy eyes. "Yes."

"Yeah. I can feel it. I can feel your pussy loving it. She's fucking strangling me."

I reach back and dig my nails in the taut flesh of his ass, his muscles bunching beneath my touch. He groans, and I clench my channel even harder.

"Fuck…"

His thrusts have become completely erratic now, just like his breaths.

Just like *my* breaths.

I'm surrounded by him. His heat. His smell.

His show of dominance.

When Simon captures my mouth in a kiss, I lose control like last night. Everything unravels inside me and I come and come.

I gush. I feel my juices slipping out of my core, sliding down my shaking thighs and quite possibly ruining the leather armchair and his pants. I can't be sure.

Simon doesn't mind though. He keeps kissing me. He keeps pounding into me, his thighs smacking against mine, his chest breathing wildly over me.

When he breaks the kiss, I open my eyes and look into his intense gaze. It is equal parts lust and desperation. Sweat beads on his forehead, and his jaw is clenched.

Slumped on the back of the chair, completely submissive under him, taking his pounding, I whisper, "I kept my slippers on my princess feet for you. L-like you told me. Won't you come for me, Simon? Please come in my princess pussy."

"Jesus Christ..."

His eyes clench shut and his words trail off on a groan. His hips jerk and twist in a final thrust and he fulfils my wish.

He comes for me.

Even though he's wearing a condom and I can't really feel the wetness of his cum, I feel the heat of it. I feel his chest vibrating and his stomach clenching over my back. I feel his random jerks and short thrusts as he straightens up.

Panting, he withdraws his cock from inside me and gathers me in his arms, bridal style. I nuzzle my nose against his warm throat, feeling all kinds of sleepy. I feel like I'm floating on a cloud, on a rainy, fluffy cloud and he's with me.

Simon takes me to the washroom inside his office and sits me down on the marble counter. I watch him with heavy lids as he takes care of the condom and straightens his clothes.

When he's done, he cups my cheek and makes me focus on him. "How many days, Willow?"

He doesn't have to tell me what he means. I already know. I come down from my high and with a hurting heart, I tell him, "Six."

Letting go of my face, he gives me a somber nod and wets

a tissue in hot water. Then, he cleans me up, my pussy and thighs.

Every second that passes with him cleaning me up, putting me to rights, I feel like he's telling me something.

Only I don't know what.

All I can do is hope that I find out before these six days are out.

Chapter 20

Every day, he asks me how many days are left before The Goodbye.

And every day I think that maybe today he'll say the words that I hear every time I look at him. But it doesn't happen.

It doesn't happen five days away from The Goodbye.

On this day, my mom calls me and tells me that she knows about Lee Jordan. She finally went to my school to get the information of the guy because of whom I jumped, and they told her that they don't have a student by that name.

She asks me why I've been lying to her. Why didn't I tell her about my struggles, about my thoughts? She says she wants me to stay at Heartstone. She says that if I've been lying for so long, then I need a longer time to get better.

"You need to fix this, Lolo," she says, crying. "How do I trust you now? How do I know that you're telling the truth?"

I cry, too. I explain it to her. I explain my struggles and how I didn't want to worry her, but she doesn't listen.

By the end of it, I'm a sobbing mess.

And that's how Simon finds me, walking out of the phone room, my eyes swollen and red. A couple of nurses find me in this state as well. He tells them he's got me and ushers me inside his office, locking the door.

"What happened?" he asks, frowny and alert.

I try to hold on to my composure and not be a bawling baby in front of him. But the thing is that I want to be, and I know I can be. I know that. I know I can cry in front of him. Not because he'll be my hero and solve all my problems. My problems are not solvable, but I know he'll get it. I know he'll listen.

"Nothing."

"Willow." His eyes track the line of my tears and his voice becomes even tighter. "What happened? Why are you crying?"

I wipe the salty water off. "I talked to my mom."

My words make him move and he almost charges toward me in agitation, heaving me up in his arms. He marches over to the windows first – it's raining so no one is outside, but we can't take any chances – and closes the blinds. He walks with me to the couch, settles down with me on his lap and asks me what she said.

I tell him everything. I tell him how my mom finally knows about Lee Jordan and all the lies. I was going to tell her. I wanted to be there to break the news. And now, she's all upset.

"I'm so stupid," I whisper in his neck, crying. "I shouldn't have said anything. I shouldn't have lied. But I got so panicked. And she was so sad, Simon. She thought it was her fault that I jumped. So I made up a story. She'll never forgive me. She'll never get over it."

"She will."

"How do you know?"

"When she sees how well you're doing, you'll convince her."

Curled up in his lap, I glance at his face, finally all cried out. "But I'll have bad days again."

"So you'll talk about it."

"I don't want to disappoint her," I whisper.

His arms tighten around my waist, like he's trying to sink my body into his. "You won't."

Conviction in his tone makes me smile and I sigh against his chest. We sit like this, entwined with each other for a few moments. I feel him rubbing his stubble over my bangs, all calm and relaxed.

"My mom thinks I should stay here longer because I clearly have deeper issues."

His entire body goes stiff. I don't know why I said that. Maybe to see if he'd say something about it. Maybe he'd ask me to stay. I would've laughed, if this wasn't so epically tragic.

Like Heartstone is a hotel and we both just happen to be here for a vacation. Like he's not my psychiatrist and I'm not his patient. He can ask me to stay. He can keep me trapped inside these white walls and psychoanalyze me and feed me meds because he can't let me go.

Because my fixer loves me.

I try to push away from him, heartsick, but he doesn't let me get away. He grabs the back of my neck and pulls me to him, to his mouth, and kisses the fuck out of me.

Then he teaches me to ride his cock. Slow and grinding and

sweaty, our skin slipping over each other. All the while our lips are kissing and our hands are roving. All the while, I'm fisting his hair and he's plumping my ass cheeks. He's looking into my eyes with his gray, passionate ones.

When we finish, he whispers, "How many days?"

"Five."

I wait for him to say something. *Anything.*

But he doesn't.

He doesn't say it the day I ask him to take his shirt off in his office during our appointment. He's looking at me like I've lost my mind.

In my defense, I did the entire meeting without trying to touch him once. I answered all his questions about my meds, my sleep, my group sessions, and individual ones with Josie. I didn't even try to kiss the life out of him when he said he'd talk to my mom about my lying and explain everything to her. Not that I can't handle her myself, but just the fact that he wants to do it makes me want to jump his bones and shower him with all the kisses.

"What? I've never seen your bare chest. Only flashes of it." I bat my eyelashes as I spring up from the chair and walk very casually to the washroom. I stop at the door and crook my finger at him. "Please? I just wanna see it once."

With hooded eyes, he stands up. But before he can take a step toward me, I chirp, "Wear your glasses."

I go in and settle myself on the counter, ready for the show. A second later, he enters, his gaze intense and sparkly behind his specs, and I bite my lip.

God, he's so sexy.

I widen my thighs for him and he settles himself between them. Arrogantly, like he belongs there. He does.

I rub my hands over his shirt-covered chest before going for his buttons and popping them up. He only lets me undo three before he snags the whole fabric in the back and takes it off.

"Oh my…" I breathe, taking in his naked chest for the first time.

Gosh, he works out. Well, I already knew he did but still.

Everything is hard and muscled and corded. His shoulders look like a hilly terrain, going down to his bulging biceps. I trace the green vein on his arm with my finger.

"I have blue veins," I whisper. "I think yours are so sexy."

"I know."

"How?"

"You're almost drooling. That's how."

"I'm not." I squeeze my thighs around his hips, making him laugh.

I bring my fingers to his collarbone, trace the triangle of his throat before moving down to the tight arches of his pecs. I moan as I sink my fingers in his chest hair.

"You're so big. God, I love how big you are." Leaning closer, I smell his skin and flick my tongue around his nipple.

He jerks and his palms cage me on either side. "Yeah? That turn you on?"

"Uh-huh." I'm now at his stomach, all ridged and grooved, slanting down in a V. "It's like you can put me anywhere. Makes me feel so small." *And cherished.*

"You *are* small," he rasps, smelling the line of my neck.

His body is all tight and carved, as if sculpted by divine hands. His flesh is so warm and darker than mine. Masculine. So fucking masculine.

Paired with his glasses, he looks so old and mature that I'm creaming my panties.

His abdomen tightens when I swirl my fingers around his tight belly button and play with the thicker tuft of hair, disappearing down his pants.

I breathe over his chest and kiss his heart, or where his heart is supposed to be. It might be weathered but it's dipped in gold. I reach up and lick the side of his neck, rubbing my nails up and down his sides.

His hands are in my hair now, undoing my topknot so he can wrap those strands around his fingers. "Are you done driving me crazy?"

Feeling super turned on and naughty, I reply, "No."

Simon's body ripples and he pulls my head back, looming over me. "Willow."

I blink up at him. "What? You never let me have any fun. Please? Let me have some fun."

He growls, his jaw working back and forth, his eyes all lusted up. "I'm going to regret this, aren't I?"

I kiss his ticking jaw softly. "Never."

His chest puffs out with his breath and before he can protest more, I slide down the counter and drop to my knees. I take off my shirt and my bra, baring my upper body to him. His nostrils flare as my naked breasts bounce into view.

"Willow —"

I don't let him talk. I don't even want him to think right now. I want to have fun.

"I'm your princess, aren't I?"

His nod is almost imperceptible, but I notice it.

"Your princess wants to suck your cock. Won't you let her?"

There's this need inside of me to show him that I love him. That I want to drink down, suck off his pain, his demons. Reward him for all his hard work. For coming to my rescue even when I don't need it. On my knees.

"Willow, you don't –"

"I do. I do belong on my knees because I want to hero-worship your cock, Simon."

"Ah, Jesus…" He groans, looking at the ceiling.

I guess that's my cue. I work quickly on his belt – I'm a fast learner so it goes much more smoothly than it did the first time. Lowering his pants and his boxer shorts, I palm his hard cock. I nose his strong thighs, kissing the warm, hairy flesh.

I squeeze his dick, making him growl, making his abdominal muscles clench. And then, I lean forward and catch his shaft in my mouth. His flavor – so musky and erotic – explodes on my tongue and it's like kissing the great depths of him.

The real him. Rather than his lips.

I swirl my tongue around the head of his dick as both my hands grip the base of his length. My mouth is getting saturated with the musky taste of him because the more I lave his head, the more I lash the vein on the underside of his cock, the more cum he makes for me.

And well, the more cum he makes for me, the more cum

I make for him. My pussy is clenching and juicing up like a fruit, and I have to reach one hand down my yoga pants and slather my own wetness, widening my thighs.

"Fuck…" Simon curses, gripping my hair.

As in-experienced as I am, I still know how to draw conclusions from the things he's done to me. The very first night I came on his cock, he asked me to smack myself with his dick. So I take my mouth off him and slap his wet shaft on my tongue, my lips.

I know he likes to see me all wet and juicy, so I even smack his dick on my face, my jaw, making myself all wet and sloppy for him. Moaning for him. Dying for him. I know he likes to lube his cock with the cream I make for him. So, I gather my moisture in the hand with which I'm playing with my cunt. Then, I take it out of my pants and rub it up and down his arousal, slathering him with my wetness.

I know he likes to be deep, deep inside of me, so I take him into my mouth again and open my jaw wide and shove him down as much as I can.

He groans above me, his entire body shaking.

God, he's so sexy, so mine like this.

I don't ever want to stop. I don't ever want to stop tasting him, tasting his dark skin, drinking down his cum.

It's mine. He's mine.

But I have to. Because I wanna do something else too.

I take my mouth off his dick and sit up straight. Making a valley of my tits, I hug his wet, juicy cock and pump it up and down. Like I think about all alone in my bed.

"Goddamn it, Willow," he grunts, his head bowing forward, his black eyes on me.

He's spurting pre-cum with my every stroke. And every time I push him up, I lick that pre-cum off his slit.

I do it over and over. Pump him up and down between my tits. Lap up his cream with my tongue, suck on his head like candy. My throat, my jaw, my chest, my entire skin smells of him, is saturated with his cream.

And my vision is filled with him, horny and aroused, shuddering and groaning.

A second later, he takes over. He pushes my tits in his big hands and hugs his own dick with them, tighter, moving up and down. His knees are bent as he pumps himself between the channel I created for him. I rake my nails on his thighs, on his clenching ass, all the while staring up at him, at his turned-on face, his furrowed brow and harsh, mean mouth.

I see him tremble massively, his fingers tugging on my nipples as he comes. Quickly, I close my mouth around the end of his cock so I can swallow his cum. It's musky and spicy and thick.

After we're done, he pulls me up gently, cleans me up, putting my clothes back on me. He looks at me like I'm so precious. It makes me wanna blurt out all my feelings for him.

He kisses my entire face and asks, "How many days?"

I stare at his sweaty, beautiful chest before looking deep into his eyes. "Four."

I want him to say something. Anything. Give me some indication of the future.

Say it, Simon. Say something.

He doesn't.

His lips are sealed, and his nod is grim and tight.

Neither does he say anything when we meet in the hallway by Beth's office the next day. He's staring at the same pictures.

Now, I understand why these photos depict the happiness instead of the crude and gritty reality. It's because they are a beacon of hope. This place can be dismal and lonely, and that's why these photos are meant to shine.

I get it now.

I stand by him and say the same thing I said a long time ago. "Interesting photos."

He faces me, and I look at him with hope. Maybe today he'll tell me about his dad. Maybe after all this time, I've showed him enough. I've showed him that I trust him and no matter what it is, my faith in him won't go away.

But when he speaks, his words aren't what I want them to be. "How many days?"

"Three."

He nods and walks away.

***

Two days before The Goodbye, there's a storm outside. Rain batters and beats this Victorian building, and everyone is cooped up inside. The girls are in the TV room, like most of the patients. I, however, am in the library.

I still can't believe Beth ordered all these Harry Potter books based on my suggestion. Like, wow. An entire shelf has been dedicated to my favorite series of all time. I need to thank her before I leave.

I'm standing by the shelves, *Harry Potter and the Half-Blood Prince* in my hands, when Simon walks in. Ever since we met in the hallway yesterday and I thought he'd talk to me about his dad, my heart has been heavy, and I have to really focus to not let it show.

Smiling is the key.

So I do that. "Hey, Dr. Blackwood."

I'm aware that the nurse is right here, sitting at the desk in the front with a book of her own.

He walks closer, watching me in that thorough way of his. I hope he doesn't find out that my feelings are in turmoil. That every night this week I've gone to sleep crying.

"Beth ordered all these books for me. I think Josie told her all the times I complained about it," I tell him, hugging my copy to my chest.

He doesn't look at the books, keeping his focus on me. "Maybe she did."

I swallow, my throat filling up with things I want to say. Things I want to ask. Maybe I should let go of my stupid vow and ask him directly. Maybe he's waiting for me to ask him.

But I don't get the chance because he reaches out and takes the book from my hands, like he usually does when I'm hugging them for strength. Perhaps he does it because he doesn't want me to hide from him.

"*Half-Blood Prince*," he reads off the title. "I've never liked Harry Potter. Actually, no. It's a lie. I did like it. I was jealous of the characters. Jealous because they all had magic. They could make things happen just by drinking a potion or flicking a wand."

Oh my God.

Is he telling me?

Is my patience going to pay off? Does he finally realize he can trust me?

I go still. Like, completely still. I'm afraid to breathe, to blink. To make any sudden movements that might spook him.

Although I do cross my fingers and my big toes inside my bunny slippers.

"My mom made me read the first three when they came out. Well, she wanted to read them herself. I was there for the company. I just kept going after that."

Simon's looking out the window to our side, appearing lost, and it's such torture to just stand here, immobile, so far away from him. But I don't know what else to do.

"She wouldn't go to sleep until we finished them. And I couldn't say no to her. I could never say no to my mom, actually. She loved being outdoors. Loved the willow tree in our backyard. I remember spending my summer vacations under that tree. When I was a kid, I used to think that my mom was so bright and full of life. I thought she had so much energy. She was always doing something, going somewhere, and I was always with her. She took me everywhere, vacations, shopping, and I thought it was because she loved me.

"She did love me, but she took me with her because she was alone. Because she needed company and my dad was always busy. He was always here. At Heartstone. With his patients. And my mom…" He sighs. "Well, my mom was lonely. She waited for him. She was good at that. Waiting. And my dad was good at saying no. So that left me. I don't know how I compared but I did everything

I could. To make her feel less lonely."

My heart's beating so loud. Louder than the storm outside. It's a wonder I can hear him. It's a wonder I can understand what he's saying.

Most of all, it's a wonder I haven't hugged him yet. This lonely, lonely man.

Simon's always been a fixer, hasn't he? Always been a hero. He's a rock.

But right now, he's a brittle one. He could break any second; he's so stiff. So devastated.

I know I said I wouldn't ask but I think he needs this. He needs the push.

"What... What happened to her?"

Simon looks away from the window at my words, and for a second I think I've ruined it all. He won't tell me.

But then, he puts the book on the shelf and shoves his hands inside his pockets. In a flash, he's back to being himself. He isn't devastated anymore. He's angry. Furious, even.

"She killed herself."

My mouth falls open as I feel the breath getting knocked out of me. "Simon —"

The look he gives me is the angriest I've ever gotten from him and I almost draw back in my place. "I'd like to see you in my office this afternoon."

With that, he leaves, and all I can do is watch him do it.

Hours later, when I go to his office and see the closed blinds and hear the two clicks of the door closing and locking, I don't feel the same satisfaction as I felt days ago.

"Simon, listen—"

"Don't say no," he rasps.

There's so much anguish packed in those three words that my tears start falling. Like I'm the rain and he's the cloud that makes me flow.

Does he really think I'll ever say no to him? If he does, then he really doesn't know the things I feel for him. The things I'll do for him. The depths I'll go to and fall in, for him.

Simon Blackwood doesn't know anything, then.

I nod and he's on me.

It's okay. We can talk later. Right now, if he needs my body to feel better, then I'll give it to him.

I become completely pliable as he lowers me down on the hardwood floor. He makes quick work of my clothes and enters me in one smooth thrust, because even agitated I'm wet as fuck for him.

It's like my body knows he needs me right now. He needs me more than he's ever needed me and every feminine part of me is loose to let him in.

My pussy makes cream for him so it's easier for him to slide in. My internal muscles clench and release so he can get the maximum pleasure. My skin becomes more sensitive, softer, more pillowy so he can dig his fingers in.

I am his playground, and he can play all he wants. I'm his medicine in this moment, curing his illness. His princess slaying his dragons.

His rhythm is choppy but even then, we move in sync. I think this is the most in sync, in rhythm we've ever been. He's staring into my eyes with such passion, such turbulence that I wind my legs around his waist and arch my back to let him in deeper. The hardness of the floor doesn't even register with how hard he is above me.

Simon has an arm braced up by my head and his other is clutched in a fist in my hair. It's like he's holding on to me because he thinks he might drown. The look in his gaze is so lost and so horny, it breaks my heart.

I won't let him drown; I tell this to him with my eyes. I tell him when I gasp his name. I tell him when he pants into my mouth, his brows bunched up in a heavy frown.

"Simon," I whimper his name and he locks our mouths in a kiss.

That's when I come, even though I wasn't looking for it. But Simon's kisses are orgasmic. They push me over the edge every time.

And while I'm clenching around him, he withdraws, takes off his condom and comes on my pussy and my wild curls, branding me like that first time.

Despite the waves of orgasm flashing through both of us, he pulls me to my feet. With glittering eyes, he puts his hands under my ass and heaves me up, taking me in his arms.

In his usual fashion, he walks me to the washroom and sits me down on the counter. The marble is so cold against my naked butt.

Then, he goes back out and gets my clothes. Wetting a tissue and cleaning me up, he puts me back into my clothes like I'm a child. I let him do it because I know it makes him happy, smoothing down my hair, taking care of me.

But I can't bear the silence any longer. "Simon —"

He looks up, his eyes cracked open in a way I can't put my finger on. "Willow, I…"

Even though he trails off, my breathing escalates. My heart races. It pounds, and goose bumps come alive on my skin.

Because for some reason I think… I think he's going to say it. He's going to say what I've been waiting for.

His chest is moving up and down, just like mine. We're breathing as one. Me and him. I bet the looks in our eyes match too because I'm cracked open in the way he is, as well.

It makes me realize what it is I'm seeing in his expression. It's vulnerability. We're both vulnerable. Flayed. Bare. Naked.

And we're both broken, in this moment. Broken and melted.

My ice king is going to say it.

He's going to say he loves me.

"I… I —"

His words get swallowed up by the ringing of the phone and I could scream with how cliché this is. How fucking cliché and unfortunate.

A cruel joke.

"Simon, don't. Please." I grip his bicep, but he shakes his head and leaves me there.

Although, he can't get to his phone on time, and I hear a man's voice when the machine picks up the call — Seriously, what era is this? Every fucking thing in this Victorian mansion is old-fashioned:

"Hey, man. Pick up your fucking cell phone. We need to talk about Claire. Two weeks are up."

I come out of the bathroom and I wouldn't have thought anything of it or the name Claire, if I hadn't seen Simon transform right in front of me.

Going all tight and icy, standing by the desk, staring at the phone. It's so startling, his change. So abrupt and so shocking, after seeing him unravel a thousand times.

My heart's racing but for a very different reason now and something like dread makes a home in my stomach. "Simon –"

He whirls to face me. "Get out."

"What?"

"Get. Out."

"But –"

"Leave, Willow."

I don't.

How can I? After everything. After what he told me and what he was *going* to tell me.

His fury rises, rises and rises, until it spills over and he lashes out, "Willow, for once in your goddamn life, will you do as I say?"

I flinch at his voice. I've never seen him like this. So cold and so heated at the same time. All the lines on his body and face set in stone. It cracks my heart, right in the middle. Crushes it, beats it into a pulp.

As soon as I feel my eyes watering, I *do as he says.*

I leave, realizing that he never asked me his usual question: *how many days.*

Chapter 21

One day.

Before The Goodbye.

And the man I'm in love with isn't even looking at me.

It's like the way he looked at me yesterday when I thought he was finally going to say something, acknowledge this thing between us, was it. He has used up all his intensity, all his passion, his heat in that one look and he doesn't have anything left now.

He's ice cold.

Or maybe it's all in my head. Maybe he wasn't even going to say anything. Maybe he never intended to say it, and whatever I've been feeling for the past few days is nothing but a delusion.

I'm delirious. In schizophrenic love.

With the man standing across the room. He's the tallest man at my party – my going away party. He's also the most aloof, tucked away in a corner. He's not even eating cake.

Renn and the girls ordered a lime cake for me, specifically. And we're all assembled in the rec room – patients, techs, nurses, therapists.

How ironic is it that it all started with a party? My eighteenth birthday party. We had a chocolate cake with fresh raspberries in the filling. The number of people who attended was bigger, but I didn't know more than half of them, and they didn't know me. They came because my family invited them, and maybe because they wanted free booze and cake.

On the Inside though, people do know me. Maybe some of them I haven't talked to personally, but still. They know I'm one of them.

So far, Annie, Lisa, Roger, a few other patients, and a couple of nurses, along with Hunter and Beth, they all have come to wish me good luck for the life on the Outside.

Ellen from the reflections group has come to hug me and tell me how proud of me she is. Hers was the group where I confessed my lies and accepted the fact I do have suicidal ideation, and that I'm a fighter.

I'm the chosen one, you see.

We all are. We're the ones who choose to fight. Every single day. Every single moment.

We don't give up when thoughts get dark. We don't give up when meds don't work. We don't give up when our inner demons overpower the demons on the outside.

We don't give up. Period.

We choose to be more than our illness and yes, it's hard. And it's fucking unfair. But when is life ever fair? You make the best of what you've been dealt and we're here because every single one of us wants to be the best that we can be.

Until six weeks ago, I never would've even thought of being here. But now, I don't want to leave. It's like I'm going to leave my family, a different, quirky family and all I want to do is break down and cry.

Will he come for me, if I do that? Will he look at me then, if I sob and wail?

Just the fact that I'm contemplating crying so he pays me some attention proves that I'm borderline psychotic.

But I do want to do that, psychotic or not. I do want to make a scene, start a commotion so he'll come for me. Maybe even keep me here, locked up.

Because I want to know what happened.

What the fuck happened?

Everything was fine – well, everything was broken because he hadn't confessed his feelings for me or given me any indication of what the future holds for us, but still, things were fine.

I thought we were making progress. Every time we talked; every time we fucked; every time he took care of me, it made me feel that we came that much closer. I thought he'd say something before I left. Or at least give me his phone number or some clue that he still wanted to be in touch with me on the Outside.

Anything.

But then one phone call about Claire and everything just shattered.

Like always, I've analyzed it to death and I think this must have something to do with his old job. I've always known something's eating at him and this must be it. Well, besides the fact that his mom killed herself. No wonder he's so cold and seemingly unemotional.

But that doesn't stop my devastation. It doesn't stop me from being sad and angry that I meant so little to him.

Before I can drown in my head, Josie finds me, and we chat for a little bit. She tells me again how proud she is of me and I tear up, thanking her.

Then I remember something. "Oh hey, I, uh, forgot to thank you for the books."

"What books?" She takes a bite of her cake.

"Harry Potter. I can't believe you actually listened to me. Thank you for that. Though you didn't have to get like, a hundred copies and dedicate an entire shelf to them. But you know, I'm not complaining."

She's frowning. "I didn't do anything."

"What?"

"I don't handle books. Or stuff like that."

"You must've said something to someone? To Beth?"

She shakes her head. "Nope. I didn't say anything. Maybe you should talk to her. She and Dr. Martin, they're the ones who handle stuff like that. Well, now it would be Dr. Blackwood."

"Dr. B-Blackwood?" I ask in a squeaky voice.

"Yeah. Since Dr. Martin isn't here right now."

"Right."

She smiles and turns away from me to talk to someone else. Or maybe it's me who turns away. I can't say.

I can't say anything right now. I don't even think I'm *thinking* right now.

Everything is a huge, giant mess in my head.

Simon ordered the books?

No.

Actually, Simon ordered a lot of books. A lot.

You guys should really do something about your library. There isn't one Harry Potter book in there.

I did say that to him. A long time ago. The day he saved Annie. I was so impressed by that. I only said it to him because I wanted to hold on to my old ways. I was being stubborn while completely crushing on him.

Did he really remember it? Did he really, *really* buy those books for me?

I mean it could be Beth, too. But somehow, I don't believe it. I don't believe that she would order multiple copies of my favorite, favorite series – the series I'm basically an infomercial for; his words, not mine – and practically dedicate a corner for them.

Simon bought those books, and he bought them for me. He did, didn't he?

My heart hammers inside my chest as I look at where he was standing before, in a corner, leaning against the wall. Kind of scowling but not really. But he isn't there anymore. He's gone.

"Oh God, where did you go?" I mutter to myself.

I feel such a visceral loss as I spin around, searching for him. Such a visceral, massive loss for someone who's only left a room. Strangely, it feels like he left my life. And I'm still here. I'm not even gone yet.

I still have one day.

I need to find him. I need to tell him. He needs to know how I feel.

Because *I* know how he feels.

Because I know he was going to say it before everything went to hell in such a dramatic fashion. I can't lose faith now when I've been such a believer this past week.

My feet start moving and I'm out the door before I can really think about what I'm doing. I left my eighteenth birthday party too. That night I wanted to jump and fall dead to the ground, just so I could shut up the voices.

Today as well, my voices are loud, and they are telling me to jump. They are telling me to take a leap.

And I'm doing it. I'm taking a leap of faith, hoping that he won't let me fall and die. Hoping that he'll catch me.

I find his retreating figure in the hallway, and I call out his name, stopping him in his tracks. He turns around and there he is.

Simon, the love of my life. A life that's always plagued me. A life I've always wanted to end. A life I'll always *want* to end, but I'll fight. I'll do what I have to do to stay alive because it's mine.

And he's mine too.

He frowns. "Willow."

His voice clenches my heart and makes my legs tremble with all the love, as I approach him.

"Can I please talk to you? In your office?"

"Actually, I —"

"Please," I say, cutting him off. I'm not going to let him hide from me. Not right now.

There's a tic in his jaw, a pulse that indicates that he's going to refuse me. But, surprisingly and to my relief, he nods.

I follow him to his office and when he holds the door open,

I step over the threshold.

Simon is still at the door, though. "Can I help you with something? I'm a little —"

I spin around to face him. "Who's Claire?"

Okay, so that wasn't my plan.

I don't exactly know what my plan was, honestly. But it wasn't this. It wasn't to blurt this out and have him go all rigid on me.

He's gone completely cold and almost menacing, and his voice isn't any better than it was yesterday when he asked me to get out of his office. "What?"

I can either take it back or I can roll with it. Fisting my hands on my sides, I decide to go for it. What's the worst thing that can happen?

Well, no. I'm not going there.

Happy thoughts.

"Who is she?" I swallow "Y-you got the phone call yesterday and since then things have been weird. I —"

"Is that all?"

There's no movement on his body. I don't even think he moved his lips when he said that. It's so unnerving to be standing here in front of him, jittery and shaky when he's so still and immobile.

"I'm sorry?"

A clench on his jaw, at last. Some sign that he hasn't frozen over.

"Is that all?" he repeats slowly, something flashing across his features. "Because if it is, I have a lot of work to do. So, you need to leave."

I take in a deep breath. There's a humming in my stomach. A swarm of butterflies and bees and wasps and dragonflies. It's a full-on plague and I want to press my hand there to calm it down. But that will mean showing him my weakness and I can't do that. Not now.

"Who is she?" I ask again. "Why did you turn all, I don't know, icy and unapproachable? Who is she, Simon? I, honestly –"

"I'm asking you to leave. Right now."

"Tell me who she is, Simon."

"Who she is, is none of your business." He hasn't moved an inch from the door. Still, I feel him and his almost-lashing voice from somewhere close. "Do you understand me?"

"I have a right to know," I say, my heartbeats getting louder and louder.

Yes, I do.

I do. I do. I do.

Please don't make me a liar. Please tell me who she is.

"Excuse me?"

God, has he ever looked more ferocious than this? His brows are bunched up and his jaw is clamped so tight. And his eyes? His eyes are shards of darkness, glinting and so intense.

Every second that passes makes me even more agitated and scared. I mean, I wasn't expecting him to be receptive of my words, but I didn't think he'd be so clammed up and tightly fisted, either.

"I have a right, Simon," I tell him resolutely, like I'm standing in a storm and refusing to back down from the thunder. "To know. And to ask."

I straighten my spine and clench my stomach. Maybe it will hurt less until we get to the point where he actually gives in and tells me.

Simon cocks his head to the side, as if genuinely curious. "What makes you think that? That you have a right to know anything."

"B-because you bought the books."

Because you love me. And I love you.

I still can't believe he did that. I can't believe he never said anything about it. At the library when I told him about thanking Josie and Beth, he didn't say anything. He didn't even mention it.

But that's the thing, isn't it? Simon never says anything. And if there was ever an epitome of actions speak louder than words, then this is it.

"What?"

"You bought those Harry Potter books."

"So?"

I close my eyes for a second before saying, "For me. You bought them for me."

"So?"

God, why does he have to be so wordless, though? Why can't he just admit it, make it easy? His stare is so lifeless and dead. As if I might be speaking in tongues. As if he doesn't understand me.

Why is he making me fight like this?

I'm so tired of fighting. For him. For everything.

I wipe my nose with the back of my hand and blink my tear-stained eyes. "So, it means that there's something between us.

You…" Another wipe of my nose, another blink of my eyes. "You have feelings for me and I have feelings for you too. I've always had them."

As soon as I say these words, I know I've made a terrible mistake. It's like watching history repeat itself.

Wasn't I here only a couple of weeks ago, saying the same thing to him? And didn't he reject me?

This déjà vu is making me want to throw up and I can't resist it this time. I put a hand to my stomach. It's fucking dizzy.

Simon squints his eyes. "I think we've had this conversation before, haven't we?"

Yes. We have.

But then, I didn't know the magnitude of feelings I'd develop for him in just two weeks. I didn't know that he was harboring the same fantasies as me. I didn't know the little things about him.

His little smirks, his sighs and groans. His heat and his skin. How he's so patient and wonderful and caring. How he can't fathom the thought of me hurting and how he beats himself up for the littlest things.

"You can't lie to me, Simon." I take a step toward him. "I know you. I might not know all the things about you. All the facts. But I *know* you. I've felt you." Another step closer, as I continue, "You're a good man, Simon. You have such a good heart and I don't know why you don't think so. I don't understand it, but I swear to God, you do. I've never met someone like you. In fact, I don't even think there *is* anyone like you."

Somehow, my voice is still steady even as my body is shivering. I reach him, craning my neck up so I can take him in.

"You're not some criminal from the wrong side of town. You're not the man on death row. You're the king, Simon. You're my king. I-I was born for you. My illness, The Roof Incident. They aren't random. I was meant to be here, and you were, too. Whatever I went through in my life, it was because I was meant to meet you. And you were meant to meet me, too."

I go to touch his face, maybe soften him up a little bit, but he grabs my hand before I can make contact. His hold is fierce, *painfully* fierce, and I clench my lips against the pain.

"Are you done?"

"Si –"

He squeezes my wrist, harder than he ever has before, and a tiny hiss escapes me. He doesn't let go, however. He watches me squirm. He increases the pressure and doesn't ease up.

On the night he took my virginity, he told me that I didn't wanna see him lose it. I think this is what he meant. This violence. "Simon, please, you're hurting me."

That's when he releases me. "Now, get the fuck out."

I rub my wrist and stand my ground. "You did that on purpose. You deliberately tried to hurt me. I know that. You're not like this. I've seen you all –"

He stops my words with a short, harsh burst of laughter. "God, I knew this was a bad idea," he mutters, almost to himself before focusing on me with lethal eyes. "I knew it the moment I laid eyes on you. I knew you were young. You were reckless. You were emotional and still, I fucked you. Let me tell you how it is, Willow."

This time, he moves in closer. He takes not one but two

steps, three. Until he's looking over me. A black, thundering cloud with gray eyes and a stubbled, hard jaw.

"I fucked you," he says rudely. "Despite my better judgment, I fucked my patient. You're young. Beautiful. There's a wildness in you that called to me. And yes, you're tight as fuck, Willow, and men like that. I'm a man, aren't I? A weak, pathetic man who couldn't resist a good fuck. That's what it was. That's what you felt. A man in heat. A man going for tight-as-fuck pussy. I don't know how else to explain it to you. How much plainer I can get but this is it, you understand? It was fucking phenomenal, but it was just that. A fuck."

I'm watching his mouth move, I'm seeing it happen, but I can't believe it. I can't believe the things he's saying.

"No," I whisper.

Or maybe I just shake my head.

Or maybe I do both.

Everything is a little confusing right now. It has been this way since I found out about the books.

"Yes. I don't have feelings for you. I never did, and I never will. You'll get out of here tomorrow like you were meant to. And we'll probably never see each other again, like we were *meant* to." He straightens up then. "But I'm not the kind of man who shirks away from responsibilities. If you feel inclined to report this, I won't stop you."

Report him?

Is that what he's thinking of right now? That I'll report him? Is that what's going through his head when he's breaking my heart?

"In fact, I'd encourage you to," he continues with a grave face. "You don't want someone like me taking advantage of you in the future."

"I-in the future?"

"Yes. In the future."

"Is that what you think about, when you think of the future? Me with someone else?"

"Frankly, I haven't thought much about you and the future at all."

I have so many thoughts inside my head. They are screaming and screaming, battering down my skull but for some reason only a whisper slips out. "You're lying."

He studies my face. His gray, harsh-as-winter eyes follow the path of my tears. Non-stop and never-ending but silent, unlike the chaos in my head.

Moving away, he walks to his desk, picks something up before turning around. I look down to find him offering me a tissue.

He carries it so casually as he replies, "I'm not you."

Something happens to me then.

Something that I've experienced before for sure, but not with this intensity. Not with this ferociousness and savagery.

For reasons unknown, Simon Blackwood has always managed to make me smile, make me happy, make me calm.

So it's probably fair, poetic even, that he's the one to awaken the hurricane inside me.

He's the one to make me fucking lose it.

All the screaming and shouting inside my head breaks free as I launch myself at him. I fucking ram my body against his like

I'm a train wreck. A wrecking ball.

I don't know what I'm doing except I know I'm screaming and my hands are moving like a windmill. My fists are colliding with something hard, something solid and all I know is that I wanna beat it, batter it, roar at it.

I wanna smash that solid, coiled strength and reduce it to what I am right now: broken and bruised.

And why not?

The man I've flown my body into doesn't seem very inclined to stop me. Maybe he knows he deserves it. He deserves every single punch, every single kick, every single scratch on his neck, on his face, every single push and tug of his shirt, his hair.

He deserves all of it. All of my wrath.

I'm hitting him and hitting him and crying and sobbing, all the while calling him a liar.

Because he is. He has to be.

If he isn't, then I'm fucking insane. I'm a psycho to think that he ever loved me.

I don't know how long I've been going at him, slapping him, punching him, but one second, I'm striking his solid frame, flaying my own knuckles, and the next, I'm flying through the air, it seems, my legs dangling, my screams louder than ever.

There's a band around my waist, a warm, alive band. Someone's arm.

Through my rage and the blur of my tears, I see the crowd gathered inside the room. I see Simon all messed up, his shirt untucked, scratches along the line of his jaw and face.

He's trying to say something to me, probably calm me

down. There are other people, too. They are saying things to me as well. But I can't listen to them. I don't want to.

I want Simon to tell me why he was lying.

Why is he breaking my heart? Why is he doing this to me? What have I done to deserve this?

A flashback grips me, then and throws me back into the past. The hospital room, my crying mom, the doctors. Everyone looking at me like there was something wrong with me. Everyone looking at me like I was an animal, needed to be put down.

But unlike that day, I'm not afraid of what's to come.

In fact, I want it. I want the numbness. I want that sting. The needle. Let them put me down. Let them fucking do it.

I'm not a hysterical patient with no rational thought. I'm an insane, heartbroken girl in full possession of my mental faculties.

Let *him* fucking do it.

I won't calm down, no matter what.

I flail my legs, my arms, until they don't let me anymore. I scream harder and harder, until I feel my throat bleed. All through this, I stare tear-eyed at my tormentor, the man I love. The man who broke my heart.

And then, I feel a slight sting.

A sting I was waiting for. It brings sweet relief. And calm and peace.

Death.

Yes. Thank God.

I feel myself going into it, getting absorbed into the black mass. At the same time, I feel myself being caged in a set of arms.

These are different from the ones holding me around my stomach.

I'd know those arms anywhere.

Simon.

He's taken me in his arms as I'm dying. I smile, or try to, because I'm slipping.

I've thought a lot about death, and how I'll die. I've made plans for it. But not once did I think that I'll die in the arms of the man I love. It never occurred to me.

It actually seems like a good way to die. The best way to die.

To draw your last breath in his arms and to look at his face before you forever close your eyes and say your last words.

"You're breaking my heart…"

Medicine

Man

"She's stable," Beth says, standing at my office door. "Sleeping."

I look up from where I'm shoving files in my bag at my desk. I'm probably crushing the papers, ruining them beyond repair but I don't really care.

This isn't the worst thing I've ruined. And there are worse things that I *can* ruin.

"I want someone to monitor her all night. In case she wakes up," I say, going back to my task.

She shouldn't, however. She should sleep through the night with Trazadone. I hope she does.

I look around the scene of the crime. My office. Everything is straightened up. Staff here at Heartstone are pretty efficient. It makes me angry. Fucking furious that there isn't any evidence of it.

Any evidence of how I broke her heart.

Scratches on my neck and my jaw, a few on my biceps sting like she's still digging her nails into my flesh, but they aren't enough. Her blunt nails didn't manage to break my skin and make me bleed. Like I made her bleed exactly seven days ago.

Where's the justice in that? Where's the justice in me going unpunished?

"You know this is it, right?" Beth says, reminding me that she's still here. "I can't help you after this. People are talking about what happened here. I can't stop it."

"I'm not asking for help."

"You're going to lose this job. I don't think even Joseph can convince the board –"

I stop what I'm doing and focus on her. "Do I look like I care about this job?"

"Do you care about her?" she asks, standing right across from me, on the other side of the desk, as if we're in a stand-off.

My hands fist around the flap of the messenger bag. "What do you want, Beth?"

"I want you to admit it. I know you've been spending time with her. Do you think I don't know, Simon?" She arches her eyebrows. "I know about frequent meetings. You haven't taken such an interest in any other patient but her."

"Then why haven't you done anything about it? Why haven't you stopped me? If it were someone else, you would've had this conversation long ago. Right?"

She nods. "Yes, I would have. I would've let them go. And if I thought they were taking advantage of one of my patients, I would've made sure that everybody knew about it, too."

"So why didn't you? Why didn't you let me go?"

Smiling sadly, she says, "Because you weren't taking advantage of her."

"Yeah? How do you know that? You've heard the rumors, right?" I cross my arms across my chest. "They say I took advantage of Claire. They say that I slept with her and when she got clingy, I told her to change doctors. There's a lawsuit against me, remember?"

She shakes her head, analyzing me. I fucking hate when she does that. Like I'm still that fourteen-year-old kid who's just lost his mother.

"I know you didn't do that."

She's right. I didn't. But everybody else thinks so.

"How? How do you know that, Beth? Maybe I've been lying to you. Maybe I didn't tell you the whole story."

"Because, Simon, you're your own worst critic. You're the height of professionalism. You're so hard on yourself," she says, exasperated. "You'd never get involved with a patient. You wouldn't even dream of it, and that's because your dad married *his* patient. Your mother."

I flinch.

I try to not think about it too much. I try to not think about how my bipolar mother was hopelessly in love with my dad. And how my dad was always too busy for her.

This is where they met, at Heartstone.

She was suffering from bipolar 1 disorder, which presents itself with full-blown manic episodes that last at least seven days.

Depressive episodes occur as well. It's easier for me to break-down her illness in technical terms rather than thinking of her as this unpredictable creature going through highs and lows, without her volition.

According to my mother, she fell in love with my dad right from the beginning. She fell in love with how calm and steady he was. How hard-working and sharp-minded. And how he always seemed to know what she was going to say before she even said it.

It always makes me wonder if my mother was making it up. She was fond of stories. Because how the fuck was it that the man who knew her so well, didn't figure out that she needed him in her life? How could he leave her alone and save the world, when his wife was fucking dying for him?

How the fuck did he not know that his absence was hurt-ing her to the point that she ended up killing herself?

"That's what drives you, doesn't it, Simon?" Beth pulls me out of my head. "Being better than your dad. So yes, I know. Ev-eryone who knows you, *knows* that you could never have done something like that."

Despite myself, I'm relieved that Beth knows. I never had to tell her; she believed me right from the beginning.

Like *her*. The snow princess. The bravest girl I know.

But it doesn't matter. I don't care about the rumors, but I do care about what happened to Claire.

Because it *is* my fault.

"What's your point, Beth?" I ask.

"Do you love her? Do you love Willow?"

I clench my teeth as anger and an unnatural fear grips me.

"I am not my father."

"That's not what I asked. Do you love Willow, Simon?"

No.

I want to say it. I want to deny it. I do.

But the fucking words won't come.

You have feelings for me, Simon. I have feelings for you, too.

I don't deserve her love. Not after the things I said to her. Not after what I made her do.

No wonder she hates doctors.

"I don't have time for this." I dismiss Beth and resume packing up all the documents that I'll need to convince Claire's parents not to take her off life support.

"Answer me. Do you love her or not?"

I snap the messenger bag shut and almost throw it aside in frustration. "What does it matter? What do I know of love, Beth? Fucking nothing. I know nothing about love. All I know is that my mother killed herself and I was the one who found her body. Do you know that I already knew? As soon as I woke up that day, I knew. I knew she was dead. I hadn't even seen her. I wasn't even out of my bed yet. I knew it as soon as I opened my eyes. There was this... fucking coldness in the house. Like she was radiating it out from her body. She was almost blue. The foam had dried out around her mouth. I can't get that picture out of my head. I can't sleep sometimes and if I do, I'm fucking terrified of waking up.

"I didn't even know that she was that unhappy. I didn't know that she was planning on killing herself. Or how long was she planning it for. I knew she felt it. She felt inadequate when Dad wouldn't come home. When he would completely disappear during her episodes. I know that. But I didn't know her end was so near."

Finally, I focus on her with grainy eyes. "I don't know anything about love, Beth. All I know is what I've seen growing up. And it's pretty fucking ugly. *I'm* pretty fucking ugly on the inside."

I don't even know why we're talking about this anymore. It doesn't matter. She hates me now, and rightfully so.

Needles freak her out, but she practically forced us, forced me to sedate her. She purposely hurt herself because of what I said and like a coward, I wouldn't even take it back. I wouldn't even take my words back.

She's better off without me.

I'm ready to leave so I can drive up to Boston, but Beth's words stop me. "Have you told him? Did you ever tell him? What you just told me, about how you found her that day?"

Breathing through my nose, I say, "Do you really think he would have cared if I told him? He went right back to work the next day. He was here for a whole week before I saw his face."

"Simon, you need to talk to someone. You need professional help."

A laugh rips out of me. "Are you really saying that to me?"

"Yes. I think these are the classic symptoms of PTSD."

"Are you a doctor too now?"

"No. But I've been around plenty of them all my life to know these things. In fact, I've been married to one since long before you were born."

"I'm fine."

"Just because you are a doctor doesn't mean you can't fall

sick," she says like she's explaining it to a kid. "You know that, right?

Sighing, I shake my head and sling my bag over my shoulders. "I have to go."

"Are they taking her off life support?" Beth asks, knowingly. "Yes."

"And you're going to do what?" She shrugs. "Ask them to not do that? Ask them to keep her going because you have this obsession with never accepting failure?"

"Are you done talking? I'm going to be late."

"Do you really think that whatever study you've dug up this time is going to help her, Simon? Or are you doing this to make yourself feel better?"

I pinch the bridge of my nose. "I'm leaving."

Striding to the door, I snap it open, but I can't take a step further without making sure Willow is safe. I turn around to face Beth. "In no way can this blow back on her. After this episode, she can't leave tomorrow. No one, not the patients, not the staff, *no one* says a word to her. Not even you. They don't even look at her the wrong way. Do what you have to do. Just take care of her. And... her mother. She's going to be upset about this, but you need to make sure that she understands. What happened wasn't Willow's fault or her illness. She was..." *Heartbroken.*

And it was my fault. She went out of control because of me.

"Just make sure her mother understands so Willow doesn't feel guilty."

Beth has tears in her eyes and as much as I hate to see her

cry, I can't bear to be in this building. After tonight, I'm not coming back. I can't stand the sight of it. I can't stand the thought of walking the same hallways as my dad did.

"Do you know what your father's biggest mistake was, Simon?"

Her words stop me in my tracks again but this time I want to hear the answer. I really do. I wait as Beth gathers her thoughts and wipes her tears.

"He let his love for her turn into a weakness. He was a great doctor, but he failed at being a man. Every time she went through an episode, he couldn't take it. He couldn't see her, so he stopped seeing her. He threw himself into saving the rest of the world because he knew no matter what he did, he wouldn't be able to fix his wife. He forgot that all his wife needed from him was love and support. She didn't need him to be perfect. She didn't need him to cure her or fix her or make her better. She just wanted him to love her.

"You want to be better than your father? Then stop being a hero. Stop being so afraid of failing. You're just a man. You make mistakes. Own them. Don't run from them. Don't run from yourself. Give yourself a chance to fall. Don't fight failure. Fight to rise from them. Fight for your future. Isn't that what you tell your patients? Fight. For once, fight for yourself. Save yourself. She doesn't need a hero. She just needs you."

That's where Beth's wrong.

Willow does need someone perfect. Because *she's* fucking perfect. She's a fighter. She doesn't need someone who's still chasing after his past and will always be chasing after it. She doesn't need someone who can't even accept his own weaknesses, right his own wrongs. Who gets terrified of accepting failure to himself, let alone to a room full of people like she did.

She doesn't need someone who can't fall asleep at night and when he does, he wakes up in cold sweats. Who throws himself into his work, in saving people because the other option is unthinkable. Panic-inducing.

She needs a true hero.

And I'm a broken one.

***

Somewhere around two miles from Heartstone, a band appeared around my chest. The farther I drive from the hospital, the tighter it becomes. Until it's almost impossible to breathe. Until I'm almost sure I'll have to stop and get help.

Just then, my phone rings. It's my father's nurse.

I manage to pick it up. "Hello?"

"Simon, it's your dad," she says. "He looks like he remembers. You should come see him."

Outside

Days since The Heartstone Incident = 93

Chapter 22

"Have you thought about it? Since we last talked."

"Yes."

I sit up on my couch. "I mean, not actively."

"Define actively," Ruth, my Outside therapist, asks.

She reminds me a little of Josie from the Inside. Blonde hair and slender, but no glasses. She's also very fond of her note-pads. She should be. Her penmanship is excellent. I've peeked into her notes, or rather tried to, and the glimpses I caught were pretty beautiful.

I cross my thighs, tapping the heel of my left boot on my right leg. "Well, you know, I didn't want to jump in front of the bus like I wanted to last month. So, yay me."

We both chuckle, and she asks, "What was it this time?"

Squinting my eyes, I try to look for the correct term. "A general wonderment," I say, truthfully. "I was walking down the street and I stopped in front of this building in my neighborhood. I looked up and I kind of thought about how it would feel to jump from it. It was for a second, I think. And then I walked away."

She nods and gets her pen ready to write something down. She's very good at not looking away from me, even when she's writing. She must have had loads of practice, which in turn means she must have a ton of clients like me.

All lost. All struggling every day. The network of all the chosen ones. People like me.

I'm not alone. And neither am I fighting alone.

"What made you walk away?" she asks.

I sigh, drum my fingers on the armrest. "My mom. She was the first thing or person I thought of. Then my grandma, my aunt. My entire family. Then I thought of all the kids at the bookstore. You know, I pictured them waiting for me to do the story-time but I wasn't there and they were crying, and yeah. That was slightly more unbearable than living one more day. So."

Ruth nods again, smiling. "Good. That's actually very good."

"Yeah. I'm reading them *Goblet of Fire*, and Harry's just about to fight a dragon. I cannot leave them hanging. That's torture."

She laughs. "One of these days, I'm going to read those books."

I feel excited, and a tiny bit sad too. I still haven't found my Harry Potter soul mate. "Oh my God, you should. Just please, please read the books. Don't watch the movies. They suck. I mean, watch them after you've read the books. But please, read them first."

"I promise I will." Then she gets serious. "Tell me about Columbia. Are you still struggling with classes?"

I deflate, sitting back. I still don't like admitting that I'm struggling either with my depression or with my courses. I don't think it will ever go away, this tiny sting when it comes to admitting things. I'll always have to remind myself that I'm a fighter and there's no shame in fighting.

It's the most honorable thing you can do for yourself.

Swallowing against the rush of emotions those strings of words invoke, I reply, "A little bit. But it's not as bad as it was in the beginning, or even a month ago."

"I'm so glad to hear that. Nothing is ever easy in the beginning, Willow. Beginning is the hardest part."

"Yeah." I nod.

She's right. It would seem that ending might be the hardest part, and saying goodbye hurts the most. But it's beginning something new *after* that goodbye that's harder to cope with. Because when you begin something new, after leaving something behind, the ghosts of that past always, *always* linger.

And sometimes those ghosts never go away. You carry them in your heart, in your veins.

"Any progress on the task I gave you?"

Sighing, I rub my palms over my jeans. They actually got wet in the rain a little bit while I was getting in. It's still raining, water and light snow. Roads are gonna be a biatch, getting back to the Village from the Upper West Side.

Maybe I can take the subway. But that would mean like, more than half an hour worth of detouring going from the West side to the East, and I'm not looking forward to that.

Maybe I should change therapists. Find someone closer to

where I live. It's about the convenience more than anything. Truly.

"Willow?"

"What?"

"Are you going to answer me?"

I bite my lower lip. "I'm thinking."

"You're stalling."

I sigh again. "No."

"No means? You're not stalling or there hasn't been any progress?"

Wedging my hands between my thighs and the leather couch, I mumble, "No progress." Then, more loudly, "But I'm working on it."

"Really?"

"Yes. Well, kind of." I grimace. "I just don't get asked out much, honestly. I'm not, you know, the popular type. Guys are not interested in me. Not that it's a bad thing. I'm not putting myself down, but they aren't really."

"I think it's the other way around. I think you're not interested in any guys. Because you're still interested in him."

A sharp pain shoots up just under my ribs, like a cramp that squeezes and clenches, until I have to make fists out of my fingers and grit my teeth a little bit.

Clearing my throat, I loosen my hands and bring them to my lap, rubbing the tattoo on my left wrist. "I'm not an idiot."

"I never said you were. You're just in love. With someone who doesn't love you back."

But what if he does?

That's always my first thought. *Always*.

You know, for a girl suffering from clinical depression, I'm a little bit too optimistic about some things. Foolishly optimistic.

Foolish. Foolish. Foolish. A love fool.

That's what I am. Probably, that's what I'll always be.

"It's time, you know," Ruth says. "You need to give someone a chance. If you open yourself up, Willow, you're going to be so surprised at what you find. I'm not saying fall in love, get married, make a bunch of babies. I'm saying give someone a chance. Go out. Have fun. You're young. Live your life." She folds her hands in her lap, putting down her notebook. "Remind me what you told me when you first came to me."

When I first came to her, I was still so heartsick and heartbroken that I didn't think I'd live to see another day. But I did. One after the other. And it's been three months since The Heartstone Incident. Ninety-three days.

Ninety-three days of living. Of getting up every day and building a new life for myself: Columbia, a job at the Thirteen Corner Bookstore, Sunday dinners with my family, hanging out with Renn, Penny, and Vi.

And every one of those ninety-three days, my first thought is always of him. Where is he? Why did he leave? Why couldn't he love me? Maybe all the horrible things he said were lies. Maybe he said one thing but meant another.

In my weakest moments, I've thought maybe if I was a little prettier or older or more sophisticated and not some fucking psycho who attacked him, maybe he could've loved me. He could've seen me as more than a girl he slept with.

I wonder what Ruth would say if I told her the man we've

been talking about for the past two months is my psychiatrist. All she knows is that I met someone when I was on the Inside and that he never loved me.

Oh and that, I attacked a doctor; news travels fast. She doesn't know why, though. I never told her the truth.

It's a secret that I intend to keep.

"I told you that I wanted to live," I reply.

"And are you living, Willow?"

Swallowing, I tell her, "I'm trying."

"Well, that's all you can do. That's all anyone can do. We can try, and sometimes we fail. And sometimes we do get where we want to go. But you'll never know if you don't try. You have to try, Willow."

She's giving me such a meaningful look, and you know what, she's right. It's been three months, and I need to let him go. I'll never know if I don't try.

"Okay." I nod, smiling slightly.

Maybe if I try, I'll get where I wanna go – a place where those weeks don't exist. That was always my goal, wasn't it? Not thinking about spending time at a psychiatric hospital. I wanted to leave it behind when I left.

But the irony of it is that I can't bear the thought of forgetting the weeks that completely changed my life. Maybe I can keep the good memories and forget the ugly ones.

Yeah, maybe that's what I should do. Remember the good times and not The Heartstone Incident.

Three hours later, I'm at the apartment that I share with Renn in the Village, lying on the carpeted floor, staring at the white popcorn ceiling.

Renn, Vi, and Penny are lying in a circle beside me, our heads on one side and our legs raised up and resting on either the yellow suede couch or on the brown coffee table.

This was another one of our poker nights and like always, Renn cleaned me out of my money that I work very hard for at the bookstore.

I hate her.

Actually, I don't. I love her and that she came to my rescue not only on the Inside but also on the Outside.

After The Heartstone Incident, I had to stay on the Inside for another four weeks. They strongly advised me that I should, and I agreed.

What happened was wrong. I did a wrong thing. I shouldn't have attacked him.

I put myself and my health in jeopardy. No amount of heartbreak should result in that. I just didn't know that heartbreak could be so powerful. But I've decided on one thing – that no matter how much it hurts, I'll never let myself do that again.

Love shouldn't make you lose your mind like that. Love could be hurtful, but it shouldn't be toxic. It's too pure for that. Too magical.

It's not an illness and I won't let it become one.

I was the last of our gang to get out and when I did, feeling all lost and afraid, Renn called me up and asked me if I wanted to share an apartment with her. She said that she was trying this new independent healthy thing and she'd rather do it with me than alone. Of course, I said yes.

And frankly, I wasn't ready to make a go at it alone anyway.

Something about stepping into the Outside world had scared me. Maybe it was the lack of structure.

On the Inside, everything is regimented. You follow a routine. You follow the rules. On the Inside, you're the most important person, the most important aspect of your life. But on the Outside, priorities change. Things are chaotic, like the New York City streets in winter. Dirty and full of sludge and jam-packed with traffic.

It's easy to lose your way. It's easy to think you're not good enough to navigate life. Every challenge is much harder on the Outside.

"Ruth wants me to date," I tell the girls.

Honestly, I'm not sure if they'd even hear me. They are drunk and high as fuck. Even Penny, who doesn't usually like to get under the influence. But it's Friday and things are relaxed.

I don't have qualms about getting drunk on Renn's vodka and practically inhale Vi's funny brownies, but tonight, I don't want to. I'm not in the mood.

"Date who?" Renn asks from beside me, her voice all hoarse.

Pot makes her horny. It makes me horny too. It also makes me dream of him.

This is why I've chosen to remain sober. So I don't dream of him tonight and touch myself and then cry. I need to take Ruth's advice. I don't even know why I'm not.

"Date *whom*." That's Penny in her giggling voice. "You're such an illiterate cow."

"You're such an ugly hag," Renn giggles.

Vi simply snorts.

Snorting myself, I shrug. "To answer Renn's question, I don't know. Someone. A guy."

"Date a girl." Renn sighs.

"What?"

"Yeah. Date a girl. Oh man, date a girl with like, big tits."

I flip on my stomach to look at Renn. She's running a finger up and down her chest and rubbing her thighs together. Her t-shirt is oversized but thin. Nothing much has changed in her wardrobe from when we were on the Inside. Except she doesn't wear pants, only boy shorts, at least when she's home.

"Is this the horniness talking?"

She shoots me a look. "It's the loneliness talking." Looking away, she continues, "I mean, how strange it is that I haven't touched another woman's tits and girly bits. Shouldn't I know my own kind intimately? It's a fucking tragedy."

Vi flips on her stomach, too. "Or it could be the fact that you're thinking about Tristan."

Now, Vi? That girl has completely changed. Her hair's pink, and instead of wearing drab and nondescript clothes like she did on the Inside, she now wears shorts like me and punk rock t-shirts. And she loves to bake. Especially brownies with pot.

We still don't know what her exact story is or how her fiancé died, but I have a feeling we'll know one day. When she's ready to tell us. I'm not as frustrated about it as Renn sometimes gets, though.

Renn flips on her stomach too. "What?"

"It's a valid conclusion."

"How is it a valid conclusion?"

"When Willow came home from work last week and said that they'd gotten a new employee by the name of Christian, you heard *Tristan*, and you completely freaked out."

"I did not!"

"You jumped a mile in your seat and you ate all the chocolate chip cookie dough laced with rum. And then we stayed up all night when you were puking your guts out."

Throwing a couch pillow on Vi's face, she snaps, "Fuck you, Vi. That was a weak moment. Such a low blow."

"It's true, though," Penny says, flipping on her stomach as well, her hands under her chin. "You did freak out a little bit."

Renn lies on her back, kicking her feet in the air. "I did not. I only knew the guy for like, three weeks tops. That's nothing. And in that entire time, he annoyed the fuck out of me, okay? I don't even remember what he looks like. The only reason I don't forget his name is because you guys won't stop saying it. So, can we please move on from this joke?"

"But –"

"Guys!" I raise my voice and my hands, deciding to jump into the conversation, still playing the peacekeeper. "Stop fighting, okay? I don't like fighting."

All three of them go quiet and look at me for a few seconds before starting back up, completely ignoring me. I sigh, shaking my head. I never should've brought up dating.

Amidst the chaos, I hear my phone ring. It's Beth.

Shooting them one last exasperated glance, I go to the bedroom and shut my door. "Hey, Beth."

"Hey, Willow. How are you?"

Ever since I got out two months ago, Beth has called me on and off, to check in with me. We've gotten pretty close, actually. At first, I thought that she did it with all the patients, as unbelievable as that sounds. But then I realized she only did it with me, because none of the other girls have gotten any calls from her.

I would've felt a little awkward and suspicious about her regular calls, but I actually don't. I never even asked her why she calls me.

I go to the window and press my nose on the glass, looking into the dark, rainy night. "I'm good. How're you? How's Heartstone?"

"It's good. Not the same without you, though."

I smile. "Ah, you're sweet. Do you miss me?"

"Of course."

"Maybe I should come back."

"Oh God, no. You stay out there."

I laugh. "Maybe we should do coffee. You should come to the city."

I hear her chuckle. "Yeah, maybe."

Then she goes quiet for a few seconds and I think that I've lost her. I look at the screen to confirm but nope, the call's still on.

"Beth?" I speak into the phone, frowning. "Are you there?"

"Yes, I'm here. I'm sorry I…" She hesitates, and my heart picks up.

So far, in all our calls Beth has never hesitated. She's usually very warm and friendly, motherly even. She asks me about my job, my therapy with Ruth, even about Sunday dinners with my family.

It's a pretty light and nice conversation. And by the end of it, I'm both smiling and hurting. Some days the hurt outweighs the smile but that's my problem. In my head, Beth is connected to him.

It suddenly hits me, though. That I can't talk to her anymore. I can't have these phone calls with her if I want to move on.

The truth is that the only reason I talk to her is because I want to hold on to him. I might even be hoping to hear something about him.

"Willow, I want to ask you something."

My heart is in my throat, throbbing, pounding as I wait for her to ask her question. I have a feeling that today I'll find out why she's been calling me.

"Will you tell me what happened that day?"

My head drops, and I stare at my bare feet. I can't bear to wear my bunny slippers anymore. They remind me of him. Of how he'd put them on my feet when he was cleaning me up and how he would ask me to *keep* them on when he was fucking me like he loved me.

"Why?" I whisper. "You've never asked me before."

It's true.

After The Incident, Beth called me into her office and told me that I needed to focus on getting better. She gave me the option to stay on, saying that she'd talk to my psychiatrist on the Outside, recommending it highly.

Not once did she ask me why I attacked a doctor. I had a feeling she knew, though. I don't know why she didn't say anything.

Josie knew, too. We never said his name out loud in our sessions, though. I told her that I never wanted to go back to that place where I could become a danger to myself, no matter how heartbroken I was.

My mental health is mine and I need to do everything to protect it. Only I am responsible for it, no one else. Not even him.

But Heartstone is a small place. Things get out. Especially since the day after The Incident, he left and never came back. Not to mention, everyone knew of our more than usual number of meetings. I was the only one who saw the doctor-in-charge every other day in his office. The rest followed a routine.

And I thought we were being so smart under the guise of medicine.

A love fool.

Anyway, they brought in another replacement doctor who stayed until Dr. Martin was better enough to join us.

She sighs, bringing me back to the present. "I'm asking because I feel like what happened was, in some way, my fault."

My head whips up. "What?"

"I knew, Willow. I knew you were spending time with him. I saw the way you looked at him and the way you acted around each other. It was my fault. I should've stopped it."

"Why didn't you?"

Her chuckle is sad. "He asked me the same thing. And I'm going to tell you the same thing I told him. I knew you were in love. By the time I found out, I knew it was too late. Maybe it was always too late. Maybe you were always in love with him."

My heart's beating so fast that I can't breathe, let alone talk. "I... I wasn't..."

I don't know what I'm trying to say. Perhaps I'm trying to

deny it.

"He tells me that I should've stopped it when I had the chance."

"S-Simon?"

"Yes and I should've. And that's how I know what you are to him. Still."

"What am I?"

"Something he wants but won't let himself have."

My knees completely give out and I have to grab onto the windowsill to not crash to the ground, instead of lowering myself to it like a dignified person.

But the thing is, my dignity is dead. It's completely gone.

God, I'm pathetic.

I'm pathetic in that in all these months, this is when my heart has chosen to race. This moment. This is the moment my body has chosen to wake up from a long-time sleep. Goose bumps, flutters, the beginnings of a storm.

"Willow? You there?"

I laugh, a short, jabbing sound. "I'm here."

"Hon, I know –"

"Why did he leave? After that day. Why did he leave? Why didn't he come back?"

I'm digging my nails on my bare knees, sitting on my ass, propped against the wall of my bedroom. I'm one step away from curling into a ball.

"You should ask him that," she replies.

Something is starting to shatter into a million pieces. It's not my heart. It can't be. He already broke it. So maybe it's my psyche.

Maybe this is how I'll lose it. Third time is the charm, isn't it?

Maybe I'll call it The Simon Incident.

"No. I'm asking you."

"He left because he was going through something and he thought he was doing the right thing."

"Does that something have to do with Claire?"

Her sharp intake of breath doesn't go unheard. "You know about Claire?"

"No," I snap. "And that's the problem. I don't *know* anything. I don't have the right to know anything, Beth. He never gave me the right."

Maybe she is choked up with a ton of emotions of her own, as well, because I hear her swallow. "I'm not condoning what he did. But at the time, he thought leaving you was for the best."

"For whom? Him or me? Because from what I remember I was drugged up and sedated and he wasn't there." I sniffle. "And you know what else? I still looked for him that morning. I woke up and I thought after everything he'd be there. He'd at least, talk to me. But no, I was wrong. He never came."

I'm just about to break my skin; I can feel it. My nails are long and sharp, unlike they were when I was locked up at Heart-stone.

Now, they are lethal.

"Do you know his mother was his father's patient?" Beth says after a while.

"Yes," I whisper.

I do. But not because he told me. It was Renn.

After everything happened and Simon left, she found a way to get the whole story. I didn't ask her to. She said she couldn't see me all broken up, so she at last got the help of her father's assistant, like she told me she would. He told her everything there was to know about Simon. Including about Claire.

But when Renn tried to tell me about her, I refused to listen. I didn't want to know. Whatever it is, it won't change the fact that I love a man who thought I was a phenomenally tight fuck and nothing else.

I hug my knees tighter, feeling so lonely. Lonelier than ever. Lonelier than when I was actually waiting for him to come back, lying awake in that lumpy twin bed at Heartstone.

"They were in love, his mom and dad. So much love. Joseph and I, we weren't very happy with it at first. But love is love. It happened. They wanted to get married and that was that. They were happy in the beginning, but things changed. Alex – Alexandra, she was a stunning woman, but she was a lot for Alistair to deal with. I'd be first to admit that he was weak. He let his marriage go and the weight of it fell on Simon. That boy was there for his mother from day one. And he stayed by her side right until the end. He was the one who found it, her dead body."

"What?"

My nails come loose from my skin as if I've lost all my strength. All my anger. My fight.

"He was fourteen. His dad was out of town for a conference."

I'm stumbling. My heartbeats, my breaths. My entire body.

"I-I didn't..."

"It's okay, not many people know. I only know because the police, they called us, Joseph and me. God knows, if they hadn't, Simon would never have told us himself."

She killed herself.

I remember his face from the day when he said it. He looked so devastated. So lost. No one has ever needed me the way he did on that day. No one has ever made me feel so useful and wonderful, like an answer to their every prayer.

A strong burst of longing catches me off guard and I press a fist to my mouth, almost biting down on the knuckles. Despite it, I manage to say, "Yeah, he wouldn't have."

I think Beth smiles. It's a little sad but I hear it in her voice. "He feels too much, Willow. And all of it is inside of him. I don't think he ever got to express anything of his own. His dad wasn't there so he took care of his mom and she was so vivacious and bright. Too bright, almost. He never got the chance to ever shine. Simon is not good at expressing things."

"I know."

"He's always been reserved, too restrained and the only time I've seen him come alive was when he was with you. The only time I've seen him either smile or even happy, was when you were there. And I know that he shouldn't have done the things he did. But he needs you, Willow. He needs you so much and that's the reason he'll never tell you because that's just the way he is. He doesn't take failures or weaknesses lightly. He doesn't ask for help." Pausing, she says, "I promised myself that I wouldn't tell you. I've already done enough damage. I've been less than professional. It doesn't matter what he's going through because I know he's hurt you. Immensely. But I know that he lo—"

"Don't say it, please."

I wipe off my tears and sit up straight, my heart beating painfully in my ribcage, breaking bones, flaying my muscles.

I don't think I can take it, hearing it from someone else. It's more hurtful. More torturous than him not saying it.

"You wanted to know what happened that day. I told him that I had feelings for him. I stupidly told him that I was born for him." I chuckle and it turns into a sob. "And he told me that I was immature. He told me that he didn't feel the same way. And I was heartbroken. Sometimes I can't stop laughing about how ironic everything is. I came to Heartstone claiming that I tried to kill myself because I was heartbroken. But I didn't even know the meaning of heartbreak until him. I didn't even know that I was capable of really losing my mind until him."

"Willow —"

"Beth, the thing is that I've been waiting for him for a long time now. I fought for him, tried to make him see that we belonged together. Tried to show that I trusted him. And I did that because I always thought that deep down, he felt the same way. I always thought that he was trying to say something to me, but for some reason, he couldn't. And he didn't. Not even at the end. And then, he left. He didn't even come back. The last thing I remember from that day is dying in his arms, with him looking down at me. Or maybe I was hoping to die, I don't know. So yeah, I don't understand what you want from me. I don't know why you told me all this. He doesn't need me. He doesn't need anyone. And trust me that he definitely doesn't *want* me. Unless they changed the whole wishing process and now, you magically get everything you wish for."

Wiping my tears again, I look at the ceiling. "And I don't think we should talk anymore because I should be trying to move on rather than being hung up on the past. Heartstone. Him."

She's silent but unlike other times, I hear her. I hear her chopped breaths and little noises of cries. I must sound the same.

Both crying for a man who probably doesn't even know that we're secretly tearing up for him.

"All right. I won't. I never should have started it in the first place. I just wanted to make sure you were doing okay. But before I go, I wanted to tell you one thing. The reason I brought it up today is because... well, Alistair, he passed away a few days ago."

"I'm sorry?"

"He had Alzheimer's and it had gotten pretty bad. We were expecting it but not really, you know. Anyway, there's a funeral to-morrow at the cemetery by the hospital. I was calling to see if you'd like to come, but I'll understand if you don't."

"I..."

"In fact, you shouldn't. You should move on," she says in a choked-up voice. "I can't even tell you how proud I am of you. How much you've grown. You were one of the best patients at Heartstone and I've really enjoyed talking to you. Please know that. And please reach out to me, if you ever need anything. You're not just a patient to me, okay?" Before she hangs up, she whispers, "Simon would've been lucky to have you."

With a click she's gone and the phone slips from my hands.

I feel dizzy but I can't do anything about it. I can't bury my head in between my knees. I can't sit there until I feel better. I have to know.

Rubbing the tattoo on my left wrist that sits right above my blue vein, I walk out of the room.

I go to Renn and say, "Tell me about Claire."

Chapter 23

When Renn told me that his mom was his dad's patient, my first thought was that I'm an idiot.

To fall for a man like that.

Of course he left me. Of course he didn't want me. Why would he want to tie himself to an illness, to a woman like his mom? He knows the struggle. He knows the burden. He's seen it, lived it.

But then, slowly, I remembered everything he said, everything he did for me. How he made me realize that I was a fighter. How he wanted me to fight and accept myself. How fondly he talked about his mom that day. How devastated he was about her death. How angry he always seemed at his father.

I went back and looked at the photo, the one Simon always stared at.

In fact, I looked at it a lot of times.

Fine, every day. On my way to breakfast.

There's a woman in that photo, wearing a red dress, who

has the most beautiful gray eyes. Her hair's all wild and dark. I'm not sure but I think that's Simon's mother, Alexandra.

I can't get her face out of my head now. Her smile and her big eyes. Beth was right. She was stunning, and she killed herself. And that would have still been tolerable if Simon wasn't the one to find her dead body.

I'm not an expert but that kind of thing just never leaves you. If I ever needed a push to move on and forget about him, this is it.

Simon Blackwood is too damaged, too icy, too unfeeling. And for a good reason. Whatever he is, he isn't for me. I can't fix him, no matter how much I want to. How much I'm dying to. And who says he wants to be fixed by me, anyway?

He left, and I can't even blame my illness because I know it wasn't that. It wasn't my damaged brain, it was my heart. He didn't want my heart.

It's done though. I'm moving on.

But I brought him flowers.

By him, I mean Simon's father. I'm attending the funeral. On the down-low, actually. Meaning no one knows I'm here, at the cemetery, hiding behind a tree.

I have only attended one funeral in my life and it became The Funeral Incident. So I am clearly not the best person to have around when someone dies.

But I couldn't stay at home, knowing that Simon would be going through this alone. Not that he *is* alone. There are people, tons of people, around him. I see Beth and Dr. Martin off to the side, among a lot of others that I don't know. Clearly, his dad was well-known.

And it's a good thing. Because not only is Simon not alone, but I have only been able to see the top of his head through the crowd.

I am afraid to see him.

I am afraid that if I see him, I'll throw myself at him and confess my love, and then I might slap him and hit him like I did that day. Only difference will be that he won't be able to have me sedated. So he won't be able to escape.

Sometimes I can't believe I did that. Attacked him and basically, goaded him to have me put down.

Yeah, let's keep the distance.

After a while, I see people starting to leave, a sea of black coats and hats and umbrellas. I huddle behind the tree, out of everyone's sight, my heart lurching in my chest. As soon as everyone leaves, I'll go put the flowers on the fresh grave and leave too.

He is right here, though.

God.

He's so close. So, *so* close that if I wanted, I could smell him.

"Okay, Willow. Relax," I tell myself. "It's okay. Things are okay. You don't want to look at him. You don't want to see his face. Because if you do then it will be harder to move on. You need to move on. You need that. Ruth is right. Listen to your therapist. Don't look. Don't look. Don't look. Okay?"

I sigh, clenching my eyes shut, and repeat, "Don't look."

Oh God. This is fucking hard.

I'm shivering. My legs won't stay still, and my breaths are

choppy, and it's not because of the winter rain.

I hear footsteps approaching me and my eyes, despite telling them to stay closed for about the ninetieth time, whip open.

And there he is, standing right in front of me.

Wearing a black suit, a tie, and his polished wingtips. Wearing the raindrops on his slightly-too-long hair and shoulders.

I wish he wasn't real, but he is. I know. I can feel it. I can feel him beating right alongside my heart in my breastbone.

"Were you talking to yourself?"

My back comes unglued from the wet bark and I stand up straight.

I haven't forgotten his voice. Not at all. It comes to me in my dreams, but I still get goose bumps hearing it. Rich, low and dense. It hits me right in the middle of my chest and sucks out all of my breath.

"No." I shake my head, finding that spot on my left wrist where the tattoo is and rubbing it to calm myself.

Simon's gaze catches my action and I stop.

He looks back up at my face and thrusts his hands inside his pockets in his signature move, and the breath that he sucked out of my body smashes back into my chest, and I almost gasp.

Clearing my throat, I say in my most normal voice, "I thought everyone was gone."

"They are. Why were you hiding?"

"I wasn't," I say quickly. "I mean, I was. Uh, I didn't know if…" I lick rain droplets off my lips. "Well, I didn't know if you knew I was coming. If Beth told you or what? Or if you wanted me here."

His eyes take me in, but only my face. He doesn't look anywhere else and I do the same. I scan his stubbled jaw, his strong brows, his stubborn chin. Nothing about him has changed.

Not one thing.

He's still perfect. Who knew perfection could make you want to cry?

He smiles his typical lopsided smile – it looks sad though – and ducks his head. "She told me, yes. I wasn't expecting you to come, however."

I rub my wrist again, now that he isn't looking at me. "I'm sorry about your dad."

Simon nods, grief flashing over his features. Suddenly, I wish that I had the right to walk up to him and hug him. Ask him things.

What happened, Simon?

A muscle jumps on his cheek and he says, "He developed a clot in his lungs. Due to inactivity. It's fairly common in Alzheimer's patients. Especially, at an advanced stage."

I'm so shocked that for a second I think, maybe I said it out loud. But I know I didn't. I didn't say anything.

Blowing on my bangs, I blurt out, "I know. I mean, Beth told me he had Alzheimer's. But that's it. She didn't tell me anything else."

"I know. She didn't tell me, either."

"Tell you what?"

"That she's been in touch with you all this time."

I didn't think she would tell him. But now I wonder if he'd have stopped her from contacting me, had she told him.

Doesn't matter. I'm moving on.

Then I remember I have flowers in my hands. I thrust them forward. "I brought flowers. You know, for him."

He throws me a little nod. "Then you should give them to him."

I move.

Moving is good. Moving means I'm not staring at him and watching him watch me. Maybe he's thinking that I might attack him again. Maybe he thinks I'm still unstable.

I'm not.

I won't do it again. No matter how heartbroken I become.

Broken heart is more dangerous than a disease of the mind, though. They give you a pill to make your brain happy, but they haven't yet made a pill for heartbreak.

So there. That should teach everyone who wants to fall in love.

With lowered lashes, I glance at him. He's looking straight ahead, his face clean and smooth, except for that stubble. No sign that he got attacked by a silver-colored hurricane. Not that I was expecting to find a sign or whatever.

But it feels like it never happened.

We reach the grave and I bend down, putting the flowers on the side. On my way back up, I catch something. The grave next to his father's.

It says: *Alexandra Lily Blackwood.*

Oh man. That's his mother.

I bite the inside of my cheek with a sudden onslaught of pain. Fisting my hands at my sides and closing my eyes for a second, I wonder again. Why don't I have the right to touch this man? This tall, restrained, grief-ridden man.

When I open my lids, I find him staring at me and my heart kicks up a notch. The gray in his eyes is so deep, so vivid and so alive.

Is that what Beth meant when she said he comes alive when I'm close?

"My dad had reserved the space right next to her when she passed away. I didn't know," he says.

"Maybe he knew."

"Knew what?"

I know Simon is looking at me, but I can't look back, so I stare at the graves of two people who were so important to him. Quite possibly, the two most important people of his life. Now they are gone forever.

If I'm hurting this much for him, I don't know how he's coping with all this. I don't know how he can stand there, all alone, with his shoulders so broad and straight.

How is he not breaking down?

"That she was waiting for him," I say in a small voice. "She was good at that, right? Waiting. Maybe he knew about it, but he didn't know how to go back to her. After everything he put her through. So, he chose this place. To finally go back to her in death because he never could in his life."

The side of my face is flaming. I'm pretty sure I'm red, scarlet. Because he hasn't stopped watching me.

Maybe he'll find my fanciful thoughts young and immature. Like he finds me.

"How are you?" he asks, after a few moments.

Gathering my courage and fucking maturity, I face him. The fact that I can look at him without craning my neck means that he's too far away.

Which is good, actually. Healthy.

Not complaining, at all.

I smile. "I'm good."

His stare is unnerving. And strangely, it feels perpetual. Never-ending. Going on forever and ever.

And I can't stop myself from telling him all the things. "School is good. I mean, I struggle with it sometimes but it's great."

"And friends?"

It makes me blush, the way he asks me about friends, with such tenderness and curiosity. Like I'm a little girl and he wants to make sure that I'm not alone.

"I do have friends, actually. Um, college is much better about it than high school. I have study partners and lab partners and yeah…" I trail off, not wanting to stop talking and hating it. "And the beach. We went to the beach a few months back. I'm not real fond of the beach and the sun but it was good."

Something strange happens to his face. It glimmers with intensity. Dare I even say… passion?

"Did you have a good day?"

I swallow. "At the beach?"

"Yes."

I open my mouth to answer but no words come out. Folding my hands at my back, I rub my tattoo.

Simon is watching. Waiting. I don't understand the way

that he seems to be so hung up on the answer. Whatever that might be.

Finally, I lie, "Yes. It was great."

I hope for him to catch me in my lie but he doesn't. He stays silent.

"Okay, well," I say, loudly. "I have to go. I –"

"I'll drop you off."

"Oh, you don't have to. I can just call a cab."

"No." He shakes his head, ready to walk to his car. "Come on."

"No, seriously, it's okay. It's like more than an hour going back to the city. And –"

"Then it'll be more than an hour."

Simon is waiting for me like he really won't move from his spot until I do.

Damn it.

I don't want to spend upwards of an hour in the confines of his car. The car I've only seen on the other side of the black gates of Heartstone. One day when I didn't have much to think about, I thought about his stupid car, the leather seats and windows fogged up by questionable activities.

It's actually one of my dreams to make out with him in the backseat of a car like a normal, horny teenager. Or was.

Shaking my head, I start to walk. And to hide my frustration, I thrust my hands in the pockets of my jacket, like he usually does.

We drive back to the city in complete silence. Yup. Not one word.

Simon is staring at the road like if he moved his eyes even for a micro-second, we'd crash and die. His hands are in a perfect ten and two position on the wheel.

God.

He makes me so mad with his stupid rule-following and precision. And the fact that he hasn't even looked my way once since he opened the door for me like a complete gentleman and we took off.

Whereas me? I've been throwing him all the glances that I can, without being obvious. But you know what? I stop there. I won't make any conversation, not until he does first.

Damn you, Beth. Damn you for giving me hope.

The rain has started to come down heavily now, and when the car comes to a stop, I literally jump out of it, feeling all kinds of caged in and frustrated. Even the cold rain doesn't do anything to bring down my heated agitation.

I throw the door closed, ready to walk away when I realize I never even told him my address, let alone the address of the bookstore I work at. But I'm magically standing in front of its yellow awning and the glass front.

How did he know –

"Are you happy, Willow?"

His voice makes me jump and halts all my thoughts. I dart my gaze to him and I have to tilt my neck up to look at his face.

He's standing much closer, rivulets of rain streaming down his thick, gorgeous hair and eyelashes. The strands are stuck to his forehead and neck and when the water sluices down his soft mouth, I want to reach up and drink it down.

Like I'm thirsty and I've been that way all my life.

I sweep my drenched bangs away from my forehead. "Yes."

I wait for him to do something. Say something. Again, catch me in my lie.

His jawline turns harsh, his eyes become dark, but then it all flickers away and he steps back.

As fucking usual. Looking down at my boots, I shake my head.

God, I'm so stupid.

What did I think? That seeing me today will change him and he'll tell me he was lying that day? That he loves me?

Sighing, I look up with a smile on my face; smiling is the key.

"Have a good life."

I take a step back too, trying not to memorize the way he looks right now. Pounded by the rain. Tall and stoic, almost grim. And handsome. A dream come true.

Then I spin around and leave.

I charge through the glass door of the bookstore where I'm supposed to start my shift. Christian, the new guy, is standing be-hind the counter with his suspenders and hipster glasses. He looks a little startled at my abrupt entrance.

"You and me." I stab my finger at him. "We're going on a date. Tomorrow. Got it?"

His eyes are wide and confused. "I have a b-boyfriend."

"I don't care," I snap. "I'm moving the fuck on. And you can't stop me."

"I-I'm not —"

Without listening to him, I march over to the bathroom in the back and burst into tears.

Medicine

Man

I never thought I'd be sad about my father dying.

I certainly never thought I'd shed tears. Not after refusing to talk to him more than in passing for years. *Especially* not after refusing to see him, while being in the same town and fixing his house. He was there all along, upstairs, being cared for by his nurse but I hardly ever stopped by his room.

My father didn't want to live in a facility. He was too proud for it. He didn't want people to know that a brilliant psychiatrist like him was slowly forgetting how to tie his own shoes and if his wife was dead or alive.

I hired the nurse because I didn't want to pack up my life in Boston and move back home to take care of him myself. I thought he deserved to die alone like my mother did.

But he didn't. I was there with him in his final moments.

I've been there with him for the past three months. I don't think it's because I've forgotten the things he did or the role he played in my mother's suicide.

It's because finally, I've forgiven him for my own peace of mind. I have finally decided to be better than him in the ways that count. He wasn't there for my mom, but I could be there for him.

Although, he didn't know. He was hardly lucid. It was okay. I wouldn't know what to say to him, even if he were.

So I said all the things I wanted to say.

I told him all the things about the girl whose heart I broke. Willow Taylor.

Standing in the rain, I watch her walk away. I watch her almost smash through the door and streak out of my sight like a falling star.

Have a good life.

It's not a question, but I'm compelled to answer her. I told her that she had no right to ask me anything; I was lying. Because when it comes to saving her, I *am* a goddamn liar.

But as it turns out, she didn't need saving. All she needed was for me to move the fuck on from the past and accept what she already knew.

That I had feelings for her. I *have* feelings for her.

I don't know how long it's been since she went inside but I'm telling her. She needs to know.

I burst through the door too, words almost bubbling on my tongue. There's a guy behind the counter and he jumps, nervously.

"C-can I help you?"

"Where's Willow?" I ask, my words rough and low. Shaking.

He looks to the side quickly before saying, "I, uh, don't know. She's not here yet."

Dickhead.

I wonder if they are friends, this moron and Willow. I wonder if he finds her fucking stunning too.

"Stay away from her," I warn him, even though I don't know if it's necessary. Even though it's me who has no right to say these things.

He throws his hands up in the air, exasperated. "What the fuck, dude? What's up with people today? I'm gay, all right?"

I ignore him even as I breathe out, a bit relieved. Not that it means much, his being gay. Willow can tempt anyone, if she wants to. But somehow, she has no clue.

I march across the space without responding to the guy's protests and make a turn where he glanced at accidentally. It's a hallway and there are doors on either side. I'm contemplating throwing every single one of them open until I find her.

But a second later, she comes out of one, halting in her tracks at the sight of me. "Simon?"

I gorge on her face, her rounded cheeks flushed with the cold and the rain, her wide eyes red with tears.

When she cries, the blue in her gaze turns bright and liquid, and my body gets emptied out of everything. I can't breathe. I can't think. Every little space inside me fills up with this need to put a stop to it. Whatever is making her cry. Or rather, whoever.

Today she's crying because of me and I swear to God, I want to destroy myself.

And I'm going to do it. I'm going to show her everything that I am so she can break me if she wants to.

"I can't," I rasp.

An adorable frown appears on her brow, and she sweeps her bangs off her forehead, stealing my breaths with her innocent gesture. "You can't what?"

I walk toward her. With every step I notice her eyes getting wider and wider. Her tiny frame is getting stiffer.

I've seen her do that a million times before. She did that the day I broke her heart. The day I lied because I thought she deserved better. She deserved someone who wasn't trapped inside his own head, reliving the worst day of his life.

Someone who isn't responsible for a death.

I stop a few feet away from her. "Have a good life."

"What?"

Her face is wiped clean. Pink and soft. There are no lingering droplets of rain or tears, but I can see their path. I can imagine them.

I clench my jaw against the avalanche of pain in my chest. It's been coming more and more, this cold, icy pain that started as soon as I drove away from Heartstone, leaving her behind.

"You said…" I swallow. "Have a good life."

Anger flickers in her eyes before it dies down. "So?"

"So, I'm answering you that I can't."

"Look, Simon. It wasn't –"

Her voice is laced with such sadness that I don't let her talk. "I killed a woman."

I've kept this moment away from my imagination, confessing my part in Claire's death to anyone. To me, confession has always meant acceptance, and I never wanted to accept that I failed.

The only time I've come close to saying these words were the day I told Willow about my mother's suicide. For some reason, I wanted to tell her that day, confess all my crimes, lay myself bare after I fucked her like an animal on my office floor. That was the least I could do after being such a savage with her, hardly showing her mercy, beating up her pretty pussy with my cock.

I couldn't then. But it's time now.

I need to accept that I did, in fact, fail, but that doesn't mean I'm a failure.

Even so, my body tightens up in shame as I see Willow's lips part. She drags in a choppy breath, and I wait for judgement, horror, anything to cross her face. But it doesn't.

She looks nothing but heartbreakingly beautiful.

Mine.

The thought pushes my words forward and I say, "Her name was Claire. She was my patient. Bipolar, like my mom. I've had a lot of patients like that but something about her reminded me most of my mother. Maybe because she was alone. Her parents had given up on her. Her fiancé had left her. When she came to me, she was very sick, and I wanted to fix that. I did everything I could. We went through a dozen therapists, med changes, dosage changes. I became obsessed with saving her. So much so that I didn't think it was wrong to let her stay in my apartment a few times or give her money if she was short on her rent. One time I even saved her from this party she went to."

I rake my fingers through my wet hair. "Christ, it sounds

like the textbook case of transference, the exact thing they tell us to beware of. I didn't see it that way, though. I got so blinded. All I knew was that I couldn't let what happened to my mom, happen to her. I couldn't be like my dad. All my life, I've been so *consumed* by that. I've hated how he made her feel less because she was ill and he couldn't stand that. I've hated that he was weak. I... When my mom died I... I even punched him at her funeral."

I chuckle harshly. "He never punched me back. I thought he would. All he did was walk away. I never understood why. Until recently. Maybe he knew he was guilty. Though he never said it."

Sighing, I put the memory out of my head. "By the time I realized what I was doing with Claire was wrong, it was too late. She'd gotten completely dependent on me. There were rumors everywhere. I told her she should see another doctor. I told her I'd help her with the transition."

I remember the night I told her that she should see someone else. It was raining. I had a list of the contenders she could see instead of me, and I discussed all her options with her.

She looked fine when she left. She was smiling, even. And then an hour later, I got the call that she'd been in a car accident.

They blamed the poor weather. They said she probably couldn't see where she was going. Or her tire must have skidded for her car to crash against the tree.

But I knew.

I knew it happened because of me. If I hadn't been so obsessed with saving her and being better than my dad, she would actually be alive today.

"Simon."

Swallowing, I focus on her. This brave, innocent girl. Her tears are falling again. I'm making her cry. That's all I seem to do.

There was a time when I could wipe off her tears, sit her in my lap, smooth down her hair and kiss her forehead, and she'd look at me like I was her hero.

Fuck, that look.

That look made me want to shake her, so she stopped doing it. She stopped looking at me like I hung the moon.

It also made me want to kiss the breath out of her, wrap her in my arms and keep her tucked by my side, slay all her dark thoughts and drink down all her salty water.

"She was in an accident," I tell Willow. "She didn't die but she went into a coma. Anoxic brain injury due to severe head trauma. And her parents filed a lawsuit against me when I told them it was my fault. The board asked me to step down from my position until the matter was resolved, and I did. I wasn't going to stay anyway. Not after what happened."

"Is she…"

She trails off, her eyes wide and so blue I want to drown in them.

I *am* drowning in them.

I am drowning in this fucking wait to see what she has to say to my confession. I know it's a distinct possibility that she'll send me away after this, and I honestly don't know what I will do if she does.

"What happened?" she whispers at last, and my next breath comes easy.

I still have time. I can still be in her presence. I can still look at her, hear her voice.

"They took her off life support. I was going to stop them. I was driving up there." I shake my head. "But I decided not to. I decided to let her go."

"Why?" she asks, frowning, so fucking perfect in her confusion.

"Because my dad's nurse called me saying that he was lucid. He seemed to remember me. She told me I should see him."

"D-did you get to talk to him?"

I smile sadly. "No. By the time I got to him he was... not lucid anymore."

"I-I'm sorry."

Even if she hadn't called, I wouldn't have been able to make the entire drive, anyway. I wouldn't have been able to leave Heartstone.

"It's okay. It was the right thing to do. Letting her go."

That night when I turned around, I felt the pressure easing off from my chest. I didn't know it then but the act of driving back to my father was my way of moving on, and letting Claire go.

Maybe that's what acceptance does. Eases off the pressure, the friction. That's why Willow started laughing more when she confessed her lies in the group a long time ago.

Beth was right. I tell my patients to fight but I, myself, forgot.

"Well." She sighs, wiping off her tears and straightening her spine. "I'm happy for you. That you've moved on. But I need to get back to work so –"

"I lied," I tell her, then.

This time when her eyes go wide, there's more than sadness in them. There's awareness. An electricity that seems to flare whenever we're close. I noticed it the first time she came into my office. That was the reason I kept asking her to meet me against traditional practices, against all reason.

"Lied about what?"

I walk closer to her and she steps back. "About everything I said that night."

"It doesn't matter."

Actually, I noticed that spark even before that. When she was on her knees, collecting pages of her book. Maybe that electricity was why I knew I had to kneel. I knew I had to help the silver-haired girl.

This is what they call fate, I think. This electricity, this magnetism. This strange call from the gut.

I shouldn't crowd her and cage her against the door she came out of, but I can't stop. I put both my palms on either side of her head and whisper, "I do have feelings for you. I've always had them."

She purses her pretty mouth. "I don't care."

I keep going, though. "I always thought that my feelings for you were my weakness. I thought every time I watched you walk down the hallways, every time I strained my ears to hear you laugh or talk, every time I called you back into my office I was failing. You were my patient, I wasn't supposed to feel that. I wasn't supposed to look for you in the dining hall or on the grounds. I wasn't supposed to hear your voice in my head or think about your skin when I saw the moon. I wasn't supposed to imagine touching your hair every time you swept your bangs off your forehead. I thought I was failing."

"Simon, I told you —"

"I wasn't failing, Willow. I was living. Waking up in the morning is hard for me too. Sometimes, I don't want to. More often than not, my first thought used to be of the day I found my mother. It would terrify me, every time I opened my eyes in the morning, going through the same cycle of emotions I went through that day. I always found it better to just not go to sleep, at all. But then I met you."

Her chin tips up and she arches toward me. Her voice doesn't have the stern cadence she probably wants to portray when she whispers, "I d-don't care."

I lean down, bringing us even closer. "I met you and every thought I had became yours. I started looking forward to waking up in the morning. I started to look forward to going to work. Walking the same hallways as my father did. It wasn't a chore. Living. It wasn't something I had to do. Living became something I wanted to do."

I hear the rustle of her soaked jacket that was draped around her arms falling to the floor. She puts her hands on my chest, pushing me, and despite the situation and the unresolved issues between us, my cold body heats up at our first contact after months.

"I told you I don't care."

Taking my hands off the door, I cup her soft cheeks. "I never believed that I could love. I never thought I even knew what the word meant. I was too broken. Too cold and buried inside myself. I was too much in hate with my past and all the things that happened. And then, you happened to me, Willow. I never thought we could have something beyond Heartstone. Every day I counted down the days I had left with you. I was counting down the days of my life. Because I knew the moment you walked out of those gates, I'd die. I'd stop living."

I wipe her tears but more keep coming, tightening that band around my chest. "You're... fucking perfect. So perfect and beautiful and innocent. A princess. You deserve a king. A true hero. Someone to fight alongside you. I never thought I could be that hero. Not with my mistakes and hang-ups and my battle with the past. But then, I realized a hero isn't someone who doesn't fall. A hero is someone who knows how to rise."

And then, I say it. The three words I never thought I'd say to anyone. I never thought I'd even *feel* them. But she knew. She always knew that we had something between us.

"I love you, Willow," I whisper, raggedly. "I fucking love you so much."

She sobs, and her hands become fists in my shirt as she tries to push me again. "Then why did you leave? Why the fuck did you leave? Why did you say all those things to me? Why did you break my heart to the point where I lost my mind?"

Her words make me bleed. Her words make me think of all the times I wanted to knock on her door and apologize. The times I've wanted to confess, to tell her everything.

"Willow –"

"No, stop talking." She shakes her head, trying to control herself. "Just stop talking. You don't get to come here and say all these things to me and expect everything to go back to normal."

She slaps my chest. "You broke my heart, Simon. You fucking shattered it. Do you know I looked for you? The next morning. I fucking looked for you. I waited for you every night in my room. Even after you said all those things to me. I waited for you. But you never came back. Not once did you come back. So I don't care if you love me because I hate you. I fucking hate you so much."

She pushes against me again, for the third time, her cheeks red with her emotions. I don't like to see her struggle like this, and I would've moved away. I would've let her go, taken my punishment without a word.

If it were true. If she hadn't said that one thing.

That one thing makes me push back. It makes me reach behind her and find the knob on the door, opening it. I maneuver her body with mine and she stumbles on her feet, gasping. I grab her arm to keep her standing and close the door, at the same time.

"What the fuck are you doing?" She glares up at me before swiveling her gaze to the door.

Stepping closer, I block her view of anything but me. I back her up against the sink – apparently, it's the washroom – and put my hands on the counter on either side of her so she can't escape.

"Simon!" She pushes at my body but it's hardly any pressure. "Get away from me."

"I did come back."

"What?"

"The night I came back for my dad," I reply. "I drove back to the hospital. I stayed the night. By your bed."

"W-what?"

When I reached home, my dad was already gone. Before I

could figure out my next move, Dean found me. His father was out of town again and he texted me. I took him and his sister out for dinner, and then I watched them until they went to sleep, leaving them with my dad's nurse. Because apparently, their father forgot to hire someone to watch them.

And then I made my way to Heartstone. Back to her. During the entire drive, I kept thinking how stupid I'd been to run to my past when my present is full of people who not only need me but want me too.

"Yeah. I left before you woke up. I didn't think you'd want to see me after what I did. But…"

For a miniscule fraction of a second, I think about how much to reveal. How much to tell her? But it's ridiculous – beyond ridiculous – to even wonder that.

I'll tell her everything.

Every fucking thing.

I soak in her features, her body, her emotions.

The agitation in her eyes, her loose, wet silver hair, her panting chest in her Harry Potter t-shirt, the mounds of her breasts punching through. Her pouty, cherry red lips turned down in anger.

She's a fucking princess. She's *my* princess. Let her see how sick and twisted I am for her.

"But what?" she snaps.

"But I underestimated how much I loved you. How much it would hurt to stay away from you, even if you hated me."

"What does that…"

She trails off when I move away from her. One step, two.

Three.

I yank my tie off. Next off comes my sodden suit jacket. I throw them both on the floor.

"What… What are you…"

"I'm telling you everything. Everything that I am. Everything that's inside of me."

I unbutton the top three buttons of my shirt before yanking it off my body. Staring into her eyes, I put my palm on my chest where my tattoo is. Exactly like the one on her wrist. The only difference is mine is on my heart.

"So I came back again. The day you went to the beach."

Her eyes go wide. Wide and blue like the ocean she went to see all those months ago. She grabs the counter, leaning against it.

"H-how," she stumbles over her words, her gaze glued to the matching tattoo on my chest.

"I watched you," I confess. "I looked through your records and I know I shouldn't have. It's confidential, invasion of privacy, but I-I wanted to know if you were doing okay. I drove into the city, insane with the thought of just holding you once. I thought I'd tell you everything you wanted to know, all my ugly parts, my anger, my mom, Claire. Everything. I wanted to tell you that you had the right to everything that I am. But then I saw you. You were with Renn and the rest of the girls. You were just coming out of the building where you live."

Pressing my palm over my chest, I rasp, "You were so fucking beautiful. So white and glowing under the sun and… and my heart started beating. After days. Weeks. I followed you like some fucking pervert. You went to the beach. I saw you on the sand. You had glasses on. A hat. I know you hated being out there but you still went. You stayed as long as your friends wanted. You looked up at the sky, as if you were not afraid of the sun anymore. And even if you were, you weren't going anywhere."

She had a white bikini on, so virginal, so pure.

Like her skin.

Like her.

"And then, you went to the tattoo shop. I went in after you'd left. I paid the guy at the counter extra to give me the same tattoo that you had. Two Ws."

It's written in a thin and tiny script, one W overlapping the other.

"W-why didn't you…"

"Because you were living. Despite everything, you were fighting. You didn't give up. What if I came back into your life and broke you again? What if seeing me brought back all the pain of that day? I couldn't do that to you. I couldn't take away your one chance to be happy, to live a life. So I kept myself away. But I kept coming back. Every day since then."

At her stunned expression, I take a step toward her. "Every morning you leave your apartment at 8:30AM. You go to the coffee shop on the corner and order a large cappuccino. You smile at the barista and he smiles back. Because he has a crush on you. He watches you when you leave. He doesn't take his eyes off you until you have completely disappeared."

I fucking hate the sight of him. One of these days, I'm going to break his jaw.

Another step closer to her. "Every Wednesday, Friday, and

Saturday you come here. When the kids arrive, you laugh. Though I can't hear it because I am always far away, always across the street, always outside looking in."

There's disbelief in her eyes, on her face, along with something that doubles up my hope. Yearning.

My confession is a balm to her. She likes it. She likes the fact that I've been watching her.

She always loved that. Being watched by me. I was so ashamed of it, tracking her movements, searching for her, knowing her habits, her quirks.

But she loves it. And I love her.

I love her with every goddamn piece of my heart, my soul.

I reach her and cup her cheeks again, tilting her neck up. "And today I was praying, hoping, fucking dying for a chance that you'd show up. I didn't want to believe it when Beth told me that she'd invited you. I was mad at her. I told her that she should leave you alone. She should let you live your life, but on the inside, I wanted you to come. I wanted one chance, Willow. Some indication that you can still stand the sight of me. That you can still stand to be close to me after I broke your heart."

Her breaths are choppy, her mouth parted and I wish I could kiss it. I wish I could bend down right now and put my mouth on her, taste her lemon flavor, lick her softness. Bite it. Make it mine.

But I can't. Not yet. Maybe not ever.

Christ. I don't know what I would do if it really turned out to be not ever.

"Willow –"

She speaks over me, "I knew about Claire. Before I came today I asked Renn. She told me about the rumors, about the lawsuit, everything. She told me not to go. She told me that you'd broken me enough. I don't need any more grief from you. You know why I showed up?"

"Why?"

"Because I thought you'd be alone. And because I didn't believe a word they said about you and Claire. I'm stupid, aren't I?"

My grip flexes on her cheek, trembles, like my heart, my fucking body. She doesn't believe the rumors. She doesn't believe any of it.

"You're fucking breathtaking."

She peers up at me through her lashes and warmth stirs in my gut. "What would you have done, if I hadn't shown up?"

"I would've kept coming back. I would've kept watching you. I would've kept watching you fight and live, and you would've kept inspiring me to do the same. And maybe, one day I would've gathered enough courage to come talk to you."

She shakes her head, sighing. "That was the hardest day after I got out. The beach. I didn't want to get up. I didn't even want to open my eyes. I was missing you so much and everything else just piled on from there. Renn told me I had to. In fact, all three of them came into my room, dragged me out, put me in the shower. They reminded me that I have to live. Because every day I live, I win."

They are right. Every day she lives, she fights, she wins.

She stares down at her tattoo, caressing her wrist. "Two Ws mean Warrior Willow. I thought I'd make a play on Weird Willow and really get a tattoo. So I did."

She throws me a wobbly smile, and I rub my thumbs around her mouth, hoping to soak that smile in. "They were assholes. They don't know what the fuck life is all about. I'm going to find them and I'm going to break every bone in their body. I'm going to…"

I trail off when she touches my chest. My tattoo, to be exact. She chases away the chill from the winter and the rain with only a flick of her fingers on me.

"You're not going to do anything," she says, and I try not to think about how my heart fucking leaps, trying to bust out of my chest and touch her.

"What if I'd gotten a princess or something?"

"Then I'd have a princess on my chest."

For the first time today, I see her smile reach her eyes. "You're crazy."

"Yes."

"And a pervert stalker."

"Yes. That too."

"Do you know what else it means? Two Ws?"

My Adam's apple bobs. "No."

"Two Ms. When I read it upside down on my wrist, which let's face it, I do several times a day." She gives me her eyes. "It means medicine man."

I cover her hand with mine and press it against my chest, trying to imprint her touch on my flesh. "Give me a chance, Willow. Just one."

"Why?"

"So I can make it right. So I can do what I should've done that day. I should've taken back my words and I should've told you that I loved you. That you've been right all along. Let me make it right, please."

She shakes her head, digging her nails in my chest. "No. I don't want you to make it right. I want you to leave."

"Don't do that. Don't make me leave, Willow."

"I don't need you. Even though I cry every night. Even though I dream about you every night and I don't listen to my therapist who tells me to date. I'm still fighting. I'm still living. I'm a fighter. You taught me that. So why should I care?"

Twin tears stream down her eyes and seep into my fingers. "You don't need me, yes. You don't need anyone. You can be whatever you want to be, Willow. But I do know one thing."

"What?"

I wipe her tears off, as I say, "When you smile, it doesn't reach your eyes. When you laugh, you don't throw your head back and do it with abandon. So I'm asking you. Begging you."

"Begging me for what?"

"To let me be the man who can make you smile not with your lips, but with your eyes. I am asking you to let me be the man who makes you want to laugh with abandon."

She trembles. "You do know that nobody and no one has ever made me happy, right? What makes you think you can?"

I rest my forehead against hers. "I can because I am not no one. I am me. I believe. You make me believe. In magic. In fairy tales. In fate. In falling and rising. In the fact that I can do it. I can be what and who you need me to be. You make me believe I was born for you."

She gasps like she can't comprehend that I remember her words. I wish I could laugh at the absurdity of it. Absurdity that I could ever forget anything she's ever said to me. I've filed it away, her words, her expressions, her touches in the furthest corners of my heart.

"I never should've attacked you. That wasn't right."

"I never should've said those things."

"I didn't know how to deal with what you said to me," she whispers, brokenly.

"Let me fix it."

She licks her salty lips. "That's what you do, don't you? You fix everything."

"Not everything, no. Not anymore. Just the things I broke."

"Like my heart."

"Like your heart."

Sighing, she rests both her hands on my chest and whispers, "Just one. One chance."

"Fuck…" I groan, clenching my eyes shut, as if she breathed new life into me.

She digs her sharp nails into my flesh and I open my eyes to find her glaring at me. "But if you blow it. If you fucking blow it, Simon Blackwood, then I'll hate you forever."

I smile, finally. "I won't let you hate me. I'd die before that."

She swats at my chest. "Don't talk about dying."

Her glare widens my smile, and I ask her what I should've asked her right from the beginning. Maybe I would have, if she weren't my patient and I wasn't too trapped in my past.

But as I said, I'm going to fix it.

"Will you go out with me?

Her eyes search mine, as if again she can't believe I said that. I can't fault her. I haven't been fair to her. I've let her fight alone for too long but I'm going to change that.

She slides her arms around my neck. "Out as in?"

"Out as in out. On a date. With me."

"Haven't we had this conversation before?"

"No." I shake my head. "Because like an asshole I never asked you. But I'm doing it now."

All my life I've wanted to be better, more, but I've only now realized that being better isn't materialistic.

It isn't about achievements on the outside. It's an inside thing. Being better or more is personal, individualistic. It's about growth. It's about me.

"You're not an asshole. You never were. You're just an idiot."

I chuckle. "Yeah, I'm that."

As I look into her pretty eyes, I know that every day I'll strive to love her better than I did yesterday. Every day I'll strive to be a better man than I was yesterday and that's the only better I care about. Loving her is my purpose. It's the thing that runs in my veins, alongside my blood.

Loving Willow was what I was born to do.

Slowly, she smiles and says, "Fine. Pick me up at seven tomorrow night."

Chapter 24

I love the rain.

I've always loved it. It makes me think of second chances. How the water flows down and washes everything away. It leaves things clean and crisp.

A clean slate.

It's very hard to get that, especially in real life. Nothing is ever clean. Nothing is ever wiped off. But there's a thing called moving on.

I'm doing that.

I took Ruth's advice. I'm dating.

It doesn't matter that I'm dating the same man we talk about during sessions but whatever. I'm moving forward with him, the one who makes me happy.

He also makes my kids very happy.

By kids I mean the ones who come to the bookstore for sto-ry-time. We're reading *The Half-Blood Prince* now, and I ask Simon to read with me, sometimes. He says it's his favorite in the series, if tolerating something could be called being his favorite.

Whenever Simon reads with me, the kids get so happy. They laugh and cheer at his deep voice and the life that he brings to the scenes.

That's what he does. He brings life.

It's so weird and a little bit sad that he still gets surprised when some of them rush over to hug him at the end. Sometimes they even ask for an encore.

He still gets shocked when my eyes well up at seeing him with them. And when I randomly stop him on the street during our dates and kiss him, his first reaction is always a light disbelief.

It's been a couple of months since he came back into my life and said all those wonderful things. Since then we've been dating.

And let me say, we've been dating in a very traditional, old-fashioned way where he comes to pick me up at my apartment. Simon is always dressed up, in crisp shirts and nice pants. He brings me flowers, chocolates, lime jello. We go to a nice restaurant and I let him order food for me because it makes me feel cherished. Fuck what people think.

He won't let me drink though. Only a couple of sips from his glass.

He likes whiskey, and his favorite food is steak. No surprise there. I've always imagined him with a tumbler in his hands and cutting into a juicy piece of meat with his big, graceful hands. Oh, and leather. I've always imagined him around oak and leather.

Like right now.

We're in his car, surrounded by expensive leather, having just come back from my mother's Sunday dinner.

My mom and I, our relationship has improved. In the sense that I told her about my fears and insecurities.

When The Heartstone Incident happened, I told her everything, except the reason I went berserk. She knew I attacked a psychiatrist, and I was so uncontrollable that they had to sedate me. Beth offered to stay with me while I explained but I told her I needed to own up to my actions and I did.

Maybe one day I can tell her why I attacked a doctor and that doctor is also the one I'm dating now. One day I'll tell her that this time I *really* did it all over a man, over something as trivial – according to her – as love. She's not going to be happy about it.

She's plenty unhappy with the fact that I'm dating at all. An older man and my ex-psychiatrist, no less. That's why she asked him over for dinner and after putting it off for weeks, I caved in and brought Simon with me.

"Willow?"

I look at him when he calls my name. He's wearing a dinner jacket that makes him look so dashing and handsome.

I smile. "Hmm?"

He tips his chin at the window. "We're here."

My apartment building is blurry through the rainy glass. Vague and distorted. And so not where I wanna be right now.

With a racing heart, I realize I don't wanna go in there. I don't wanna leave this car.

"I don't wanna go," I repeat my thought to him.

"What? Where?"

His voice is concerned, and it makes me bite my lip and lose my breath. He still does that to me. *Still.*

Every time I hear his voice roughened with concern or see his gray eyes darken with worry, I fall in love with him all over again. I feel so feminine, so fragile and so cherished that I want to crawl in his lap and ask him to fix everything for me.

And he will, or he'll die trying.

"I don't wanna go back to my apartment," I whisper, studying his features.

He reaches up and turns on the overhead light, making his concern and his frown even more evident. "Why not? What happened?"

"Did you mean what you said?"

"Said what?"

"To my mom."

His face tightens up in anger.

So yeah, the dinner was a disaster, in more ways than one. First, my mom – my entire family, actually – couldn't stop grilling him about my stay at Heartstone and all about The Heartstone Incident. Basically, showing how overprotective they are and how I'm the baby of the family.

Simon answered the best he could without giving his part away. He hated it; I know. And that's why I specifically told him beforehand not to reveal anything.

I already know that Simon is big on consequences and if it were up to him, he would've taken all the blame in a heartbeat. But we have enough to deal with right now without adding family censure to the plate. At least more than whatever is on there already.

And second, my mom didn't make it a secret that she doesn't like Simon for her one and only daughter. She grilled him about his intentions. At one point, she even went on about leaving me a virgin for my future, real, age-appropriate boyfriend.

That ship has sailed, Mom. So fucking sailed.

It was so painful to watch. Well, until Simon put his foot down and said, "With all due respect, Miss Taylor, your daughter is more than capable of making her own decisions. About her life and about her body. In fact, you'd be surprised at how capable she is. It's one of the many things I love about her. Her capability. It's also the one thing that scares me the most. Because I know she doesn't need me. At least, not as much as I need her. I'll always respect her decision. That being said, I won't go down without a fight either. So unless you have more to say, let's move on to dessert."

Oh gosh.

This man is so swoony, isn't he?

Now, I ask him again, "Did you mean what you said to my mom? That you'd fight for me?"

His stormy eyes rove over my face. "Always."

My breathing escalates, and I take off my seat belt before hopping out of the car, into the pouring rain. The sidewalk is almost empty because it's the middle of the night and the storm is something fierce.

Simon jumps out after me, all frowny and upset. "What the fuck, Willow? It's cold. Either get back in the car or get inside your building."

He is right. It is cold. I'm only wearing a thin pink sweater and my jacket is in the car. But I don't care. I have to ask him something.

I crane my neck and look at his drenched face. "Do you

know why I love the rain?"

"Willow –"

"Because it reminds me of second chances. It makes me think that if this ugly world can be pure after a heavy shower, I can be pure too. I can get all the chances that I want."

When he asked me for a chance, I wasn't even reluctant. Every beat of my heart wanted to give him all the chances he wanted.

Maybe it's stupid to trust someone this much but I do. I've always trusted him. I've always believed in him. It's the way he carries himself, with such confidence. It's the way he cares about people, with such passion.

It's the way he looks at me, with such intensity and tenderness. He's always looked at me that way, even when he was keeping parts of himself aloof. That's what made me believe back then that he loved me too.

He puts his large hands on my arms, rubbing them, instantly warming me in my sweater. "Willow, what –"

"Will you marry me?"

There. I asked him.

I've been meaning to ask him this… well, ever since we left my mother's house.

I know. I *know* that we just started dating, like, two months ago. We haven't even jumped back into sex yet. And it was my decision to take it slow. Imagine that.

But every time he comes to my door to take me out, right on the clock, and every time he listens to me when I've had a bad day or reminds me about my pills like I could ever forget, or every time he talks to me about *his* bad day, it makes me think that we're meant to do this forever.

Every time he opens up about his past a little more, telling me how his mom's favorite color was red – I definitely know that woman in the photo is his mom, or that she was the one who taught him to climb trees – I now, know that the girl he mentioned in our first appointment, the one he was trying to impress with his tree-climbing abilities was his mom, he immerses me even more in his life.

I even got to see his house, the house he was fixing while working at Heartstone. He hired people to fix it for him and it's on the market now. He found himself a nice apartment here, in the city, instead.

I put my hand on his chest and go up on my tiptoes to kiss his parted lips. "Will you? Marry me, I mean."

It was supposed to be a small peck on his wildly breathing lips, but he winds his arms around my waist and crushes me to him. My breasts flatten against his hard chest and he thrusts his tongue inside.

Sighing, I let him mold me to his body and invade my mouth.

I'm his, anyway. He can do whatever he wants with me. Just as I start to kiss him back though, he pulls away.

"No," he growls.

"What?"

"My answer," he pants, staring into my eyes, "is no."

Gasping, I sputter, "What... why... why not?"

"Because it shouldn't be your question. It should be *my*

question. I should be asking it."

I can feel his chest punching into mine with his out of control breaths. His erratic breathing rhythm is messing with my rhythm, and I shove at him.

"Then why haven't you?"

He looks at the sky as if he's exasperated. "Because, Willow, you're young. You're so fucking young. And you're impulsive."

I glare at him, though it's hard to do that in the rain. "Are you saying I'm not your type?"

Simon cups my cheek, tilting my neck. "I'm saying that you're asking me to marry you and you haven't even said it yet."

His rainy, musky smell is driving me wild. God, I want this man with every cell, every single atom in my body, and he's saying no to me.

"Said what?"

"That you love me."

I'm taken aback. "I... I haven't?"

His laugh is humorless. "No."

I know he tells me every day. I know that. That's the best part of my day. He says it right when he's about to leave me for the night and go back to his apartment. I take those three words and sleep with them under my pillow. Well, after I make myself come with his name on my lips.

But I didn't realize that I hadn't said it yet. I say it to myself all the time.

Oh my God, does he not know?

His expression is a little ticked off, and I realize that maybe he's been waiting for me to tell him all this time.

Idiot. How can he not know?

"Maybe I haven't said it yet because..." I search for words. "Because what I feel for you is more than love. It's... it's happiness. You make me happy, Simon. I mean, as much as I can be. I know you said that I could do whatever I wanted to. I could be happy, if I wanted to. You said that I don't need you for that. And maybe that's true. Maybe I would've been happy someday. Maybe my smile would've reached my eyes. But I would've always, *always* looked for you. I would've stopped laughing just to search for you because I would've wanted to share it *with* you. But more than that... I would've wanted to share my tears with you. And you know what, even if I were crying and you were there, my world wouldn't look so dark. So bleak. I would find some sliver of happiness even when I was sad. My mind wouldn't be able to get my heart down because you were with me. Don't you know that already, you moron? That's, like the biggest, most gigantic thing anyone could ever do for me. You make my sadness not so... sad."

I'm crying now. He knows it, even though it's raining, and you can't tell. He can always tell, though.

My hero.

"Fuck, Willow. Stop talking," Simon groans against my lips.

Of course, I don't listen. "*I love you* seems so little for what you are to me, Simon. But I do. I love you and I wanna be your wife. Even though I ruined everything for you."

"Stop talking, Willow."

The Heartstone Incident wasn't only bad for me. It was bad for him, too. Simon hasn't gone back to work because this time the rumors are worse. There's a hint of truth to them. He says he doesn't want to go back to work – not yet, at least – and he's focusing on writing a book about bipolar patients and their care.

Not to mention, he's spending some time in therapy about the issues relating to his mom's suicide, and how he spent his childhood taking care of her.

But what if they never take him back? The lawsuit has been settled by Mass General, but what if this time around, even without the legal repercussions, his career is basically over?

I fist the lapels of his jacket. "I'm sorry, Simon. I can't tell you how sorry I am for putting myself in danger and basically outing our secret. I never wanted anyone to find out. I never wanted to do that to you or to myself. I'm so sorry, Simon. I'm an idiot."

"Stop. Talking."

Obviously, I keep talking. "I-I know how difficult I can be. I know that. I know living with me, with someone like me won't be a picnic. And I can't ask anyone to do that, you know. Like, marry me and have babies with me because you never know if my babies are gonna come out like me or –"

He presses my cheeks together, almost making duck lips. "Shut the fuck up, Willow."

I still try to open my mouth but his glare cuts me off.

When he's satisfied that I won't say another word, he eases the pressure off my cheeks. His jaw is working back and forth and a second later, he asks, "Are you trying to hurt me?"

I shake my head, quickly.

"Then stop fucking blaming yourself for what happened that day. It was me. I said all those things to you because I was a coward. Your love scared me so much that I lashed out. I pushed you away. But it's over now. It's fucking over, and the last thing I care about is a job. I can get another one. Do you know how famous I am in the psychiatry field?"

I shake my head again.

"I'm pretty fucking famous," he tells me. "And that's because I worked my ass off to get where I wanted to go. Yeah, I've made mistakes and yes, some things take a bit longer to blow over, but whatever. I can make my way back, if I want to. Right now, I don't care so much. I'm happy with some time on my hands and focusing on me and you. Do you understand?"

With wide eyes, I nod.

His lips twitch.

"Can I talk now?" I whisper.

"You *are* talking."

I glare at him but decide to let it go. "So are you going to marry me?"

His fingers bury themselves in my sopping wet hair and he leans over me. "Are you going to have my babies?"

A quickening starts up in my belly. "Y-you want to have babies with me?"

"Fuck yes, I do. In fact, I think about it constantly. The baby-making process, I mean."

It moves down, that quickening, way, way down in my stomach. "You'll have to come inside me, then. Without a condom."

"I'm looking forward to that. So fucking much."

Actually, me too.

I can't help the blush that overcomes my face, my body. "Okay."

He kisses me, possessively. "Then, yes. I'll marry you."

Grinning, I kiss him back. "So I have some time over my Christmas break. Would you like to do it then?"

Groaning, he drops his forehead on mine. "Christ, Willow. We're not getting married while you're in school. You need to finish college first."

"Why not?"

He shakes his head, looking up at the sky again. "I won't feel so ancient, for one. And second, I can't believe I'm saying this, but your mom will kill me."

I grip his hair in a fist. "I don't care about my mom. I can't wait four years."

Another possessive kiss. "It's not up to you."

I rub up against him, making him groan once more. "You like to boss me around. But you do know you're not my dad, don't you?"

A lustful glint enters his eyes, his hands going to my ass and squeezing the flesh through my soaked jeans. "You like to act bratty, but you do know you aren't a little girl, don't you?"

Before I can react to his statement and his dominating hold on my butt, we hear a couple of guys and their hooted laughter coming from behind me.

Immediately, Simon pushes me toward his car. He gets us in the backseat and shuts the door, with me sitting on his lap.

It all happened so fast that I have to take a second to catch my breath.

Panting and sprawled on him, I ask him, "Wh-What was that?"

Simon's eyes are focused on the guys that just passed us by. He's glaring at them. I try to look but he doesn't let me, grabbing the back of my neck, keeping my gaze glued to his face.

"They were looking at you. Those dickheads."

I laugh. "What?"

His jaw ticks in anger but he remains silent, making me shake my head. My ice king thinks everyone watches me like he does.

Before, he was the king of the castle, roaming its corridors to keep an eye on me, and then, he became my broken hero, looking for me in this big, bad city.

Gah. I love him so much.

"Not everyone watches me, Simon," I whisper, tracing his stubble.

His grip flexes and he growls, "If you think that, then I need to lock you up somewhere and tie you to the bed so you can't even go to the window."

I rock my body against his, getting unbelievably turned on by his possessiveness. There was a time when I wanted to stay back at Heartstone, all trapped and ill, just so I could stay close to him.

And the truth is that being trapped with him doesn't sound so bad because being with him sets me free.

Simon's hands go back to my ass as I keep undulating against him. "Are you still gonna be this possessive when we get married over Christmas?"

He begins kneading the flesh, as he thrusts his hard cock

into the juncture of my thighs. He leans up and bites my lower lip in a show of pure dominance. "No. I'm going to be even worse when you officially become mine. Four years from now."

I laugh again, and Simon grabs my face, looking at me with such intensity that I blush. "What?"

"I… I can't stop looking at you. I can't… You're so fucking beautiful, Willow. So stunning and…" He swallows. "So white and pale and like a snowflake."

I study him with my watering eyes. That slant of his jaw and that stubborn chin, his perfect nose and those stormy eyes.

"I'm your snowflake."

"Fuck yes, you are."

"I love you. I love you so much, Simon."

And then, he kisses me.

I love this man with every piece of my brain, heart, and soul.

This man who thinks I'm beautiful and a warrior. Who doesn't know that he's so getting laid in the backseat of his car like a teenager. And that no matter what, we're definitely getting married over my Christmas break.

Epilogue

Five years later…

I'm losing my mind.

Well, not really but it feels like it. And of course, it's happening at a birthday party.

Her birthday party, no less.

It's not my usual bad day. At least, it didn't start out as one. I was perfectly calm when I woke up this morning.

I opened my eyes with a purpose, a clear goal set in my head. I'd taken the day off from my job at the local high school where I work as a guidance counselor, since I had a few things to get done before the party.

Over the past few years, I've learned that whenever I get overwhelmed, making lists helps. It started out as an exercise for Columbia when my exams overwhelmed me. But now I use it for almost every aspect of my life.

My husband seems to find my little lists amusing and sexy,

all at the same time. But that's beside the point.

So yeah, I had my list and I was ready to face the day and the party but then she started crying.

God, the sounds she made.

They were so excruciating, so painful to hear. Her soft chin wobbled and her beautiful face scrunched up as big, fat tears streamed down her pink cheeks.

And the worst of all was that she wouldn't stop.

No matter what I said to her, she wouldn't stop crying. She went on and on. I tried everything. Talking to her, soothing her, playing her music, reading to her. But nothing.

I even thought of calling my mother, which in itself shows how frazzled I was. I never call my mom for help. Mostly because she thinks my life is a series of bad choices. Besides, Simon hates it if I reach out to her for things.

"You're coming to me with anything and everything from now on. You got it?" he said to me once.

I remember being mad and, obviously, turned on by his authoritative statement. "Oh yeah? Why?"

He looked at me like I was crazy, and not the useless kind. "Because you're mine, Willow, and I'm yours."

Needless to say, I jumped his bones. I almost always do that when he says things like this.

But I didn't want to bother him today. He was at a meeting with his editors that he couldn't get out of, and in any case, he was going to be home soon for the party.

Somehow, I got her to calm down enough so she could tell me why she was crying. Turns out, it was because she'd lost her favorite toy and she couldn't find it.

And here I thought her world was ending.

It would be a hyperbole to some but it's a very real thing to me.

We did find her toy – a little snow owl inspired by Harry Potter – but her gut-wrenching cries knocked me off my positive mojo. I needed space and I needed happy thoughts.

All the fucking happy thoughts.

I hear footsteps, sure and confident. His.

He's back.

My ears perk up. In fact, my entire body has perked up as I hear him climbing up the stairs and walking toward our bedroom. He knows that if I'm not downstairs, helping with the arrangements, then this is where he'll find me.

When we moved to this house, I remember having one of my ugliest bad days. I couldn't get out of bed. I didn't even have the energy to breathe. The sun was burning me, sucking off all my energy. So I hid myself in here where it's all dark and the air is saturated with his rainy smell.

He knows this is my happy place, or at least this is where I go to *find* it.

The door to our bedroom opens and in three short steps, he's here. He opens the door to the closet, bringing the sunlight in.

I blink a few times, trying to adjust to the light even though I've only been inside for about fifteen minutes. I'm much more suited to darkness and closed spaces. But strangely, I don't mind the sun now that it's illuminating my husband's massive, toned body, his dark hair, the sharp, mature lines of his face.

He's wearing a light blue shirt that brings out his eyes. I picked it out for him this morning before his meeting. He also wore a gray tie to go with his gray suit, but he isn't wearing the tie or the jacket right now. Probably took them off on his way back home.

He does that after a long, hard day. Like he can't wait to rush back and relax. Like he can't wait to be the Simon I know – warm and safe – after being all cold and professional, Dr. Blackwood.

Biting my lip, I look up at his towering form that somehow still makes me lose my breath after all this time. "Hey."

Without looking away from me, he closes the closet door, but not all the way. He leaves it slightly open, so the sunlight can stream in. I don't mind. He's here; the sun can't touch me.

Taking off his glasses – he wears them all the time now, he settles himself on the floor beside me, where I'm huddled, almost hiding between his clothes. I crawl up to him, putting my head on his chest. He gathers me in his arms and kisses my forehead. "Hey, baby."

I close my eyes and just breathe that word in. It's a seemingly ordinary endearment but from his mouth, it's the magic word. Like he made it just for me.

I pop open a couple of buttons on his shirt and nuzzle my nose in his bare chest. It makes him chuckle softly.

"Here."

He fishes something out of his pocket and offers it to me. A lime jello.

I smile. "You brought it for me?"

"Uh-huh," he almost purrs, as if he's finally at peace now that he's back home. "I knew you'd need it."

I take it from him and dig in. "Thank you."

Sighing, he kisses my hair again, his fingers going up and down the bare skin of my arm, calming me, making me feel steady.

Tucking my chin in his chest, I ask, "How was your meeting?"

"They want me to expand on a few things. I thought the book was done. But apparently not."

I can hear the slight frustration in his voice and setting my lime jello aside, I pop open a few more of his shirt buttons so I can really touch his naked chest, and that tattoo he got for me. I rub my hands in circles, tracing that inked spot, trying to soothe him, like he soothes me. He groans and his head falls back to rest on the wall.

"I'm sorry," I almost coo. "I know you want it to be over."

His arms snake around my back as he plasters our bodies together. "It's just taking longer than I thought."

I know. My poor baby.

Kissing his chest, I whisper, "Do you wanna tell me about those changes?"

His lips twitch, telling me that he's onto me, and that he's amused.

I know that it helps him when he talks. Not that I understand anything. Most of the time, I don't get what Simon is talking about. Like, at all. But I always offer to be his sounding board.

I become one now, as he tells me about all the little tweaks he has to make in his second book.

His first book did great. Obviously. Like there was ever any doubt of his capability and awesomeness. The publishers asked him to write a second one. It's based on the same topic, bipolar patients, but this time, it's really from the perspective of a patient rather than a provider. I think its Simon's way to pay homage to his mom.

It doesn't stop with his book, however. Over the last few years, he's participated and consulted in various studies that deal with bipolar patients and their care all over the country.

Yup, my husband is pretty fucking famous.

There were rumors about him and his conduct for a long time, but things simmered down. He doesn't want to go back to practicing, however. He says he likes the research aspect of medicine. But maybe one day.

When he finishes, he slants me a look. "Did you get all of that?"

I peek up at him through my lashes. "Uh-huh."

"Yeah?"

"Yup. I got that my husband's brain is fucking sexy and I'm in love with it."

He shoots me a smirk. "Just his brain, huh?"

I nuzzle my nose in his hard chest again and flick a tongue over his tattoo. My hands wander and go down the grooves of his sculpted stomach. "Well, I can't deny that I love his body, too."

He puts his hand on mine, stopping me from playing with his belly button and the dark trail that leads down to the best thing in the world: his dick.

"Willow," he rumbles.

"What? It's true."

He rubs his stubbled jaw over my forehead. "Don't start what you can't finish."

"I can finish." I lick my lips and his pupils flare. "I can finish you, at least. I know you need it."

Maybe this is the answer right now. A quickie in the closet. A simple fix. Endorphins from an orgasm. God knows my husband gives me the kind of orgasms that put me in another dimension, where everyone is always happy and mellow.

His grip tightens over my hand. "Tell me why you're sitting up here."

Or not.

I frown. "It's stupid."

"Tell me anyway."

Sighing, I sit up, or try to. At first, he tightens his hold, but then reluctantly he lets me go.

Swallowing, I whip my bangs away from my forehead and whisper, "She was crying." I blink my eyes, trying to clear out the flashes that my words have caused. "And I got so scared. She wouldn't stop, Simon. And I thought she was like me. I used to cry like that. On my birthdays. No one could get me to calm down. My mom used to get so frustrated and angry and sad. And I was…"

"You were what?"

I look at his big, sprawled form. He looks so king-like, sitting like this. His shirt half open, his one leg stretched out and the other folded at the knee, his expression all alert and focused. He looks like he could do anything. Anything at all. He could protect me and her, all with his bare, healing hands.

"What if she's like me?"

Anger flashes through that alert expression of his. "So what?"

"It's going to be hard. So hard for her."

His jaw clenches. "And?"

I wring my hands in my lap, an urgency taking over me. Ever since her, I get anxious very easily. Simon knows this. He helps me calm down. He helps me see reason, but when she cries, something comes loose inside my chest. My anxiety can't be controlled even though I know I'm not being rational.

As a person suffering from depression, I know anxiety. I've lived with it all my life. The hopelessness sometimes takes a more dangerous form. It becomes sharp-edged, laced with fear and paranoia.

Paranoia that I might have made her like me.

"I'll teach her everything," I say, with my eyes on the man I love. "We'll teach her everything. We'll never let her feel less, Simon. She has to know that we love her, no matter what. She has to know that she's strong. She can do this. She can fight. She has to…" I trail off, not knowing how to convey this to him, my fears.

"Baby."

I focus on him. "Yeah?"

"Come here."

His arms are open and I don't wait for even a second before I crawl back to him. This time, he maneuvers my thighs to straddle his lap.

He takes my face in his hands and whispers, "Breathe with me, all right?"

I nod, my lips parting and grazing his. He parts his lips too and soon, we're breathing as one. He's giving me his air and I'm giving him mine.

He's purging me like he always does. Curing me with his breaths, with his intense gray eyes and his touch.

It doesn't take me long to calm down after that.

"I can't watch her cry, Simon. It makes me feel so helpless," I whisper into his mouth, lax in his arms.

"Me too," he confesses, kissing the tattoo on my wrist. "You know what else makes me feel helpless?"

"What?"

"Seeing you like this. Hidden away." He fists my hair and I feel a tug in my belly, a different kind of pull, a delicious kind. "Why didn't you call me?"

"You were busy."

"Willow —"

Pressing a finger on his soft lips, I stop him. I know it's hard for him when I don't tell him things. He doesn't like it when I keep secrets. Especially secrets about my moods and thoughts. I hardly ever hide anything from him but still. He gets agitated, and I don't blame him. How could I, after what he went through with his mom?

God, I love this man so much. Sometimes I just wanna squish him to my chest and keep him tucked away.

I kiss him softly. "I was going to tell you once you came back home, I promise. You know I'd never keep anything from you."

His jaw is still clamped so I kiss him again, until he presses our mouths together and takes over.

As always, I let him. It's his turn to be medicated. He needs this kiss, so he knows I'm okay. He needs to know that he owns me, possesses me. That he runs in my veins. He needs the reassurance that I won't ever keep any part of myself hidden away from him.

Breaking our connection, he rasps in my mouth, "She's a fighter just like you. Just like me. So yeah, if she needs it, we'll teach her everything we know."

I sigh.

The confidence in his words makes me feel even better. He's right. If she is, in fact, like me, we'll teach her everything. It will be hard but we'll fight.

My hands trace his broad shoulders, the tendons of his neck, his hair and back again. "Hmm. I always knew you'd make the best dad."

"Yeah, you did, didn't you?" he murmurs, throwing me his lopsided smile.

"Uh-huh." I bite his lower lip, feeling reckless and in love. "In fact, I think I wanna have more of your babies."

He stills.

I don't know where it came from. I wasn't planning on saying it. I wasn't even thinking about it but seeing him like this, all-powerful but also vulnerable, it just hit me.

"Are you joking?" he asks.

"Nope."

He gives me a look and I'm compelled to add, "I'm serious. I promise."

In his signature style, he grabs the back of my neck to bring our faces even closer. "And when did you decide this?"

"Just now."

Simon is silent, but I can feel the heat radiating out of his body. I can feel his hardness bumping against the empty space between my legs. He's turned on.

"One of these days, Willow, I'm going to fuck all the impulsiveness out of you," he growls and smacks a hard kiss on my mouth.

I moan.

I know he loves my impulsiveness. It's the reason we got married over my Christmas break five years ago. He kept saying no but I convinced him. It's the reason he took my virginity in that room, so long ago. Not to mention, my impulsiveness is what made me ask him out on a date a long time ago.

"You're welcome to try. Maybe you should start now." I rock against his erection, my panties getting damper and damper with each passing second.

"Yeah?" Moving his hands down to my ass, he presses our lower bodies together. "Is that what my princess wants? To get fucked in the closet while everyone else is downstairs, waiting for her?"

Closing my eyes, I shiver. Will I never get over it? That he calls me princess in that raspy, possessive voice of his.

I guess not. But it's okay. I'll ride the high of his endearments as long as I can.

"Yes, please. Fuck me. I'm gonna pretend this is the dark alley and the floor is the brick wall you fucked me against that one time."

A few months into our marriage, he grabbed me a couple

of blocks away from our building, pushed me against the wall and almost fucked the life out of me with his delicious violence. It was exactly like I told him in our session long ago. Even better, actually.

His chuckle is thick and dark, like the air around us. "I'll do you one better this time. I'll fill you up with so much cum that when you walk out of here, it'll seep out of your tight hole and drench the little girl shorts you like so much."

"Oh God, Simon…"

He lowers me to the floor, hovering over me as he makes quick work of our clothes. "And you're going to have to clench your pussy and keep your legs closed to stop all my cum from leaking out. You know why, princess?"

"W-why?"

"Because if my princess wants a baby, then it's my fucking job to give it to her."

With that, he enters me, all bare, and seals our mouths so my moans don't reach downstairs.

See, impulsiveness pays off.

People have labeled our relationship. My mom, my therapist, *his* therapist. They have tried to diagnose it, analyze it because of what we were to each other when we met, and what we've been through in our lives. But we've come so far. We've been so content and happy. Well, as happy as you can be while living with clinical depression. Unfortunately, love isn't a cure for it, but the love of my life is there with me every step of the way.

So yeah, impulsiveness definitely paid off for me.

Twenty minutes later, I change into a fresh pair of little girl shorts and a Harry Potter t-shirt, and go downstairs. I've ignored my mommy duties long enough.

Simon is already there; I sent him down before me. And in his arms is my entire world: Fallon, our daughter.

The name Fallon means daughter of a king. And well, I couldn't have named her anything else when I've always thought that her daddy is a king.

Standing at the foot of the stairs, I take them in. Fallon has her chubby arms around her daddy's neck as she gives him a very detailed account of everything she's done today. Her breakfast, her bath. Her struggle when Mommy made her sit still to do her hair. Her panic at losing her favorite toy.

And her daddy listens to everything with such rapt attention. He gives her all the reactions she wants, disbelief, dismay, chuckles. He even asks questions.

Then he tells her – seriously, with all of his fatherly authority – that she scared Mommy with her cries, and she shouldn't do that.

Fallon pouts and lisps, "Sorry, Daddy."

And well, there goes his stern expression.

I bite my lip as I watch them together. Simon is so good with her, such a softy. Not that I ever doubted, but still. Every time I watch him with Fallon, something inside of me just melts. I love him even more. His arms look even stronger to me when they are holding our baby girl. His eyes look even shinier when he looks at her with all his love. His shoulders look broader, he looks taller.

Frankly, Simon Blackwood, as a father to our child, is lethal, irresistible. More of a breath-stealer. More of a man.

I place a hand on my tummy. Maybe we did really make a

baby upstairs. I hope so. This time, I want a boy like him, dark hair, polite, kind of nerdy, and a little arrogant.

Finally he notices me and my hand on my belly. His eyes smolder behind his glasses, and my sleeping arousal wakes up a little bit. I can't wait to get him alone so we can get on with our baby-making.

He whispers something to Fallon.

She whips her eyes over to me and squeals, "Mommy."

She's wiggling in his arms now, so he bends down and lets her go. She runs over to me on her pudgy legs, her pigtails flopping. Her pink dress flutters around her knees and her bunny slippers flap against the floor.

I meet her in the middle, and going down on my knees, I say, "Hey, baby. Were you good for Grandma Beth?"

When I needed a little breather after Fallon's crying, I called Beth to come over a little early so she could watch her.

My baby girl jerks out a nod. "Gramma Beth gave me a cookie. She the best."

I chuckle. "She is, isn't she?"

She puts her small hand on my cheek. "You crying, Mommy?"

God, why does she have to be so perceptive? Her gray eyes watch everything and she's so precocious. She's like her daddy in that way.

She's a mixture of Simon and me. Her silver hair and chubby cheeks come from me. But her penchant for tree climbing and her eyes take after her daddy.

Fallon is also the result of impulsiveness. Well, she's the

result of me getting a sinus infection four years ago and my birth control not working alongside the antibiotics. Simon knew having sex was risky but I told him I didn't care. Maybe I really wanted a baby. Maybe we *should* take a risk. He obviously liked that very much and voilà, we have a little baby girl. I never took birth control after that.

I clutch her soft hand on my cheek and whisper, "A little bit."

Frowning, she says, "Why?"

Blinking my eyes to get rid of the moisture, I kiss the middle of her palm. "Because you're getting so big."

It's true. My baby is turning three today and I can't bear it. Soon, she'll be off to school, then college. I don't know what I'll do without her.

"But I wanna get big," she insists, nodding, her bangs fluttering around her forehead.

I sweep them away so they don't poke into her eyes. "Yeah? Why?"

"So I get married, silly."

I laugh. "Really? You wanna get married?" Another enthusiastic nod. "Who are you going to marry?"

She scratches her nose, still red from crying, as if thinking about it. "Daddy."

"You're going to marry your daddy?"

She grins. "Yeah."

I look at her daddy. He's helping Beth in the kitchen, but at my stare he turns his attention to me. There are so many things written in his gaze. Most of them have to do with desire, though.

He can't wait to get alone with me either.

"Yeah. Daddy's amazing, isn't he?" I wink at him before turning to our daughter. "Good choice, baby."

She frowns again, chewing on her lip. "No. Wait, Mommy."

I extricate her lip from her teeth before she brutalizes it. "What, honey?"

Going on her tiptoes, she looks around as if searching for something.

We're in the living room, so we have a direct line of sight to the rest of the house, including the backyard where the party is going to be.

When I got pregnant, Simon decided to buy a new house outside of the city. He thought the city wasn't good for raising a baby. Plus he couldn't baby-proof his apartment because it was a rental.

There are a couple of people in the backyard right now and Fallon points to one in particular. "No. Not Daddy. I gonna marry Dean."

I purse my lips so I don't burst out laughing.

Yeah, Dean. He's the boy Simon met five years ago at the cemetery. He's grown up now and he's a part of our family.

I met him when I was dating Simon and I loved him immediately. Hello, the guy loves Harry Potter. How could I not love him? His dad isn't there most of the time, so Simon likes to check on him and his sister.

Dean loves Fallon. In fact, he's super protective of her. He can't see her upset or crying. Good thing he wasn't here when she was throwing her tantrum. The guy wouldn't have liked it.

Most days, Fallon won't go to sleep unless she hears his voice on the phone. Also, she needs to see him every day or she gets really unmanageable. So he stops by for a little while before going to his job at a local restaurant. He's the one who taught her to play ball, ride her tricycle, and all the other outdoorsy stuff. Simon sometimes gets jealous; it's cute.

Fallon looks at me with large, shining eyes, wiggling in place. "Please, Mommy? Please? Can I marry Dean?"

I don't know what seventeen-year-old boy is best friends with a three-year-old girl, but I guess Dean is different. Perhaps because he's been taking care of his little sister for so long. But even so, I don't think he was expecting to be the very first crush of my baby girl.

Clearing my throat and getting my laughter under control, I say, "Honey, I think you're gonna have to ask him."

Her eyes get even wider, if possible and she jumps up and down. "Okay! I gonna ask him now."

She's ready to run to him where he's chatting with Dr. Martin, but I stop her. "Fallon, I think you should wait. Because –"

"But Mommy, I got a plan."

I'm suspicious. "What plan?"

"I gonna ask him a gift. And he has to gimme it 'cause it's my birthday."

"What gift, honey?"

"I gonna ask him to marry me." When I still don't understand, she says, exasperated, like I'm the kid, "As a gift, silly! I gonna ask him to marry me *as a gift*."

And then, she's running away before I can say another word to her, and I can't help it. My laughter comes out.

Oh my God, she's going to trick him. Not gonna lie. I'm kinda proud of my daughter.

When I come to my feet, Simon sidles up to me. His arm goes around my waist and together we watch Fallon dash up to Dean. She stumbles in her path and my feet are ready to move and rescue her. But Dean is there. He gets to her in a flash and gathers her in his arms. His face is bunched up in a frown as he says something to her, smoothing down the wayward strands of her hair. Fallon shakes her head in response, and he kisses her forehead, smiling at her.

As I watch them together, I realize I know a thing or two about crushes on lonely, dark-haired guys. Not that my sweet girl's crush is going to amount to anything. Obviously.

Right?

Before I can really think about it, Simon asks, "What was that about?"

I switch my focus from them to my husband. If I tell him, he's not going to like it. He is possessive of his daughter. He's going to be upset knowing that Fallon chose Dean over him for her marriage plans.

"Nothing."

Simon looks down at me and I trace his stubble, causing him to squeeze his arm around me before placing his splayed palm over my belly. I almost moan at his touch, squeezing my thighs together, keeping his cum from leaking out like he told me.

"Don't look at me like that," he whispers.

"Like what?"

He presses his palm over my stomach. "Like I'm a hero or something."

"But you are a hero," I say, bringing my hand over his and threading our fingers together. "You're my hero. And Fallon's. And you'll be his hero, too, when he comes."

"It's a him, then."

"You know it."

He chuckles, and I go up on my tiptoes to kiss him.

When his lips are moving over me like this, with love and passion and promise, I'm not afraid of the future, of what's to come.

I'm happy. Excited.

In fact, I'm excited about this party, too.

In a little while, our house will be full of people I love. I'll get to see Renn and Tristan after a long time. They travel a lot because of Tristan's paintings, so sometimes it's hard to get ahold of them. I hope they'll finally decide to get married this year. I can't wait to be her maid of honor. Matron of honor. Whatever.

I'll see Violet with her husband, Graham. I'm especially excited about that because I just love how they met. Every time we see each other, I make Vi tell it to me, right from the beginning. They're such an unlikely pair. Vi with her ex-fiancé's super-hot dad. I love how Renn gets all hot and bothered whenever Graham, the silver fox, walks into a room. Tristan hates that.

Even Penny isn't immune to Graham. Not that she's interested in dating anyone because she's busy with her residency. Maybe tonight, along with Renn and Vi, I'll change her mind.

Not to mention, maybe Dr. Martin will finally convince Simon to come work at Heartstone again. I know one of these days, Simon will break and go back to the job he really loves.

So yeah, life is full of possibilities, even for me.

A silver-haired, blue-eyed girl who takes a pill every day for an illness that can't be cured.

Because I was born with more than blood in my veins. I was born with strength. I was born with courage to fight.

I'm a warrior.

And that's what I've passed on to my daughter, as well.

That's what I'll pass on to every single child of mine.

Strength and courage and the ability to rise even when they fall.

THE END

Coming Soon

God Amongst Men

Enemies to Lovers Romance

Coming 2019

Dopamine

Renn & Tristan's story

Coming 2019

Nicotine Dreams

Violet & Graham's story

Coming 2019

Author's Note

Disclaimer II

As a writer, I get my inspiration from a lot of things. Medicine Man is inspired by my love for the novel, Girl, Interrupted and Harry Potter series, along with my uncle who suffers from depression.

When I was little, I could never understand why everyone was so worried about him or why his hands would shake while writing or why his visits to the hospital lasted for weeks.

While I will never grasp the hardships he went through and still goes through, as an adult, I know that I admire him immensely. I admire his will to fight and stay steady and strong in the face of his illness.

My goal in writing this book is to acknowledge this very strength that resides in millions of people who battle it every day. I hope you know that you're not alone, and you don't have to be.

You're strong.

You're a warrior.

I'd also like to take this opportunity to point out that a stay at a psych ward is more often than not a very intensive and sometimes, grueling process. I found several articles depicting both harrowing and hopeful experiences. With this work, my aim is to focus on the light at the end of a dark tunnel. Please be aware that I do not intend to make light of this experience.

But at the same time, I'd also like to disabuse anyone of the various myths surrounding an open-unit, medium-term psych ward such as Heartstone. Generally, patients staying at such facilities have a full life on the Outside, and are admitted with the goal of helping them resume it as soon as they are able.

Thank you for reading this story!

PS: In case, you want to connect with me, please email me at: storiesbysaffron@gmail.com

Acknowledgments

My husband: He's the man behind all my hard work and every single book I write. He's also the kindest, most genuine man I know.

My family: Thank you for supporting me, always. Thank you for being there for me and teaching me to always go for my dreams.

Ella Maise: I'm so, so thankful that we connected this year and that we've been chatting almost every single day since our first few messages. Thank you for taking this journey with me. Thank you for being my sounding board and a source of inspiration. Love you!

Bella Love: Can you believe that we started this journey together? It seems so surreal. Thank you for being with me since the beginning. I love you so much!

Autumn Davis: Thank you so much for all your faith in me. I'm so sorry I bug you with my little insecurities and anxieties. I'm so very grateful for your support and your trust in me.

AM Johnson: Thank you so much for putting up with my constant questions. Thank you for holding my hand when I was freaking out about every little detail. I adore you!

Beta Readers: Renate Thompson, Bella Love, Ella Maise, my agent: Meire Dias, Mara White, Ellen Widom, Cynthia A. Rodriguez, Autumn Davis, Melissa Panio-Peterson, and Veronica Larsen. Thank you so much for your invaluable comments and insight into my story. Your thoughts have made this story the best that it could be.

Candi Kane: Thank you for being on my team and being so very sweet. Releases scares me and you made everything so easy.

Readers: Thank you for reading my books and waiting for them with all your enthusiasm. I'd be nothing without you.

About the Author

Writer of bad romances. Aspiring Lana Del Rey of the Book World.

Saffron A. Kent is a Top 100 Amazon Bestselling author of Contemporary and New Adult romance. More often than not, her love stories are edgy, forbidden and passionate. Her work has been featured in Buzzfeed, Huffington Post, New York Daily News and USA Today's Happy Ever After.

She has an MFA in creative writing and she lives in New York City with her nerdy and supportive husband. Along with a million and one books.

She is represented by Meire Dias of Bookcase Agency

www.saffronkent.com

An Excerpt from

THE UNREQUITED

Chapter One

My heart is not an organ.

It's more than that. My heart is an animal—a chameleon, to be specific. It changes skin and color, not to blend in, but to be difficult, unreasonable.

My heart has many faces. Restless heart. Desperate heart. Selfish heart. Lonely heart.

Today my heart is anxious—or at least it's going to be anxious for the next fifty-seven minutes. After that, who knows?

I'm sitting in the pristine office of the school's guidance counselor, Kara Montgomery, and my heart is going haywire. It's fluttering, dipping up and down in my chest, bumping against my ribcage. It doesn't want to be here, because it takes offense at seeing the guidance counselor, which is really just a euphemism for therapist.

We don't need a therapist. We're fine.

Isn't that what crazy people say?

"Layla," says the guidance-counselor-with-a-psychology-degree/therapist, Ms. Montgomery. "How was your vacation?"

I glance away from the window I've been staring out of, forgoing the scenery of the snowy outdoors to focus on the smiling woman behind the desk. "It was all right."

"Well, what did you do?" She is rolling a pen between her fingers, and then it slips out of her hand and falls to the floor. She chuckles at herself and bends to pick it up.

Kara is not a typical guidance counselor/therapist. For one, she's clumsy and always appears frantic. There's nothing calm about her. Her hair is never in place; strands are flying everywhere, and she's forever running her fingers through them to make them behave. Her blouses are always wrinkled, which she hides under her corduroy jackets. She talks fast, and sometimes things she says aren't very therapist-like.

"So?" she prompts, giving me her full attention. I want to tell her that her glasses are tipped to one side, but I don't; she is less intimidating this way. My heart doesn't need any more threats than what her degree represents.

"Um, I took walks, mostly." I shift in the cushioned chair, tucking a strand of my loose hair behind my ear. "Watched Netflix. Went to the gym."

Lies. All lies. I binged on Christmas candy my mom sent—or rather her assistant sent, because my mom didn't want me to come home for the holidays. I sat on the couch all day and watched porn while sucking on Twizzlers and listening to Lana Del Rey in the background. I'm addicted to that woman. Seriously, she is a goddess. Every word out of her mouth is gold.

I'm not addicted to porn or Twizzlers, however. Those are

just for when I get lonely…which is most of the time, but that's beside the point.

"That's great. I'm glad." She nods. "You didn't feel lonely without your friends, then? It was all good?"

Now, this is what I don't get: why is she smiling at me? Why are her eyes curious? Is she trying to dig deep? Is she trying to fish for answers?

Her questions could be a cover for other loaded questions, like, *Were you good, Layla? Were you* really *good? Did you do something crazy, like calling him in the middle of the night? Because you've done this before when you were lonely. So, did you call him, Layla? Did you?*

The answer to all of this is a big fat no. I did not call him. I haven't called him in months. *Months.* All I've done is stare at his photo on my phone—the photo no one knows about, because if my mom knew I was still pining after him, she'd send me to a real therapist, a real live one who would ask all sorts of questions rather than disguising them with euphemisms.

So *no*, I did *not* call him. I have only stared at a stupid picture like a pathetic lovesick person. There, happy now?

I shift in my chair and open my mouth to tell her exactly that when I realize she hasn't even asked the question. I'm only *thinking* she has. It's all in my head. I tell my anxious heart to calm down. *Relax, would you? We're still in the clear.*

I exhale a long breath and answer, "Yeah, it was good. I kept myself busy."

"That's great. That's good to hear. I don't like when students have to stay back for holidays. I just worry about them." She laughs and her glasses become even more crooked. This time she straightens them up and folds her hands on the desk. "So have you given any thought to what electives you'll be taking this semester?"

"Sure."

Of course not. I'm not made for education. The only reason I agreed to college was because I was given the choice between school in Connecticut and the youth rehabilitation center in New Jersey, and I'm not setting foot in New fucking Jersey *or* going to a rehab center.

"Well?" Kara raises her blonde eyebrow in question.

I lick my lips, trying to think of something. "I think I'm gonna stick with the regular courses. College is hard as it is. I don't wanna pile on new things."

Kara smiles—she's always smiling—and leans forward. "Look Layla, I like you. In fact, I think you're great. You have great potential, and to be honest, I don't think you need these thinly disguised therapy sessions with me."

I sit up in my seat. "Really? I don't have to come here anymore?"

"No, you still have to come. I'd like to keep my job."

"I won't tell anyone. It could be our secret," I insist. I don't like to keep secrets, but this one I'll take to the grave.

"It's tempting, but no. Cookie?" She chuckles, offering the chocolate chip cookies sitting on her desk, going all friendly on me again.

She gives me whiplash and sometimes I want to ask her, *Are you here to analyze me or not?* Not that there is anything to analyze. I'm a simple girl, really. I hate winters, Connecticut, and college. I love the color purple, Lana Del Rey, and him. That's all.

I reach out to take one cookie but then change my mind and take three instead. I never say no to sugar.

Kara watches me carefully and I am about to snap at her when she speaks up. "So as I was saying, I think you have great potential, but you need set goals and you need to work on impulse control." She gives me a pointed look as I take a bite out of my cookie. "You don't have any, or at least, what you have is very little."

"Huh." I sag back in the chair. "Well, I knew that already."

Kara threads her fingers together on the desk. "Great. So we've already conquered the first step: acceptance. Now we need to work on the next step."

"And that is?"

"How to control it."

I hold up my finger. "Way ahead of you there. I've totally got it under control." Kara raises a skeptical brow and I continue, "I've been going to all my classes even though I wanna walk around aimlessly all day, and I've got C's across the board even though I hate college. Not to mention, I'd kill for a drag or a drop of Grey Goose, but I haven't touched any of those things. I don't even go to parties, because we all know parties are just breeding grounds for pot, alcohol, and sex."

I shoot her an arrogant smirk then finish my cookie. She can't get me after that. I've been good. I've busted my ass to be good.

"That's commendable. I appreciate your restraint, but that's also the bare minimum. You shouldn't be drinking and partying it up anyway." She pushes her glasses up. "College is your time to learn, to discover yourself, to see what kind of things you like, and for that, we have electives. So, I ask you again, any thoughts?"

Sighing, I look away. I'm back to staring out the window. The grounds are white and the trees are naked. It's all desolate and sad, like we're living in a post-apocalyptic world where things like electives are mandatory.

"What are my choices?" I ask.

Kara beams at me, swatting at a wayward curl that's getting in her eyes. "Well, we've got a great writing program. Maybe you should try some of the writing classes."

"You mean, like, *writing* writing?" At her nod, I shake my head. "I don't even like reading."

"You should probably pick up a book sometime. Who knows, you might end up liking it."

"Yeah, no, I don't think so." I sigh. "Do you have anything else? I don't think I'm cut out for writing."

"In fact, I think you'd be great at it."

"Really?" I scoff. "What do you think I should write about?"

This time her smile is both sweet and sad. "Write about New York. I know you miss it. Or maybe something about winter."

"I hate winter." I wrap my arms around my body and hitch my shoulders to huddle in my purple fur coat. Another thing I like: fur. It's soft and cuddly, and it's the only thing that can somewhat keep me warm.

"Then why do you keep staring at the snow?" I shrug, and she dips her head in acceptance of my non-answer. "How about you try writing something about what you felt when Caleb left? About the way you acted up?"

Caleb.

I'm jolted at the mention of his name. It's not an outward jolt, more a tremor on the inside, like when you hear a sudden loud sound in a quiet apartment and you know it's nothing, but your body tenses nonetheless.

I don't think I've heard his name spoken out loud since I moved here six months ago. It sounds so exotic in Kara's voice. On my tongue, his name sounds loud, shrill, wrong somehow. I shouldn't be saying it, but hey, I've got no impulse control, so I say it anyway.

I hate her for bringing him up. I hate that she's going there in a roundabout way.

"I didn't act up. I just…got drunk…every now and then." I clear my throat, pushing my anger away when all I want to do is storm out of here.

"I know, and then *every now and then*, you went shoplifting, crashed your mom's parties, and got behind the wheel."

Should therapists be judgy like this? I don't think so. And why are we talking about these things, all of a sudden? Mostly, we stick to neutral topics like school and my teachers, and when things get a little personal, I evade and make jokes.

This one time when she tried talking about the days leading up to Caleb's departure, I took my top halfway off and showed her my newly acquired belly button ring, and maybe even the underside of my bra-less boobs.

"I didn't kill anyone, did I?" I say, referring to her earlier comment about drinking and driving. "Besides, they took away my license, so the people of Connecticut are safe from the terror that is me. Why are we talking about this?"

"Because I think you can channel all of your emotions into something good, something constructive. Maybe you'll end up liking it. Maybe you'll end up liking college." She lowers her voice then. "Layla, I know you hate college. You hate seeing me every week. You hate being here, but I think you should give it a chance. Do something new. Make new friends."

I want to say I do have friends—I do, they are just not visible to the naked eye—but I don't, because what's the point of lying when she knows everything anyway?

"Fine."

Kara looks at the clock on the wall to her right. "Tell me you'll think about it, *really* think about it. The semester starts in a couple days so you've got a week to think about the courses, okay?"

I spring up from my seat and gather my winter gear. "Okay."

"Good."

It takes me a couple of minutes to get ready to go out in the snow. I snap my white gloves on and pull down the white beanie to cover my ears.

Winter is a cruel bitch. You gotta pile on or you'll get burned by the stinging wind, and no matter how much I pile on, I'm never warm enough, not even inside the heated buildings. So, I've got it all: hat, scarves, gloves, thermal tights, leg warmers, fur boots.

I'm at the door, turning the knob, but something stops me.

"Do you think…he's doing okay up there? I mean, do you think he misses me?" I don't know why I ask this question. It simply comes out.

"Yes. I do think he misses you. You guys grew up together, right? I'm sure he misses his best friend."

Then why doesn't he call? "Boston is cold," I blurt out stupidly, my throat feeling scraped. A chill runs through my body at the thought of all that snow up there.

"But I'm sure he's fine," she reassures me, with a smile.

"Yeah," I whisper. I'm sure Harvard is taking good care of their genius.

"You know, Layla, falling in love isn't bad or wrong or even hard. It's actually really simple, even if there's no reciprocation. It's the falling out that's hard, but no matter how much you convince yourself otherwise, reciprocation is important. It's what keeps the love going. Without it, love just dies out, and then it's up to you. Do you bury it, or do you carry the dead body around? It's a hard decision to make, but you have to do it."

I know what she's saying: move on, forget him, don't think about him—but how can you forget a love of thirteen years? How can you forget the endless nights of wanting, *needing*, dreaming? *I love you.* That's all I ever wanted to hear. How can I let go of that?

With a jerky nod, I walk out of her room. Outside the building, the air is cold and dry. It hurts to breathe. My heart is still fluttering with residual anxiety when I take my phone out, and stare at the last picture I have of him. He's smiling in it. His green, green eyes are shining and his plump, kissable lips are stretched wide. It's fucking beautiful. I don't think I can ever delete it. Not in this lifetime.

I put the phone away when I see a couple. They are up ahead of me on the cobblestone pathway, and they are wrapped around each other. The girl is cold, her cheeks red, and the guy is rubbing his hands over hers, trying to warm her up. They are smiling goofy smiles, reminding me of a smile from long ago.

Caleb as the ring bearer and me as the flower girl. Caleb stopping in his confident but boyish stride to take my small hand in his, me looking up at him with a frown. Oh, how I hated him in that moment. Caleb flashing his adorable smile and me returning it, despite the frown, despite the strange surroundings, despite the fact that my mom was marrying his dad. I hated getting a new brother. I hated moving across town to a new house with no roof-top garden.

At the fork, the couple takes a right turn and I'm supposed to go left, but I don't want to go left. I want to go where they're going. I want to bask in their happiness for a while. I want to see reciprocation.

What does requited love look like? I want to see it.

I take the right turn and follow the couple.

***

It's cold, *so* fucking cold. Also, dark—super dark, and the Victorian lamps flanking the street don't do shit to light up my path.

But none of that deters me from taking a harried pace. I'm walking down Albert Street, heading toward Brighton Avenue where the university park entrance is. Sleep is hard to come by, especially after Kara mentioned writing about my unrequited love.

Once upon a time, six-year-old Caleb Whitmore smiled at

five-year-old Layla Robinson. She didn't know it then, but that was the day she fell in love with him. Over the years, she tried to get his attention without success. Then one night, in her desperate, desperate attempt to stop Caleb from going off to Harvard, she kind of, sort of... raped him a little bit. She's not entirely sure. Caleb went off to college one month earlier than he was supposed to and Layla was stuck acting up. The end.

Two years later I'm here, walking the streets, feeling ashamed of my love, ashamed of having ever fallen for my step-brother and then driving him away.

For the record, Caleb Whitmore isn't even my stepsibling anymore. My mom divorced his dad a few years ago, but I think some stigmas never go away—like, you don't sleep with your best friend's ex-boyfriend, and you don't date your friend's brother. Caleb will always be my stepbrother because we kind of grew up together.

I don't even have memories of the time before him. I can't remember the house I lived in before I lived with him, except that it had a rooftop garden. I can't remember the friends I had before he came along. I can't even remember my own dad before his dad came into the picture.

All I remember is one day when I was five, Mom said we were leaving, and that I was going to get a brother. Then the dark days followed where I cried because I hated the idea of a sibling.

And then a burst of sunlight: a tiny six-year-old boy holding the rings on a velvet cushion, standing next to me. I remember thinking I was taller than him in my frilly, itchy dress, flowers in my hand. I remember thinking that I liked his blond hair and green eyes as opposed to my black hair and weird violet eyes. Together, we watched our parents get married, and together, we grimaced when they kissed each other on the lips.

It was beautiful, with white lilies and the smell of cake everywhere.

Now, I make my way toward the solitude. Slipping and stumbling on the transparent patches of ice, I enter the park. The cold wind curls around my body, making me shiver, but I keep going, my booted feet trudging through the snow. I'm looking for a particular spot that I like to frequent during the nights when I can't sleep, which happens often.

Unrequited love and insomnia are longtime friends of mine. They might even be siblings—evil and uncaring with sticky fingers.

Frustrated, I stomp and slip, falling against the scratchy bark of a tree. Even through the thick layer of my fur coat, I feel the sting.

"Motherfucking…" I mutter, rubbing the burn on my arm. My eyes water with the pain, both physical and emotional. I hate this. I *hate* crying. I wipe my tears with frozen fingers and try to control my choppy breaths.

"It's fine. It's totally fine," I whisper to myself. "I'm gonna be fine." My words stumble over each other, but at least I'm not crying now.

Then I hear a sound. Footsteps on the iced ground. A wooden creak. Fear has me hiding against the tree, but curiosity has me peeking out.

A tall man dressed in all black—black hoodie and black

sweatpants—is sitting on the bench, my bench, under my tree with the network of empty branches.

That's my spot, asshole, I want to say, but I'm mute. Terrified. Who is he? What's he doing here at this time of night? People sleep at night! I'm an exception though; I'm heartbroken.

He sits on the edge, head bent and covered by the hood, staring at the ground. Slowly, he slides back, sprawls, and tilts his face up. His hood falls away, revealing a mass of black hair illuminated by the yellow light of the lamp. It's long and wavy, almost sailing past the nape of his neck and touching his shoulders. He watches the sky and I do the same. We watch the moon, the fat clouds. I smell snow in the air.

I decide the sky isn't interesting enough. So, I watch him.

He is breathing hard, his broad chest puffing up and down. I notice a thick drop of sweat making its way down his strained throat, over the sharp bump of his Adam's apple. Maybe he's been running?

Without looking down, the dark man reaches back to get something from his pocket—a cigarette. He shifts, brings his face down, and I see his features. They are a system of angles and sharp, defined lines. His high cheekbones slant into a strong, stubbled jaw. Sweat dots his forehead and he wipes it off with his arm, stretching the fabric of his hoodie over his heaving chest.

Any moment, I expect him to light the cigarette and take in a drag. I realize I'm dying to watch him smoke, to see the tendrils of smoky warmth slip away into the winter air.

But he…doesn't.

He simply stares at it. Wedged between two of his fingers,

the cigarette remains still, an object of his perusal. He frowns at it, like he is fascinated. Like he hates it. Like he can't imagine why a blunt stick of cancer is holding his attention.

Then he throws it away.

He reaches back again and gets out another cigarette. The same routine follows. Staring. Frowning. My anticipation of seeing what he does next.

This time he sighs, his chest shuddering up and down as he produces a lighter from his pocket. He throws the stick in his mouth and lights it up with a flick of his finger. He takes a drag and then lets the smoke seep out. His eyes fall shut at the ecstasy of that first pull. He might've even groaned. *I* would have.

Watching him fight his impulse to smoke was exhausting. I feel both sad and happy that he gave in. I wonder what I would've done in the same situation. Kara's face comes to mind, her saying I need to work on restraining myself.

I know the smoke coming out of his mouth is virgin, not a drop of marijuana in there, but I want it in my mouth too. I *so* want it.

Abruptly, he stops and shoots up from his seat, pocketing the lighter. This guy is tall, maybe 6'3" or something. I have to crane my neck to look at him even though I'm standing far away. He skips on his feet, takes one last drag, flicks the cigarette on the ground, crushes it, pulls the hoodie over, and takes off jogging.

I come unglued from the tree, run to the bench, and look in the direction where he vanished -- nothing but darkness and frosty air. I might as well have conjured him up, like a child makes up an imaginary friend to feel less lonely. Sighing, I sit where he sat. The place is cold as ever, as if he never sat there.

My exhaustion is taking its toll and I close my eyes. I breathe in the lingering smell of cigarette and maybe even something chocolatey. I curl up on the bench, my cheek pressing into the cold wood. I hate winter, but I can't fall asleep in my warm bed. It's one of those ironies people laugh about.

Drifting into sleep, I pray that the color of the stranger's eyes isn't green.

Chapter Two

I live in a tower.

It's the tallest building around the area of PenBrook University, where I've been banished to go to school. I'm on the top floor in a two-bedroom apartment overlooking the university park. In fact, I can see the entire campus from my balcony—the umbrella of trees, red rooftops of squatting houses, spiked buildings. I like to sit up on my balcony and throw water balloons at people down on the street. When they look up, outraged, I duck behind the stone railing, but in those five seconds, I feel acknowledged. They knew someone was up there, throwing things at them. I like that.

The lower floors will be rented out in a few months, but currently I'm the only person living in this posh, luxurious, tower-like building. Henry Cox, my current stepdad, is the owner, hence the early access. My mom thought living in a dorm would make me more susceptible to drugs and alcohol. As if I can't score here if I want to.

Since my heart is lonely today, I decide to go to the book-

store and get the books on my course list. Might as well since classes begin tomorrow.

I throw on some sweatpants and a large hoodie, then cover
myself up with my favorite purple fur coat, a scarf, and a hat. My
dark hair falls around my face for extra protection from the cold.

Ten minutes later, I'm at the campus bookstore, pulling up
the list of books on my phone. One by one, I collect the required
texts in the nook of my arm. I'm sad that it took only a few minutes
and now I'll have to go back to my tower.

Then I get an idea. I walk toward the literature section of
the store. Rows and rows of books with beautiful calligraphy surround me in shoulder-height wooden bookshelves. There's a smell
here that I can get used to, warm and sharp. Heaven must smell
like this.

Unlike Caleb, I'm not much of a reader. He's a great lover
of books and art.

With Lana crooning in my ears about "Dark Paradise," I
run my fingers over the edges of the books, trying to decide how
best to mess things up. My lonely heart perks up. It flips in my
chest, telling me how much it appreciates my efforts to fill this
giant, gaping hole.

Don't mention it.

Then I get to work. I trade books on the G shelf with the
ones on the F. I laugh to myself, cackling as I imagine people getting confused. It calls for a little twerking so I move my ass—only
a little, mind you—to the sensual beats of the song.

As I turn around, my movements halt. The book in my
hand remains suspended in the air and all thoughts vanish from

my head.

He is here.

Him.

The dark smoker from last night.

He stands tall and intimidating with a book of his own in his hands. Like last night, he is frowning at the object. Maybe it pissed him off somehow, offended him with its existence. If not for the ferocity of his displeasure, I never would've recognized him under the industrial light of the bookstore.

He looks different in the light. More real. More angry. More dangerous.

His dark hair gleams, the strands made of wet, black silk. The night muted their beauty, their fluidity. I was right about his face though.

It is a web of square planes and valleys, sharp and harsh, but regal and proud. Nothing is soft about him except his lips, which are currently pursed. I picture the cigarette sitting in his full, plump mouth.

Then, like last night, he sighs, and the violence in his frown melts a little. He hates the book, but he wants it. I think he hates how much he wants it.

But why? If he wants it so much, he should just take it.

My heart has forgotten its loneliness and is invested in this dark stranger now. I study him from top to bottom. A leather jacket hangs from his forearm. He's wearing a crisp white shirt and blue jeans and…

Oh my God! He's wearing a white shirt and blue jeans.

He's dressed like my favorite song, "Blue Jeans" by Lana

Del Rey.

My heart starts to beat faster. Faster. Faster. I need him to look up. I need to see his eyes. I will him to do just that, but he doesn't get my vibes. I'm just about to go up to him when a girl skips into my vision.

He looks up then. In fact, he whips his eyes up, irritated.

They are blue—a brilliant blue, a fiery blue, like the hottest part of a flame, or like the water that puts out that flame.

"Um, hi," the girl says as her blonde ponytail swishes across her back.

He doesn't reply but watches her through his dark, thick lashes.

"I was wondering if you could help me get a few books from over there." She points to the tall wooden shelf across the room that almost touches the roof. A couple of girls are standing by it. They giggle among themselves when he looks over.

Really? That's so cliché, hitting on a guy like that at a book-store.

Well, who am I to judge? I've done things like that multiple times with Caleb, playing the damsel in distress just so he'll come save me.

The girl is waiting for him to say something. He's been holding his silence for the past few seconds, and I begin to feel embarrassed for her. Silence is the worst response when trying to get someone to notice you.

Then he breaks his tight pose and shrugs. "I'd love to help you, but I forgot my ladder at home today."

Low and guttural—his voice. It's a growl, really, and it

makes me shiver.

He delivers the line with such dryness that even I'm confused. Don't they have a ladder here at the store? But then the complete, yet fake, innocence on his face tells me he's making a joke, and despite the shivery skin, I chuckle quietly.

"They have a ladder here. Look," the girl says, pointing to the dark brown wooden ladder slanting against the bookcase. Her friends are still staring at the exchange between them.

"I see," he murmurs, scratching his jaw with his thumb and then drumming his fingers against his biceps.

There are tight lines around his eyes, flashing in and out of existence. He's trying to control himself yet again. He hated the interruption, and now he's deciding how to deal with it. It's all guesswork on my part, but I'm right. I just know it.

"I'm totally scared to climb it in my heels," the blondie explains.

"You shouldn't be," he encourages. "I do it all the time."

"Do what all the time?"

"Climb ladders in my heels," he deadpans and studies something on the floor—her shoes, maybe? "Ah, I can see where you're having trouble. Pencil heels. You don't want to mess with those. Dangerous contraptions. People have lost their lives."

There's a moment of silence. Then, "You're kidding, right?"

"No, I never kid about heels." He rubs his lips together. "Or skirts that make my calves look slimmer. I never kid about them either."

"What?" the girl screeches.

He draws back, looking affronted. "You don't think my

calves can look slim in a skirt? Are you calling me fat?"

"Wh-What? I'm not… I never…"

"Yes, so I just had a tub of chocolate ice cream, and yes, I promised myself I'd cut down on sugar"—a sharp, dramatic sigh—"but I slipped up. You think just because you're blonde and pretty you can question a man's wardrobe choices?" The blue in his eyes is amused, as are the crinkles around them. I press my lips together to stop the snort from bursting out.

"I don't…I don't even know what you're talking about. I just came here asking for help." The girl is irritated and indignant.

The crinkles around his eyes snap back into tight lines. "Let me tell you a little secret." He lowers his voice and I find myself inching closer. "I'm not the helping kind." He tilts his head to point toward her friends. "You should run along and play with people your own age and IQ level."

Then he throws the book on the shelf, looks at his watch, and strides away, leaving us both stunned. The blondie huffs and heads toward her friends.

So the blue-eyed smoker is a giant asshole. I feel bad for the girl, even though a trapped laugh escapes me.

If that was his show of control, I don't know what he'll do if unleashed. I walk to where he was standing and pick up the abandoned book. *A Lover's Discourse: Fragments* by Roland Barthes. It looks harmless enough with an unassuming black cover. I wonder why he was mad at this book. I wonder how our conversation would go if we ever talked. I wouldn't even know what to say to him, except, *Hi, I'm Layla, and you remind me of a song.*

Hours later, I'm back at home. I'm tired and want to go to

sleep. I don't even want to watch porn, which I would normally do while munching on my Twizzlers. I don't watch porn to get myself off, no. I don't even touch myself. I watch it to feel something, a sense of closeness to someone, maybe. I study the naked, writhing bodies, the erotic frown on the girl's face, the look of focus on the guy's. I listen to the sounds they make, albeit fake.

I try to understand their dynamic. It looks surreal to me. I try to compare it with the one time I had sex. It was nothing like that. The guy didn't look at me like he'd die if he didn't get inside me, and the girl—me—wanted him to get out as soon as he got in.

Well, that's what you get when you force someone to sleep with you.

***

First day of the spring semester. I wonder why they call it the spring semester; it's still January and freakishly cold. The snow is sprawled around like a white nightmare and the wind blows it sideways, slapping our faces with chilled flurries.

Even so, there's an enthusiasm in the air. New classes, new professors, new love stories.

The street outside my tower is flooded with people carrying book bags and wearing puffed-up multicolored jackets. I'm bombarded with shrieks of laughter and conversations as I walk down the street to Crème and Beans, my favorite coffee shop.

It seems as if it's become everyone's favorite overnight because it's jam-packed this morning. I wait in a long line that stretches to the back of the store.

The line moves slowly, like molasses, and as I take a step forward, I see him. Again. The blue-eyed smoker. He is up ahead at the counter. I can only see his profile—square jaw and untamed hair—as he steps out of the line, fishes his wallet out, and pays for the coffee.

He walks out, clenching a cigarette between his teeth, and lights it up. No hesitation this time. Has he already lost the battle?

My legs move of their own volition and I abandon the line, running after him. Even the blast of the cold wind isn't enough to deter me from pursuing the dark stranger.

He is eating up the distance, leaving a trail of smoke behind. He is more lunging than walking with his long legs, and I have to speed-walk to keep up. He walks toward McKinley Street where the quad is located, dodging the stream of people easily. I'm not as graceful. I bump and crash into bodies.

But somehow, I keep the broad line of his shoulders in sight. It's hard not to, really. He's taller than most people, his back broader, and I bet when that black sport jacket is peeled off, that back is an expanse of thick cuts and sleek lines, much like his face.

The chilled breeze ruffles his hair and scatters the smoke billowing out of his cigarette. I can taste it in my mouth, taste the ashy smoke and languid relief that only nicotine can provide. This man makes me want to buy a pack of cigarettes and smoke my day away. He makes me want to whip out my fake ID and get liquored up.

That reminds me—I am a good girl now.

So what the fuck am I doing? I've got class, and I should be scrambling like everyone to get to it.

But we want to follow him, my heart whines.

Fine. Just this once.

I keep following my smoker. We cross the quad and he climbs the steps leading up to the bridge that stretches over the two sides of campus. I hardly ever take it since all my classes are on the south side, where I live, but we're going to the north side, I guess.

The other side of campus is quieter. Cobblestone pathways and benches are almost empty. There are hardly any stragglers here. Even the air is sharper as it blows through my loose hair and swishes around my red-checkered skirt. Here, the leafless trees are dense as they line the path, making it seem like we're walking through woods.

At last, he stops in front of a building and I stop a few feet behind him. The golden letters on the red-bricked high-rise building say *McArthur Building,* and on the side in a smaller cursive font, it says *The Labyrinth*—whatever that means.

I enter the building behind him and sounds bombard me from every side. Murmurs, laughter, footsteps. A phone rings somewhere. A drawer is snapped shut. A door thuds closed. It is a hub of activity in contrast to the quietness outside, as though every soul on this side of campus resides within this archaic building.

The floors gleam under my feet and the unpolished brick walls give the space a homey feel. I want to look around and see what exactly this place is, but I don't dare take my eyes off him. He walks down the hallway and enters the very last room.

I follow him and as I'm about to enter the room, it happens.

He turns and looks at me.

His mysterious, otherworldly blue eyes are on me, and I'm rendered paralytic. I can't move. I can't think. His stare lulls me into a foggy stillness.

He leans against something…a table. The windows in the wall behind him let the sunlight in, which dissolves as soon as it touches his body, making him glow. He takes a sip of his coffee and watches me over the rim of the mug. Somewhere along the way he got rid of his cigarette, and oddly, I mourn the loss.

"Hi," I say breathily.

"Are you going to take a seat?"

His rich, mature voice slides over my skin, causing a slight sting, like that of an aged liquor.

"What?" I ask stupidly, thoughtlessly.

"Take a seat," he says again, sighing.

"I don't…"

He stands up straight. "Take. A. Seat." He enunciates every word like I'm an imbecile. "Or get the fuck out of my class."

Class. That word pierces the bubble around me, making me wince. I break his gaze and look around. Sure enough, we're in a class with twenty or so people, and they're all staring at me.

I look back at him, frowning, and study his features. The *aged*, *mature* features. The lines around his mouth and eyes. His confident manner. The fact that he is intimidating when he wants to be.

He doesn't look like a college-going guy…because he is not.

This blue-eyed smoker is a professor.

Made in United States
North Haven, CT
06 December 2021

12104373R00311